*Praise for* MA

---

"Lloyd is so paranoid! My daughter loves it when I read him in a funny robotic voice!"

-Amelia, Mother of Two

"This book is amazing! My imagination was tickled by the soft kisses of playful baby seals as I was reading."

- Julia, 8th grader

"I laughed so much my mom called the ambulance!"

- David, 7th grader

"Chapter 17. Incredible fight. (spoiler) is WICKED!"

- Mike, Accountant

"Favorite part? Hhhmm, tough, I'd say when Mark discovers the (spoiler), but then Lexe uses it to (spoiler) that (spoiler)."

- Justin, College Student

"(spoiler) (spoiler) (spoiler), then (spoiler). (SPOILEEEEER)!"

- Marco, Artist

"#1 Interstellar Bestseller."

– The Galactic Gazette

Copyright © 2013 by R. G. Hauxley

Illustrations © 2013 by Tomas J. Quaid

All rights reserved worldwide. No part of this book may be reproduced or transmitted in any form or by any means without written permission from the author, except in the case of brief quotations embodied in critical articles and reviews.

MARK FROM EARTH, M, and associated logos are trademarks and/or registered trademarks of R.G. Hauxley.

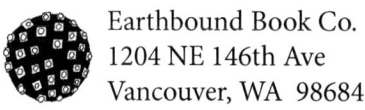

Earthbound Book Co.
1204 NE 146th Ave
Vancouver, WA 98684

Book Design: Amy Pogue of Irving Street Press

Library of Congress Cataloging-in-Publication Data:

*Hauxley, R.G.*
*Mark from Earth, 1st ed.*
*ISBN 978-0-9895475-0-5*
*1. Fiction. 2. Science Fiction. 3. Action & Adventure*

First edition paperback: June 2013

1 2 3 4 5 6 7 8 9 10

Printed in the United States of America

# MARK

# FROM EARTH

## R. G. HAUXLEY

ILLUSTRATIONS BY TOMAS J. QUAID

Earthbound Book Co.
Vancouver, WA

*Dedicated to…*

*My sisters, Sara and Julia, who inspired Ella with her adventuresome spirit and sharp wit.*

*My brother, David, who inspired Mark with his humorous, gigantic heart.*

*My parents, for two years of encouragement and four years of patience.*

*MJ, an artist, a thinker, a brother from another mother.*

*Brian, a friend with faith in me from the beginning.*

*Shawna, a goofy yet poignant muse.*

*Debra, the professor who believed in me.*

*Mike, an old soul with a penchant for prose.*

*The red ink pen wielders: Elizabeth, Lisa, Tammie, Justin, and Erin.*

*And to you, curious reader. Whether you're making mischief with Mark for the first time or for the last time, we share these wild adventures, and I am grateful for this.*

# CONTENTS

Chapter 1: The Last Recruit .................................................................. 1

Chapter 2: "That's Not a Tractor!" ...................................................... 17

Chapter 3: SPIFF .................................................................................. 37

Chapter 4: Heath and Lexe .................................................................. 55

Chapter 5: The Last Recruit ................................................................ 79

Chapter 6: The Black Pearl Bazaar .................................................... 101

Chapter 7: The Seven Site ................................................................. 121

Chapter 8: RUN .................................................................................. 139

Chapter 9: "You Tryin' to Kill Me?" .................................................. 161

Chapter 10: When Alarm Clocks Attack .......................................... 183

Chapter 11: How to Build a Flarejet .................................................. 197

Chapter 12: Junkrider ......................................................................... 209

Chapter 13: Wargame ......................................................................... 225

Chapter 14: Worlds Apart .................................................................. 243

Chapter 15: "Let's—Get—Dangerous." ............................................ 261

Chapter 16: The Obliv ........................................................................ 283

Chapter 17: Mistakes .......................................................................... 295

Chapter 18: The Fighter ..................................................................... 313

About the Author ............................................................................... 330

# CHAPTER 1

# CHAPTER 1
## THE LAST RECRUIT

"Hey . . . Let's get in trouble!"

"You're already in trouble!" shouted a voice over a pair of earbuds.

"Then let's get in more trouble," yelled the boy piloting the small red stunt plane. He pushed the controls forward. The plane dived.

Out of the hot Australian sun and into billowing white clouds, the propeller pulled the boy and his plane forward, faster. He breathed deep. The air up here in the clouds was always different: the scent of apple orchards mingling with the salty sea; wafts of ancient sands from the far-flung Great Victoria Desert, even the tropical rainforests of distant Tasmania lingered up here. The plane's old engine roared on, pouring exhaust out of its two steel pipes. He loved filling his lungs with it all.

The open-top stunt plane and its lone thirteen year old pilot burst out of the cloud.

"Woooo yeah!" crowed the boy, leveling back into steady flight. "Did you see that, Tom?"

"That was intense!" said Tom, whose light brown eyes avidly watched everything through the front-facing webcam taped just outside the plane's rattling windshield. "Went by too fast, but still intense." He paused. "You know what it reminded me of, Mark?"

"The rollercoaster incident?" Mark guessed with a rueful grin as he throttled down the engine, which chugged on like an old tractor.

# CHAPTER 1

"Yeah. Front seats. I looked over and you were chewing a lemon while looking through binoculars."

Mark laughed. "It was our eighth ride. I was getting bored." To highlight this troublemaking love of never being bored, he careened the plane into another cloud.

The dense white fog enveloped the perfect cherry red plane, obscuring those big yellow looping letters on both sides that spelled out its name: Thunder. A vintage Pitt's Special from the late 1940s, it had been lovingly restored by someone with time and money who never intended it to be more than a trophy piece. But today, the trophy piece had done eight barrel roles and three dives, buzzed a herd of cattle, and could currently be seen cutting across an endless sky.

"What's it like? Flying?" asked Tom as his computer screen went from rushing white clouds to dazzling blue sky again.

Mark scrubbed the droplets of cloud water off his aviator goggles and thought. From way up here, he could see several of his favorite surfing spots along the Australian coast. The gold sands and the foam of cresting waves looked calm and peaceful at this great height. The taste of salt water and the rough surfboard under his bare feet were his childhood.

"You know that moment—when you're surfing under a wave," said Mark, closing his eyes to remember, "and you look up, and you see the sunlight melting through the curling ocean?"

"Yeah," said Tom, who had joined Mark on many a surfing adventure that summer.

"It's almost like that," said Mark, and relaxed into the leather pilot's seat. The late summer sun went playing across his closed eyelids. He felt at ease. The farm fields hundreds of feet below were gliding along smoothly; the glimmering Pacific Ocean was busy making tubular waves for surfers of all ages; and he'd be back home and parking ol' Thunder before Dad even noticed. In short, he was having the best joyride ever.

Sputter.

"What was that?" said Tom.

Mark sat up. His eyes focused on the dashboard. It bristled with round gauges and metal switches and black rubber knobs. He didn't quite understand it all, but he knew that sound wasn't normal.

Sput-sputter.

"You're starting to sink," said Tom.

Mark focused on the controls. Tom was right. The altitude gauge kept creeping lower; he could hear the engine making odd gurgling noises; and when he looked back up, the sight of the propeller's choppy spin made him start sweating.

"Land it," said Tom. "Glide down and land it."

Mark fought the controls. The controls fought back. "I . . . I can't."

"What do you mean you can't?"

"Something's jammed."

Tom's voice grew panicked. "What do you mean something's jammed?"

"I mean I'm trying to convince the plane to go steady and it's ignoring me like Katy Jones in seventh grade!"

Ka-CHUNK . . . BOOM.

The engine seized and backfired. Mark began coughing as coal-black smoke poured out of the exhaust. Tom panicked and began yelling even louder. Mark couldn't hear a word. His ears were ringing.

"Tom," said Mark. "Tom, the engine hates me and the propeller is on fire."

"Do something!"

"Well . . . it's on fire. Don't know what you want me to do here."

"Anything! Something!"

"How about randomly mashing buttons while spinning out of control?"

"Right, perfect."

## CHAPTER 1

Mark began punching all the buttons, flicking all the switches, and mashing all the knobs while his world filled with clouds of black and sounds of fire. Suddenly, to Mark's surprise, a whole lot of nothing happened. He grew a tad frantic as all that nothing continued to happen.

The late summer's joyride had turned from hours of flying around having fun into a frantic struggle.

Tom's voice traveled into Mark's headphones in a low and serious tone. "Bail out man, get that parachute strapped and jump."

"I can't let Dad's life savings eat dirt. He'd dedicate a whole cemetery to me!"

"I'm serious, you're almost too low to even parachute out!"

The vintage plane screamed out of the brilliant blue sky. Turbulent winds whipped Mark's dark brown hair into more of a mess. He set his jaw and tried fighting the controls through the burning smoke and roaring noise and confusing blur.

Tom nearly fell off the edge of his seat as screamed at Mark. "Bail out or you'll be fertilizing those farms with your face!"

"I—" Mark said, forcing the controls hard back, "can," throwing the tail rudder to the right, "do," his teeth clenching, all his muscles aching from the effort, "this."

"Then pull up!" Tom raged at him. "Pull up, pull up, PULL UP."

"What the junk do you think I'm doing up here? Kissing pandas?" Mark screamed back at him. The farm fields were so close, he could see individual trees. Panic hit, making him lose focus and breath hard. The buffeting wind burned his eyes and blurred everything. He kept choking on all the diesel smoke. Flames from the stuck wooden propeller engulfed the front of the plane.

The throttle was useless, engine shot, but Mark still fought. With all his might he pulled and pulled on the control rod. He could hear treetops scraping the plane's belly.

Tom started jumping up and down in front of his computer screen. "Land in that pond! Land in that pond!"

Mark tried to focus. A large body of murky water glimmered in the approaching distance. He aimed for it. Clouds of engine smoke made this difficult. Closer and closer, lower and lower.

"Steady . . . steaaaaady" Tom stressed as he ran sweating fingers through his short, curly black hair.

This was it, do or die. The controls were slick with sweat. Wind wild in his ears, Mark was a fragile little thing sliding around in a slippery leather chair. Eyelids closed, he felt the blistering heat of the engine fire, the gritty taste of oily smoke, the rush of being alive. Goosebumps, deep breath, eyes snap open and focus.

Impact.

Mark miscalculated. With a grinding metallic shatter, the tip of the right wing hit the ground just before the pond. Shards of red-painted metal splintered apart, spraying across the water as the whole plane violently rotated. Like a big skipping stone it splashed sideways once. It then crunched hard, tail first, into the opposite shore, nose way up in the air. The whole plane creaked, steel straining against the steep angle. Mark looked up into the sky. He gripped the seat's edges.

"WOOOOOWW."

The nearly vertical plane fell flat onto the slimy water with a huge splash.

Mark sat there, breathing hard in disbelief as the world rocked.

Tom whispered in equal disbelief over the earbuds, "You landed . . . alive."

All Mark's senses rushed back in a flood of exhilaration. "YEEEEAAAAAAAAAAAAA," he yelled at the top of his lungs, fists in the air. Tom, watching his computer screen, did the same.

Then the plane started to sink.

## CHAPTER 1

"Whoa, whoa, WHOA!" Mark shouted as he untangled the knotted seatbelt, got up, was yanked back by the earbuds, tore them off, and clambered out of the plane. His feet pounded over the hollow metal wing. A quick jump onto the muddy shore sent him tumbling.

He stood and turned. Bubbles rose from the murky green as Thunder slowly sunk, nose first. The charred propeller disappeared, and then half the engine, sizzling as it sunk. Then the grime gave a loud burble and stopped sucking in the lovingly pampered 1940s Pitts Special. The red stunt plane stayed stuck, tail in the air, wings just below the scummy water. Splattered mud now covered the proudly painted looping yellow letters.

"Sure," Mark said to himself, surveying the damage. "Pat on the back. I survived. Now Dad will kill me. Mmmm hmmmm, look at it. Sticking up at me out of its watery grave like a big fat middle finger." Mark's frown became a grimace as he dropped his eyes to his muddy shoes. He was dreading the moment his dad would find out. His stomach hurt.

The world took no notice of Mark's painful plight though. The rude interruption being over, nature settled back into its usual rhythm. Sunlight warmed the little heads of turtles basking happily on logs; birds sang their sweetheart songs; and gentle summer breezes lifted the scents of freshly tilled earth into the air.

Mark sighed under the weight of disappointing his dad for the last thirteen years. He kicked a stone into the pond, watched the ripples travel to the mess he made, and started the long trudge back. Another walk home—alone—He hated being a failure.

■ ■ ■ ■ ■ ■ ■ ■ ■ ■

"Seventy thousand sunspots in a supernova!" exclaimed a grizzled man. He looked as if he had traveled halfway across the solar system just to see a plane in a ditch. This was because, in fact, he had.

THE LAST RECRUIT

"I'm amazed the kid didn't die," said a woman with straight brown hair. She looked like a well-trained starfighter pilot. This was, in fact, because she was.

"Yes, he crashed quite naturally," said the bulky man. He had a short square beard, the color of salt and pepper. His wrinkled brown eyes balanced many good-natured laugh lines.

"And you want to recruit this kid, Captain?" she said, her sharp amber eyes open below raised eyebrows. The tone of disbelief in her voice reflected what she thought about the mess of splintered wood and painted metal that was still leaking oil into the murky pond, two weeks after the crash.

The old captain rocked back and forth on his heels. His hands were clasped behind his back, holding a Pan-Galactic captain's cap.

"Fishing" he stated. "I've never been fishing."

The woman's eyebrows rose further, this time in confusion.

"Once, time and time ago, while flying with the Three-O-Three in the Carpaus wars —a dastardly war—I got to know my copilot. He talked about fishing the lake planet of Gyradosia. Said the squids were the size of sunspots. Have you ever had spicy squid chowder, Lieutenant Landeth?"

The straight-backed military woman did not know quite how to respond.

"Luke Blevins was his name, as I recall," continued the gray-bearded captain. "He almost crashed every starfighter he ever piloted. The boys started calling him Lucky Luke . . . because he'd always pull through in the end."

Lieutenant Landeth, a rather strict and disciplined woman, never quite understood the captain's fondness for his food-obsessed war stories. She decided to change the subject.

"Yes . . . well . . . I'll just have Lloyd activate our cloak system, shall I?"

"Hmmmm?" he said, lost in nostalgia. "Ah yes, yes," he chuckled. "We must look a strange sight."

## CHAPTER 1

Indeed, the whole scene was a bit strange. Two people, both in sharp Pan-Galactic military uniforms, standing on the muddied shore of Pond Placid, gazing out at the crumpled wreck of a 1940s Pitts Special—was a sight to make any passerby do a double take.

Stranger still was the Orion-9 class starfighter sitting in the field behind the two individuals. It looked like a wingless military jet. Hot air rose in shimmering waves from dull gray metal vents. It would have made the passerby who did a double take do one more, just for good measure.

The strangest, however, was the sight of a bunch of small bumble-bots hovering all over the place, scanning everything, even the turtles (who were rightly ticked at being lifted off their sunny logs for a quick scan and drop). Indeed, the whole cacophony was so bizarre that any passerby—after having done a double take twice—would probably wig out and drive straight to the nearest doctor. The lieutenant would soon solve this.

"Lloyd?" she said, turning towards the starfighter.

An android slipped and fell from the top of the ship, landing with a tremendous clamor. Lloyd appeared to be a short, wide-eyed, multi-colored android, who happened to be very, very paranoid. This made him rather skittish.

"Yes Lieutenant Landeth, ma'am, officer person sir!"

"Fire up the UBF generator," she ordered.

Lloyd scrambled to the side of the starfighter. He started futzing with a small gray box labeled Uber Boring Field Generator. Lloyd finished programming what he thought would be a very boring disguise.

A pulse of static emitted from the gray box. It rushed out in a wave to envelop the captain, lieutenant, all the bumblebots, and the entire pond. Then it faded away.

# THE LAST RECRUIT

Now, any passerby who happened to see the pond would not give the place a passing thought. This was simply because everything appeared incredibly boring.

Two boring old fishermen were standing on the edge of a boring old pond, out of which protruded a boring old tree surrounded by a boring bunch of—flying turtles— clearly, Lloyd had a few circuits missing.

Lieutenant Landeth turned back to the grizzled man. "Captain Zumski, the bumblebots," she scrunched her nose in disapproval at the silly name, "are not cloaked properly."

His brown eyes twinkled at the sight of all the little scanners zipping around disguised as flying turtles. "Ah, let it be. Get the Admiral on the line, please, Lieutenant."

"Captain."

Moments later a clear, life-size holographic image of a tall, commanding woman with raven hair and piercing green eyes stood opposite the captain.

"Good afternoon, Admiral," said Captain Zumski in his usual cheery voice.

"Good afternoon, Captain," replied the admiral in her usual formality.

"How about final approval to recruit this kid?"

"Stan" said the admiral, using the captain's first name in heartfelt emphasis, "the boy is an ill-advised choice."

The captain tried to interrupt. He was stopped mid-protest by the admiral.

She continued, unhappy to deny his request, but firm: "We do not recruit Earthers. Unless they are exceptionally skilled and promising, they will fail. No," she raised her hand against another of his interruptions. "I know you've been trying to recruit this kid for some time now. But he failed today. He lost all control. He will fail at the academy."

# CHAPTER 1

"I understand, Admiral. But the kid didn't parachute out. He fought to recover."

"Stan, he wrecked on a basic emergency landing that our novice cadets can pull off."

"There is potential and possibility in the kid."

"This young Earther has not attended any proper schools. His grades indicate an average level of intelligence, even by earth standards."

Captain Stan Zumski would not be deterred. "There is fight in the boy, willpower and grit."

The admiral would not relent. "Mark has no training, shows no skills, lacks talent, and has no natural ability. He will fail. He will make mistakes and he will fail. And you want to recruit him as a pilot into the Cadet Core?"

"No, Admiral. I understand he does not have the money or the talent to join the Core. And I am not asking for him to. I am only asking that he be recruited into the Support Crew."

The high-ranking woman weighed his request. "That may be possible. Consider, however, that this will change the boy's life forever. He will never be the same. He will never be able to tell his family or his dearest friends. Most Earthers go home broken, Stan. Tell me, why would you recruit him?"

"My gut tells me so."

The admiral's green eyes were touched with warmth. "My old friend, your gut is bloated with half-digested leftovers."

The captain's belly shook as he chuckled at the truth of it.

Her seriousness gave way to a small smile. She considered the battle-worn man's request. He had been a captain before she was a lieutenant. He had fought through unfair wars and insincere peace pacts alike. She knew he had witnessed the dark heart of humanity alongside all a person could become. Her small smile became serious once more.

THE LAST RECRUIT

"You believe this boy can succeed?"

"I believe that when he fails, he will stand back up."

After a pause she shook her head in disbelief at her own decision. "Then recruit him, Captain Stanislaw Zumski, wing commander of the Three-O-Three."

The veteran of a hundred battles saluted.

"But Stan," she continued. "Try to keep him on school grounds. The city has become a dangerous place to wander."

In another moment the admiral had signed off, her holographic image dissolving into the summer air.

Landeth walked up to stand beside the captain. They both stood looking out at the wreckage. She clasped her hands behind her back and spoke up. "Bold move, recruiting this young Earther. Too bad he doesn't have the money to get into the Cadet Core."

The captain's twinkling eyes drifted to the wreckage. "I have a sneaking suspicion he will find his own way."

"Still," continued the lieutenant. "We did have several far more qualified Earthers selected."

Stan just smiled. "Do you remember the best recruit from Earth we've ever had?"

Landeth glanced at the captain. "Amelia Earhart was different."

"I remember when she rushed out to save Ruth, even though that meant ending up third instead of first at that air derby—that was the first time I tried those—what did they call 'em? Elephant ears?" That faraway look warmed his eyes again. "Isn't she commanding the Electra Wing Breakers now? In the Solvus system?" He paused. "Funny way of exiting Earth, making up her own mysterious disappearance like that." He concluded with a short chuckle. "She always was an adventurer."

Lieutenant Landeth looked up and away into Earth's blue sky. A flock of birds soared below billowing white clouds; endless fields of barley

# CHAPTER 1

swayed in the warm breezes; and pond water rippled from the splashes of turtles frantically swimming away from bumblebots bent on scanning every last one of them. It was a peaceful, serene, and untroubled scene.

Her gaze moved back to the crumpled plane and then out towards the path Mark had taken home.

"Soon everything will change for that kid. All he knew about his own home planet, his own solar system—the whole galaxy." She frowned. "You think he can handle it?"

The old captain looked at the lieutenant. "Yes," he said, with a confidence only gained from living through a life of difficult decisions.

Lieutenant Landeth, always abiding by the military chain of command, put the matter away with a curt nod. "Then I will make preparations for depar—"

"Excuse me officers, ma'am and sir?" said Lloyd, rushing up.

"Yes, what is it?" barked the lieutenant, not keen on being interrupted.

"Sorry, sorry, Fleet Commander Eli Exor is reporting another death-wish attempt on his life—And he is calling the Captain."

Stan's eyes sharpened. "Patch me through."

Fleet Commander Exor did not consider himself to be a patient man, believing action solved everything. His tall nose and high forehead set in a gaunt face spoke of a ruthless intelligence; while his square shoulders, rigid on a lean frame, were made from decades of discipline. He stood, sleeves rolled up, waiting in a gray concrete control room, wiping his bruised and beaten knuckles with a damp cloth. Several dark-clothed bodies lay where they'd fallen with cracked rib cages and broken jawbones. Two were breathing heavy, unconscious but alive and three lay crumpled, burned alive.

"How can I be of service, sir?" said Zumski, appearing as a hologram in front of the tall commander.

# THE LAST RECRUIT

Commander Exor finished wiping the blood off his knuckles and tossed the stained cloth to one of his waiting soldiers. "Attempted murder in my own personal command center. Five Syn'Crux Operatives, all highly trained elite men. They knew where to find me, how to bypass all security, and where I keep the Obliv key."

"It is good to see you standing," said the captain.

Exor began to roll down his right sleeve. "The Obliv is no longer safe. As soon as Director Shaw gives me its location, I will move it to safety aboard my Dreadnaught Battle Cruiser. Unfortunately," said Exor as he rolled down his left sleeve, "he refuses to give me the location. He claims that keeping the Obliv hidden is far more effective than fully armed and armored protection." The tall man scoffed as he snapped the cuffs of his shirt. "Foolish man."

The captain's voice urged caution. "The Galactic Council entrusted the Obliv to Director Shaw and entrusted the key to you, sir. No one man should have the Obliv's power."

A soldier standing next to Commander Exor held out the Commander's black military coat. Exor took it, dusted off the gold embossed shoulder pads, and slung it on. "Captain," he began while buttoning up the dark military jacket, "the Obliv is an unethical, hazardous, depraved kind of interrogation machine. Why the Galactic Council did not destroy it upon its creation remains their burden. Keeping it from the hateful hands of those who would abuse it remains my burden. Your job," he continued, stiffening the gold edged collar, "is to convince the foolish director that the Obliv would be far safer on my Dreadnaught."

"Commander," said the captain. "I urge us to trust Director Shaw. Syn'Crux Daemon's have tried to find the Obliv before. They have failed."

"There is a new Daemon." Eli Exor locked his intense silver eyes on the captain's hologram. "Unlike any before. Inspiring loyalty until death and

## CHAPTER 1

demonstrating a ruthless power over others as I have never witnessed." Exor swept a hand over the dead and dying Syn'Crux Operatives. "His deathwish attempts on my life are evidence enough of that."

"Even if this new Daemon should find the Obliv," insisted the captain as his hologram floated to follow the commander's firm stride across the room, "he could not move it, let alone access it. You have the key."

The commander stopped in front of a scale model of the Milky Way galaxy. "I must secure the Obliv, Captain," he said as his fingers connected several solar systems in a pattern. A mechanical hiss and the center of the galaxy opened. A small sphere of red and blue slowly rose from the center, glowing faintly and carved in strange symbols. He grasped it in his fist. "I will carry this Obliv key with me. I will find the Obliv with or without Director Shaw's cooperation. And I will destroy this new Daemon." Exor's fist glowed as he gripped the spherical key. He pointed at Stan. "And you best get onboard."

Back by the shallow waters of Pond Placid, Commander Eli Exor's hologram blinked away, leaving the grizzled old Captain standing with a darkened grimace. The hot Australian sun had formed beads of sweat on his forehead. One bead rolled down past his focused brown eyes. He absently dabbed at it with a worn out red and white cloth. The commander's ominous words did not bother the captain as much as the man's reckless pride.

"Director Shaw is a fool," said Lieutenant Landeth. The sharp angles of her face highlighting her own angered grimace. "Why does he not see the danger of a new Daemon?"

Captain Stanislaw Zumski turned to her, a curious concern in his voice. "You have experience with the Syn'Crux, Lieutenant?"

"When I was young, the Syn'Crux took my little sister," said Landeth, trying to control her voice, as it was unprofessional to show so much anger. "That is experience enough."

The old captain placed a comforting hand on her shoulder. "We will fight, as always."

The lieutenant—forever trying to appear cold and distant—saluted the captain, pivoted, and marched away to do her job.

He watched her disciplined strides take her to Lloyd. She began barking orders at the short android, who scurried around fulfilling them.

The captain combed through his square salt and pepper beard. The wrinkles around his brown eyes were folded in far away thought. He put his captain's cap back on and flicked its brim for luck.

"We must always fight—or Mark may be the last recruit."

## CHAPTER 2

# CHAPTER 2
## "THAT'S NOT A TRACTOR!"

Mark stood gazing out the window of his bedroom. He wasn't so much grounded as confined to barracks. It was solitary confinement in a room emptied out by his dad. The second story window overlooked endless rolling hills under an endless sky that his imagination filled with endless stunt planes. His imagination was out there, doing barrel roles and loops and midair gun-blazing dogfights. It hurt, because freedom had never looked so sweet, and so far out of reach.

When Dad found out that Thunder—his ten-year-long weekend project and one true love—was lying in a cold ditch all by itself, well, an ambulance could not have sped faster to find it. And then, when he'd seen it sticking out of the muddy pond like a single-fingered salute—Mark decided to stop thinking about his dad's reaction. Instead he walked back to his empty desk, wincing as he sat down.

Mark's bedroom stood barren. Bookshelves empty, video games gone, surfboard locked in the basement, not a trace of fun remained. Instead, his parents had left his great-grandfather's set of dusty encyclopedias. They were so old he couldn't find the definition of a computer, and the only entry listed under electricity—black voodoo magic.

He stuffed his left hand into a half-empty box of fruit loops. Then he uncapped the pen in his right hand with his teeth. Volume B lay open on his lap. He smudged the definition for boredom, thought for a minute, and wrote: "chewing a stale piece of gum."

## CHAPTER 2

A light knock on the bedroom door interrupted all the nothing he was busy doing.

"Still here," he called out. Then added in a mutter, "rotting away."

Mark's mom opened the door. From her round face to her well-worn apron, she was covered in splotches of flour. Wafts of delicious baked goodness drifted in. She looked at the five empty cereal boxes strewn about the room and waggled a finger at Mark.

"You've eaten more junk food in the last two weeks than over the whole year." She walked over and took the cereal box from his hand. "No more mister. You'll get diabetes."

"Mom," said Mark, his head thumping back against the window pane. "Is my coffin ready? Any minute now, any second, I will die of boredom."

She laughed and hugged him, her chocolate-brown hair touched with the aroma of warm cinnamon apple pie. "Dinner is almost ready. Wash up and scoot to the kitchen."

"I can't. I'm sorry, mother dearest. Please forgive me."

"And why is that?"

"My leg muscles have atrophied. My legs . . . my legs . . . they are useless now."

"I'm baking apple pie and left the mixing spoon all gunky with cinnamon and apple chunks."

Mark jumped up and bolted out the door, thumping down the stairs in a beeline for the kitchen.

His mom arrived to find him done with the spoon and scraping pie batter from the bowl in the sink. He couldn't help it, being powerless against the deliciousness and all.

"Clean the dishes for me, will you dear?" she said, heaving a tired sigh as she sat down on a stool by the counter.

"Only for two extra slices of pie," Mark joked, grabbing the sponge and running the faucet to find a good water temperature.

# "THAT'S NOT A TRACTOR!"

"The principal called today," she said. "He will be visiting this evening after dinner. He said there are two very important people joining him. Apparently they need to discuss certain matters with us before the school year starts."

"Awesome! Maybe I'm getting expelled," said Mark, crossing his fingers.

"No, you are not. And don't dare think that way."

"But school sucks porcupine balls," He said, furiously scrubbing a plate.

"Hello?"

Mark raised a confused eyebrow and glanced at his mom.

"Yes, hi, this is Mary from Victoria Point Real Estate," she continued, business phone in hand. "I have a wonderful young couple who are interested in your beautiful home. Hmm? Yes, absolutely. . . . Great! When could we arrange a showing?"

Mark went back to washing the measuring cups. His absent-minded gaze wandered out the window. They lived on acreage out in the farmlands of Southern Australia. A short walk from the house was Dad's home business. It was a small red airplane hangar. Mark was only seven when his dad built that hangar. It was big enough for two small stunt planes or one larger crop duster. He remembered how happy and proud his dad had been, opening his own business like that. Norman & Sons was painted in big looping yellow letters above the bay door.

Mark put the measuring cups on the drying rack and began scrubbing the mixing bowls. He remembered walking into the hangar while his dad fixed the small crop dusters and hobby planes belonging to all the local farmers. Back then the concrete floor had been spotless. Shelves lined with clean tools in neatly organized bins had lined the walls. Every week Dad would be working on a new airplane. And he'd show Mark and his older brother, Nick, how airplane engines worked. Dad used to be so patient, explaining how a propeller pulled the airplane through the air

## CHAPTER 2

and how the wings made it fly. He'd even let them sit inside the planes and press buttons and flick switches and make engine noises while pretending to fly in the great big Australian sky.

Mark sighed. He missed those days. The dish water was getting too hot; he turned down the hot water tap. The red paint on the hangar had faded by now. The bay doors squeaked when opened. The hangar smelled of used axle grease and old oil. Smudged tools and spare parts were strewn about. It wasn't that Dad didn't care. He cared very much. He was just too overworked and so stressed, constantly trying to make ends meet. Mark's eyes stayed on the tall tree next to the hangar, the one with the half-finished tree fort in the shape of an airplane.

Nick walked out of the hangar and crossed the lawn. Tall and built, with black hair in a short buzz cut, Mark's sixteen year old brother was growing up to become the spitting image of their father. Everyone said so, especially the older town's folk who'd known Mark's family for decades.

Nick opened the patio door and stepped into the kitchen, grease stained from rebuilding a PZL-Kalisz nine-cylinder engine with Dad. He appeared quite proud of that fact, strutting over to the fridge like a dirty peacock. "Helping Mom with the dishes there, little sis?"

Their mom covered her phone with one hand and said, "Nicky, don't be mean to your little brother." Then she added, with even more firmness, "and don't you even think of opening the fridge with those filthy fingers. Wash up first, it's time for dinner."

"Mom, don't call me Nicky. I ain't five anymore." He said and opened the fridge. The dirty peacock rummaged around, leaving greasy hand prints on anything he moved aside. He pulled out a six-pack of beer.

"Where are you going with that?"

"What? Me and Dad worked hard all day. We're having a couple o' cold ones."

"No, you are not having 'a couple o' cold ones'. Put it back."

"We worked hard and we earned it."

"You're too young."

"Don't be such a nanny, Mom," he retorted, walking away with the pack.

"I'll call you back, Judie," she said and snapped her phone shut, storming after him. "You are not going anywhere with that beer, young man," she scolded and closed the patio door before he got there. "Now give me that case, go wash up, and tell your father dinner's ready."

After a short staring contest, the scowling peacock shrugged. "Whatever," he said, thumping the six-pack onto the counter. Opening the patio door, he strutted outside.

A look of sad concern filled her eyes as she watched her eldest son walk back to the hangar.

Mark wanted to say something funny to cheer his mom up. "So do I get his piece of pie?" he quipped.

She brushed flour off her apron in an absent-minded way. "Set the table, dear," she said and went back to her laptop.

He loaded his arms up with the usual. Four square glass plates holding four stacked square bowls filled with a bunch of different spoons and forks. Mom liked to keep the dinnerware modern. He didn't mind that the bowls were square, because the food that filled them was always delicious. No matter how much Mom worked, she always made sure her family was well fed.

Tendrils of steam were rising from the pot of chunky chicken soup. The evidence of delicious home baked goodness was everywhere: in the apple peels twirled up on the counter, in the cracked egg shells by the open bag of flour, and especially in the sunlight glinting off the sugar glaze that covered those delicious pies on the window ledge. Best place in the whole house, in Mark's humble opinion.

The patio door slid open again. Mark's dad strode in. Standing six-foot-four with arms the size of barrels and a chest large and flat, the man

## CHAPTER 2

was a small mountain. His close cropped gray hair was the old snow on a craggy glacier of a face. Thick cords of forearm muscles flexed under skin tanned deeply in the Australian sun. He was unaffected by the magic of the kitchen. In his opinion the best place was his shop, where all the real work happened.

"Mary," his dad said, "I asked Nick to bring those beers. Why didn't you let him?"

"Norman," she replied, just as calmly while closing her laptop lid. "He is too young to be drinking. It'll stunt his growth."

"The boy did fine work today. Replaced all the valves on his own. He is growing up to be my right-hand man. One beer won't kill him." Dad opened the fridge and took out the pack.

She stood her ground. "Norman, no. Nicky still has high school to finish. Don't start him drinking. I want our son to make it to college."

"I'm teaching the boy responsible drinking, Mary." He set the pack on the counter and took out two bottles. "He is learning that a day's hard work deserves a drink with his father, in moderation. That is how our son will make it to, and through, college."

"If you start him drinking this early he'll turn into a drunk," she said, voice rising.

"Your overbearing ways will turn him into a drunk," he retorted.

"I'm trying to raise him right, Norman."

"Mary, you are sheltering our boys so much they'll rebel. Look at Mark." His dad pointed at him. "Stealing ten years of my life for a foolish joyride, then crashing it. He's rebelling against your overprotective parenting by going after me!"

"If you would just spend some time with him. Teach him all you're teaching Nicky—"

"That boy doesn't know a wrench from a hammer. Every time he

## "THAT'S NOT A TRACTOR!"

picks one up, I spend two hours fixing his mistakes." Dad's voice was rising now too.

"If you'd just take the time to teach him!"

"I don't have enough blood pressure medicine for that!" He shouted back.

"But you'll drink with Nicky?" she exclaimed. "I won't allow it."

"Don't tell me what I can and can't do for my son!" Dad's heavy palm slammed down on the counter, shaking everything.

Mom knew there was no use arguing and with eyes watering, she walked away.

Dad watched her go. The frustration in his face eased, touched with a moment of sadness. He heaved a sigh. Without looking at Mark, he picked up the pack and went back outside.

Mark went back to washing dishes. All the magic in the kitchen was gone. The apple rinds seemed rotten; the soup was lukewarm; the pies looked fake, like plastic. Everything was hushed. A wall clock ticked on, hollow and empty. All that sunlight that had danced in through the window over the set table and fresh-baked pies was now stark, stiff, and fake.

The scruffy-haired boy finished cleaning, vacant eyes staring out the kitchen window. He watched his dad and brother "crack open a couple o' cold ones." He watched them start grilling up some ribs and toasting to work well done. Their laughter drifted in.

Mark made a decision right then and there. "Time for more fruit loops."

■ ■ ■ ■ ■ ■ ▬ ■ ■ ■ ■

Late afternoon took its time turning into early evening. Song birds returned to their nests in trees that were busy making long shadows. Aus-

## CHAPTER 2

tralian alligators slipped into swamps and swam under lily pads where bull frogs practiced croaking. A gentle breeze ruffled the curtains at the sides of the open window, carrying the faint buzzing of the lone streetlamp outside as it flickered. In an increasingly inky violet sky, a yellow moon was rising. Meanwhile, Mark was busy planning out his calendar.

"Hmmmm, tough one, that is." Chewing on the end of a pen, he stared at the calendar on the wall. Every day's square box was filled with one word: nothing. He put the pen to the last week in the month. "I'm booked on Friday evening with being grounded sooooo, I'll have to move all that nothing into Saturday." He wrote the word nothing in Saturday's box. "That should work. I'll finally be able to get all that nothing done."

Zip. Bang.

Mark jumped out of his chair. Something had whizzed in through the open window and thudded into his closet. With narrowed eyes, he crept to the dark closet. There, in a pile of messy clothes, was a small rock.

Zip. "Ouch!" Mark cried as another small rock flew in and beaned him on the back of the head. He whirled around, raced to the window, and leaned out. "Oy! Show yourself!"

Tom, who had been bent over next to his bike looking for more rocks, stood and looked up. "Keep your hat on, it's just me."

"What happened?" said Mark. "I'm sneaking the phone past my dad, but every time I call, your mom hangs up on me."

"Yeah. She said you're a bad influence."

They both laughed.

"Get out here," said Tom. "I've got some news."

"Can't. Mr. Kennedy brought over two top brass people. They've been yakking it up in the living room with Mom and Dad for hours."

"The principal? What does he want? Who did he bring?"

# "THAT'S NOT A TRACTOR!"

"I don't know," said Mark, folding his arms on the windowsill. "But Dad's been arguing and Nick's been yelling about wanting to get accepted somewhere. Anyway, hopefully I'll get expelled or something."

"Hmmmm," said Tom, looking away and rubbing the back of his neck.

"What? Are you getting expelled too?"

Tom paused. He heaved a sigh and looked up again. "Mom's shipping me off to Canada to live with Dad this year."

"What?" said Mark, almost tumbling out of the window. "Why?"

"A hundred stupid reasons," said Tom, kicking a rock. It bounced off the house with a dull thud.

"That's stupid."

"Yeah."

The coolness in the evening air was unwelcome. All those creek-jumping, video-gaming playing, lazy surfing days of summer were over now. School would start in a few days, and middle school without a friend was, well, too horrible to imagine. They stood in silence, looking out at the fading sun.

"Well," said Mark, "at least she's finally letting you see your dad."

Tom shrugged. "Yeah, he's pretty happy about that. Wants to teach me guitar."

Another silence followed. Mark wished the stone in his stomach wasn't so heavy.

"Plus," he continued, "I bet all your friends back there are super excited."

Tom kept looking away, torn between places. "I dunno. It's been two years. It'll be fun going back. But it won't be same."

That stone sunk further into the pit of Mark's stomach.

"Anyway," said Tom. He stopped and looked around absently. "I gotta go. Mom's probably back from groceries and on the warpath to find me."

"She didn't make you go and help?"

## CHAPTER 2

Tom smirked. "I locked myself in the bathroom and said I had explosive diarrhea."

They shared a good laugh, the kind that's followed by a sigh and a shake of the head.

The mirth ran dry faster than usual though. Tom stood his bike up and got on. He looked at his best friend of two years, did that salute they'd made up, and pedaled away.

Mark held his end of the salute until the small dust cloud from Tom's bike disappeared in the dusk.

The yellow moon had climbed the sinking rays of the setting sun and could be seen touching the wings of sleepless bats with a pearly white as they flew into the growing night. Dry winds mixed the scents of Mom's herb garden, steeped in mint and boronia flowers, with the distant chirps of cicada's, cries of sugar gliders, and the occasional haunt of some strange creature from the Australian bush. Any other night, Mark would have breathed in the mystery and nocturnal life and let his lungs swell with imagination and adventure. Not tonight.

"This sucks," he said, his voice dripping with bitterness. He shook his head in disbelief at life. "What's the point of making friends if they go away?"

This thought, and all its tangents, kept him resting on the windowsill and thinking and replaying good memories for longer than he knew. In the end, though, he realized he'd been staring at the glowing moon for what seemed a very long time. A whisper came from inside and he said, to no one in particular, "I wish I could go away."

As if on cue, a light knock on his bedroom door brought him home.

Mom opened the door and stood with a sad, proud smile. "Mark, honey," she said and took a few steps in. "The principal and his guests have been discussing some very important things with us and it's time for you to come down."

# "THAT'S NOT A TRACTOR!"

Feeling like an inmate leaving his jail cell to be interrogated, Mark opened the door, walked into the hallway, and started downstairs. His mom, the sympathetic and loving jail warden, followed.

"Three hours is a long time to discuss the terms of my jail sentence. Will they at least allow you to send me fresh pies? Maybe you could hide a crowbar in one for me."

Mom laughed. "Nothing like that, dear."

"Well did they bring a taser?" he asked. "Because I'm not going quietly."

She laughed in that soft way when her thoughts were both happy and sad. Stopping him at the bottom of the stairs, she tried combing his forest of messy brown hair. "Be polite. Mr. Kennedy's guests are important people."

Mark heaved a sigh in response.

To his surprise, Mom sighed too. Then she wrapped him up in her cinnamon scented arms and said, "I'm going to miss you." She hugged tighter. "But I'm so proud of you!"

Mark, frowning in confusion, entered the interrogation room to find everyone sitting and eating apple pie from little plates with little forks. Mr. Kennedy was there, bald and business faced as usual; Dad was there, reclining in his big easy; Nick had brought in a dining room chair and flipped it around, straddling it to look cool. The couch was occupied by two people Mark didn't recognize.

Mom put a hand around his shoulder. "Mark, this is Captain Stanislaw Zumski," she said, gesturing at the man with the square gray beard and captain's cap. "And this is Lieutenant Alice Landeth," she said with a smile to the military lady, who didn't smile back.

Captain Zumski stood up with an extended hand and hearty smile. "Thundering comets! It's good to see you in person there, ace."

Mark walked over and returned the man's firm handshake. "Aye, aye Captain."

## CHAPTER 2

Stan chuckled and good-naturedly clapped Mark on the shoulder. "Take a chair, ace, there are matters for discussion."

Nick refused to give up his perch, so Mark dragged in another dining room chair.

Lieutenant Landeth went straight to the point. "We are here to recruit you, Mark, for SPIFF. Leaving immediately."

"How's that now?" said Mark, right eyebrow clambering up his forehead.

"S-P-I-F-F," said the Lieutenant, her fingers folded in an authoritative way across her lap. "SPIFF is the School for Paragon Cadets Excelling in Trans-stellar Neomechanics, Intersolar Starfighter Tactics, and Pan-Galactic Fleet Command."

"That—those words don't even match the letters," said Mark, confused. "And . . . and they don't make any sense!"

His mom spoke up. "Oh honey, we're so proud of you! Mr. Kennedy says you've been accepted into the most prestigious academy there is. He already filed your transfer papers and we have decided to let you try for the first year."

"We have decided no such thing, Mary," said Dad from his big recliner. His voice was calm, deep, and firm in resolve. "I will not permit Mark to go to a school I know nothing about. We don't even know where this school is!"

Lieutenant Landeth cut right in. "I am sorry, sir. But I must remind you once more, that besides informing you of SPIFF's name and purpose, all else is and will remain classified."

"Nothing to fear, Norman," said the captain in a reassuring, authoritative way. "As we've said, your son will be safe. He will be trained by the best. It is an honor."

"I fear nothing, sir," Norman replied. "I simply do not understand why my eldest son has not been chosen for such an honored recruitment."

# "THAT'S NOT A TRACTOR!"

"Norman," said Mom in an appeasing tone, "please don't bring this up again. Can you just be happy for Mark and let him join?"

"But I should be the one going, Mom!" said the peacock with the buzz cut.

"It's true, Mary. I still do not see why Nick could not go in Mark's place." Landeth went to answer, but Mom cut in first.

"Norman, you've punished Mark enough. There is no reason to punish him further by denying him an opportunity to improve his future."

"There is every reason, Mary. You know how much time Nick and I spent restoring that plane. Then that rebellious son of yours up and decides to vent his adolescent disobedience by wrecking our retirement investment. That plane was our nest egg, Mary, our investment for our future. Mark will not be attending."

She narrowed her eyes at him. "May I see you in the kitchen?"

Dad, ever ready to argue for his point of view, stood up and went with her. They began whispering in that low, vehement way that Mark knew would always end up in a shouting match. He sighed.

Mr. Kennedy cleared his throat, clearly uncomfortable, and stirred his Earl Grey tea. Mark stared at the carpet, confused and hurt because he'd once again been the spark to an angry fire. He didn't know what to do or say.

"How about it, Mark?" said the Captain, his warm voice breaking the tense silence. "Adventures across the Alpha-Azimuth, schooling in stellar starfighter tactics, experiencing all manner of vertical horizons, and savoring the most delicious foods from across the galaxy? . . ."

Mark glanced back at the kitchen. Sure enough, the vehement whispers had become a low-voiced argument with overtones of a shortly approaching scream fest. His shoulders felt laden with the stones of guilt. "Can I go in a couple years? Maybe pay back my dad first . . . somehow. . . ."

## CHAPTER 2

Captain Zumski gave a somber shake of his head. "The Admiral may not grant acceptance."

"What happens if I stay?"

Mr. Kennedy answered with an awkward joke. "I'll have to file a bunch more paperwork getting you transferred back." He gave a short, uneasy laugh, then cleared his throat and went back to moving the lemon slice around his tea cup.

"Staying is an option," said the lieutenant, stiff even in the way she sat. "You are under no obligation or pressure to join."

The old captain, with his worn captain's cap and all those weathered wrinkles around his intuitive brown eyes, saw the struggle in Mark's heart. He knew that fight, the guilt for family against the call of adventure.

"It's your choice, ace," he said in earnest. "Living like no adventure ever came your way or," he shrugged, "changing—everything."

The boy looked up from the spot on the carpet. His steady gaze traveled between both important people.

"I have one question."

"Just one?" Stan said with a light chuckle.

"Just one."

"Alright, shoot."

"This SPIFF academy school thing sounds rather science, yes?"

"Right."

"Okay, here's the question, if this school is so science. . .are there . . . hoverboards?"

Stan gave a good-natured laugh. He set down his third plate of apple pie so that Mark could see how serious his reply would be. He looked the boy square in the eyes and said, "Yes."

Mark threw his hands in the air. "Welp, that's me then."

The peacock puffed up, feathers ruffled. "This isn't fair!" he shouted and stomped into the kitchen to argue on his dad's side.

# "THAT'S NOT A TRACTOR!"

The captain stood up with a happy sigh, brushed apple pie crumbs from his belly, and slapped his cap onto his head. "Good! Pack a rucksack and let's set sail!"

"Right now?" said Mark.

"Yes," said Lieutenant Landeth. "We are on an urgent time table."

Mark looked back towards the kitchen where the shouting match he predicted was now in full force.

"Don't worry," said Captain Zumski, flicking the brim of his cap, "I'll talk to your dad."

The next couple of hours raced by in a blur. Mark stuffed his backpack full with a few pairs of jeans, some of his favorite shirts, a couple hoodies, and a bunch of mismatched socks along with all the clean unmentionables he could find. Faster than any other time in his life—even when he had to pack for that theme park day trip—he was by the door, ready to go, because. . .hoverboards.

Dad strode up to the door, a scowl of resignation on his sun-wrinkled face. "You lack discipline," he growled. "This military academy will whip you into shape."

Mark's mom joined them. She just smiled happily and gave her son a big hug. "You know how I worry," she told him, "but I couldn't be happier. Just stay safe OK?" Her warm eyes met his with loving care.

"I will," he said and smiled back. "Can you please tell Tom I'm going to some crazy science academy? And that I'll see him when he gets back next summer? Oh! And that he should try fruit loops mixed with apple pie. Just a thought. It sounds delicious."

Mom promised that she would and Dad gave him a firm handshake and Nick yelled that it just wasn't fair and stomped off. And so, before Mark knew it, his steps were carrying him out onto the front porch and down to the road where the captain and lieutenant waited. A warm evening breeze tussled his unruly hair. He breathed in, filling his lungs

## CHAPTER 2

with the swirling aroma of apple trees, sage, and eucalyptus. The solitary street lamp flickered and buzzed. Adventure drifted in the wind.

Stan clapped him on the shoulder. "Good to have you onboard, lad."

"Let's get going, then," said Landeth, brisk and businesslike as always.

Mark looked back at his house, the warm lights behind closed curtains were comforting and familiar. "I guess I'll need a new calendar. I won't get to do all that nothing after all," he said with a small smile.

They marched out into the nearby field. After a short walk underneath a starry sky, they stopped. Directly in front of them and illuminated by bright moonlight, was the most boring thing Mark had ever seen: a rusted heap that used to be a tractor.

"Liftoff in two minutes. Stow your luggage," the lieutenant ordered.

"What? In that busted old tractor?" asked the perplexed new recruit.

Zumski, tapping the brim of his captain's cap, smiled and said, "That's not a tractor!"

In a moment all the air around the boring old piece of farm equipment started to shimmer and sway. Like an evaporating curtain of water, the tractor dissipated to reveal the strangest thing. Jagged fins protruded from the hull, yet the craft looked sleek. Solid steel panels made it heavy, yet the engines looked powerful. Never had Mark seen such an aggressive machine, yet it looked . . . beautiful.

Captain Zumski had walked up to the gray starfighter and was searching around. "Lloyd?" he looked underneath. "Lloyd!"

A short android was crouching underneath, looking suspiciously at Mark.

"Saddle up an extra seat in the starfighter and stow the boys bags away when you're done hiding, will you, old chap?" Stan said, standing back up.

Lloyd scrambled up from his hiding spot, never taking that suspicious gaze off Mark. "Is he contagious?"

"THAT'S NOT A TRACTOR!"

Mark took a step back, eyes wide. It was an actual, real android. Funny cylindrical head, metal body parts, and all—and it could talk!

"Not of anything that'd affect you," chuckled Zumski, "you paranoid bag of bolts."

Lloyd stared at Mark, still very skeptical. "What if he's a Syn'Crux, sir?"

"Burn my biscuits! He's no more one of them than you are."

Lloyd's camera-lens like eyes widened. "What if," he paused in horror. "What if I am?"

Stan chuckled again. Landeth ignored the whole exchange. She went about preparing for liftoff. Lloyd scooted over to Mark, grabbed his backpack, and scooted away. Mark was dumbfounded by the little robot. The captain had to say Mark's name twice before he looked up. Soon, though, Mark was sitting in his own seat next to the captain while Landeth made final calibrations.

"Sir," Mark asked Stan. "Who is Lloyd? And why did this starfighter look like a tractor?"

"Invisibility is highly overrated, you see," the captain began. "An uber-boring-field generator projects a hologram over whatever it's attached too. The hologram is something so ordinary, so very boring, that nobody gives it a second thought." He settled in his seat and adjusted his cap "And Lloyd . . . Lloyd is the most loyal android you'll ever meet. He may have a few circuits missing, but beyond his paranoia, he's a rather swell chap."

Landeth looked back at them and said, "Prepare for departure."

Two seatbelts automatically crisscrossed Mark's chest and clicked tight. A dull thud rumbled his seat as the engines fired up. Soon, Mark would leave house and home behind for unimagined adventure. A curious thought occurred to him all of a sudden. "So, where is this SPIFF anyway?"

## CHAPTER 2

The lieutenant pointed somewhere up and out the glass canopy covering them. Mark followed her outstretched hand. She was pointing straight at the moon!

He fell back into his seat. "Whaaaat?"

A deep hum filled the cabin. Both thrusters spun up. A curved black control panel blinked on in front of the lieutenant. Cryptic neon-yellow symbols sprung up in between crisp blue lines. Her hands flew over the controls. The starfighter responded.

Mark gulped. His confusion turned to surprise, and then to awe, before settling on complete enthrallment. The whole starfighter had lifted off the ground and was racing over everything at ever increasing speeds.

Captain Zumski relaxed into his chair and pulled the brim of his hat down. He yawned. "Take us to the moon, Alice."

The high-pitched whir that had been building suddenly thudded into a deep roar. Gravity sunk Mark's stomach. The starfighter tilted upwards. The cabin filled with bright moonlight.

## "THAT'S NOT A TRACTOR!"

CHAPTER 3

# CHAPTER 3
## SPIFF

Up, up, above the clouds and through the atmosphere they sped. Mark's hometown became a glowing dot among hundreds of glowing dots across the night-shrouded Australian continent. All the rumbling turbulence faded as the starfighter broke through Earth's upper stratosphere and soared into space. His ears rang from so much sudden silence. Mark gulped to clear his ears. Then he gulped out of awe-struck amazement. Stars, everywhere, brighter than diamonds scattered in a gigantic, endless pool of spilled ink. The universe was vast and open, . . . forever. And he was traveling out into the void.

"Whoooaaa," he breathed. It was magic made real.

Then he felt a strange sensation, right around in his stomach area. All that food in there felt like it was—floating!

"Whoa-hahaha!" he laughed as he saw the captain's cap float off the man's head. "We're completely weightless?"

"Sure are," Captain Zumski said as he snatched his cap out of the air.

"So if I," said Mark and spat in his hand. "Awesome!"

His spit had become a floating blob. He poked it with a finger. It wobbled and floated down. He poked it again. It wobbled sideways. He poked it again. It wobbled up. For a solid twenty minutes the boy from Earth kept poking that blob of spit and watching it wobble around, snickering like an elementary school kid mixing all his leftover food together at the end of lunch.

## CHAPTER 3

"Wait." Mark paused poking his spit blob. He'd been struck by an abrupt realization. He turned to the captain. "How is SPIFF on the moon?"

"It's up on the West Ridge of Crescent City. Great views."

"A city?" Mark exclaimed. "A whole city on the moon?"

"The capital city of this solar sector, in fact. It sits at the lowermost edge of the star side of the moon. No cities on the Earth side—you guys would notice." Stan smiled to himself. "Fancy all the ruckus that would cause."

"A whole city full of people from Earth." Mark imagined it all. "Whoa. . ."

"Full of Earthers? No, well, perhaps one or two in a million."

"Only one person in a million is from Earth?" said Mark, with a confused frown. "Where's everyone else from?"

A nostalgic smile parted the old captain's gray-flecked beard. "Many, many years ago—when my bones were still young and restless—I traveled the oceans of space for years and years at a time. I wouldn't land on a planet or moon for ages. I wouldn't see a normal horizon for years!" He scratched his beard. "And you know what? My mind settled to thinking like that. I thought in only one way, one opinion, one idea. But then you know what happened?"

"Huh?" said Mark, all curious.

"After years in space, an adventure took me down to a rocky, dusty old planet. I landed. The starship doors opened . . ." Stan's hands shot forward. "There! The horizon! Looming, massive, solid, infinite, flat." His hands illustrated it all as he continued. "My brain didn't know what to do. Everything went sideways! A vertical horizon! And I puked my guts out on the tarmac . . ."

"Whoa," Mark breathed.

"Magical," replied Stan with a grin. "And so, Mark old chap, perhaps what I'm about to tell you will make you feel like you've seen a vertical horizon, or," Stan continued with a shrug, "it won't. But the fact remains this," he paused to look at Mark with a twinkle in his eyes, "our galaxy is filled with people!"

Mark's eyebrows scrunched together in surprised confusion.

The captain continued by pointing out the window at all those twinkling stars. "From the famous bakers of cloud cakes served only in the neon sky cities of Alpha Centaurie, to the street-side sellers of gringly grumbakes in the space colonies of Stragl-minus—there are people, people everywhere!"

Mark was shocked. The whole Milky Way Galaxy was filled with people? "That's so crazy it," Mark paused, dumbfounded. "It must be true."

"Indeed it is, my boy. Earth is only one planet out of many, many planets filled with many, many civilizations—each with their own food specialty."

"But how?"

"Ah. Hmmm." Captain Zumski turned to the lieutenant. "Alice, hand me the star chart, will you? The galaxy one."

Without looking away from her controls she reached into a nearby compartment and produced a neatly folded map. It was blank and made of a semitranslucent, soft plastic.

"Thank you," said Zumski. He unfolded it and held up the top left corner. He gave the top right corner to Mark to hold up. They stretched the star chart between them.

Mark's eyes widened. The clear, blank plastic flickered on to display the whole shimmering Milky Way galaxy. The galaxy floated a couple inches off the dark blue plastic sheet, rotating.

"I'll illustrate it this way, our whole galaxy is like your home planet," began the well-traveled captain. "Tell me, on Earth, what are the most populated places? The continents with the most people?"

## CHAPTER 3

Mark thought back to geography class. "China . . . well but that's part of Asia. So Asia. And Europe too, I bet."

"Right," he said and pointed to the center of the Milky Way. "All around the center of our galaxy are millions of the most populated solar systems. Alpha Centaurie," he pointed at one end of the center, "is thought by most scholars to be the cradle of civilization." His finger moved to the other end of the center. "Others think it's Beta Centaurie." He turned back to Mark. "Now, you see all the galactic arms that spiral off of the center?"

Marks eyes wandered around the galaxy map. He looked at the curved glowing arcs that spiraled out from the center. If people lived there, it must be like living on the outskirts of a big city. "Suburbia?" he guessed.

"In a way, in a way," Stan replied. "Once humanity figured out how to travel and settle the stars, people moved out into all these galactic arms."

"What's this really dark area?" asked Mark, pointing to a large sector that seemed to blot out the light of the galaxy the way a menacing storm blots out the light of day.

The old man grunted, disgust in his voice. "The Dead Arm. Severed from its galactic arm eons ago. With few ways in and fewer ways out, it became a haven for outlaws, shadow corporations, convicts, and worse. It is dead space. And it is overseen by the Syn'Crux."

"Oh."

"Moving on. Last question, what is the most isolated, unexplored jungle on Earth? The place with all those primitive, undiscovered tribes who still use bows and arrows and would use an iPod for a hammer because technology never reached them?"

Mark smirked. "My grandparents' house?"

The old captain waggled a finger at him. "Respect your elders."

"Okay, okay . . . hmmm . . . the Amazon Jungle."

Zumski pointed to an area on the outskirts of the galaxy. It was at the end of one of the longest spiraling arcs. "There you have it, the Amazon Jungle of our Milky Way: the Phoenix Massive."

Mark stared at the large fiery mass. A sense of wonder enthralled him.

"It's one of the great Uncharted Areas," the captain continued. "Along with the Alpha Azimuth, the Typhoon Nebula, and several smaller locations. The Phoenix Massive is one of the oldest unexplored Galactic Quadrants." He turned back to the new recruit. "Galactic humanity wasn't able to send voyagers to this area until several thousand years ago. And you know what they found?"

"What?" said Mark, curiosity piqued.

"A long lost, primitive, uncivilized bunch of fellow humans living on a small blue planet—which they called Earth."

"Whaaaaaatttt?" said Mark. "Me? Everyone from Earth? Our whole planet is a long lost tribe in the Milky Way galaxy?"

"Indeed," said the old captain. "Compared to the rest of galactic humanity, Earthers just invented fire. No trans-galactic travel, no planetary Tera-formation, your cars drive on the ground, and not an interstellar buffet in sight! Tragic really, but there you are."

"Why? . . . Why don't we know about all this?"

"Disease, mainly," replied Stan with a sad shake of his head. "The 'Black Plague' as you call it."

Mark frowned. "Yeah. Killed millions of people." He grimaced. "After festering sickly black boils full of puss on their skin."

Stan's tone stayed solemn. "And it was all started by a galactic tourist with a cough."

Mark gave a weak laugh. "Really?"

"That is why the Galactic Council ordered Class 1A protection for Earth shortly after your planet was discovered. Otherwise, your whole civilization would have ended up like the Mayans or Aztecs after the

## CHAPTER 3

Conquistadors. Or like so many of the Native Americans after the colonists. You remember?"

"Dead of disease."

The Captain nodded. "Yes."

Mark thought for some time. This was heavy. He looked out the window at all those stars out there, really looked at them this time. To think those stars had planets, planets with people—people like him.

The old Captain could tell that the new recruit needed time to think. He folded the map back up. Landeth took and stored it.

"Get some rest, ace. It's a long flight and you have a big day tomorrow," said the old captain. He settled down in his chair and pulled the cap over his brow once more.

Mark leaned back in the seat and sighed. His mind spun. Feelings of amazement and awe and adventure began warming his blood. The diamonds glowed with a red hot fire now, out there in the spilled ink of the universe. He couldn't really understand all he'd learned yet, but he felt the truth of it, the truth of a galaxy filled with life. His eyes darted between one glimmering pinpoint of light to another.

"Life all out there," he whispered to himself. "People. Old people like gramps and gran, who look up at the stars and remember all the fun they had; people like dad who are so busy that they never really look up at the stars anymore; and kids, kids like me, who always, always look up at the stars and dream and dream." The truth of it all had only just begun to sink in, and Mark felt, no, he knew, that this was only the beginning. His eyes wandered the void and forever. "Someday, I'm going to see a real vertical horizon. . . ."

A silence settled around them. Mark thought and thought. He wondered what Crescent City looked like. He wondered if he'd make new friends who'd go exploring with him. He wondered if the classes at his new school would be mind-blowingly weird. But most of all, he wondered if that was really the lieutenant who was softly humming what sounded like a lullaby.

The song rolled from her lips in notes that were other-worldly and beautiful, happy yet haunting. A listing verse, a lulling melody, it told Mark of a family long broken apart, of childhood memories shattered at heart, of an unforgiving past that would never depart.

She seemed to be humming to herself while checking the instruments and gauges, lost in her own thoughts. He thought about leaning over to Stan and asking, but the old salt had started snoring. Lloyd was stuffed somewhere out of sight too. So Mark just settled back in his chair and gazed out the dark window.

Earth was behind them, the sun was too, and the moon was yet a long way off. He tried to remain awake. He tried getting lost in the wonder of his adventure, but the dull, steady drumming of the engines made him feel warm and comfortable. And he had lived through so much today. Alice's quiet lullaby began pulling him away. His eyelids drooped. Sleep beckoned. He followed.

■ ■ ■ ■ ■ ■ ■ ■ ■ ■

"Something's wrong."

The captain's voice came from a distance. Mark grimaced. His neck hurt from trying to sleep while sitting. The glass against his forehead felt cold and hard. That steady hum of the starfighter's engines had become an accelerating roar.

The lieutenant's voice reached in through his cobwebs of sleep. "Alert, unidentified hawk class ship, alter your course away from the starliner."

Static.

Mark slowly sat up. He rubbed his hazy, hurting eyes. How long had he been asleep?

## CHAPTER 3

"Repeat. Unidentified ship, your bearing is on a collision trajectory. Respond."

More static.

Mark blinked furiously. His eyes focused. A blaze of neon exploded into sight. Far below, a crescent shaped city filled his entire field of vision. And, ahead of them, highlighted by the harsh lights of the city, were two spaceships. One could have been a Boeing 747 from back home, except its wings were swept underneath it in the shape of a closed pair of scissors. The other was a small ship with short wings; it seemed to be heading straight for the larger ship.

"Final warning! Change course!"

Mark looked at the captain.

The man remained focused forward. Then, "Lieutenant, intercept that hawk, now."

Mark gripped his seat as the starfighter pitched forwarded and down, accelerating hard. Heart thudding loud in his ears, he kept his eyes on the two ships. Crescent City shone below them, a brilliant backdrop.

"Get on the com and alert that starliner," the captain continued. "They have a rogue inbound."

"Starliner Delta-10, respond."

Once more, static filled the line.

Mark felt overwhelmed. He could see the tension around Stan's eyes, the lieutenant's sharp hand gestures over the controls, the panic they were trying to control. Sweat and stress filled the little air there was in the small cabin.

"Delta-10, respond," Landeth repeated. "Respond, Delta-10!"

Nothing.

She looked at the Captain. "That hawk's on a suicide course, sir. Collision imminent."

Stan's eyes rested on her for a moment, then snapped towards the hawk. "Take care of it."

Alice took them into a hard roll that made Mark's head bump against the glass. Her fingers danced over the glowing controls. The starfighter responded.

Crescent City so far below spun in a dizzy blur of green, blue, and yellow neon. Mark squeezed his eyes shut. His fingers were going numb from gripping the seat.

"Guns hot."

He opened his eyes just as the starfighter leveled out behind the hawk. The rogue ships thrusters were burning an aggressive red.

"No warning shots," said the captain. "Aim for the engines."

Mark gulped as the starfighters guns came into play. He could feel each shot leave the barrels on each side of their ship. A magnetic rushing, a thick buzzing whoosh, and crimson bolts of electrified plasma streaked right by him.

Alice aimed flawlessly. No misses, no losses, each bolt met the hawk's shields with punishing force. The shield warbled and swayed, unable to absorb everything. The few shots that struck the ship tore into its hull. Jagged splinters of burning metal ripped off, dashed into space.

Mark blinked as Alice took them straight into the shards of glowing debris. He heard the pieces hit and bounce off their starfighter.

"Hawk's shields at sixty and dropping," said Alice.

"Good," Stan replied.

"Delta-10 sees us," said Alice. "They're trying an escape."

Mark strained to look over her shoulder. Sure enough, the large starliner had seen the firefight and was racing away, bright blue engines on fire. He tried relaxing. This crazy wakeup call would end soon. But then the hawk's shields blinked off.

## CHAPTER 3

"He's going full burn!" said Alice and rerouted all their shields to the front.

All the power from the hawk's shields had gone into its thrusters. Both rectangular engines went from glowing red to scorching crimson. Mark instinctively threw his hands up in front of his face. Their cabin filled with harsh light. He could see their shields boiling.

"Follow at full," the captain commanded. "Cripple those engines!"

Landeth slammed the throttle. Mark cupped his ears as the snarl of their engines became a high-pitched scream. Each breath he took, he felt the reverberations from the magnetic coils of their guns firing.

The hawk dove and twisted to avoid being ripped open. It never slowed in its suicidal pursuit of the escaping starliner. Alice plunged and rolled and never let off the trigger. The night filled with neon embers as electrified plasma bolts streaked above the shimmering city.

Mark gulped again. This chase was about to end, one way or another. The bulky starliner could not escape the relentless speed of the Hawk.

"Sir, we won't make it," said Landeth, grim in voice.

"Steady on, Lieutenant," said the determined captain. But he too saw the inevitable.

In a final burst of insanity, the hawk blitzed straight at the starliner's passenger side.

It was unstoppable.

Then, the hawk made an odd maneuver. Instead of smashing straight into the passenger-filled hull, it aimed a bit higher, right at Delta-10's roof.

Mark could not look away. The bottom of the hawk hit the top of the starliner, ripping its roof clean off. In silence they saw shards of metal from both ships shatter into space. In silence they saw the oxygenated air from the starliner start rushing out into the void. In silence they saw the people inside panicking, screaming, holding on. Both broken ships fell towards the neon city.

Alice dove after them, careening their starfighter into the shattered mess. They fell into a red metal storm of jagged scraps. Mark's tight grip on his seat renewed. He could hear the clatter of sharp pieces against the hull. He saw chunks of broken metal bash against their windows, leaving long scratches. The starfighter lurched around glowing debris, arced above the burning wreckage, and twisted to avoid fiery fragmented remains. Landeth—steady at the helm—flew her ship through the wild maelstrom.

"Come on, come on," Stan growled.

Mark looked at the captain. The man's eyes were locked on the broken starliner tumbling ahead of them. He didn't feel the bent masses of hull metal breaking their shields and gouging their starfighter. He didn't see the hawk as it plummeted away in a haphazard tumble of fractured steel, its red engines seeping black smoke. He focused only on the ripped open Delta-10, and all its panicking passengers as their air streamed into space.

"Throw your emergency shields up already!" He shouted, fists clenched.

Mere minutes after the hawk had torn the starliner's roof off, a transparent silver-blue pattern of hexagons blinked on.

"Yes!" cheered Zumski. "Good show!"

The shield intensified, enveloping the whole starliner.

"I don't believe it," said Landeth, amber eyes darting between her controls and the crash ahead. "My scans shows not a single casualty. Everyone is safe."

"Spot on, Alice," Stan said as they burst out of the storm of debris and into the calm void of space.

She didn't respond, her hands flying across the controls. She looked back up, searching for something out in dark void. "It's gone. That hawk is gone and our communications are back up."

Mark felt his muscles unclench. The tension started to dissipate. He breathed a sigh of relief and craned his neck to see the starliner. The

## CHAPTER 3

large swept wing ship had stabilized. Three of its four diamond shaped engines were running. Two of the engines stayed steady while the third flickered; the fourth remained dark. Delta-10 was flying normal now. Just like that, all those passengers were safe.

"Patch me through to Delta-10's con," said Stan.

Landeth flicked a few switches and hailed the starliner.

"This is Captain Stanislaw Zumski to Delta-10 control, respond."

"This is Delta-10 control," said a disciplined man's voice. "Thank you for getting ready to back us up, Captain Zumski."

"What was that all about?" said Stan, leaning forward in his seat to hear better.

"We aren't sure," replied the man's voice. "But we think it has something to do with Fleet Commander Eli Exor being on board."

Stan's concerned tone changed to irritation. "What is the Commander doing without a proper escort? And on a civilian ship no less?"

"He claims to be traveling alone and in secret on a mission to find the Obliv."

"Secrecy be damned," growled Stan. "He risked the lives of every soul on board!"

"I agree, Captain. I tried to— "

"Captain," interrupted Landeth. "Port Authority is hailing us."

"Switch lines."

A gruff male voice spoke up over the intercom. "Captain Zumski, this is Port Authority Officer Steve McCroskey. Please land at Hangar 42 and immediately report to my office."

"What is it?" said the captain.

"My office?" said McCrosky. "Why, it's a room with a desk, coffee maker, and picture of my wife. But that's not important right now. Go to hangar 42 and report for debriefing on this situation."

"We have a passenger on board for SPIFF," said Alice. "Please advise."

"Drop passenger at SPIFF and report immediately for debrief."

"Understood," Landeth replied, banking them in another steep dive, this time towards the West Ridge of the neon city.

Mark looked between the lieutenant and the captain. Both were focused, the military woman on speeding them down into the city and the captain on distant thoughts that made his brow furrow.

"Captain," said Alice, breaking the brief moment of silence. "That was the strangest collision I've ever seen . . ."

"I agree."

"Sir," she continued. "Was this another deathwish attempt on the commander's life?"

Zumski remained silent, a pensiveness having sunk into his craggily face. "We may know at the debrief."

"What happened then?" said Mark.

Stan turned to meet Mark's searching gaze. He could read the worry and confusion in the boy's eyes. But the only answer he could give was the truth. "I don't know yet, ace. The lieutenant and I will be looking into it. Thankfully everyone is safe." He looked back towards the neon lights. "But Alice is right, that was a very strange crash. The way that hawk pulled up at the last instant," he trailed off for a moment. Then, slowly shaking his head, he continued. "Coupled with the fact that there hasn't been a collision—accident or otherwise—in Crescent City for decades, and we have ourselves somewhat of a mystery."

Mark heard the honesty in the man's voice. There was no answer. Not yet. Not right now. But he couldn't get the crash out of his mind. It kept replaying in slow motion, that horrific moment when metal and air ruptured out into space, all the more gruesome with the eerie silence. He tried to forget about it by looking at the city they were speeding into.

They broke into the atmosphere. All the turbulence scattered Mark's thoughts.

## CHAPTER 3

"Hold onto your seatbelts," Stan suggested as their ship descended, bobbing and rocking in the winds. Clearing his throat and adjusting his captain's cap to clear the tension, he said, "We'll be in full view of your new school soon."

Mark clutched onto his seatbelt, feeling a sense of anticipation building. "Lloyd will show you to the Mess Hall. It's about lunchtime right now."

"Lunchtime?" said Mark. "But it's dark outside!"

"The way the moon turns, we get two weeks of night and two weeks of day."

Mark's brain tried processing that. Two whole weeks of darkness. Two whole weeks of daylight. It was going to be either really creepy or dangerously exciting.

"There she is," said Captain Stan with pride. He pointed out the window. "Our grand academy, our illustrious institute, our School for Paragon Cadets Excelling in something stellar, neo-something, something something, and something else."

Mark's forehead clunked against the window as he strained to see. The vibrating glass shook his head, making his "whoooaaa," sound like he was breathing through a fan. His eyebrows rose as he opened his eyes wide to see absolutely everything. "My school is a gigantic old starship?"

"Indeed it is," Captain Stan rejoined. "The GSS Final Frontier," he said with immense pride as they drew nearer. "It crashed right into the top of the West Ridge more than a thousand years ago. That's why the front sticks out like that while the rest is buried in the crater—never made it all the way through."

Mark responded by hyperventilated. The galactic starship, with its broken front spearing out the top of the mountainous West Ridge, looked like a massive shark bursting out of an enormous wave with its jaws wide open. It was colossal. At least seven stories high and hundreds of feet long, the old starship dominated the hill.

"Yes, it's served many, many different purposes. But that was before my time. SPIFF has been there for more than five hundred years now."

Mark could only respond by pointing at it. Glowing windows covered the sides; From classrooms to hanger bays, the tall curved sides were aglow with life. The yawning front was filled with offices at the top level, a few levels of classrooms, a two-story cafeteria with a curved exterior wall made of glass, and below all that stood a high glass entrance with a long flight of stairs descending from it to the ground. But they weren't flying to the entrance.

"Yes, yes, it's a sight to see," said Stan as they flew to the lower left side of the starship school. "My office is at the top too. I can see all my favorite restaurants."

The lieutenant interrupted with a sharp, "Prep for landing."

Mark held his breath as they zoomed in. He was wondering where they were going to land when they slowed. A large set of hangar bay doors opened at the side of the massive school. The starfighter hovered in place until the doors opened, then they drifted inside.

Landing in a cavernous bay where mechanics rushed between ships of every shape and size, their starfighter settled down with a groan.

"Alright, ace," said Zumski, voice bespeaking his urgency. "The lieutenant and I are expected for debriefing."

Mark nodded. "Okay, well thanks." He shook their hands. Then the starfighters glass canopy lifted. A wall of sound slammed into Mark's eardrums. Noise from the starfighter's humming engines, mechanics using power tools, and people shouting commands all echoed in the deep landing bay.

Mark scrambled down the side. Lloyd joined him, walking over from somewhere behind the starfighter. He looked as if he had spent the flight crammed in the luggage compartment.

## CHAPTER 3

"Stuffed like a sardine," said the android, shivering. "The horror . . . the horror."

"Lloyd, get Mark to the Mess Hall," said Zumski.

"Sir, yes sir," saluted Lloyd, "Captain, sir."

"Oh! I almost forgot," said Stan with a raised hand stopping Mark. "Got this for ya." He reached below his seat and pulled a sleek red and black metal box from underneath. "It's your new lunchbox. Makes forty-two hundred different types of food."

"Thank you," said Mark, catching the box tossed down by the old captain. With a salute, Zumski turned and spoke to Alice.

The starfighter's engine's spun up and the glass canopy slid closed. Mark watched the craft lift and turn. With a burst of speed, the sleek gray ship rocketed back out of the bay doors.

Mark tucked the red lunchbox under his arm, his eyes following the starfighter as it faded from view across the neon city. Then he jogged out to the edge of the landing pad to see the city he'd call home for a whole school year.

Crescent City came into full view even before he reached the ledge. He could see the whole city, and the funny thing was, it didn't look strange. No big glass bubble dome, no floating pods, no stupid sci-fi stuff; just, you know, hovercars and junk. He honestly thought it looked like any normal city. From the center rose a downtown of soaring glass skyscrapers designed by pompous architects with inadequacy issues. Just south of downtown was a large lake bordered by sandy beaches and overpriced restaurants; below that stood the busy Crescent City Spaceport where luggage was being lost. Surrounding all this was a suburban jungle of homes, stretch malls, and little parks. Enveloping everything, like two arms hugging the whole city, were the tall ridges of the crater rim.

He could see hovercars dipping down out from translucent highways that were stacked on top of each other, some seven rows tall. There were hovercars streaming all across the city in zigzagging patterns of red taillights and yellow headlamps. People. People traveling to and from work and home and the grocery store. All across the valley people were living their lives.

A breeze gusted in through the bay doors. It was hot and muggy and filled with strange thick fumes. He could smell the grime and dirt, and the metal and glass, and the diesel and electricity of the neon city. He knew he was someplace else, someplace far from home—someplace different.

Mark breathed in deep. He filled his lungs with the dense, sultry air and sighed happily. "If this is where adventure lives . . . I'm home."

# CHAPTER 4

# CHAPTER 4
## HEATH AND LEXE

"Sardines," said the short android as he led Mark through school hallways. "Have you had sardines?"

"I've had tuna," said Mark, trying to walk straight while lost in the awesomeness of being inside a galactic starship. The hallways were long triangle-shaped corridors. The slate gray floors were illuminated on each side by an orange glow; smooth white walls curved upwards in a sophisticated yet efficient design; colorful rectangular banners hung from ceilings adorned in bare steel pipes. The banners displayed simple symbols on backgrounds of solid colors. There were a variety of symbols: curved, sharp, straight edge, or rectangular. They resembled helmets, spacecraft, and solar systems.

"No, not like tuna," Lloyd continued. "Tuna is mashed up. I was a sardine. A sardine!"

Mark kept politely murmuring in agreement. But he wasn't paying attention. He was gazing up at those banners, trying to figure out what the symbols represented. Then, a high-pitched buzz like miniature jet engines echoed down the hall.

"Do you hear that?" said Lloyd, camera lenses open wide.

Mark saw something small streak by overhead. He whirled around. A flash of orange metal disappeared down the hall.

"The Calvien Rebels escaped again!" Lloyd shouted, ducking behind Mark.

## CHAPTER 4

Two high whines filled the air. Mark turned back to the corner where the first jet had flown in from. Around the corner raced two small black starfighters. They looked like miniatures or models or something put together by a hobbyist with way too much time, except these were—alive!

Mark stopped, his eyes wide open and following both miniature black starfighters as they chased after the first in hot pursuit.

Lloyd stood up on tiptoe and whispered, "The Volde Empire's given chase." Then he sprung away, shouting, "Run while covering your head!"

Mark laughed, watching the android sprint down the hall in the opposite direction. Then a frown of realization sunk in. He looked around. "Aaaannd now I have no idea where to go."

The corridors stood empty . Everyone was at lunch already. He did walk by a few students but didn't ask for directions, hoping to find the lunch room on his own. But after a few turns down random hallways, his stomach pressured him to ask.

A group of guys were walking by, talking and laughing together.

"Excuse me," said Mark, "where's the cafeteria?"

The group stopped and turned to him. They looked like a bunch of guys who regularly skipped classes and lied to any teacher who caught them. One of the guys, older than the rest, said, "What's that you're looking for, friend?"

"Bad food, worse smells, bearded lunch ladies, you know, the cafeteria."

"Oh," said the older boy with a chuckle, "the Mess Hall."

"Right, yeah."

"Next left. The tall metal doors. Can't miss it."

"Thanks," said Mark.

"Sure," he replied before he turned to his snickering friends. They left, talking in low whispers about "Earthers."

Mark squinted at their suspiciousness. Then shrugged it off and decided to try it out. A left turn and a few short steps and he was confronted by a tall metal door. Hesitation stalled him, but hunger goaded him on. He reached for the long metal door handle. His hand sunk through!

"Weeeeiirrrrddd," said Mark. He wiggled his fingers inside the holographic door. Then, he took his right hand out. He put his right hand in. He put his left hand in, he took his left hand out, he put his right foot in, and shook it all about.

"So awesome," he said again, grinning. Deciding that lunch could wait, he put his left arm in; he took his left arm out. He put his backside in, he took his backside out. He closed his eyes and put his whole face in and shook it all about.

"WHAT are you doing?" bellowed an irritated man's voice.

Mark, head still through the door, opened his eyes. Gasping, he ducked his head back out.

The door dissipated. A whole classroom, big as half an assembly hall, waited with older students staring right at him. On the lecture floor, behind a large table, stood the professor. White hair fell straight past his square shoulders; his jaw was rectangular and face rigid.

"Step on in," he motioned to Mark, "and enlighten us, please, as to why you felt compelled to shake your rump in front of one hundred and eighty of my advanced bio-augmentation students."

Mark cleared his throat and fidgeted with the lunchbox under his arm. The professors stare was hard to keep. "Welp, it's like this" said Mark, stepping in. He was about to make a wise-cracking comment but stopped. The professor had walked out from behind his desk—on what appeared to be four metal legs. Each leg ended in a square point; two on each side of a black metal torso, they looked efficient and far more effective than normal human legs. The man's face was just as efficient at conveying his disciplinary intent. Mark mumbled, "I was looking for the Mess Hall."

Most of the class laughed, the rest scowled at him.

## CHAPTER 4

"And here I thought we had a policy against recruiting Earthers," said the augmented professor. "Get out of my class!"

Mark shrugged an apology and backed away. As soon as he was out in the hall, the metal doors reappeared behind him.

"That wasn't the food factory," he said, adjusting the lunchbox under his arm. "Maybe I'll just eat in the hall."

The box's lid had a picture of a red bagel with little horns and a spikey tail. Turning the box over, he tried to find a way to open it. No lid, no seam, nothing there to give him a clue. The hunger made him quickly loose his patience. He stopped trying.

"I'll prove it!" said a kid who had walked out of a set of green doors further down the hallway. "But save my seat!"

Mark heard the loud noise of lunchroom chatter drift out before the doors reappeared in place. He strode forwards. A few short steps and he was confronted by vegetable-green doors. Above them were large block letters that read: "Mess Hall, South Entrance."

He approached the door. But, not seeing any door handles—and still goaded on by his hunger—he decided to just walk through.

"Nice," he said as they disappeared to let him through. Once inside, he turned around. The doors reappeared as if closing behind him. "Never walked through a door before. Ghosts have it good."

Noise, students, and the smell of food filled Mark's senses in an instant. He turned and looked out across the large room he'd entered. Recruits of different ages sat around circular tables. Some were laughing in between bites of food; others leaned in whispering over empty lunchboxes; most were just talking and eating.

Standing in that one spot, gazing out across the packed Mess Hall, he suddenly felt very alone. Energetic conversations floated in the air around the large domed lunchroom; he wanted to join in, but he didn't know anybody. In a lunch room filled with people, he felt stranded on a

HEATH AND LEXE

deserted island.

The curved walls to his left and right seemed to be gigantic screens displaying videos. There was one video of older students in modern aviatorlike jackets flying through space doing barrel rolls in small, sleek ships. Another showed younger recruits working on those ships and smiling. There was even a looping video of a round escape pod soaring across the city with a big red X over it and warning letters.

His stomach growled.

"Yeah, yeah, yeah," he responded. Looking around, he didn't see a food pick up area. He started walking, hands shoved into his pockets, feeling lost and out of place. Should he ask someone where to get food? But everyone looked so happy and busy talking with their friends and eating lunch and laughing at inside jokes. As he walked around he tried to figure out how people were getting their food. All he saw were open lunchboxes with every type of tasty goodness inside. His stomach growled even louder.

"I heard you the first time," he growled back.

He felt stranded without a map or a clue. It was making him hungrier. For a few minutes he went wandering between cheerful groups. Snippets of conversations would reach his ears. Words like wargame and flarerider and Lance's blacknova, were new and confusing. Other conversations were less confusing but still strange. Mark didn't know how to join in groups discussing "my terraforming class," and "Professor Elgor's grading is rough."

A minute more of wandering and Mark caught an interesting conversation. It was about "board's modded with three kicks need at least an eight cell crank," and "Jack broke his foot trying that last stunt."

Those topics were coming from a table with a couple open seats. Four guys around his age were seated at it. Mark decided this might be a friendly place to park it.

## CHAPTER 4

"So how about those hoverboards, eh?" he said with a smile. "I'm going to get one ASAP."

They looked at him with a mixture of pity and laughter.

"You do that," said a guy who was trying to grow a mustache.

"Yeah, maybe mod it out," said Mark.

Everyone at the table tried holding back a laugh.

"With what?" the failed mustache kid said. "A straw to help it suck more?" He laughed. The others didn't join him though. A girl with long dark hair said, "That was lame, Bobby. I can do better than that."

Everyone at the table started topping each other's jokes about Mark and hoverboards and Earthers.

Mark left them to their tittering and walked away with his back straight. It was his first day here. He didn't want his empty stomach pushing him into a fight, at least not this week. But the hungry frustration was really setting in now. He decided to just ask the next table how these baffling lunchboxes worked.

"Hi," said Mark, standing at a random table. "Do you know how these confounded things work?" he asked, shaking the red lunchbox in his hand.

"What are you? From Earth?" said someone at the table. They all laughed.

Mark turned and left. He silently cursed Lloyd for leaving him alone. This wasn't a great start to the day. Feeling alone among laughter, an outcast among people, an outsider in a strange new place—he decided to find somewhere quiet and just sit down.

He made his way to the back of the Mess Hall where a wall made entirely of curved glass looked out over the Crescent City valley below.

SPIFF, sitting at the top of the west crater rim, held a commanding outlook. Suburban homes stretched down the hill, aglow with warmth in the darkness. Further away, the glimmer of downtown skyscrapers

HEATH AND LEXE

reminded him of a distant bonfire of neon colors. Connecting all this was an intricate web of stacked flyways where hovercars zipped to and fro, faster than fireflies in the night.

Mark sighed. "No. One more try."

He turned, eyes wandering around the lunch room. He saw a boy about his age walking up to various tables and talking to the students there. This peaked Mark's curiosity. Each table greeted the kid with enthusiasm, clapping him on the back and giving him a chair. The kid had sandy blonde hair that curled and friendly olive-colored eyes set in a round and good-natured face. Square glasses sat on his lightly freckled nose and a solid blue tie hung from the collar of his white button-up shirt.

Mark saw him taking an odd assortment of things from the worn brown satchel slung across his left shoulder: a pair of brand new sneakers, a handful of sunglasses, and several packs of chewing gum. The other kids would check out the stuff while the boy told stories that made them laugh. Then—and this is what peaked Mark's curiosity the most—they would buy an item or even three. After a two more tables of salesmanship, the kid found an empty table, slung his satchel on the tabletop, and flopped down in a chair with a sigh.

Mark decided to walk over.

"Hey new guy," said the kid, who had noticed Mark walking up. "How goes?"

"Picture this," Mark began, scrapping a chair to sit down, "Your mindkey being exploded to smithereens by a lemon grenade. Then the truth shanking you between the ribs like a gazillion knife-wielding fireflies. Then falling asleep. Then being slapped awake by a juicy pomegranate detonated in your face. Then landing on a derelict ship populated by no one but howler monkeys. Then being crazy hungry. Take that feeling and sing it—dramatically."

## CHAPTER 4

The boy laughed while loosening his blue tie, "Holy tobuscus sauce. That's intense."

"And emotional," Mark pointed out, "as long as nobody understands it."

The kid considered Mark for a minute, then extended his hand, "The name's Heath — Heathcliff Dodger Robinson."

Mark shook Heath's hand, "Mark, from Earth."

"I knew you weren't normal!"

"Never said I was!"

"How's it feel?" said Heath, eyes lit up curious like, "seeing all this?"

Mark leaned back in the plastic cafeteria chair and said, in all seriousness, "Have you ever lived under a rock?"

Heath adjusted his black rimmed glasses. "Not that I know of."

"I have. For my whole life—crawled out yesterday."

"Unreal," said Heath. "Is it true that all your cars drive on the ground?"

"Four wheels and four tires," said Mark.

"Radical!"

"So, riddle me this," said Mark, then rattled his lunchbox. "How do these diabolical things work?"

"Ah." Heath grinned, "Easy." He pushed his satchel away and held out his hands. "Here let me see."

Mark handed over the red lunchbox. Heath turned it over to the side with the evil bagel. He then held his thumb on the top right corner. The cover lit up! A picture of a raspberry bagel appeared below the words Evil Bagel Box. After a moment it disappeared, replaced by a menu screen. On the left was a list of foods, and on the right, pictures of the foods.

"Whoa," said Mark, salivating.

"Yeah," agreed Heath, kicking his feet up on a chair opposite the table, "and you've got the Evil Bagel edition," he continued enviously.

HEATH AND LEXE

"Cakes soft as clouds and twice as delicious; spicy noodles famous for burning tongues right off; creamy soups that warm up your tummy for hours and hours."

Mark marveled at all the scrumptious foods scrolling down the screen. He stomach grumbled in anticipation. But first, he looked up at Heath. "Thank you."

Heath just chuckled and shrugged. "Sure."

"No really," Mark continued, and then looked out over the noisy Mess Hall. "The rest of these howler monkeys just flung their feces at me."

Heath didn't look around the Mess Hall. His olive eyes considered Mark a bit deeper. "Yeah. My family just immigrated to the Sol sector too." His lenses reflected the round tables he had just come from, full of kids eating and happily chatting. "Everyone has their own circle of friends by now. Can't break into a circle."

Mark heard the tone of dismay in Heath's voice. "But I just saw you making them laugh and selling stuff."

Heath's eyes stayed on those same tables. "Sure. They all want what I'm selling, but none of them want another friend. They're good with the ones they have."

Mark felt stuck. After all that rejection, he hadn't expected this seemingly popular kid to share something like that. "Oh—well—you want to share some food?" He rattled the Evil Bagel Box.

An idea lit up Heath's round face. "Hey, you mind if I transfer some food codes to my box?"

"Go for it!" said Mark, happy to be generous to the first kid who'd been friendly.

"Thanks!" said Heath. "I don't know how to transfer codes myself. But I know who does. Want to go with me?"

"Sure," said Mark, his desire to meet new people won over his desire for food. Heath had slung his old satchel around his left shoulder and

## CHAPTER 4

stood up. Mark followed suit by tucking the lunchbox in the crook of his arm and standing.

They wove among tables, stopping whenever someone would say hi to Heath. Lots of people seemed to know him. They would ask if he had anything new for sale or if he could get them something in particular and for how much. But Mark could see that's all they were interested in. He watched Heath smile politely and promise to get them things and that's it. Mark could tell that this amiable kid wasn't trying to make friends, because no one wanted or needed an extra friend. They soon arrived at the corner of the Mess Hall where the video wall met the tall windows.

Sitting casually on a bench, one leg folded up and the other dangling, was a girl with a cold sort of personality. Two bright yellow highlights fell on either side of her oval face, offsetting the rest of her dark hair; her clothes were of the comfortable variety; and she seemed so focused on some intense game playing across the small handheld glass square in her hands, that to her, the cafeteria didn't exist.

"Hey Lexe," said Heath as they walked up.

"Hey Heath," she said without looking up.

Heath sat down on the bench by the window and spoke to Mark. "Lexe Haxler is the digital mechanic to know." He dug in his backpack while talking, pulling out his lunchbox and putting it on the table. It was bumped and dented all over with signs of beloved ownership. "Anytime a kid forgets the password to their Lemonsquare, they come to me—and I go to her."

"Nice," said Mark, sitting down next to Heath. He leaned against the cool window glass. "I lost all my iPod stuff once. My brother jacked my iPod, changed the password, and threw it against a brick wall."

"You're from Earth?" asked Lexe, still concentrating on her game, from which they could hear guns ripping through something big.

"Flew up today."

"In what?" she said with a smirk. "One of those floppy Earther space shuttles?"

"Yeah," said Mark, his voice standing against her sarcasm. "A space shuttle made of rusted bits held together by Neil Armstrong's chest hair and fueled by old school Earther awesomeness."

Lexe chuckled without looking up.

"She's a cold snapfish," said Heath with a warm look at Lexe, "but once you get to know her,. . . " he trailed off for a moment, then shrugged, "well, she's still pretty cold."

Lexe grinned. A moment later, from the sounds of it, the game's boss died with prejudice. A level-up chime followed. She pocketed her handheld and looked straight up at Mark. Her eyes were an intense violet. "Let's see those lunchboxes."

They handed their boxes over to her.

She held one thumb at the top right corner of the Evil Bagel Box and the other thumb pressed to the bottom left corner. It powered down. She restarted it the same way. This time though, during the loading image, she flicked her fingers over the screen and somehow pulled up a white command prompt. After entering several commands she did the same for Heath's box. In a matter of minutes both boxes were transferring codes.

"Brilliant!" Heath exclaimed.

"There you go," she said, handing Heath's box back but holding onto Mark's.

Heath had a hungry, happy look about him while scrolling through all his new food choices. Mark leaned over to see, amazed at all the strange new foods and eager to try them all. Lexe joined them in taking turns taste testing through the long list of everything sweet and delicious.

"Pop pastry from Parsoo," she read on the screen of Mark's lunchbox, and then went on to read the description. "Pop one in and jam out, Parsoo style."

## CHAPTER 4

She pressed the foodify button. The box hummed. It beeped. She lifted the lid. Inside was a sugary pink pastry in the shape of a tiny guitar. Lexe lifted it out between two fingers. She took a bite.

"Well?" said Mark.

"What?" replied Lexe, chewing.

"How does it taste?"

"What?" Lexe repeated, louder, covering her mouth so crumbs didn't fly out.

Mark tried to show the question by pointing at the little half eaten guitar, then rubbing his belly, all the while making a rather silly questioning face.

"It tastes like music!" Lexe shouted back. She scrunched her nose and added, "not the good kind of music either."

"Check it out!" said Heath, pointing to his box. "I can make those cerebral cake clouds now!" His box hummed. It beeped. He opened the lid with eager anticipation. A puffy white cloud floated out. It looked like cotton candy. All three reached for it and tore off pieces.

"Yeesss!" he exclaimed, olive eyes alight with delight.

"Now this is music!" said Lexe. "I'm listening to a song so good the hair on the back of my neck stands up!"

"I'm flying!" said Mark, "on the wings of eagles, but backwards, while orangutan's lick my face."

"No, no," said Heathcliff, taking another bite, "It's like making bank on a killer deal."

"Better," said Lexe, grabbing more, "like turning the music up until your teeth rattle."

Mark had tears in his eyes. "Piloting the fastest starfighter straight through the most dangerous radioactive nebula to fearlessly fight against the most murderous mercenaries who just kidnapped the most gorgeous girl I've ever seen." Obviously, Mark had eaten too much.

They gobbled the floating cloud of favorites and were about to order another when a sharp bell sounded. An automatic announcement chirped over the loudspeakers. "Classes begin in T-minus five minutes."

"Aww, buzzkill," said Mark.

Heath and Lexe slowly nodded in agreement.

"Hey what classes do you two have next?" asked Heath.

"Pan-Galactic History," said Lexe, "Liquid programing 102 and then basic starfighter repair after that."

"Huh," said Heath. "I'm in the first and last, and flex fuels in the middle."

"I have no idea," said Mark.

"Here," said Lexe and took out the glass square she had been gaming on before. "My Lemonsquare." She handed it to Mark.

"How do I use it?" he asked, holding it rather carefully. It felt like glass, light and smooth and cool. It was clear but had a faint yellow tint to it.

"Thumb in the center."

Mark pressed the glass. It lit up! His schedule started scrolling across the smooth surface. "Jump point calculations 101," he read. "Core cosmic languages, then lunch, then Pan-Galactic History, Milky Way waypoints, and basic starfighter repair."

"Hey, looks like we share two classes: history and starfighter repair."

Another announcement sounded. "T-minus three minutes."

"Come on," said Heath, packing up his stuff.

Lexe didn't have anything to pack, so she just waited. Mark closed his awesome new lunchbox and they walked out of the lunchroom.

The hallways after lunch reminded Mark of middle school back home: crowds of students talking, laughing, and jostling each other as everyone made their way to their classrooms.

"Trade up anything good today?" Lexe asked Heath as the three of them moved through the crowd.

## CHAPTER 4

"No," said Heath. "The headphones are too expensive. I need to find a rich kid. Sold a few things though."

"What do you do with the money?" asked Mark.

"Saving up."

"For what?"

"My own hovercar," said Heath in all seriousness.

"Wow, that'd be the sauce."

Mark had more questions for Heath, but a shrill sound echoed from down the triangular corridor. He soon saw what kept making it: a miniature starfighter.

"Whow!" said Mark, ducking as an orange streak raced overhead. "Why am I under attack by miniature orange starfighters?"

"Those Tinus scouts must have flown down from the eighth grade wing again," said Heath, hitching up his backpack, not having ducked or slowed down.

"Nope," said Lexe as they continued, "those were the Calvien Rebels from the sixth grade wing. Yellow helmet on orange background. "

"What are they?" Mark asked.

The shrill screams of more jet engines answered. Four black miniatures the size of Mark's fist came tearing around the corner, banking hard against the walls.

"Those would be a few Volde Empire guards from twelfth," Lexe commented. "All the models fly around the whole school, attacking each other," she added as they walked on.

"Cooooool," said Mark, like a five-year-old.

Pushing through the crowded hallway, they soon reached their destination: a square door with several history dates scrawling down it. Mark sincerely hoped the class was not as boring as the door looked.

They entered the room along with thirty or so other recruits. Mark looked around as he followed Heath and Lexe. He sat down at a desk between them. The well-organized room was a long rectangle. Both side walls leading up to the front had tall niches carved into them at equidistant intervals. Inside each niche was a statue or a pedestal with a trophy. Mark noticed that all the statues seemed to be of the same person.

"Good afternoon, class!" said the well-dressed man who walked in. He strode over to the desk at the front and pivoted on his heels to face all his pupils. His hair flowed in pure white. It did not match his middle-aged face. Mark guessed the man must color it white to look wise or something.

"I am positively enthralled that everyone made it for another day of history." He then waggled a finger. "Additionally, whoever scrawled 'Mr. Barrie is a snob-bag' on my desk, remember, my name is Doctor Barrie, not Mister Barrie. Also, when I find you, I will personally expel you. Good? Spendid!"

Mark sat back in his chair and folded his arms.

"Let us begin our history lesson by first watching a video that will give context to a special picture that is very dear to my heart." His desk lit up and he swiped past a few videos. Finding that special one, he flicked his fingers out.

Mark's eyebrows jumped up as the top of his desk lit up to play the video in 3D.

"This is a clip from five years ago when our illustrious Fleet Commander Eli Exor, the hunter of Syn'Crux, the Daemon Killer, brought order to Sector Six. Here he is with a troop of his personally trained guards, demolishing, absolutely demolishing a Syn'Crux swarm."

Mark avidly watched as the tall, lithe commander led a charge of armored guards. The guards, all dressed in identical full body armor, marched into the launch bay of an enemy starship. Burning starfighters lined the bay. A few exploded, blasting several guards away. The frontline guards never flinched, just dropped to one knee. Shields

## CHAPTER 4

of blue hexagons snapped in front of them. A second line of guards took cover behind them and aimed their long rifles. A third line stood behind these, aiming higher. This execution would be flawless. Perfect discipline.

One long, loud roar filled the chamber. A raging mass of disordered men and women poured from the other side of the bay. These were Syn'Crux. Each one wore a different type of armor, attacked with a different kind of weapon, and fought in their own individual way. Many were heavily augmented, having replaced their arms with guns for ripping through their enemies, or their legs with hydraulics to give them the speed of machines, or their eyes with ghastly lenses for reasons unknown. A few of the Syn'Crux were spliced, having combined their DNA with the agility of animals and the brutality of predators; these men and women charged first, ripping into the front line of guards like beasts. A storm of gun fire erupted.

"Notice," said Doctor Barrie, "how our fleet commander deftly wields his powers. Marvelous! . . ."

The video showed torrents of dark purple energy powering out from Eli Exor's right hand. He moved in a deadly dance, right hand making strange, sharp motions to lift Syn'Crux attackers in midair, then clenching his fist to crush them or spreading his fingers to burn them. Through all this, Mark noticed that Eli did not wear any armor, not even a dark commander's coat, choosing to fight in a plain, stark white, rolled-sleeved shirt.

"Pay particular attention, students, please, to how quickly our fleet commander thrashes, just trounces," the professor shivered with excitement, "their daemon."

Mark stared as an abnormally large, muscular man, clothed in flowing gray garments with a fine cut black beard, blasted away his own Syn'Crux people to stand in front of Eli Exor. The gray man held an arcing silver sphere of energy in his left hand. He roared and hurled it at Exor. The fleet commander deflected it with a swift slice of his right hand. The silver orb tore into the floor and disintegrated a nearby cargo ship. Another silver blast raged at Eli. Again Eli deflected it, continuing his menacing strides towards the gray man. The gray man stood his ground, attacking furiously and with much anger. Nothing touched Eli. Then, Eli stopped, shifted into a wide stance, balled his fist and thrust it forward, breathing out in a sharp attack. A blistering tidal wave of rolling lightning surged at the gray man and consumed him whole.

"And that!" said Doctor Barrie, pausing the video on the nothingness left by Eli's attack. "Is why we call Commander Exor. . .the daemon killer." He flipped his fingers over his desk. "Now that you all are thoroughly impressed, you will no doubt be even more impressed by this!"

Mark frowned in confusion as a picture came up. It showed Barrie shaking hands with Eli Exor.

"Yes, this is me personally shaking hands with the hunter of Syn'Crux, the daemon killer." His sparkling smile matched the color of his hair. "Yes, impressive, I know."

Mark glanced around the classroom. Everyone's desk displayed the same picture of their pompous professor. Mark wasn't sure if everyone was being silent out of genuine interest or genuine shock at the size of their professor's ego.

A curious girl with curly hair spoke up from the front of the class. "Mister Professor, is it true that there is a new daemon leading the Syn'Crux in our solar sector?"

"It's Doctor Professor," corrected their white haired teacher, "and that's not important. No, it's not, put your hand back down and look at this picture of me with the Nu Aquilia Senator, Mr. Veneti."

Another picture of political handshaking appeared. Doctor Barrie looked at himself and smiled with pride.

## CHAPTER 4

An inquisitive boy with freckles raised his hand and asked, "What's the Obliv?"

"You best learn to address me properly," said the infuriated man, "and not interrupt my lectures! How will you learn the names of all four thousand and ninety current solar system senators?" He glowered at his students. "Now, next, this is me, Doctor Barrie, with Senator Volrind. He presides over the Omega Centauri colony out on the Dark Fringe." Barrie's eyes widened for effect as he finished, "Working on something dangerous!"

Someone behind Mark whispered to some other kid. "My dad says if the Syn'Crux get the Obliv, they'll make it into some strange war machine."

Mark didn't pay much attention to all this, though. He was staring at the desk and thinking about the video of Eli Exor. He turned to Heath and whispered, "Hey what's with those wicked powers Exor used?" Then he raised his right eyebrow, adding, "And where can I get such freaky thunderbolts?"

Heath glanced at Mark, and then whispered back, "That's Syn'Crux technology he's using. He says he stole it from them and learned to use it against them."

Mark gave a quiet whistle. "I can see me now, blazing around shooting bolts of crazy out my fists while riding a hoverboard." That last word popped his eyes wide open with realization. He snapped his fingers and shouted. "Hoverboards!"

The entire class turned to look at him.

"Pardon?" said Doctor Barrie with a scowl.

"Erm—I meant—holy balls," he replied and added a thumbs up. "Great handshaking there."

The professor squinted his beady eyes, but then smiled. "Thank you!"

Mark didn't have to wait long for the fashionably dressed man to resume staring at himself shaking hands with famous people.

He turned to Heath on his right and whispered, "hoverboards, man."

"Are lame," said Lexe from his left.

Mark's chair squeaked as he whirled to face her. "What?"

Lexe didn't look up from her Lemonsquare, which she was hiding and playing with the volume off, just below her desk. "Hoverboards are lame," she repeated. "All they do is hover around."

"That's awesome though!" he said in a furious whisper.

Heath snapped his fingers this time, adding in a low voice, "That's what hoverboards remind me of!" He leaned past Mark and whispered to the dark haired girl, "Local Culture Studies last year, remember? Segways?"

She looked up at the blank far wall. "Oh yeah," she said and snickered, then went back to gaming. "Snazziest Earther invention ever."

Mark felt his stomach seize and collapse in on itself. A bitter taste soured his tongue. He gulped. "Hoverboards are like Segways?" he murmured. "But... but... but," he kept quietly whimpering. He tried to tell himself it just wasn't true. But then he went into shock.

The benefit of being in shock was that the entire rest of history class passed by his deadened eyes. Thus, he was spared the details of Doctor Barrie's walrus-sized ego. No slogging through endless pictures of the good doctor shaking hands with the Solar Senate secretary of defense; no wading through piles of news articles; no need to pretend as everyone made fake ooos and aaas when Doctor Barrie proudly showed more pictures.

The unfortunate side effect of being in shock was that Mark didn't snap out of it until the middle of the next class: Milky Way waypoints. This class, besides being in a different classroom where the gray walls curved into a dome, was taught by a very old android who droned as he lectured. Heath and Lexe were not in this class to ease the boredom either, since it was a beginner's class.

## CHAPTER 4

"Hey," said a red-haired kid sitting at the desk to Mark's right. "Hey, dare me to eat this waypoint finder for a quark?" He wiggled a small black box with a screen.

"What?" said Mark, startled out of his stupor. He looked at the freckled kid with the toothy smile. Then he looked all around him. The classroom was round and full of people he didn't know. In the middle stood a tall lanky android who looked old and wheezy.

"There are five hundred waypoints in Ursa Majjooorrr," the android professor droned.

"I'll eat two waypoint finders for three quarks and a qubit," offered the boy.

Someone behind them hissed, "Shut up, Gus!"

Gus turned to him. "I'll shut up for a quark."

The guy grumbled and said nothing.

Gus turned back to Mark and held up the small box again. "How about I bean the professor with it for ten quarks?"

"Why?" said Mark.

"OK, three quarks."

Mark just stared at Gus and his strange words.

"All right, all right. Two quarks and a couple qubits. But I'll only throw one, and only if you take the blame."

"Riiiiiight," said Mark, edging away in his seat.

"Nearly three huuunnndred and thiiiiirty twwooo of these waypoints are," continued the old rusted professor.

"Hey, why do hoverboards suck so much?" Mark suddenly asked.

"Because skyboards rock so much," said Gus with a quizzical stare at the new recruit, as if Mark had lived under a rock until now.

Mark's eyes widened as he sensed another big revelation. "What are skyboards?"

Gus squinted at him. "I'll tell you for five qubits."

"I don't have any money."

"One qubit."

"Never mind," said Mark with an exasperated sigh. He'd wait until the next class with Lexe and Heath. He'd ask them then. And so, once again, Mark spaced off through another class. Milky Way waypoints wasn't too difficult anyway. It was like a geography class, except instead of learning about various places around the world, he learned about various places around the galaxy.

As it turned out, the last class, basic starfighter repair, was cancelled that day. So Mark stood outside the door waiting for Heath and Lexe to show up.

"Basic repair is cancelled?" asked Heath as he walked up to Mark.

"Yeah," Mark nodded. "Hey, what're skyboards?"

Heath grinned. "Not segways."

"Flying and stunts and junk?" said Mark, then narrowed his eyes. "You're not having a laugh, are you?"

"No no," Heath replied with a sincere shake of his head. "I'll bring my board 'round after school in a couple weeks, if you like?"

"Bring it today!" Mark continued in his overly excited enthusiasm.

"Can't. Still modding it out."

"Hey guys," said Lexe, joining them.

"Skyboard mods," Mark continued. "I love it. What kinds are there?"

But at that moment the familiar voice of one anxious android could be heard.

"Mark! Mark," said Lloyd, running up to him. "Let's go. I'm showing you to your dorm room and then hiding. Come on."

"But it's not even the end of school," Mark protested.

"Never mind that, never mind that," said Lloyd, tugging at Mark's shirt. "Come on. Out of the hallways."

"Fine! All right," said Mark, giving in before Lloyd ripped off his shirt.

## CHAPTER 4

He looked back around to Lexe and Heath. "What dorm wings are you guys in?"

"I live at home with my family, actually," said Heath. He turned to Lexe, "you too right?"

"Yeah," she nodded, "most of the students do," she said as Mark was leaving.

"Oh, all right. So you're heading home?" Mark called back.

They nodded. It was a bittersweet ending to a really awesome day. He waved as Lloyd led him around a hallway corner. They waved back.

After several flights of stairs and much trudging around various hallways, they arrived in front of a door in the shape of a solid round circle.

"Here you are," said Lloyd. "Dorm room WD-40."

The circular door spiraled apart with a fluid shunk. Mark walked into the room he'd call home for the school year. The sleek white walls arched over the plain white floor. A screen curved above the short metal desk to his left; an empty, polished metal bookcase curved to his right. On the opposite side of the room, a one-person bed rested on a shelf with four drawers; and above the bed was a round window, perfect for daydreaming.

"Don't touch any buttons!" Lloyd rushed in shouting. "All the dorm rooms used to be this starship's escape pods." He pointed at a row of knobs, switches, and levers on a large panel above the desk. "Do. Not. Touch." he commanded, emphasizing each word with heavy caution. "You'll launch yourself halfway across the city!"

"Really?" said Mark.

"Well—no—But I worry—so much!"

"All right," said Mark with a chuckle. "Well thanks, Lloyd."

"Don't touch," Lloyd emphasized again, his camera lens eyes narrowed at Mark. He made the I'm-watching-you hand motion as he backed out of the door. It spiraled closed after him.

Mark smiled and shook his head at how crazy this new—everything—was.

A huge yawn cracked his jaw as he stretched involuntarily. The whirlwind of the day hit him pretty hard. Continuing to yawn, he walked over to a small round window at the opposite end of the room. The city outside looked glorious: dazzling lights everywhere, cold blue skyscrapers soaring in the distance, twinkling warm lights dotting the valley, streaks of hovercar headlamps painting the night in zigs of yellow and hovercar taillights painting opposite zags of red. In the distance the east hills shimmered. He laughed quietly, imagining what it'd be like launching himself and his whole escape-pod-turned-dorm-room across the city. He stayed pressed up against the round window for hours and hours, watching the world outside—far too excited for sleep.

# CHAPTER 5

# CHAPTER 5
## THE LAST RECRUIT

Mark's dorm room slowly filled with the aroma of fresh-baked French bread and the gentle chirps and warbles of singing song birds. A weak ray of light came in from the little round window. It shone onto the flat yellow rectangular alarm clock that busied itself trying to wake Mark up. The alarm's display scrolled glowing words: 7:30 A.M., French bread aroma & morning birds. Mark snored through it all.

The alarm clock increased the volume a gentle amount and puffed out a few more clouds of fresh baked delight. For some reason it was compelled to wake up the target.

"Mmmmppfff," Mark muttered. His left hand took its time sliding out from under the sheet. The hand waved around trying to feel for a snooze button.

Small wheels sprang out the sides of the yellow box and it zipped away behind a book shelf. It peeked out. The target had gone back dreaming about things and not waking up. The clock noticed a bit of drool hit the pillow from the targets big snoring mouth.

"Battle stations! Battle stations! All hands on deck!" shouted a gruff voice from the alarm clocks speakers.

Mark jerked up out of bed. Frantically looking around he saw— nothing and nobody. After his wheezing lungs stopped burning and his vision cleared, his blood-shot eyes settled on the alarm clock. It was now

## CHAPTER 5

displaying "7:38 A.M." with scrolling green words flashing "Get up, you gullible fool."

The red-eyed new recruit dove at it. Quick as a bird, the little thing ducked behind its favorite hiding spot: the narrow space between the control panel and the wall.

"Every day! For two weeks!" the sleep-deprived boy shouted. "Why must you invent a new heart attack for me every morning?" He took a few deep breaths, trying to steady his breathing. Sitting down heavy on the edge of his bed, he said, "At least give me the weekends!"

After another heavy sigh he stood back up and shuffled around his room getting ready for school. A look outside the round window revealed something new: a dim violet hue on the horizon beyond Crescent City. Mark wondered if that meant the two weeks of night would be over soon.

The school day passed by in sleepy stupor. Classes were a bunch of notes made from boring lectures. Strange math had to be done in Jump Point Calculations 101. Lieutenant Landeth, the teacher for that class, was as strict and formal and cold as a professor as she was a starfighter pilot. Core cosmic languages confused his tongue with a bunch of odd sounds mixing nasal snuffs and throaty grunts and rolling Rs. At least he could doze off a little in history and that waypoints class; though Doctor Barrie did catch him and—for the remainder of class—Mark had to polish a statue of a local dignitary the professor once met at a conference.

Finally, Mark met up with Lexe and Heath as they walked to their last class of the day. They hadn't attended basic starfighter repair yet. Nobody had. The class had been cancelled each day for the last two weeks. But no one knew when it would begin, so they had to check.

"So you're telling me," said Lexe, fixing Mark with a disbelieving stare, "that on Earth—food is grown in the ground?"

"Yup," said Mark.

"Unreal," Heath remarked as Lexe shook her head.

"Next you'll tell us that cars drive on the ground," Lexe quipped.

"And movies are in boring 3D," said Heath, joining in the banter.

"And—and that there are no skyboards," continued Lexe, snickering.

"Or even hoverboards!" said Heath.

"Yes," said Mark with a nod.

His friends gasped and stopped in the middle of the crowded hallway.

"Mark," said Lexe, wide-eyed, "you're a caveman."

The boy with the messy dark brown hair shrugged. "Grunt? Grunt grunt GRUNT grunt?"

"You know, I think I'll start calling you Caveman Mark," said Lexe, pretending to ponder this thought by tapping a finger on her chin. "Or Caveman Johnny—or just, Cave—yeeaahh."

Mark ducked as three white and gold painted miniatures blazed overhead. Nobody else had ducked, but he still wasn't used to it all. He could see why Lloyd skittered around all paranoid.

"Have you guys noticed it's getting light outside?" Mark asked Heath and Lexe as they continued bumping through students down the packed hallway.

"Yeah," said Lexe in a disappointed voice. "Sucks."

"I can't wait," responded Heath, turning to avoid an eleventh grader barreling down the hall like he owned the place. "Growing up on an orbit colony, nights are nice and short. These long ones on the moon are creepy. I just wish sunrise didn't take eight hours."

"Eight hours?" said Mark. "Wow." He dodged another eleventh grader who was following the first. "Hey, so can you guys kick it after school today? Maybe bring your skyboards?"

"Still not finished modding mine out," said Heath.

"Oh give it a rest, Heath," said Lexe. "You're spending more time modding than riding. I'll bring mine too. We'll show our grunting caveman how it's done."

## CHAPTER 5

"Yeah!" Mark rejoined.

Heath glanced between them. Their stares were unrelenting. "OK, OK. I'll pick it up after school."

"How about now?" Mark suggested. "I bet basic repair is still cancelled."

"Nope," said Lexe, pointing to the door of their destination.

For the last two weeks the door of their last class, the one that looked like a small hanger bay door, had been closed. Today it stood wide open.

"Huh," said Mark, as they followed a few students in. The classroom appeared unlike any they had been in before. It was cavernous, it was empty, it was like walking into a large airplane hangar.

Standing against solid gray walls were dozens of rolling tool boxes larger than most trucks Mark had seen. These were dwarfed by thick steel beams holding up a truss ribbed ceiling high enough to bungee jump from. About forty students, all Mark's age, were shuffling around. Nobody knew quite where to stand or what to do in all that empty space.

The three of them decided to lean up against the high right wall.

"I wonder why the prof was gone so long," Mark commented as they stood there.

"Had something to do with that crash above Crescent City a couple weeks ago, I think," said Heath, always in the know. "The captain had him inspect that damaged starliner."

"Good, because I saw it happen, and it was messed up."

"You—" said Heath before Lexe shouted, "you saw that crash!"

"Yeah. It was eerie. No sound. Everything went in slow motion. Just this small ship ripping into that big one, shredding its roof right off."

Heath and Lexe alternated questions, cutting each other off.

"What was it like?" said Heath.

"Did you see the people inside?" said Lexe.

"Did chunks of metal hit your ship?"

"Did any of them float away into outer space?"

"Did the pilots recover?"

"Did you wet your pants like a frightened caveperson?"

Mark arched an eyebrow at Lexe.

She shrugged. "Fair question, I'd say."

"It was scary strange to see. So many people almost died."

That sobered Lexe and Heath right up. They frowned. Lexe stared at the blank far wall. Heath fidgeted with his backpack straps.

"Yeah," said Heath with a sigh. "The new Syn'Crux daemon is ruthless."

"Daemon?" asked Mark.

"Their leader," said Lexe.

"That's a name?"

"A title," Lexe clarified. "Nobody knows the name of a daemon."

"So that crash wasn't an accident?" said Mark.

"No," said Heath. "Eli Exor was on that starliner. It was another death-wish attempt on his life. They tried killing him."

"Why? And why along with so many normal folk?"

"They threatened Director Ernest Shaw and Commander Exor, saying if neither gives them the Obliv and its key, then," he paused to emphasize the quote he read, " 'you desire death—and the daemon will visit death upon you and those around you and will then take the Obliv from you.' "

"That's heavy," said Mark. "But so what? Seems like they've failed to kill Exor a couple times already."

"Yeah," said Heath in a perplexed tone. "It's always been one threat, one shot, one kill. Strange that Exor's survived—awesome, really great—just weird."

"So it's nothing to worry about," said Mark and shrugged it off.

Heath scoffed. "My family wouldn't think so." He looked at Mark. "The Syn'Crux bring chaos. They corrupt every level of society. They corrupt everyone. They seize control over entire solar systems, slowly,

## CHAPTER 5

planet by planet, city by city, person by person." He looked away. "There is everything to worry about."

Mark's face skewed with confusion. "What the hell are they?"

"People," said Lexe, firm in her own beliefs, yet not meeting their eyes. "They're just people."

"No," said Heath, rounding on her. "They've chosen to become spliced, chosen to be shifted. What healthy person would replace their arms with weapons? What sane person would splice their DNA to have snake eyes or legs bent backwards. It's sick. It's not right."

"But it's a choice," Lexe argued back. "You said they chose it. They don't force people to choose it."

"Do I have a choice to go back to my home planet or not?" Heath pressed. "Do I? No, I don't."

Mark, right eyebrow raised, looked from Lexe to Heath. They refused to acknowledge each other. Standing apart, Lexe had her hands shoved in her sweater pockets and Heath had pressed his fist against the concrete wall. Mark wanted to say something to reconcile them, but he didn't know quite what had happened in the first place.

Then, a door opened at the far left of the immense hangar. Whether it opened out of respect for the man who walked in or out of cowardice was hard to say. Quiet, well-oiled gears and hydraulics made the man's right arm and left leg. His long strides did not carry him towards his students, but towards the center of the room.

"Well?" He called out to them, his voice surprisingly jovial for being as rough as the black stubble covering his anvil of a jaw. "Don't stand around like a bunch of greenie grease monkeys! To the center with ya!"

Everyone started shuffling towards the middle of the hangar.

As the man approached, Mark heard the sound of gears from the mans barrel sized right arm; from fingers to shoulder, it was an augmented piece of machinery filled with cords of steel cables acting as muscles and thin metal power strands in place of veins. Everyone could see this because he had no skin to cover it. The sound of hydraulics came from the man's tree-sized left leg as he walked; from a single metal stub on the ground to past his knee, it was a working set of cylinders compressing air with each step, then hissing it out. None of that noise was loud, but in this echoing hangar of a classroom—where all the kids were silent—the man's machinery was everything. He reached their huddled half-circle, stopped, and faced them.

"Welcome to basic starfighter repair. I'm Otto McMaluch. You can call me Otto. I'll call you whatever comes to mind." He continued with a stern, yet high-spirited seriousness. "I don't believe in textbooks. I don't believe in sitting behind desks. I believe in dirty hands and clothes covered in grease stains."

Two guys high-fived. A prissy girl grimaced.

Otto noticed, and continued with a caution. "Don't get to thinking this'll be easy. You won't be calculating jump points or memorizing who discovered the backside of Jupiter; but you will be working harder than both those classes combined." He paused and surveyed his new recruits. "By years end I will teach you to know an engine by the touch of your hand; I will teach you to know if it needs tuning by listening to the exhaust. You will learn that machines are not chunks of metal bolted, greased, and rusted together, but are alive and breathing." The gears in his right leg clicked and the hydraulics hissed as he turned and took long mechanical strides that carried him further than everyone else, who jogged just to keep up.

"Today, little grease monkeys, today we crack open some flarejets!" said the half-augmented man. He stopped by the four-story hangar bay door and punched a flat red button. A loud chunk reverberated through the floor.

## CHAPTER 5

Mark felt large gears clacking beneath his feet and saw the bay door begin to roll up. Early daylight cast a harsh slant against the opposite wall. He gazed out at a sky dotted with scarlet clouds drifting in a fading pale darkness where only the brightest stars remained.

"Here they come!" cheered a rosy-cheeked girl at the front, pointing up at the sky.

Three squads blazed across the brightening blue in a V formation. They raced just below the clouds, leaving streaks in their wake. Following the pilot at the front, they dove.

"That's Lance leading Alpha Squad," squealed the same rosy-cheeked girl to her equally excited friends.

"He's piloting a Blacknova-AX, he is," said a tall boy to their right whose mouth stood agape.

Before the bay door fully opened, Lance roared in doing a barrel roll. His flarejet was chrome black, fluid, and made of more aggressive angles than an overpriced exotic sports car.

Mark felt dumbstruck. "That thing flies like a smug bald eagle riding a snarling winged jaguar into battle against armored elephants—while playing chess—blindfolded," he whispered to no one in particular.

The boy whose jaw had gone unhinged nodded vigorously. "Yeah, it's a Blacknova—AX," he said, then didn't continue, as if that was all that needed to be said.

Mark's hands itched with a new and sudden longing as the Blacknova banked a sharp right, did another barrel roll, and then stopped in the middle of the hangar bay floor. Dust billowed while it landed. Mark's imagination clouded in dreams of high-flying adventure. He saw himself racing up and up and up, through cloud after cloud, chasing the stars while screaming his lungs out. He saw himself weaving through asteroid fields with a concentrated frown as a bead of sweat rolled down his forehead. He saw himself flying with his squad mates, his friends; he saw himself—happy.

Mark's green-blue eyes snapped into focus, into determination, into purpose.

"I am going to fly that thing. I'm going to get in it, and I'm going to fly it," stated the boy from Earth.

The rosy-cheeked girl in front of him glanced back and did a quick up and down check. She then snorted and said "as if," and turned back to watching Lance.

Mark, feeling unexpectedly offended, stuck his tongue out at her.

Lance's three squad mates blazed in. The first flarejet appeared to be a big box with smaller boxes stuck to it. Mark could see a chunky guy sitting, barely fitting, inside the rectangular cockpit. The second flarejet was thin like a wisp but flowed and snapped like a whip; a blonde boy with tanned skin and an angelic face piloted that one. The last flarejet was sharp, precise, and covered in so much chrome that nobody could see inside. All three circled around Lance's flarejet and landed facing him. Everyone around Mark ooo'd and ahh'd. The only person who wasn't impressed stood wearing a disapproving grimace.

"Toffee-nosed gits," Otto growled. Then, in a bellowing command to his students, "make room on deck! Beta and Foxtrot Squads need room."

Beta Squad flew in; they piloted far less flashy flarejets but seemed far more disciplined in their maneuvers. A second cheer went up for them, though not as enthusiastic as for the Alphas. There were no cheers for Foxtrot Squad, the third and last squad, which flew in on rather old and clunky machines.

A buzz of chatter began even before those flarejets had shut off their engines. Mark heard phrases float around he didn't understand: "This year's Wargame'll be intense," "Did you see the mods on Galantine's

## CHAPTER 5

Fistbreaker?" and "Lance is soooo cute, oh my god, I can't believe he's in your class, Becky." That last one came from the rosy-cheeked girl. Mark guessed she was not in this class to become a mechanic.

"Listen up!" said Otto, talking over the sounds of engines winding down. "Today and for the next month you'll be examining and getting a closer look at these flarejets."

That rosy-cheeked girl in the pink dress turned to her friend and said, "I'd like to examine and get a closer look at those FlareRiders." Her friend giggled and whispered something back.

Heath glanced at Mark. They shared a rather queasy grimace.

"Everyone will be in groups. Each group will be partnered with a FlareRider. The FlareRider you are assigned to will explain his or her flarejet's specs and systems."

Mark watched the pilots climb out. They were a diverse bunch, but they did have one thing in common: their flight jackets. Each was made from brown leather and looked like a modernized version of those classic aviator jackets worn by daredevil pilots. Mark grinned to himself, thinking he'd look quite snazzy all suited up.

"Becky! Gloria!" the girl was whispering to her friends, both as prissy as her. "It's Lance. There he is!"

Surprise mashed Mark's eyebrows together as he saw Lance climb out. The boy was Mark's age, though taller. He had glossy black hair combed back to reveal a rectangular face with a strong nose and high cheekbones and solid blue eyes. No wonder the girls fawn over him, Mark thought, he looks like a young version of Superman.

"At month's end you will each be given a test. You must identify critical systems, their functions, and give repair solutions," McMaluch was saying. "The exam will not be pudding. So don't be afraid to take off engine parts and get dirty; it's the only way to learn."

THE LAST RECRUIT

The rosy-cheeked girl turned back to her friends. "I'd like to take off Lance's engine parts and get dir –"

"Shut your gobbey gobbling gobs!" Lexe shouted at them, startling Mark and Heath. "Your voices makes me want to Q-tip my brain until I die!"

All three girls harrumphed and crossed their arms.

Mark and Heath exchanged a discrete low-five.

"Group assignment time," said McMaluch to everyone. Apparently he had noticed that little exchange, because he pointed to the girl and her friends. "Miss prissy girl number one, two and three. You three will be assigned to—hmmmmm, the Boxtron piloted by Dinzdale over there." He thumbed towards the heavyset eleventh grader from Alpha Squad whose twin chins were sweating.

"Uuuuuh!" said the three girls in unison, putting as much disgust and unfairness into the word as possible.

"Next," continued Otto. "Flashy backpack kid, that guy zoned out on his gaming thing, and the girl in overalls. You three get the Volks-52 piloted by Ashley Higgins."

The three new group mates looked at each other, then looked at Ashley, who was waiting with hands clasped militarylike behind her straight back. McMaluch went on forming groups of three and assigning them to flarejets.

Mark leaned over to Heath. "So what's the big deal with Lance?"

"The guy's a doofnozzle," Heath retorted without adding anything else.

The prissy girl whirled around and started spitting out facts. "Lance is the youngest cadet recruited to the Cadet Core," said the defensive fan-girl. "He won last year's Wargame, was awarded the badge of the Golden Falcon, and is the youngest cadet to become a wing leader. He's the best."

## CHAPTER 5

Heath scoffed. "Aaaaah, that pinprick just has the fanciest flarejet around. Without it, he's a hack."

The girl's rude hand gesture was not very ladylike.

"Excuse me, professor?" said Mark with a raised hand.

"Yes, what is it, lad?" said Otto.

"Could my friends and I be assigned to the Blacknova AX?"

"Right, off you go."

That sent the raging fan girl and her friends into a hissy fit.

"Nice," said Lexe as they crossed the hangar bay floor.

"I just need to climb into that stupid thing," said Mark, his pace picking up.

Upon reaching the sleek, almost liquid Blacknova, they paused. Mark thought it was truly a beastly machine. He could tell it was built for a singular purpose: to win.

They walked up closer. It smelled like a machine: cold and raw.

"Whoa there, guy," said a heroic voice behind them. Lance's easy stride brought him over. "No smudging the surface now, it's covered in Shade Skin."

"Name's Lance," he continued while making a point to shake Lexe's hand first. "Wing leader of Alpha Squad." His pearly whites beamed from that young Supermanlike face. "I've escaped many a jam, cloaked and unnoticed, by keeping the surface clean," he informed them while giving Mark and Heath a hearty handshake.

"So you're my group of kids—cool," he said and looked them over. "What would you like to know?"

"How'd you get into the Cadet Core?" asked Mark.

"Raw talent," Lance replied, placing a hand on Mark's shoulder. "Raw talent, my friend."

Heath snorted.

"Can we look inside?" asked Mark.

"Sure," said Lance. He went to the front and placed a finger toward the top of the curved middle. A line appeared; it raced along the top in the shape of a glass canopy. They heard a hiss and click as the glass lifted an inch and slid backwards. Lance grinned, watching them crane their necks to see inside.

Mark's eyes glazed over. He could see himself sitting in that single, racecar-yellow leather bucket seat; he could see himself facing that curved black glass control panel, inputting flight commands like a real pilot.

"She has a Graybox VI with a full holograph interface," said Lance, not bothering to point it out. "Let's me track and lock onto ten enemy combatants in real time. Best part?" He paused for dramatic effect, "No lag." He continued doing what was clearly his favorite thing ever: listing, one by one, the cutting-edge technology in his flarejet. "Single cell, symbiotic Blacknova drive core into an Asymmetrical Xenon thruster out the back." His offhanded wave towards the engine was only pretending to be casual. "Cold Plasma cannons—two on each wing—and Thermix missiles stacked up inside the main battery for, you know, special occasions." He winked at Lexe, who blanched. "And of course, the Shade Skin: nano sized particles of rare-solar adaptive—"

"Nobody cares," said Lexe, sweeping an arc with her hands. "Open it up, I want to dig around inside."

Lance appeared slightly phased. No one had interrupted his favorite speech before. "Erm, no."

"Why not?" Lexe demanded.

"Because no one touches Helen except certified specialist technicians," the blue-eyed boy said, and then grinned. "And you're a bit young to be one hhmmm? Yeah."

Heath stepped in front of Lexe before she did something that would get her expelled. "Our instructor told everyone that we needed to know

## CHAPTER 5

the critical systems, hands on. He also said the cadets would help us out—and—also—Helen? Really?"

"No can do, little buddy. Certified only."

Mark stopped Heath from saying something inappropriate. He had an idea.

"Lance is right, guys," said Mark. Then to Lance, "All the stuff you've told us, man, We are deeply thankful for your help."

Heath stared. Lexe's foot itched to meet Mark's shin.

Lance threw a heroic smile at Mark and said, "Hey thanks! I'm glad you recognize."

"Yes, indeed," said Mark. "In fact, I think we've taken up enough of your valuable time, Alpha Squad wing leader. We'll just take some notes on all you said and do some research on our own."

"Now that's being a rather swell chap! I am a busy guy. Not easy being wing leader, after all. I'm glad to have helped you kids out." He made a snappy salute and went off to join his Alpha Squad friends.

"Pffsh, calling us kids!" Heathcliff exclaimed, olive eyes glowering with indignation. "He's our age!"

"What gives?" Lexe demanded of Mark.

Mark didn't answer, just watched Lance rejoin his squad mates to a round of cheers. Then, with a mischievous grin, he said, "Well, you two ready to crack on?"

"Ooohhhh haha, I see what you did there," said Lexe.

Mark shrugged, feigning innocence. "Whaaat? I just want to sit in the stupid thing," His eyes filled with desire. "The sweet sweet stupid beast of a machine."

Mark clambered up into the pilot's seat, not caring to check if anyone saw. Heath began studying the engines; Lexe, interested in the Graybox VI, ducted under the wings to find an access panel.

Mark let out a sigh of pure contentment as the yellow racing seat molded itself to match the curve of his spine. He reached out to the control panel. When glowing yellow symbols popped out of the black glass to float half an inch above the surface, he didn't flinch. Instead, tracing the controls with his hands and feeling his heart quicken and breath catch, he realized a natural truth.

"I want to become a FlareRider." It was the most solid thing he had ever said. "Ya hear that!" shouted Mark over the side. "I will become one of those blokes who rides these flarejets into meteor-filled sunsets!" Then he turned back to the control panel and wiggled his butt into the chair. "Now, how do I get this baby to START?"

The Blacknova heard him. A mechanical hiss and the solid glass canopy closed. A high hum began.

"Siiiiiick," he whispered as the Heads-Up-Display blinked on. Small red info boxes popped up above each of the flarejets on the hangar floor. They listed each flarejet's weapons, shields, and combat info.

"Please input flight point," said a calm, pleasantly computerized female voice.

"Warp speed!" said Mark with glee.

"Error 404: Warp Drive not found."

"Then rocket us out of here!"

"Compliance."

Mark heard no loud engine sounds, felt no gut feeling of hard gravity, nothing but soft, sleek movement as the Blacknova burst out the hangar bay door. They left behind a surprised crowd, a cursing McMaluch, and an infuriated Alpha Squad wing leader.

Mark found out the Blacknova was almost entirely voice controlled as, streaking through the purple sky, he kept repeating, "barrel roll! Barrel roll! Baarrreelll Roooooooll!"

## CHAPTER 5

The black flarejet spun and spun and spun, making Mark wonder if this was what riding in a washing machine felt like. "Urp—I'm having so much fun I think I'm going to hurl."

The digital female voice responded, "Projectile vomiting not recommended."

"Only joking! Sort of—Now dive! Dive, dive, dive!"

"Compliance."

Leaving shredded clouds in their wake, they cut through the sky. Flying straight down, Mark kept yelling until he could see the tiles on suburban homes.

"Now climb! Climb! CLIMB," he hollered.

The Blacknova responded by flipping 180 degrees in midair, burning hard, and rocketing back into the sky.

Mark felt more independent than the time he was home alone for a weekend; more grown-up than when he bought that one video game with his own money and against his parents' permission; more alive than when he stalled and then dive bombed in the little red stunt plane. This was living.

The inky void of space loomed just beyond the clouds. Mark wanted to see it again. To taste and touch those dark sky diamonds would be — would be — freedom.

"Get your thieving backside back in the hangar!" shouted a mean voice over the intercom.

But Mark didn't want this high flying adventure to end, so he happily shouted back, "I don't know how!"

"You get your cowardly hide ship-side or I'll have you expelled!"

He was so close to touching space. "I'm telling you, man, I don't have the faintest!"

"This is Sergeant Vance Hammerstrom, commander of the Cadet Core. You WILL do as I say!"

THE LAST RECRUIT

"All right, all right," Mark said and sighed in disappointment. The stars were just out of reach. Then to the nice digital lady, "take us home, please."

"Compliance."

They flew back below the clouds, back into the open hangar doors, back to landing in the center and being swarmed by people. Daylight made Mark squint as the canopy opened with a swoosh.

Lance jogged over shouting, "get out! get out! GET OUT!"

"I AM!" Mark shouted back and jumped down. He returned Lance's furious glare.

That disciplinary voice cut in, "Who is responsible for this?"

Mark turned to see a tall, fit, and bald individual making sharp military strides to the new recruit. Mark stood his ground.

Otto McMaluch placed his bulldozerlike bulk right into the warpath the sergeant was carving. "Vinny, you bald-headed badger, how've you been?"

Vance Hammerstrom stopped so hard and so close to Otto's face that the medals on his sergeant's uniform jingled. His lead-colored eyes narrowed. "I outrank you, Petty Instructor Otto McMaluch. You will respect me," he growled.

Then the man who must have been a cruise missile in a past life rounded on Mark. "And who are you to steal my BEST cadet's flarejet for an airheaded joyride?"

"Go easy on the lad," said Otto, putting a restraining hand on Hammerstrom's shoulder. "I should have had a closer eye on my students. I take responsibility for this. Stand on me."

"I will walk all over you for this," snapped the wolf at the bull. "I will speak to the admiral. She will agree with me. Any damages will be cut from your pay."

The bull stood calm, amused by the wolf's bared teeth.

## CHAPTER 5

Hammerstrom snarled at Mark again. "And you, what have you to say for yourself?"

Mark met his mean eyes, set back in that long gaunt face of dry skin. "I want to become a FlareRider."

Only a brief moment of stunned silence elapsed before the sergeant roared with laughter. Almost everyone in the room joined him. Mark's bold statement was heard as an ignorant joke. Only Heath and Lexe weren't laughing. They winced instead. Otto wasn't laughing either; his rough face stood stoic and without emotion; his gray eyes, however, rested on Mark with an idea.

Hammerstrom stopped laughing, his voice snapping into harshness. "As acting commander of the Cadet Core, it is my regrettable duty to inform you that, unfortunately, you are not accepted."

A fresh round of jeers and unprintable remarks struck Mark, who stood defiant.

The sergeant turned back to glowering at McMaluch. "You will pay for this." With a last sharp look at Mark, the sergeant turned heel and marched away with his chest out, medals furiously jingling.

McMaluch faced his students. "Listen up! Class is cancelled for the rest of the day."

The grumbling crowd of students threw dirty looks at Mark as they left to pack up. Overly loud conversations sprung up about "backwoods savages ruining everything," and "wasn't there a thing about not recruiting Earthers?"

Mark went to leave with Heath and Lexe. Otto stopped him with a heavy metal hand on his shoulder. Lexe and Heath stopped too, but Otto told them to go pack their things. He then faced Mark.

"The captain told me about you. He failed to warn me that you'd try to get my metallic butt fired on the first day."

Mark grimaced. "I'm sorry, professor."

"You pull a stunt like that again and we'll both be rusting in the junkyard."

"Why?" asked Mark. "Why can't I be a FlareRider?"

"You're not in the Cadet Core. You're in the Support Crew."

"What does that have to do with anything?"

The earnestness in the boy's voice helped the half-augmented man calm down a notch. He heaved a sigh and took a moment to glance around his hangar bay classroom. His students milled about talking to the remaining cadets. He looked back at Mark.

"Our illustrious academy separates everyone into three groups: majority of kids get put in the Support Crew, where they learn to become mechanics, technicians, and other good worker bees. The kids who've got piloting skill and money, they get put in the Cadet Core. Their parents buy them a flarejet so that they can be FlareRiders, and that's how they learn to become starfighter pilots. Last and least are the kids who've got money and prestigious, famous parents. They get into the Commanders Club—you can guess who they learn to become."

"When did this selection happen?" said Mark. His voice rose. "Why wasn't I put into the Cadet Core?"

"Before you even step foot at school on your first day—you are measured, labeled, and shelved," said Otto with a snort of disgust.

"I don't give a custard gobstopper," said Mark. "I want to be a FlareRider."

"No Support Crew recruit has changed their stars in decades. What makes you think you can?"

"I don't know. But I'll keep trying until I'm in the Cadet Core, flying a damn flarejet."

"You have the money to buy one?"

"No."

"Then where do you plan to get it, hotshot?"

## CHAPTER 5

"I'll build it if I have to."

Otto chuckled at Mark's doggedness. "Out of what, exactly?"

"Out of a lawn chair, two used hairdryers, mountains of duct tape and a flarejet."

Otto laughed, his big belly shaking. "You're a tenacious little bastard, aren't you?"

Mark's eyes glowed above a roguish grin. "I try."

Otto looked Mark over. "Huh, well" he said, in that way when someone is considering an idea that just struck but isn't ready to be revealed yet. "I tell you what. You stay after class each day and clean, organize, and work off all the trouble you caused today—and I'll think about making a few calls."

Mark started slowly nodding, then sped up the head bobbing as a spark of hope returned and said, "OK."

"OK," said Otto with a hearty clap on Marks shoulder. Then, the half-augmented man strode away, his gears turning and his hydraulics hissing as he went.

Lexe and Heath stepped over.

"You get expelled?" asked Heath.

"No," said Mark as he looked after the professor. "I have to stay after school and work for him for a month."

"But that means no skyboards for a whole month."

Mark heaved a sigh. "Yeah, I know. But if there's even a sliver of a chance I can handle one of those beastly flying machines again—I'll work my fingers off."

McMaluch called him over, a bucket and mop in hand.

"Welp, that's me."

His friends watched him go. They noticed he didn't trudge or shuffle over, instead walking with a resolution to work hard for a chance at something. This made them feel better. Mark was not a friend to feel sorry for, or one to worry about. He was a friend that would stand back up after being knocked down—and that earned him a small measure of respect.

# CHAPTER 6

# CHAPTER 6
## THE BLACK PEARL BAZAAR

The month did not go by in the blink of an eye. Mark mopped and swept floors, cleaned and organized tools, and then moved onto degreasing engines and making simple tune-ups. Sometimes he wondered if Otto was teaching him; but most times he went home in the evening too exhausted to slog through homework. But he did slog through the homework, because this place was awesome, and he'd fight to stay.

Each morning Mark's diabolical alarm clock would conceive of another bait and switch scheme to get him out of bed. Sometimes it was songbirds that would become snarling werewolves, other times it was the scent of fresh-cut grass that quickly turned into raw sewage. He started sleeping with a shoe under his pillow, and his aim was improving.

Classes were getting more interesting too. Gus was still trying to convince people to pay him to do strange stunts. A week ago he'd gone around asking if anyone would pay him to tackle a Volde Empire frigate. SPIFF's in-school surgeon, Doctor Mildred Mueller, complained about running out of burn ointment after that one. But Gus showed up to class to collect his bet money, grinning and covered in bandages.

Milky Way waypoints was becoming easier to understand; Mark felt awed by how huge their galaxy really was. Even with the most advanced FTL warp drives it'd take several lifetimes to travel across it. That meant if someone started from one end, only their great-great-great-great-grandchildren would reach the other end.

## CHAPTER 6

But where Milky Way waypoints blew Mark's mind, jump point calculations only made his brain hurt. Lieutenant Landeth taught jump point math the way a falcon teaches it's young to fly: by dropping them from a hundred feet in the air and expecting them to soar.

At least in Dr. Barrie's class he could tune out and give his noggin a chance to recoup. Barrie would begin the class with a video of himself receiving a prestigious history award; this would be followed by holding up the award for the whole class to see, then passing it around so each student could note how heavy and shiny the award was. The heavier and shinier the award, the more prestigious it was, claimed the good doctor.

The end of the month finally arrived. Apparently, Otto's office wasn't in the school like all the other teachers'. Instead, it stood several miles away just outside the Port District. Mark was walking there with Lexe and Heath after school that day. They were bundled in sweaters against the late autumn cold.

"It's not a question of where the engine grips it!" said Heath to Lexe as they all walked down Monty Grail Street. "It's a simple question of weight ratios." He continued his line of reasoning. "A five ton landracer could not benefit from a one kiloton thruster."

"It doesn't matter!" Lexe argued back. "Will you go and tell your brain that speed from the land of thrill seekers is here?"

"Listen, in order to maintain air speed velocity, a landracer needs to hover at forty-three feet, right?"

"Please," Lexe scoffed.

"Am I right?"

"I'm not interested in ratios."

They were arguing about the Need for Nebular Speed game that Mark couldn't stop playing. Lexe had let him play it on her Lemonsquare. In the game you drove a landracer—an exotic type of hovercar with a huge engine—across harsh terrain for trophies, upgrades, and fame. He kept his eyes glued so hard on the screen that he'd walked into a garbage can, two advertisement boards, and gotten tangled in the leashes of several dogs being walked by a floating robotic disc.

"Yes!" he shouted with a fist pump in the air. "I got the scramjet engine upgrade!"

Lexe, still wrapped in her conversation with Heath, said, "It could benefit an Afrian landracer."

"Oh yeah," said Heath, "an Afrian landracer maybe, but not a five ton, that's my point."

Mark's gameplay was interrupted by a beep from the Lemonsquare and a voice that said, "Destination on your right."

They stopped and looked. A tall two-story brick building with a single door and two garage doors stood across the street. A large flat roof jutted out as if the place had once been a gas station. Above the flat roof blinked a neon sign that read Otto's Hovercar Repair.

"Check out the car above the sign. It's cut in half." Lexe pointed at the classic looking hovercar that helped advertise Otto's garage by sticking out of the wall near the top of the building.

"Huh," said Heathcliff, "who'd cut a sweet '67 Maverick in half just to stick it on a building?"

They stood staring up at it for a few minutes.

"All right," said Mark. "Let's go see if Otto got me into the Cadet Core!"

Lexe snorted. "Maybe he bought you a pretty pink flarejet?"

"Hey," said Mark, pointing a finger at her. "I'd fly one even if it was the color of a unicorn's toenails, after being manicured by pretty pink fairies."

They crossed the street. The metal garage door rattled as he knocked on it. Nothing but more noise returned. He knocked again.

## CHAPTER 6

A metal bolt grated open. Chunk, chunk, chunk, chunk went the door as it rolled up, revealing a beautifully grease-stained woman with black hair tied in knot.

"Yes?" she asked in an icy voice.

"Eerrrrr," said Mark.

"Uuuhhhhhmmm," joined Heath.

"We're here to see Otto McMaluch, our basic repair teacher," Lexe said in a clear, purposeful voice.

The lady with the metal colored eyes paused on each of their faces. Then she turned and shouted into the shop. "Hey, Topps! Get Otto."

A short man turned off his paint sprayer and went towards the back of the garage.

Mark looked around as they waited. His eyes widened at the whole sight. The place smelled of welded metal with a hint of melted plastic. Fumes from caustic chemicals burned inside his nose as they evaporated off a floor stained by neon green and blue fluids that leaked from hanging hovercar engines. He counted seven cars lifted on stands in diagonal disarray across the large garage. Two more mechanics were busy with their own projects. One was a heavy set guy with large mechanical arms and legs who was towing away a truck by himself. The other was also heavy and had just as many augments; he was wrestling an engine out of its place with his bare metal hands.

"No need to scare them off, Miranda," said Otto as he walked up to where they all stood.

"We're not scared," said Lexe, folding her arms.

The big man's warm gray eyes reflected his light-hearted chuckle. "And there isn't any reason. Miranda simply enjoys scaring kids," he jested.

She frowned at him, shrugged in admittance, and then grinned at the kids before heading back to the modern hovercar she was repairing.

"I see your brave friends joined you. Eh, hotshot?" He then opened his arms wide. "Welcome! Welcome to my humble repair and restoration shop. Follow me," he said, heading inside.

They followed, weaving their way around rivulets of unknown liquids that glowed as they dripped from hoisted engines. Mark could hear classical music playing over the hiss of blowtorches cutting into neoplastic frames. "Is that Beethoven's Fifth?" he shouted above the din.

"Yes," said Otto. "Tchaikovsky, Chopin, Brahms, help my crew and me work. Let me introduce you." He stopped next to one of the heavy set fellows whose hands were busy being screwdrivers. "This is Phil. He's my engine guy."

"Hi!" said Phil, waving his fingers-turned-screwdrivers at them.

"Had both his arms augmented into all the tools he'll ever need. Show 'em, Phil!"

The heavy-set, round faced man proudly displayed both arms. Click, click, click, click went the tools in each arm as they rotated from hexheads to hammers and more. "This way—I never have to look for anything!" said Phil with a happy grin.

"Over there's his brother, Ratchet." Otto motioned towards the other heavy-set fellow.

"Topps is our auto body guy." He pointed at the energetic short man who waved back with a paint sprayer that was still on. "And you've met Miranda. She works on anything electric. Damn good driver too."

They continued to the back of the shop where hovercar parts were stacked on neat and labeled shelves. "My office is right upstairs. Mind the steps, the heights are all different."

Mark, Heath, and Lexe took the stairs with their heads down, trying not to trip. Otto opened the only door at the end of the stairs and they all walked in.

"Have a seat," he said, pointing to a low sofa made of steel and cloth.

## CHAPTER 6

"Is that a Harley?" Mark said, standing in the doorway while Heath and Lexe went to the sofa. His eyes were fixed on the pan-head chopper parked against the opposite wall. It had a single studded crocodile leather seat and ape-hanger handlebars.

"Yeah." Otto chuckled. "Only thing I've ever smuggled up from Earth. Had to, you know. It spoke to me. Anybody want tea?" He asked and walked over to his desk, which was made out of old, used engine parts.

They nodded, busy admiring the black and chrome motorcycle. Otto rummaged through several shelves stacked on the left wall. Mark looked around. The office had two large floor-to-ceiling windows and a glass door on the back wall. These looked out onto a short deck jutting over the bustling garage floor below.

"Yup," Otto continued while tossing glowing purple tea leaves into the eight hollow cylinders of an engine block. "The admiral sent me down there to check on some things a while back." He poured boiling water into each of the eight cylinders. "After the job was done I stopped by a local pub for a drink. Had to cover up the arm and ol' peg leg o'course." He let the tea simmer. "But my looks didn't sit too well with that crowd anyway. One thing led to another and I'm sliding a porky fellow across the bar while several more try to bash my head in with beer bottles. Long story short, I throw the last guy through the only window; he lands on the first parked Harley of many, and hey! Dominoes!" He said with a reminiscent chuckle. "But for some strange reason, the dominoes didn't touch the last bike. It stood there, defiant—spoke to me, it did." He smiled in satisfaction and poured them each a mug from beneath the engine block. He handed out the mugs—which were upside down pistons from the engine-turned-teakettle—to each of them.

Mark took a slow slurp. He licked his lips in delight.

"What's it like?" whispered Lexe, reluctant to try anything from an old engine.

"Sour," Mark whispered back. "Like that little tickling zap when you put your tongue on a nine-volt battery. But it's sweet too! Mmmm, friendly raspberries."

Lexe took a tentative sip, loved it, and went on sipping.

They enjoyed their mugs of tea for a few quiet moments.

"Aaahhh," McMaluch sighed, content enough with his tea to put it down. "Now we need to talk, hotshot."

Mark put his cup down too.

"Last month's stunt nearly cost you your enrollment. And I nearly got sacked."

Mark lowered his eyes back to the glowing tea.

"You've been doing a fine job after class every day, though. And I've been discussing certain matters with Captain Zumski and the admiral."

Mark felt a tremor in his heart.

"Here, step out on the deck with me."

Mark followed him out onto the deck. He glanced back through the windows at Heath and Lexe, who tried their best at encouraging expressions. He sighed and looked at Otto. The augmented man's imposing bulk made the thin iron railing creak as he leaned on it. For a few quiet moments, he surveyed the bustling scene of blowtorch fires and whirring power tools.

"Mark," he said without looking at the new recruit. "This is the time to speak honestly, as men. Why did you steal Lance's flarejet?"

"I didn't steal it!" Mark responded. "I wanted to fly the stupid thing is all. . . ."

"Lance claims that you tricked him. Claims you were jealous."

"What? No! I barely know the guy—I mean, he acts like a right hero of some bloody battle but—"

"To this school Lance is a hero. Many people believe he'll lead them to the Wargame Championships in a few years."

## CHAPTER 6

"That's great. I'm happy for him, great stuff everyone loving the guy and all, but I only wanted to take one of those flarejets for a spin. Believe me. I would have tried flying whichever one I had climbed into."

"I see—so you wanted to show off, is that it, hotshot?"

"No, honestly no. I really just wanted to fly, just—just—I don't know how to explain it."

"Try," Otto said and locked his hard gray eyes onto Mark's lost green-blue ones.

"I—it—hhhmm," he stammered and looked away. Visions of flying through meteor-filled sunrises in uncharted solar systems gripped his mind. How to explain that being a FlareRider simply—spoke to him?

Mark's eyes focused. He knew. Looking back at Otto, he said, "For the same reason that pan-head, crocodile seat, chopper of a Harley is sitting in your office—flying that flarejet spoke to me."

Otto harrumphed. "Well played hotshot, well played." He turned back to looking over his garage floor. Light from hissing blowtorches flickered over his weary face. "But the admiral doesn't believe you have the skills. And you know you don't have the money."

Mark looked away. He felt defeated.

Otto still did not look at the boy. "You must work to change your stars."

"Then I will."

They stood above the clamor of the busy garage, not saying anything, but lost in their own thoughts.

"I will, Otto," said Mark with a slow nod. "I'll work and I'll make it."

The half-augmented man turned to consider the resolution in the boy. "Good," he said with a wide smile. "Then I'll haul out that old shell of a flarejet I have sitting in my scrapyard."

Mark couldn't quite process what he'd just heard.

McMaluch clapped him on the back and Mark nearly fell over the rail. "It's nothing new. In fact, it's a piece of junk! But hey, if you can get the rest of the parts to build it, then, well, you might just make this year's Wargame—and get into the Cadet Core."

Mark was stunned. "I—don't know what to say—"

"Say no. After all, you'll need to spend every day after school in the garage fixing it up."

"I'd spend every day after school scrubbing dried plums off elephant bums just to pilot a flarejet one more time."

"Then I'll have Phil and Ratchet clear a space for you at the back of the shop. And here's a list of all the parts you'll need."

Mark, dizzy from shock, nearly missed taking the piece of paper Otto held out to him.

"But why, Otto? Why help me?"

Otto's gray eyes twinkled above his black stubble covered jaw. "Because damn what everyone else thinks! I believe that with solid stubbornness and a rebellious spirit, you can learn the skills for anything you want to become." He rested his augmented right hand on Mark's shoulder. "And if you stay true to that fighting heart of yours, you just might change your stars."

"I won't let you down, Otto."

Otto only shook his head. "Don't let yourself down, hotshot."

Mark left the office and walked downstairs with his mind churning out ideas. He marveled at the unexpected turn of events. His vision was already clouding with racing against comets through asteroid belts. Lexe and Heath followed, pestering him with questions.

"Mark! Hello? Moon to Mark," Lexe was saying as she raced down the stairs after him.

"Huh?" he replied with a blank stare.

"Look at him," said Lexe to Heath, who was jogging down the stairs behind her. "He's either won the lottery or gotten himself expelled."

## CHAPTER 6

"No," said Mark with a face still lost in high flying visions. "No, I'm building a flarejet."

"WHAT?" Heath said, stopping at the bottom of the stairs.

Mark stopped too. "Crazy huh? I thought I was getting the boot or something. But he was only testing me—I think." He started weaving between hovercars towards the garage door.

"For what?" Lexe asked as they followed him. "And why?"

"Not sure. But he's got a flarejet shell. All I need to do is find parts."

Heath and Lexe were too stunned to do more than duck under hoisted engines and avoid stepping in neon yellow puddles.

Mark stopped at the open garage door and whirled to face them. "I—am—going—to—build—my own piece of almighty junk!" He pumped both fists in the air for emphasis.

Lexe stood there, confused. "How are you going to get the parts?"

Mark's arms fell. "I don't know."

"I do," Heath simply stated.

They turned to him, Lexe skeptical and Mark curious.

"I know a guy," he continued. "Twenty minutes away, in the Port District."

Lexe grinned. "That seedy part of the city where my parents never let me go? Let's kick it then!"

"And," said Heath, making a point to look at Mark. "This guy sells some core skyboards."

"Stop it," said Lexe to Heath. "You're overwhelming our caveman. Look at him. He's about ready to either wag his butt or start drooling on your shoes."

But she couldn't hide her own eagerness for long. And as they drew nearer to Heath's 'one guy who sells everything,' they all quickened the pace.

After several blocks of increasingly dilapidated buildings, they entered a part of the city that could only be described as—suspicious. The Port District was not a tourist destination. Each building had at least one boarded up window; the dirty glass in the remaining windows reflected empty, hollow street lamps. Pubs and bars were not far apart, announced by the glare of harsh neon signs above doors from which sounds of rowdy laughter, beer bottles shattering, and angry words emerged. The air felt humid, burdened by hard labor and broken spirits.

"Where are we, exactly?" asked Mark, his sense of risky adventure tingling.

"Someplace dangerous!" whispered Lexe, violet eyes opened wide.

Heath chuckled, "not that dangerous to us locals."

"You live around here?" said Mark.

"Down a few streets in that apartment block," he replied, pointing to a squat thirty story building made of dull gray concrete that had been constructed in the most efficient and cheapest way possible. "It's not too ritzy, but it's home."

Mark looked at the apartment block again; it seemed a dismal place.

"OK guys," said Heath, "we made it."

They had stopped in front of a small brick and mortar store nestled between two other venerable establishments: O'Ryan's Pub and Credits 4 Crap Pawn Shop. In front of them, in curvy letters, blazed a purple neon sign: Black Pearl Bazaar.

"My skyboard's waiting inside," said Mark. "I can feel it!"

The excitement made him rush ahead, going straight for the door as if it would dissipate like all the others. It didn't. The way the glass shook from the impact Mark's face made threw Lexe into a laughing fit. Heath shook his head while Mark rubbed his nose and muttered curses.

"Dude," Heath said, reaching for the door handle, "it's a normal door."

## CHAPTER 6

They walked into the Black Pearl Bazaar with Mark still muttering and Lexe still laughing. The bazaar had the feeling of an Arabian desert. An intoxicating aroma lingered, musky and laden with the dreams of exotic treasures from strange solar systems; the floor was sprinkled with grains of sand fallen from the shoes of cloaked travelers who walked in from dusty planets orbiting distant suns. Around them, shelves bent under piles of oddities that, seen close up, whispered of mysteries waiting to be unraveled.

They walked up to a polished wooden counter at the back. Heath rang a small bell. Somewhere behind the beaded curtain to their left, a crash of things was followed by a cheery, "one minute, honorable customer!"

The beaded curtain opened with a clatter. A short man bustled in with a welcoming smile and opened arms. His eyes were mocha brown, just like his swarthy self. His clothes were billowing, puffy, and composed of every rich, bright color.

"Aaahhhh, salaam and good evening esteemed friends." He bowed with a flourish. "Welcome to my humble bazaar of the bizarre. My name is Perfidious Funk, purveyor of paradoxical presents most pleasant."

"Hey, Funk." Heath greeted him with a grin and an extended hand.

The short shopkeeper clasped Heath's hand in both of his for a hearty handshake. "Ah, Mr. Dodger Robinson, thank you for new customers."

"Oh no, these are my fr—"

"Sssshhhhh ush ush ush. I know," the mysterious little man said, turning to Mark with narrowed eyes. "I know why you are here. What you seek—I have."

"A skyboard?" said Mark, trying to act casual. "Nothing fancy or expensive, just, you know—awesome—and insane—and crazy and fast and delicious and AWESOME!"

"Follow me!" Perfidious exclaimed. Then, with another swirl of his gold-fringed cloak, he took a few short, quick steps to the left side of his store. They followed.

They stopped and stood in front of a wall that held a long row of beautiful skyboards.

Mark's face lit up at the sight. He looked at Heath. He looked at Lexe. He looked at Funk. He looked at his pants to make sure that, in his excitement, he hadn't wet himself.

It was like looking at a row of neatly stacked surfboards. Except these skyboards had small jet engines the size of soda cans attached to the back.

Lexe glanced over at Mark. "He's making that drooling face again."

It was true. Mark's hungry eyes were roving around the row of boards, making it difficult for his friends to tell if he wanted to ride a skyboard—or eat it. Mark was simply star struck by how many different designs there were. Some boards were sharp razors meant to cut clouds, others were wings meant to soar; each had different designs, engravings, and colors.

"Yes," said Mark with a vigorous nod. "Someday, straight to Earth, I'm smuggling all of everything right here in front of me."

Heath chuckled. "I know a guy for that too."

Funk, who'd been trying to tug a long thin skyboard out from the row, succeeded in tipping it over. It clattered to the floor. He hastily picked it up and made a show of polishing the red and silver board. Then, tilting it up for display, he smiled proudly.

"The Comet Chaser," said Perfidious with that gold-toothed smile of his. "Fast. Very fast."

"Whoa," Mark breathed. He wanted to grab it and run outside for a ride.

Funk, being an astute businessman, noticed and leaned the board towards him.

Mark grabbed it and held it close. The board felt heavy, solid, real. The surface was rough, like a skateboard, but more metallic, as if covered

## CHAPTER 6

in magnets the size of sand grains. Turning it over revealed a smooth underside. A silver grid of wires covered the bottom, along with images of comets racing through outer space. The top of the board was jagged, with edges that appeared as though a shark had bitten through. The bottom held a single engine in the shape of an inverted triangle. The whole board even smelled new, like plastic and aluminum.

"I—I can't breathe," said Mark, hyperventilating.

"I don't know," said Lexe, looking at the inverted triangle of an engine. "That's a First Form kicker on the back. Might be too much for Cavemanski over here."

"No," said Mark, bear-hugging the board.

Funk pulled a different skyboard out. This one was thick and wide like a big fat paddle board. It was a plain oval painted a solid baby blue. "Sol-Glider," he said with a flourish. "Best for beginner."

Heath looked it over. He ran a hand down the silver grid on the underside of the board. "It's got a solid flux field," he commented with a shrug.

"It is Novix circuitry," Funk said with another proud nod. "Stable. Very stable."

"Nah," said Lexe. "Looks lame."

Heath nodded.

"So?" said Mark. Dragging the Comet Chaser under his right arm, he grabbed the second board under his left arm.

"Nooooooo problem," said Funk and took a few brisk steps down the row. He pulled out another board. Its shape was a mix of the first two, except painted black with a gold edge down the left side. "Razor-Nine. Has two Invus kicks," he pointed at two pop-can sized engines on the back. "And an Invus flux field," he pointed to the silver grid across the bottom of the board.

"How's the crank?" Heath asked.

"Much power," answered Funk and unlocked the middle of the board. He opened it to show four glowing circles, like batteries. "Charge up only once every week."

"No," said Heath. "That's only a four-cell crank. It won't be enough power for two kicks."

"But it looks awesome!" said Mark and dragged both previous boards over to grab the Razor-Nine. He tried balancing all three in his arms.

"You getting all three?" asked Lexe with a smirk.

"Yes—maybe—well no, but I want to see them ALL!"

"Nooooo problem," said Perfidious Funk. "I have many boards. Many, many boards!"

"Maybe later? After the flarejet stuff?" Lexe suggested.

Mark blinked. His mind had forgotten everything once he'd seen that row of skyboards. "Right, right, good. Flarejet parts." His head swiveled to Perfidious. "Do you have flarejet parts?"

"Yes! Of course! Perfidious Funk has everything in the galaxy!"

Mark kept balancing all three boards in his arms while jutting his butt out at Heath. "The list's in my pocket."

Heath arched an eyebrow. "You want me to get it out of your back pocket?"

"Yeah," said Mark with a vigorous nod.

"I'll hold the boards and you get it."

"No," said Mark with a vigorous shake.

Heath sighed and reached into Mark's pocket. He pulled out the crumpled piece of paper, unfolded it, and held it in front of Mark's face.

"I need a shield generator," said Mark, reading the list. "What kinds do you stock?"

"Yes—yes yes—mmmm. I do not have one of those."

"Oh, but you just said everything in the—nevermind. OK, how about a HUD?"

## CHAPTER 6

"Mmmm, yes—no."
"A tracking system?"
"Probably—maybe—also no."
"An engine. Please tell me you at least have a flarejet engine."
"Yes! I have one of those. Funk does have one of those."
"Perfect! What kind?"
"Top of the market. Brand new. Made by Invertix Inc. Five hundred kilotons thrust force, nine vectors of breaking power, fueled by proto-ion core."

"Sahweeeeet," said Mark in his delighted voice. "Faster than a Blacknova AX?"

"Ten times faster! Or I eat my swirling purple pants!"

"Sahweeeeeeeeeet," said Mark, nearly out of breath again.

"For you special price. Not one million quarks. No. Nine hundred ninety nine thousand quarks!"

Mark's face flattened as if someone had walloped it with a shovel. "I can't afford that," he muttered to himself. Then a realization dawned. A hard truth he had forgotten. A panicked expression sunk his eyebrows. He looked around the room as if in a daze. "I can't afford anything."

Heath winced and lowered the list. "You don't have any money?"

Mark looked up at him with pain in his eyes. "No."

"No money?" asked Perfidious in a businesslike tone. The shrewd and clever black market dealer sensed an opportunity. But he had to play it up first. "No sale," he said and took the Razor-Nine from Mark's arms. He made a show of placing it back in the rack.

The boy flinched as the shopkeeper took the second skyboard away. The boot heel of money driven reality proceeded to grind the remaining pieces of Mark's hope into dust.

"Your parents didn't give you anything?" said Lexe.

Mark slowly shook his head. "Just for the school. That's it."

Nobody spoke. Lexe had stopped talking as soon as she saw Mark's sunken face. Heath remained silent out of respect for Mark's dead hopes and dreams.

Perfidious reached for the Comet Chaser. He had to tug it away from Mark.

"Someday," said Heath with a reassuring hand on Mark's shoulder.

Mark didn't budge. His eyes, though sad, kept roaming the rack of skyboards.

"No money?" Perfidious asked again, breaking the boy down further. Mark slowly shook his head, still fixated on the boards.

The short shopkeeper looked between the three friends. He had built the moment up enough. Leaning in with a low voice, he said, "Then I have different deal for you."

Mark's wounded expression refocused. Heath raised an eyebrow. Lexe tilted her head.

Perfidious Funk's voice became lower. "Very good deal—profitable," he had Heath's attention. "Risky," he had Lexe's attention. "With much flarejet technology," he had Mark's attention.

"What is it?" asked Mark, cautious but eager.

"There is a broken place. It was city's most guarded industrial area. Now it is city's most guarded wasteland." Perfidious paused to make sure they understood the inherent danger's they'd be facing. "Orion Industries made powerful engines there. Deep Intersolar Enterprises made powerful weapons. Shattered Sky Interspace had headquarters there—making powerful—hhhmmm—things." He paused again, fiddling with the edge of his gold-fringed sleeves. "It is abandoned now. For thirty years—quarantine. No person in—no person out. But," he adjusted his purple robe in a watchful way. "I know how to get you in. I give you locations to profitable loot inside this place. Inside the Seven Site."

## CHAPTER 6

The three friends exchanged excited glances. The dangers hadn't deterred them. Silently, they had decided to go.

"How do we get there?" asked Mark.

"Follow map I give."

"How do we get in?" asked Heath.

"Follow instruction I give."

"Let's go!" said Lexe.

"No. Not now. In one month, at solar zenith. Force field will be weak. I will tell you when," said Perfidious Funk. Then the shrewd dealer had another idea. "But you get my stuff first, understand?" He picked up the Comet Chaser and held it out to Mark. "For mutual good business. You borrow Comet Chaser. You get my stuff first. You keep Comet Chaser."

Mark tried keeping a cool, calm face. His willpower lasted all of half a minute.

"STUNTS!" he shouted, grabbed the board, and ran outside.

He did not understand that he had just agreed to a curiously dangerous deal.

# THE BLACK PEARL BAZAAR

# CHAPTER 7

# CHAPTER 7
## THE SEVEN SITE

Canapki's Deli, at the corner of Marrian Street and Zena Avenue in the Port District, was famous locally for serving the choicest meats, best cheeses, and bread so fresh with crust so crunchy and insides so fluffy and warm that people on a diet had to move out of the city.

Late autumn had turned into early winter and Heath sat on the curb outside the deli with his boots in a mixture of slush and puddle water. But he was happy. He was munching on a zapiekanka. The top half of a bread roll, flipped over, toasted and piled up with slices of pan-fried spicy sausage, radish, and covered in three types of melted cheese—for him, this was heaven. He looked up into a cold sky, his mouth stretching a string of cheese from the steaming zapiekanka.

Lexe was diving on her sliver thin, Seven-Zero-Seven skyboard; it left a fading streak of neon yellow against the gray winter clouds. Her face was set in one of those focused scowls of serious fun. A minute before hitting the ground, she wrenched her board up. The silver grid on the bottom of her board blazed as it created a flux field. Slush and street water sprayed out as her board came inches from crunching into the pavement.

"Oh come on!" said Heath, sheltering his toasted deliciousness with his arms.

She grinned, flicked her board up, tucked it under her right arm, and walked over.

## CHAPTER 7

"My zapiekanka in there too?" she asked and sat down on the curb next to him.

He bit down on his and, holding it between his teeth, opened a brown bag.

"Thanks," said Lexe, taking her wrapped zapiekanka. "Mmmmmm yeah," she breathed, tearing it open. The aroma of warm, diced ham under melted gooey cheese escaped in the tendrils of steam rising from the crunchy bread.

They sat and ate in blissful silence. Their breath misted from the warm zapiekankas.

"How's Mark up there?" asked Heath.

Lexe shrugged. "He's got the leaning turns and tilting stops down." She took another bite and chewed between words. "But his cut and slash turns suck. My grandmother could cut faster. And she's dead. "

"It's only been a month," said Heath, almost finished with his zapiekanka.

"And if he doesn't learn to turn faster he's going to keep leaving snot on brick walls."

"What are you teaching him today?"

"Dives."

"Dives?" said Heath, choking on his food. "But you just said he hasn't learned to turn fast enough. How's he supposed to tilt up fast enough?"

Lexe took another big bite. "No better motivator to learn than the hard ground threatening to kiss your face."

As if on cue, Mark's excited hollers could be heard along with the sound of his Comet Chaser ripping through the air.

They looked up to see the boy crouched on his plummeting skyboard, one hand holding the edge, the other flailing. His eyes were wide open and fixed on the approaching pavement.

"Fiver says he shorts it," said Lexe.

"Ten he sticks it," Heath replied.

Mark's dive looked steep. The red streak left by the First Form engine was aggressive. He was the picture of fearlessness. But the pavement was approaching too fast, and it did not look fun to make out with.

"Holy sheeeee!" he yelled, wrenching the front of the board up. It began to wobble. He kept speeding down towards Heath and Lexe, skyboard swinging out of control. He lost his sense of balance.

Lexe and Heath leaned apart. Mark sped between them and slammed into the deli window. His skyboard flipped and clunked onto the sidewalk.

"He tilted too soon," said Heath, going back to munching.

"Way too soon," agreed Lexe, taking another big bite.

From somewhere behind them, Mark groaned.

"You know, I love these," said Heath, holding up the last bite of his zapiekanka. "You can't make them in lunchboxes—well, you can," He gobbled up the rest. "But they don't taste the same."

Lexe, mouth full of warm toppings on toasted bread, nodded and mumbled in agreement.

A grumbling Mark slowly got up behind them.

"Know why?" Heath continued. "Because the cook grilled up something else before making your zapiekanka. And the flavor of whatever he had made before gets grilled into your zapiekanka." He licked the salt and spices off his fingers. "Tastes different—every time."

"Sounds like you should open your own deli," said Lexe.

"Huh—maybe," said Heath, considering this thought. "But I'd have to name the zapiekanka something else. Something catchier."

Mark, who had stumbled up behind them, made several huffing noises as he gingerly sat down. "I think I'm renaming my board," he said. "I'll call it: the Vomit Comet."

## CHAPTER 7

Heath slapped him on the back and, reaching into the brown bag, took out a third zapiekanka. "You're doing better and better. Here's your reward."

"Thanks," Mark wheezed. He unwrapped it. The spicy aroma of a bread roll slice loaded with that awesome kind of pepperoni that's toasted to be crispy at the edges, instantly made him feel better. He took a big crunchy bite, savoring the minced chives sprinkled on melted cheddar cheese. "Oh yeah. That's the stuff."

"And dude," said Heath, picking at his teeth, "Don't worry. Starting out is always rough."

"Like learning to ride a bike, huh?" said Mark in between spicy mouthfuls.

"A what?" said Heath with a puzzled look.

"Is that a caveman thing?" said Lexe.

Mark's mouth was full of zesty sauce, but he had to laugh. They didn't know what a bicycle was. "Two wheels and a lot of bruised shins and scraped ankles."

"Heeeey kids," said a creepy voice behind them.

Mark spluttered out bits of chives and bread crumbs; Heath jumped and whirled around; even Lexe yelped. They hurried to stand up and look who was behind them.

"I've been waiting for you to fly down," said the short, gaunt man who had startled them. His appearance was intimidating, unapproachable, and menacing. Dressed in all black clothes with spiked purple hair and piercings in his eyebrows, ears, and nose, he could have looked quite scary. Unfortunately for him, his frightening persona was somewhat diminished by the shockingly pink ballerina's tutu around his waist and those large fake fur boots.

"How—um—how can we help you?" asked Heath.

"Oh!" said the thin man, as if he'd forgotten something. He reached over to his right wrist and twisted the dial of a black watch.

Heath's eyebrows clambered up and Lexe's eyes widened as the punk rocker ballerina guy blinked away. He was replaced by an android with a backpack.

"Hi, Lloyd," said Mark.

"I'm in disguise, you know," said Lloyd, raising a finger as if to make a point.

"Not a very boring one," said Mark, crunching into cheesy bread.

"Different disguise tech. But never mind that, never mind that," said Lloyd. "Got something I'm supposed to deliver. Your hands only." He took off the gray backpack and held it out to Mark.

"From?" said Mark as he took the backpack in his left hand.

"I didn't ask."

"What's in it?" said Heath.

"I didn't ask."

"Then wha—" said Mark, confused, his half-open mouth showing chewed up food.

Lloyd shook a finger at him. "Ask no questions—get no lies." Then he darted a look to the left and right. "I must go," he said. "Or else they'll see me."

"Who?"

The droid's camera-lenslike eyes widened as he reached up to Mark's face. Gripping Mark's shirt in both hands, he whispered, "Them!" Then, with a twist of the dial, he became a punk ballerina once more, and bounded away down the street.

Mark took another bite and shook his head in wonder.

"So what's in there?" asked Lexe, leaning in for a look.

Mark handed the shell shaped backpack to her. She opened it.

## CHAPTER 7

"A map and a bunch of these things." She held up a black palm-sized disk with a red button in the middle.

"Proxy ports," said Heath. "They're for teleporting stuff."

"Huh," said Mark. "Think it's from Funk, then?"

"Yeah," said Lexe, "Look." She held up the unfolded map. It was a sheet of thin plastic currently displaying one sentence: Remember! My stuff first!

"Want to go?" asked Heath, eager for profitable loot.

"Does a bear frump in the woods?" exclaimed Mark, stuffing the rest of the zapiekanka in his mouth. Then he tipped an imaginary hat at Lexe and said, "yes, yes he does."

She shoved the backpack at Mark, picked up her board, and rocketed skywards. Heath did the same. Mark slung the backpack on and followed. Their skyboards left shimmering streaks of color in the deli windows.

Deeper and deeper into the Port District they raced. Squat brick buildings scowled against the bright daylight and dirty neon lights fought to be seen. The air sat heavy in their lungs and tasted of cold, bland factories. This far into a city's industrial area and the crisp breezes of early winter choked on concrete factories and steel mills.

They sped fast and high above dirty streets and gritty sidewalks where grass grew in pavement cracks. Flying far above all the buildings, they cut diagonally across Carmine Road, then Bunker Hill Road, Ironbind Street and then Colburn Street.

Lexe had the map open while riding, rarely looking down, maneuvering her board with ease. Heath too didn't seem to be paying much attention; his feet moved his board in slow, easy adjustments as he followed. Behind them, Mark was moving in a zig-zag, still learning how to maneuver on his board. It didn't help that he was distracted. The dirt and soot of the Port District called to his sense of adventure.

Traveling high above these mean streets, he breathed the cold grimy air and listened to the sounds of traffic and factories.

"What do you think of this?" said Heath. "A roasted chicken zapiekanka with bacon bits and Thousand Planet sauce."

Mark stabilized his board to fly next to Heath. "I'd eat it."

"You know—I was telling Lexe this—I've always thought more people would eat zapiekankas if they had a snappier name."

Mark hooked his thumbs in the backpack straps and gave a thoughtful frown.

"Something more marketable," Heath continued. "Like kankas."

Mark snickered. "I dunno. That sounds a bit—dirty."

"Yeah, kinda, huh?" said Heath with grin. "Hhmm—how about meatwiches?" But then he shook his head at his own idea. "No that sounds gross."

Mark nodded. "And they're not really witches."

"Yeah, no, something simpler anyway. Hmmmmmm."

They rode on for a minute, following Lexe over Thermite Road.

"Hey," said Heath, face alight, "Hey how about—a zippy?"

"Zippy?"

"Zippy."

Mark mulled it over. "Zippies."

"Zippies!" said Heath, rocking his skyboard back and forth out of excitement.

"Not zip pies," Mark clarified.

"No no. Zippeeees," Heath enunciated by extending his fingers with the E sound.

"Mmmmm. Yeah," said Mark, slowly nodding. "I like it. I like the way the word tastes. Like a strip of deep fried bacon riding a motorcycle made of crunchy bread."

## CHAPTER 7

"Yeah," Heath breathed, cold air turning his breath into mist.

They rode on, getting hungry from the thought of delicious zippies.

Soon the map had them hang a right above Menhir Street and head toward the West crater ridge. The roads began leading upwards. After a short uphill journey they stopped at Kogan's Cliff. It was an imposing and steep cliff that made Mark's head spin as he looked down upon the valley they'd traveled from. They rode on, hanging close to the cliff edge until they arrived at Kogan's Creek. Following the creek upwards, they didn't stop until the edge of a peculiar sort of forest.

"Look at all the fallen trees," said Mark. "I wonder why . . ."

"What is this place?" asked Heath.

"The Fallen Forest," said Lexe, showing them the map.

They wove between the few standing trees in silence. Mark noticed that for every standing tree there were five fallen. Some of the rotted trees were only half fallen, being gently supported by the bare winter branches of the few living trees.

The further in they traveled, the more the moss became a sickly green. Lexe grimaced the entire time and Heath put a hand on his stomach. Mark wondered if it was the air that made them feel nauseous; it was slimy sweet like rotting leaves.

But, being at the lowest edge of the forest, their journey was short. And after many broken trunks and hollowed logs, they reached the other side and burst out onto a steep slope. The three friends stood on their boards and gazed at the hazardous wonders just down the hill. It was like a faraway place. City noises couldn't be heard over the creak of swaying timber and the cry of a rare bird.

"There it is," said Lexe, folding up the map, "the Seven Site."

"Look at all those tall piles of scrap," said Mark, eyes darting around the rectangular plaza. It was too large of an area to see all at once.

"Must be from those four factories that are still standing," said Heath.

# THE SEVEN SITE

Mark pointed. "And from those two half-sunken buildings at the edges of that gigantic lake. Think it's an acid lake?" he mused. "Must be an acid lake. Nothing but bright yellow, red, and even the green looks like melted plastic."

"There's a small spaceship half sunk in it too," Lexe pointed out.

"Where?" said Mark, straining his eyes.

"There," Lexe pointed.

Sure enough, at the edge of the acid lake was a small spaceship, half-sunk with its right wing sticking out of the acid-colored water.

"Huh, you're right," said Mark. "Looks familiar too—but it's too far to tell."

They stood for a few minutes surveying all the trouble they'd be getting into. Piles of scrap lay heaped up on old streets alongside abandoned factories. Long ago, there were seven large factories here. They researched and developed new technologies, cutting edge circuitry, and even military tech. Now, they were filled with broken things.

"Shall we?" said Mark, tightening the backpack straps, eager to find flarejet parts.

Heath grinned and Lexe said, "Race you down!"

All three sprinted on their boards so fast and so close to the steep ground that the flux fields on their boards kicked up dry dirt. They were dodging hollowed black stumps in a game of skillful speed when Heath shouted, "Oye!" and pointed to the bottom of the hill. "Force field coming up quick!"

A cloud of chalk-white dust billowed as Lexe skidded to a stop only feet in front of a transparent wall of pulsing turquoise-colored energy. Heath, who'd seen it first, calmly stopped behind her. Mark, being more about speed and less about remembering how to stop, slipped, skidded, and nearly met the stiff force field with his face, stopping only an inch away.

## CHAPTER 7

"So close," he said, coughing from the cloud of dust he'd made.

"Good cut," said Heath. "Leaned back nice and heavy."

"Yeah, not bad," said Lexe.

"Thanks!" said Mark, beaming.

They hopped off their skyboards and went up to the force field. Block-like words were scrolling across the slowly pulsing force field.

"Dead Valley Quarantine," Mark read in between coughs. "No entry."

"How does Funk say to get through?" Heath asked, turning to Lexe.

"Fly over!" shouted Mark, feeling overly encouraged by his recent good performance.

Lexe unfolded the map again. She zoomed in on the location. Perfidious Funk's instructions popped up. "Well, first thing he wrote was: no skyboards," she read. "So no flying over."

Mark put the backpack on the ground. He folded his arms. "Challenge accepted."

They watched him soar straight up.

Heath looked back down at the map. "What do we do then?"

She tapped twice on the little holographic symbol of the force field. A list of words popped up. She frowned. "Instructions say to run through it."

"Run through it?" said Heath. He looked at the slowly pulsing curtain of energy and raised a skeptical eyebrow at her.

"Yeah. See," she started reading. "Do not touch or walk. Run. My stuff first.'"

Mark shouted from way up high. "Hey! Hey guys! I'm over! Check it!"

They both looked up and saw the bottom of Mark's skyboard a few feet past where the curve of the force field faded away. "Haha! Watch this!"

Bbrrzzzaaapp!

THE SEVEN SITE

Mark learned, right then and there, that when a field of energy seems to fade away, it doesn't mean it's actually gone. His lightly electrocuted body rolled down the curved dome of the force field, making hard spots of crimson energy appear each time he bounced.

"Watch out for his skyboard," said Heath and moved out of the way. "It's rolling down next to him."

Lexe didn't hear, being busy doubled over with laughter. This made Mark's landing softer.

The Vomit Comet clunked down in the dust. Mark fell on top of Lexe.

"Gerrr-off!" She said, shoving him. He rolled onto the ground, laughing.

"That was fun," he said with a grin, laying there as if he'd just made a snow angel. His brown hair looked like a charred forest.

"Lumpy dingbat of a cave idiot," grumbled Lexe as she stood and dusted herself off.

"You all right?" asked Heath, offering a helping hand.

"Just gotta walk it off," said Mark as he coughed and laughed and stood up on wobbly knees. "So how do we get in?"

"We'll leave our skyboards here," said Heath and propped his Galaxy-Ten against an ash covered stump. He rubbed his hands together and stared at the force field. "Then we run right through. No walking or touching, apparently."

"What? Like platform nine and three-quarters?" said Mark.

"Like what?" said Heath, distracted from his nervousness.

"Movie reference," said Mark.

"Ah," said Heath. Then he took a few quick breaths, glanced at Mark and Lexe, and sprinted at the force field.

A wobbling sound, a ripple across the turquoise surface, and Heath was through! He looked back at them through the solid force field, amazed.

## CHAPTER 7

"My turn!" said Lexe, and sprinting at full speed, she jumped through.

Mark picked up the shell shaped backpack and ran through. "Felt all cold and fuzzy, didn't it?" he asked when on the inside. "Like hugging a polar bear."

"Let's find some loot!" said Lexe.

They leaned in as she held the map open, zooming in on their corner of the Seven Site. Eleven red dots appeared.

"Funk's stuff looks close," Heath commented, pointing at a few of the dots.

"Or," Mark interjected. "OR — we go into the first building we see and sack the place."

They considered this proposition.

"We've got the rest of the afternoon to find Funk's stuff," said Lexe with a shrug.

Mark nodded. "Then off we go!"

They turned their backs on the force field and headed into the maze of scrap piles. Lexe held the map while they walked. The fuzzy hologram bobbed with the rhythm of her footsteps.

"Check out that tall crane sitting there." Lexe nodded toward a machine taller than most houses, painted yellow and rusting.

Strange, huh?" said Mark. "The grabber claw still has junk in it. It's like the guy operating it just left his job one day and never came back."

A mysterious atmosphere sunk in. The first scrap pile was composed of old office chairs, broken desks, rusted filing cabinets, and other office furniture. Papers were scattered across the streets, soggy from recent rains. The streets themselves were cracked, with weeds and dirt growing between faded yellow lanes. Everything looked dull and bland in the gray light of an overcast day. A stale smell hung in the air, like mold and decay.

THE SEVEN S!TE

They passed the first pile and walked among other looming heaps of ordinary things. Once in a while Mark or Heath would rush to a pile and dig around, thinking they saw something good. They would always come back empty handed and grumbling about how it wasn't what they thought or it was broken.

There were no signs of nature. Not living nature anyway. Once, when this place was alive, workers would gather for some rest and relaxation on little lawns under tall trees that dotted the Seven Site. Now those tall trees were twisted trunks, wreathing up in agony from burnt grass, their stumps bleached like dry bones.

They rounded another rusted pile of junk and stopped in front of a single story science building from which leafy vines draped and obscured the faded white exterior.

"Our first treasure trove," Lexe announced. "Orion Industries."

"Place looks haunted by Frankensteinish dust bunnies," said Mark as his eyes roved the empty windows and empty doors.

Gravel gritted beneath their feet as they walked up the front entry steps. Mark ripped away the slimy vines covering the door and they stepped inside. A cool, clammy darkness enveloped them. Their ears adjusted to the silence before their eyes could adjust to the black—and from somewhere inside, the roof was leaking.

"Darker than an Orc's bum, innit?" said Mark, feeling around in the dark.

"I've got an app for that," said Lexe. She handed the map off to Heath and took out her Lemonsquare. Pressing a button, it lit up like a flashlight. They ventured inside.

"Strange. Nothing's out of place," she said, picking up a single sheet of glass from a round end table. It blinked on to show colorful advertisements for perfumes along with scrolling headlines. "Look at this magazine. It's dated fifty years ago."

## CHAPTER 7

"None of the chairs are overturned. No rush, no hurry out of here. Weird," said Mark. He subconsciously adjusted the backpack on his shoulders.

"And we'll leave it that way," said Heath and spread the map on the table. He double-tapped on the building they were in and the map responded by displaying a hologram of the floor they were on. "All right, this place has two subfloors and a vault."

"Vault first!" said Lexe.

The glow of her Lemonsquare faded from the cold lobby along with them. Silence began to settle back in as the lighthearted voices of the three explorers traveled down the hall. The room sank back into chilled darkness and shadowed obscurity. All was as it had been for many years.

Then, in the growing silence, five small unblinking LED eyes appeared. Set haphazard in a flat featureless face, the eyes stared after the three kids. Once the silence was complete, a rusted skeletonlike droid scuttled through the shadows, following them.

■ ■ ■ ■ ■ ■ ■ ■ ■ ■

"Nothing!" said Mark, smashing open the glass double doors leading out of a six story concrete building.

"Let me see the backpack," said Lexe, following Mark's brisk stomp down the stairs.

"At least we've got most of Funk's stuff," said Heath, trying to be encouraging as he joined them in the littered street.

Mark dropped the backpack on the cold ground. He held up three fingers. "We've been to Orion Industries—nothing," he ticked off one finger. "We've been to two manufacturing plants—nothing," he ticked off another finger. "And we've just gotten more of Funk's crap from this

THE SEVEN SITE

place without finding jack squat for us!" He shook his last finger back at the concrete building.

"Yeah," said Heath with a sigh. "Looters, man. Everything worth anything has already been sacked."

"Nothing. This bites," said Mark, kicking a chunk of concrete down the street.

"Not many proxy ports left," said Lexe. She closed the backpack and put it on. "Where to next?"

"Anywhere," said Mark. "Anywhere with jacked up engines that barbeque so hard marshmallows turn into fossilized candy."

"Nobody understands half the things you say," Lexe grumbled.

"Flarejet engines, Lexe. Flare—jet—engines."

"Here, maybe you'll find one," she retorted, giving him the map.

Mark took it, but only to wave it around while talking. "We've been through all the standing buildings. Nothing. So let's try one of the half-torn down factories by that acid lake."

"Lead the way, Captain Caveman," said Lexe.

Their shoes went on crunching concrete bits and their eyes went on searching for something worth their time. Several piles of worthless rubble later and the acid lake came into view. In the distance the half sunken spaceship jutted out. They walked in silence, staring at the lake's slowly swirling magentas, violets, yellows, and reds. It was a peaceful place, like one of those romantic lagoons in the movies. Only this lagoon was surrounded by blood-crimson shallows. All three explorers felt chills run down their spines. Not one of them noticed the three rusted skeletal droids skittering on top of the junk piles, following them.

"There it is," said Lexe as they rounded another rubble pile.

A long, dilapidated eight story building began filling their field of vision. The entire left end of it was gone, having fallen into and been dissolved by the acid lake. Numerous docking bays and several loading

## CHAPTER 7

cranes stood off to the side, half of them snapped and dangling. Large block letters at the top of the factory announced what this place once was: Shattered Sky Interspace.

"Isn't this the place Perfidious was all sketchy about?" said Lexe.

Heath nodded. "Yeah. So—careful, right?"

They trekked along the crimson lakeside until they reached the left end of the crumbling building. Standing on the narrow shore between the acid lake and the severed building, they looked up. All eight floors were exposed, as if a knife had cut the end of the building off, leaving a jagged opening.

"Can you imagine falling from up there?" said Mark. "I would literally die."

"Give me a boost," said Lexe, turning to Heath.

Heath cupped his hands and crouched. Lexe stepped in and reached for the floor hanging above them. After she scrambled up, Heath helped Mark. Then Mark lay on the floor and reached down to him, pulling him up to join them.

"Let me see the map," Lexe said, reaching out to Mark.

He dug in his pocket and gave her the folded sheet of plastic.

She unfolded it against the peeling wallpaper of the nearby wall. It blinked on, showing the blueprint of the building. "I bet this place has a skunk works," she murmured, eyes roaming the floor plan.

"A what?" said Heath, staring at her.

"A skunk works. Large research factories like this sometimes have an off-the-books R and D." Her hands were moving around the map. "It's the place where they make tech off-contract and off the books. Experimental tech, stuff so bleeding edge or so military that almost no one knows about it—not even the regular employees." Her hands swiped the map, switching between floors; on each floor she zoomed in and out of rooms that caught her attention, then, with a few flicks of her fingers, she stopped on a large area labeled "Waste Disposal Tanks." Snapping the map shut, she said, "Top floor, come on."

"Waste Disposal?" said Mark with a skeptical frown.

She just blazed ahead, leaving them to follow. They did, walking behind her down the empty, tilted hallway. Mark looked into the offices they passed. This factory was above ground and lined with windows. The daylight showed him offices ready and waiting. The people who used to work there could have strolled right back in and started complaining about their jobs to their coworkers.

Heath noticed this too. "Doesn't look like this place was sacked like the rest, huh?"

"I wonder what happened," said Mark.

"I heard that parts for the Obliv were made here," said Heath while looking into the offices they passed. "Made by Shattered Sky Interspace. They say all this happened because something went wrong. . ."

The three young explorers were so far down the hallway, they didn't hear those quiet rusted scrapes. Five skeletal droids were climbing in, following them through the shadows like cockroaches.

# CHAPTER 8

# CHAPTER 8
## RUN

"Wow," said Lexe, the first to walk into the soaring circular entry chamber.

Heath was next and also gaped in awe as he craned his head back to see the immense empty space where daylight rained in from a gigantic broken glass dome. A museum's worth of rocket engines were floating in mid-air at various levels around the entry chamber. Each cast jagged shadows onto a floor made of sleek tiles set to read "Shattered Sky Interspace."

"I'm a dizzy ant stuck at the bottom of a blender," said Mark, looking up into the streams of cold daylight as dust motes floated by.

"This way," said Lexe, heading up a flight of stairs that circled the chamber.

Taking two steps at a time for eight flights of stairs and they were out of breath. Lexe couldn't be persuaded to slow down. Reaching the top floor, she marched them down a hallway where large doors were clearly labeled "Waste Removal," "Waste Recycling," and "Waste Processing."

"Lexe, where are we going? Seriously?" said Mark as he jogged next to her.

"Right here," she said and stopped in front of a black and white round door. She pointed above the door. A skunk had been painted in place of a room label.

Mark squinted at her. "You're going to shove me down a stank sewer hole filled with hardened keester cakes for a laugh, aren't you?"

## CHAPTER 8

Lexe laughed. This made Heath back away. Then she said, "Why didn't I think of that?" She folded up the map and stuffed it in her backpack. "That would've been fun! But no. Didn't you think it was odd that, just to get to this door, we had to go through eight—now deactivated—security grids?" she said, pointing behind them. "Now help me open it."

Mark made sure Lexe was in front of him as they slid the doors apart, just in case this was a dubious prank. The doors scraped open, revealing a dark void.

"What's in there, ya think?" Lexe turned to them with a suspicious grin. "Who wants to find out?"

Mark looked at her sideways, eyes narrowed. "You first. I don't want to end up tumbling down the tunnel of tangy butt nuts."

Heath chuckled. "That sounds like a carnival ride at the Amusement Park of Unfortunate Names."

"It's been fifty years," Mark stated. "The corn chunks have probably become sentient and formed their own turd-fueled society complete with famous poopstars and a president elected by how well he can BS."

Heath laughed. Lexe shook her head at their immaturity. She strode into the dark room with her Lemonsquare glowing. They followed. The dark air had a clean, plastic smell to it.

At first, the light from her Lemonsquare reached only as far as their footsteps. Then, when their footsteps took them a stone's throw into the room, a deep hum began. It reverberated through the black and white checkered floor.

"Bright!" yelped Mark, shutting his eyes tight. The deep hum had clicked into a flood of pure white light. All three began blinking and rubbing their eyes.

"Wholly scrumptious gearboxes!" Mark said after he could see. "We hit it! We hit the mother lode!"

They stood in awe, basking in wonder at the treasure trove. Mark didn't know where to look first. He turned round and round in the large, star-shaped laboratory. His eyes darted around the tables that stuck out of each of the five corners. The tables were stacked with all manner of strange gadgets. An air of unspoiled technology filled the place. This was a laboratory where the greatest minds worked to create new machines. Mark felt as if this stark white and black room required him to wear a lab coat and serious frown at all times while present.

"Load up, boys," said Lexe with a proud smile, shoving the backpack into Mark's arms.

Heath made a beeline for the table with the most loot. Mark began to wander around, reading labels. Lexe gravitated toward a wall with eight computer monitors stacked to form a large screen. All three became preoccupied with happily rummaging around.

Heath in particular was enthralled with a crystal orb. It had long tubes coiling around the bottom. Gray particles floated about inside. "I don't know what this is!" he gleefully shouted, "But it looks expensive!"

Mark, knowing what was up, dug a proxy port out of the backpack and tossed it to him.

"Thanks," said Heath, catching the palm-sized disc and pressing the red button in the center. Small triangles sprung out along the edges of the disc. A hazy green glow emitted from the bottom. Heath stuck the disc to the gray orb. The triangles clamped down. A single beep and the whole crystal dissolved into a transparent hazy green, then blinked away.

"You need any, Lexe?" asked Mark, offering a few proxy ports.

"Nope," she replied. "I'll be downloading all these gadgets' blueprints."

"Sweet," said Mark. "Let me know if you find any flarejet tech. Oh! jetpack!" he shouted, holding up two long cylinders with straps attached. "How much you think Funk will pay us for it?" he asked while sticking a proxy port to it and teleporting it away.

## CHAPTER 8

"Or," said Heath, pointing to Mark. "How long do you think we could fly around with it?"

"Yes," Mark replied, pointing back at Heath.

"That wasn't a jetpack, guys," said Lexe, focused on those eight monitors, which displayed information around three dimensional diagrams and a download bar at 10 percent. She pointed to a blueprint of what Mark found. "It was their portable coffee maker."

"Oh," said Mark. "Well—look at me filling up Funk's teleport bay with useless crap."

"Pro tip," said Heath, waving around a sheet of glass that looked like a screen, "if it looks easy to break, it's gotta be expensive."

The two would-be looters spent the next several minutes happily teleporting random things from random tables. Whatever looked expensive, high-tech, or profitable, disappeared.

"You guys find anything for my flarejet?" Mark called out again.

"Not yet," said Heath.

"Nope," said Lexe, her download bar at 48 percent.

Mark went back to sifting through odds and ends, reading labels in hopes of finding flarejet components. Heath kept on using up their stock of proxy ports on anything shiny and easily breakable he could find. And Lexe kept adding digital blueprints to her downloads, which hovered around 70 percent. All three young treasure hunters were having so much fun that they didn't notice the seven rusted droids lurking outside the door.

"Hey what's this?" said Mark, standing in front of a thick glass case. Inside, suspended in mid-air and slowly rotating, was a small jagged blue cube the size of two dice smashed together. Mark put his hand against the thick glass case. It was ice cold. "Hey Lexe, you know anything about this creepy cube thing?"

She turned her head to look, then went back to her monitors. A few hand swipes later and her voice had a note of confusion in it. "It's coming up 'high-grade restricted.' "

"Is it shiny?" asked Heath.

"It glows," Mark replied.

"Even better," said Heath. "Port it."

Mark looked around the glass case. He found a small indention at the bottom left. A light press and the front glass panel swung open. The air inside was cold, like opening the freezer.

He pulled a proxy port out of the backpack, pressed the button, and covered the cube with the glowing green underside of the disc. It buzzed twice and flashed red and nothing happened. He tried again. Nothing happened.

"Something's wrong," he muttered. He gave the disc a good shake and tried again. It buzzed and flashed red and the cube stayed put. Mark frowned at the cube. He frowned at the disc. He shook the proxy port, mashed the button, and then stuck it onto the corner of the nearest table. The triangles gripped, the disc beeped, and the whole thirty foot long table dissolved green and vanished.

"Whoops!" said Mark as everything that was on the table clattered down and spilled across the floor.

"Yup," said Lexe. "A table, exactly what Funk wanted. Nice."

"Pffffffff, tssshhh, huh, yeah!" said Mark. "Go well with his," he waved his hands about, "purple pants."

Lexe shook her head, going back to tracking her downloads, which stood at 89 percent.

Mark sighed. He frowned at the cube. It was so small. Such a small thing. Such a strange thing—turning and turning, jagged little edges glimmering, radiating. He felt thirsty. It could satiate that thirst. An

## CHAPTER 8

aura of cold power radiated from it. It could forgive his hunger. Was he hungry? Why was he ashamed to be so hungry? He felt guilty. The longer he looked, the more he wanted it. Wanting. Yes, guilty and wanting. Yes, he decided, he was quite hungry. He reached in.

"Sssss, ow!" he yelped as the cold cube burnt his fingers. He jerked back. It fell out of the case. The entire room plunged into darkness.

"What the frik, man!" said Lexe from somewhere in the pitch black. "I was at ninety-seven percent!"

"Sorry! Sorry!" Mark frantically shouted, diving after the faint glow of the cube. He grasped it in his right hand. It hurt. "Ow," he breathed. The cold bit. He tried throwing it away. Nothing fell out.

"No." The cube was half melted into the skin of his palm. "No — no." It kept melting into his hand. The jagged little edges were unfolding and unfolding. Small blue and purple squares in a digital pattern went creeping and sinking through his skin. He rotated his glowing hand. From fingers to just past his wrist, the skin had become a hazy network of digital squares. It felt cold. It felt powerful. He flexed his fingers. He didn't feel hungry anymore.

"What happened?" asked Heath as he and Lexe rushed through the dark to the glow coming from Mark's forearm.

"I don't—know," Mark replied, the blue and purple glow casting shadows across their faces.

Krrrrrrreeeeeeeeeeevvvvvvvvv. A piercing shriek ripped into the room.

"What the bleeding earlobes?" Mark yelled.

Lexe whipped out her Lemonsquare and shone a faint beam across the room.

From the darkness, nine long, lithe and bent droid bodies slunk in. Each had a flat, angular rusted metal face. The white plastic covering their slender arms and legs had hardened and broken over the years, exposing metal bones corroded and pitted with rust.

The one in the lead fixed on Mark with its five pin-sized eyes. Another starred at Lexe with only three eyes, the rest burnt out. The remaining droids could not be seen in the darkness, only their beady eyes pierced through.

"All right," Mark began in a whisper. "Try to— "

The five-eyed droid lunged at Mark. Lexe screamed as it knocked him to the floor. Heath grabbed its slimy plastic body, trying to pull it off Mark. All the other droids began rushing at them. Mark's crystalized hand hit the floor. Blue sparks scattered across the tiles. Where each spark landed, a deep crack formed. The fissures raced outwards. The entire floor underneath Mark, Lexe, and Heath, shattered.

They screamed as they fell to the floor below. The landing flattened their lungs. In a haze of rubble and dust they tried standing. Their coughs were drowned by the robotic shrieks of the five-eyed droid. A large concrete slab pinned its left arm. It screamed and slashed out at them with its right. A second droid lay crushed underneath a fallen beam. More shrieks came from above.

"There!" shouted Lexe, "Down that way!"

They scrambled up and over concrete chunks with Lexe leading the way. Behind them they heard the thuds of metal bodies landing. Mark's glowing forearm was the only light as they sped down the dark hallway. Racing, feet thumping, their lungs rasping, the distant light source grew.

"It's the big chamber with the engines!" said Lexe.

They burst out of the dark hallway, skidding to a stop against the steel railing. Their eyes hurt from all the daylight pouring in from the broken glass dome overhead.

"Down the stairs," said Heath, making to dash away.

## CHAPTER 8

"No!" said Lexe, grabbing his arm. "Look." She pointed to the entry floor below all the floating engines. Two more droids ran up the flight of stairs. Behind them, demented shrieks echoed closer.

"We're surrounded!" said Mark. He tore open the backpack. "Quick, slap a proxy port on my butt and hold my hand!"

Lexe glared at him. "They don't work like that."

"Then we're jumping on the engines to the other side," said Mark. And without waiting, he vaulted himself over the rail.

"That guy's coconut is rotten," Heath grumbled.

"Come on!" said Lexe, jumping over the railing next.

Heath was the last to land on an old rocket engine the size of three stacked barrels. It floated nearly seven stories above the ground, swaying under their weight.

"Four more to go," said Mark. "Next one's a bit higher, so aim up."

Heath looked back to the railing. But there was no going back. The three-eyed droid had crashed into the rail. It was going to leap right onto Heath if he didn't move.

The circular entry chamber was filled with frightened shouts and robotic screams. Mark, Lexe, and Heath jumped from one engine to another, keeping mere steps away from their hunters. Two droids, both eager for a kill, fought each other. They ended up falling, making sickening thuds on the floor far below.

The kids kept jumping. Some of the engines were high up, making the leaps frightening; other engines were low, making the landings painful; but they finally tumbled onto the other side of the seventh floor together.

"Down that hall!" said Mark, as he and Lexe helped Heath up.

They dashed toward a dimly lit hallway. Those piercing robotic shrieks followed, like psychotic digital voices gone mad. In the distance, bright sunshine illuminated the Seven Site just beyond the torn end of the factory. They were seven stories above where they had first climbed in.

"But it ends," said Lexe between running breaths. "Nothing but a seven story fall into acid."

"I know," Mark panted.

"Let's just hide," Heath suggested as they dashed past office after office.

"No," Mark replied. He wanted out of this place. His cold right hand was going numb.

"We'll be cornered," Heath protested while wincing and holding the stitch in his left side.

"No," said Mark, "we'll climb down."

The Seven Site filled their vision as they stopped at the end of the seventh floor. Far below, the acid lake swirled, a colorful cauldron brimming with caustic chemicals.

"Ready?" Mark asked.

They nodded. Climbing down was going to take skill and speed. The droids were almost upon them.

A deep crack shook the floor. Steel screeched. They yelled, falling onto the quickly tilting floor. Heath and Lexe, flat on their stomachs, grabbed onto bent steel rods. Mark, however, slid all the way down the tiled surface, hands flailing. Just before falling into the sky, he snagged a beam. Broken chunks of concrete and rubble joined the backpack as it sailed past, plummeting through the air before splashing into the shallow acid pool.

Mark tried thinking of a way out of this. The fractured floor didn't give him any time. With a final metallic screech, the remaining beams began splintering apart. Then the whole slab of concrete and steel they were hanging on, plunged.

Panic rushed through Mark's veins, dilating his pupils so that he could feel everything at once. He lost his grip. He went tumbling through the

## CHAPTER 8

air. An entire concrete slab was falling below him. Lexe was screaming. Heath's face was twisted in terror. Slivers of bent metal pricked their skin. Arms flailing, legs higher than their heads, they fell.

Down past the sixth floor; down past the fifth floor; then the fourth and third, falling fast in a rain of metal and debris. Mark could hear the plunks and plinks of the pieces falling ahead of him hitting the acid pool. Cold ice seized his right arm.

The cube had taken control.

Blue cords made of digitized squares began arcing out of his right hand. Some gripped onto the falling concrete slab; others fixed onto the nearby crane, most slammed into the first floor and solidified. Instantly, Mark's descent slowed. All those attached cords were holding him by the arm, slowing him down. Four feet from the acid pool, he stopped. For a moment, everything was dangling from an exploded web of digitized energy. The next instant all the blue tendrils shattered. The slab splashed onto the lake's edge and Mark fell on top, not far from Heath and Lexe.

"It's not over," said Heath, as they heard the angry screams of droids far above.

"Back to our boards," said Lexe, standing up and jumping onto the shore. Heath followed.

Mark grunted as he picked himself up. "I can't, I can't," he said. "This cube is freezing my hand."

"Behind a scrap pile then," she said. "Before they find us. Quick."

They ran down the crimson shore to a nearby rubbish heap. Crouching behind it, Lexe and Heath acted as lookouts while Mark tried to make his hand normal again. He tried peeling the blue squares off. Nothing. He clenched and unclenched his fist. Still nothing. Flipping his palm up, a glint of red caught his eye. Looking close, he saw a small red hexagon in the center of his palm. He knew he had to press it—but a whisper crept inside his mind. He didn't want to. But it burned. It was so cold. He pressed it. Warmth began returning.

"Whoa," said Heath and Lexe at the same time. They'd stopped being lookouts to see what was happening to Mark's arm.

Starting from the middle of his forearm, the little blue squares began folding in on each other. All the way down past his wrist and down from his fingers, like water draining, they folded. Soon, the small, jagged blue cube sat in the palm of his hand.

Mark sighed in relief, flexing his fingers—all warm and normal again.

"Can I try?" said Lexe, looking at the cube with a thirsty glimmer in her violet eyes.

Mark raised an eyebrow. He didn't quite want to give it up. But he also didn't want to keep it. Odd, these mixed thoughts. "No, those droids will find us any minute now."

She took it from his palm anyway.

"Hey!" said Mark, reaching out after it.

But it was too late. The cube began unfolding and sinking into and through Lexe's right hand. She winced, gritting her teeth as small digital squares crept up to just past her wrist. "Freaking cold."

Krrrrrrrreeeeevvvvvvv. That haunting robotic scream pierced the afternoon air.

Heath quickly peeked around the side. "They're back. And that five-eyed droid's leading again."

"I thought he was stuck," Mark hissed.

"He's missing his left arm. And he's looking for us."

"The boards," said Lexe, forgetting her hand in a moment of panic.

"No," said Mark, "the half-sunk ship."

"Why?" Lexe challenged him.

Heath's voice was frantic. "They're coming this way!"

## CHAPTER 8

The pile shook as the five-eyed droid leapt on top. It crouched, supported by its right hand. A small avalanche of broken rubble rolled down.

"RUN," Mark shouted

Behind them, the droid's screech sounded like an uncontrolled battle cry.

Running, zigzagging past piles of debris, dodging beams sticking up from the ground, their feet pounded the cracked pavement. Howls, frenzied howls pursued them; the demented digital screams of sentient machines leaping from one pile to the next, hunted them.

Lexe began coughing from the dust each step kicked up. Heath's feet kept slipping on the weeds that grew out from all the potholes. Mark's legs, not given any time to recover, were on fire. But he could see the upturned wing of the half-sunken space ship. It was so close. Then, his eyes caught site of something.

"Wait, wait, wait!" Mark shouted and skidded to a stop. His fascinated eyes were locked on to the front of a red landracer. It stuck out the middle of a rubble pile on their left.

Heath and Lexe stopped further on and whirled around. Four rusted droids were almost upon them, and two more were quickly catching up. The five eyed droid with the missing left arm led the way with the three-eyed droid lopping along beside it.

"Heath!" Lexe shouted, "grab Mark and go!"

"No, wait!" Mark yelled, he glanced down the road. The six droids were a minute away. He formed a new plan. He began a frantic scramble up the rubble pile.

He wasn't half way there when Heath bellowed, "Maaarrrk! Get back down NOW."

Mark followed Heath and Lexe's terrified gaze down the road. The five-eyed leader had understood they were up to something. Its machine-like scream sounded guttural. On command, the three-eyed droid began a fast assault. Charging on all fours, it looked like a large, deformed dog. It would rip through Lexe, and then Heath, in seconds.

Mark would need to do this fast. He tried jumping the last few feet to the red landracer. Instead, he failed. Slipping and falling, sharp things slashed into his jeans, cutting into his knees. He stumbled for a foothold, rasping and wincing from the burning pain. That droid was almost upon his friends. Eyes blurring, he looked at the scene below.

Lexe and Heath had started running, but the three-eyed droid kept charging hard.

"Lexe!" Mark screamed as it pounced at her.

She turned her head. Her violet eyes went wide in horror. Instinctively, she raised her right hand against the coming assault. Five seconds away from contact and the little blue squares covering her forearm began to float inches above her skin. Four seconds away and a vicious dark purple field snapped into existence around her hand. Three seconds and the dark force began streaming from her open palm in a raging torrent. Two seconds and the burning torrent made contact with the three-eyed droids rusted chest. It then stabbed clean through. One second away and a lifeless metal skeleton plowed into the dirt, crashing at her feet. Three dead eyes stared at her shoes. The stench of melted plastic made her gag.

"Lexeeeeeee!" Heath hollered, pumping his fists in the air.

But the tremendous show of force had drained something from her. She slumped down on one knee. Heath rushed over to help her up; she pointed down the road. The remaining five droids were charging faster with greater hunger.

Mark grappled his way back up to the landracer. Stabilizing himself, he popped open another proxy port, pressed the button, and slammed it onto the sleek red metal. "Come on, come on," he muttered as it blinked. A look back showed Heath helping Lexe stumble away. The droids were

## CHAPTER 8

closing in. "Work already!" Mark shouted at the disc. The disc began to dissolve the landracer into a translucent green. Mark grunted as he jumped off the small ledge. Sliding down the pile, he heard the proxy port finish with the sound of something large vanishing. All the junk resting on top of the large red landracer fell.

Mark tumbled onto the ashen shore. An avalanche of rusted steel beams and heavy concrete slabs rumbled down behind him. He bolted up and dashed after Heath and Lexe.

They ran. Ground shaking, knees nearly giving in, and every breath ragged, they ran. Mark only looked back once. The heavy avalanche rolled onto all five hungry droids. It did its job, pushing two droids into the acid pool and covering the other three completely.

The exhausted adventurers stopped. Heath had his hands on his knees, taking rasping breaths; Lexe held her sides; and Mark began wheezing.

"That was rough," said Heath, spitting in the dirt.

"Nice idea, Mark," said Lexe, heavy breaths misting in the cold air.

"Thanks," he said, wiping his forehead. "You too. Going full Zeus— god of thunder— on that demented jackrabbit. Solid."

They stood by the crimson shallows for a minute, filling their lungs with winter air.

"I can't take the cold," Lexe said, pressing the small red hexagon on her glowing blue palm. The digital squares melted down her forearm, folding back into a jagged little cube.

"It burns, doesn't it?" said Mark, looking at the cube. He wanted it back. "Maybe I should hold onto it?"

She put it in her pocket.

Mark shook his head to clear the hunger. "Come on, let's get to that ship."

"What?" said Heath, breathing heavy. "Why?"

"Just come on."

They dragged themselves the few feet down the shore to the wreck. Its short, flat wing protruded out of a long white cabin lined with small rectangular windows. The tail was buried beneath the acid waters; the front stuck up at a shallow angle.

"The wing's close enough to jump onto," said Mark. "Let's go in." The ship shuddered as he made the leap onto the wing.

"But why?" Lexe pressed.

"I recognize it," said Mark, walking on the wing towards the cabin.

Lexe muttered something about stubborn cavemen, but they followed.

Mark squeezed through a broken window and led the way to the front of the spaceship. It smelled fairly new, like it hadn't been at the Seven Site for more than a few months. He opened the door to the cockpit, and then stumbled backwards with a "yeesh!"

A dead android, different from any he'd seen, sat staring at him. It didn't move. The light filtering in through the broken windshield revealed it to be the autopilot. Mark poked it. Nothing. Satisfied, he turned back to the cabin. "Over here!"

Heath and Lexe, having just squeezed in through the windows themselves, walked over.

Lexe stumbled back when she saw the autopilot.

"Yeah." Mark laughed. "Got me too!"

"So why aren't we running for our boards right now?" Heath asked as he walked in.

"This was the hawk that hit Eli Exor's ship," Mark replied.

"What?" said Lexe, turning to stare at Mark.

"This was the hawk-class ship I saw—the one I can still see—that crashed into the starliner Eli was on."

"You're sure?"

"Yes."

Lexe whistled and Heath combed through his sandy hair.

# CHAPTER 8

"We shouldn't be here," Heath said.

"Why's the ship here, you think?" said Lexe, stooping down to check out the autopilot.

"Maybe we'll find out," said Mark, turning to examine the ships controls.

"You dragged us here to look for clues?" said Heath from the door jamb he was leaning against. "While more of those things might be lurking out there?"

"Yes."

"Why? Why? What for?" said Heath, throwing his hands up out of frustration. "We are not going to solve some sort of diabolical mystery and nab the villain in the end. We are going to get ourselves killed in the end."

"Listen," said Mark, rummaging through a lower shelf, "we've found a major piece of evidence here. Who's to say we won't find out the name of the Syn'Crux daemon, huh? We might even come out looking like heroes. I could see myself being a hero."

Lexe, who had remained preoccupied with the androids wiring during this great debate, decided to weigh in. "How about we ask the autopilot?"

Heath and Mark calmed down out of curiosity. Lexe connected a couple wires. The leads sparked. They watched as the androids round head snapped up, both lens shaped eyes adjusting and clicking like camera shutters.

"Hello, world," it said in the voice of a pilot through a microphone.

"Hi," said Heath. "Can you tell us how you got here?"

"Searching," the small android replied. Then, "Self-destruct sequence activated. Reverting to basic start-up functions. Hello, world."

"Why?" said Mark.

"Self-termination required upon mission success."

All three exchanged bewildered looks.

"Your deathwish mission was a success?"

"Correct."

They all frowned at each other again, muttering, "But Eli Exor didn't die," and "nobody died."

Mark turned back to the pilot. "Your mission was to crash into Exor's starliner. You were supposed to kill him."

"Incorrect. Mission parameters specify zero casualties."

Lexe stood up and faced the pilot. "What do your mission parameters specify?"

"Searching," The pilot's internal memory whirred. "Nonfatal collision with starliner. Eli Exor fake deathwish attempt number three."

"Fake deathwish?" said Lexe out of shock. She looked between Mark and Heath, who mirrored her surprised confusion.

"Why a fake deathwish?" she pressed on.

"Retrieving," The pilot hummed again. "Error: 401. I am unauthorized to access."

She let out a frustrated sigh and combed her yellow bangs. "OK. Who issued your command? Who ordered this mission?"

"Retrieving," The android took longer this time. "Error: 403, forbidden."

They all were frustrated now. Heath leaned back against his doorjamb; Mark sat heavy on the control panel; and Lexe started pacing, arms folded in thought.

"Why would the deathwish attempts be fake?" Lexe muttered aloud.

"So Eli hasn't been in any danger at all?" said Mark. "This whole time he's been raging about the Syn'Crux trying to kill him—and he's been perfectly safe?"

Heath and Lexe looked at Mark, realizing the same thing.

"Huh," said Lexe, crinkling her nose in confusion. "Yeah."

## CHAPTER 8

"Doesn't make sense," said Heath with a frown. "Why would the Syn'Crux fake it if they're the ones who want the Obliv and key so much?"

"Seems to me," said Mark. "That all I've heard is Eli Exor raging about wanting the Obliv so much."

"Yeah," said Heath with a dismissive shrug. "But that's because the Syn'Crux are after it."

"Who said they're after it?" said Lexe, a serious idea brewing in her violet eyes.

Heath turned to her with a concerned tone. "What are you driving at?"

Lexe cleared her throat. "Exor said the Syn'Crux are after the Obliv. Exor demanded the Obliv be moved to his personal Dreadnaught battle cruiser. Exor is going on the news all the time about how we aren't safe, that we should trust him to take away the Obliv."

"Right," Heath responded. "And. . .?"

Lexe looked him square in the eye. "What if Commander Exor is faking these deathwish attempts? Faking them to convince everyone to give him the Obliv?

Heath vigorously shook his head. "There's no way Eli Exor would have faked his own deathwish like that. He'd have to be a Syn'Crux to put all those lives at risk."

Lexe's response came out low and serious. "And if he is?"

This shocked Heath, who sputtered and looked at Mark for support. Mark, not knowing enough to take sides, responded with an apologetic wince and shrug.

"No!" said Heath. "Eli Exor is our fleet commander. He's the hunter of Syn'Crux, the daemon killer! He can't be a Syn'Crux himself."

"What if he is?" Lexe pressed. "He's been demanding the Obliv. He already has the key. Maybe these fake deathwish attempts are his way of covering his tracks?"

"Covering his tracks?" Heath shouted. "No. No, Fleet Commander Eli Exor is going to use his key to get the Obliv so he can protect it."

"Protect it? Or use it?"

Mark, who had been listening and considering said, "That's an interesting thought."

"Yeah!" Lexe continued, getting excited by this revelation. "What if Exor is the Syn'Crux daemon? He's got the key to the Obliv already. All he needs is the Obliv itself. But he needs to look innocent until he gets it. So, . . ." she smacked her fist to solidify her case "he has his Syn'Crux make fake deathwish attempts against him!"

Heath didn't have a response and kept his brow furrowed in doubt. Mark kept considering these thoughts. Lexe's eyes darted between them.

THUMP.

The small ship trembled.

"What was that?" said Heath, rubbing the goose bumps on his arms.

THUMP. Another shudder rocked the ship. They looked up at the ceiling. Heavy metallic steps were slowly scraping across the roof.

THUMP. Krreeeeeeeeevvvv. A third heavy body landed, this time on the ships nosecone. Through the windshield they saw the five-eyed droid.

"It's that armless bastard!" Mark shouted.

The droid rushed at the windshield, shattering the remaining glass out of the frame. They bolted out of the control cabin as its arm slashed inside. Its metal fingers gripped the pilots head and began pulling. Lexe stopped. "No, damn it, we have to save him!"

"It's just a robot," said Heath, jumping on the seats to get by her.

"No, we have to!"

A rusted arm ripped through the ceiling above them.

"Heath, toss me a proxy," Lexe shouted.

## CHAPTER 8

Without stopping, Heath tore a palm-sized disc out of his pocket and chucked it at her.

The rusted arm disappeared, replaced by metallic hands ripping away the roof.

Lexe ducted underneath, rushing back toward the control cabin. Metal was being torn apart above them; below them the ship was swaying in the murky acid; all around were horrendous noises, burnt smells and digital screams.

Lexe tumbled into the cabin, flipped the proxy port, activated it, and stuck it on the autopilot. A green translucence began melting the pilot. It melted the rusted claws digging into the robots head. It melted what was attached to those claws too, which was a very demented—and very angry—five eyed droid. Both the autopilot and the droid teleported away to a quiet little storage bay at the Black Pearl Bazaar.

"Funk's in for a nasty surprise," said Mark with a chuckle as Lexe joined him. They ran to Heath.

The two remaining droids finished tearing open the hole in the roof. A dull thump shook the floor as the first droid jumped into the ship. A second thud followed, throwing Mark off balance into a nearby seat. Robotic screams came from the droids as the kids scrambled over arm rests and seat buckles to reach Heath, who was waiting by a broken window.

Heath dove through the window first. He tumbled onto the wing and helped his friends up after they leapt through. The spaceship tipped and sloshed in the acid as they ran down the metal wing.

Desperate sounds came from the remaining two droids as they began ripping through the rectangular window frames, not able to fit through.

Heath jumped to shore first, followed by Lexe and Mark. Their knees buckled as they each hit the ground. Heath tried picking himself up to get ready to run again; Lexe was trying but her coughs were doubling her over; Mark, also coughing, simply sat back to watch.

The small spaceship, rocked out of its settlement, began sinking. Screams, angry screams from the two broken droids pierced the cold afternoon air. Their manic attempts to escape grew frenzied. Swirls of boiling magentas and hissing crimsons ate into the white hull. Neon yellow chemicals poured into the windows. Tendrils of steam curled around the broken wing as it tipped into the artificial colors. The lake was devouring the ship whole, and as the acid poured into and around the rusted droids, their screams grew tormented.

The three friends sat together. They sat and watched the small ship as it gently slipped beneath rippling neon waves. They sat and listened to the rage of the droids as acid silenced their digital voices. They sat on the crimson shore and breathed the dusty air and felt the grit beneath their palms and existed.

Mark combed a sweaty hand through his hair. "Well, we almost died. . . ."

Lexe attempted a tired laugh. "Yeah."

Heath took a proxy port out of his pocket. He waved it in the air. "Last one . . . ?"

They all looked at each other. Exhausted and wanting nothing more than a quiet return home, they shook their heads. "Nah."

With triumphant grins and shared stories and favorite highlights—all in dog-tired conversation—they stood up, dusted their knees, and walked back to their boards.

# CHAPTER 9

# CHAPTER 9
## "YOU TRYIN' TO KILL ME?"

"Yes? Hhmm?" demanded the short, swarthy, silk-draped shopkeeper while putting out the last small fire in Teleport Bay 13. "Tryin' to kill ol' Funk, yes? No more Perfidious Funk, what he good for anyway?"

"We're sorry," said Lexe, "but we had to. That thing was going to kill the pilot!"

"It nearly kill me!"

"Why didn't you warn us," said Heath. "There were eighty of those bloodthirsty things trying to kill us."

"Baaahhh, then you won't go! You scared. Like little babies."

"But we nearly died."

"You not die!" he said with a dismissive wave. "They only hunt other androids. No humans."

"Then why were they chasing us?" Heath demanded, then turned to Mark. "Right?"

Mark eyes were locked on the entry door with a thoughtful expression. "Did you get a look at those two girls and that guy walking away across the street as we entered?"

This derailed Heath's train of thought. "Not really, no. Why?"

Mark sighed, unable to catch a fleeting memory. "No reason. I thought I saw one of the girls somewhere before. . . ."

"Anyway," said Heath and turned back to Funk. "Look at all this loot we brought back," he said, proudly surveying the piles of stuff in Teleport

## CHAPTER 9

Bay 13. "I bet we made a small fortune for ya here, huh, Funk?"

The purple and gold bejeweled shopkeeper stopped spraying extinguishing foam everywhere and gave Heath a blank stare. "All junk."

"Wait, what?" said Mark, suddenly alert.

"Not all of it," said a disbelieving Lexe as Heath worked hard not to faint.

"Not all," Perfidious said with a nod, "but much." He pointed to several objects. "That glowing box is failed experiment; that silver brick is toolbox; those tubes are leftover parts; and this," he kicked the glowing orb Heath had been so happy to find, "is forgotten janitor's vacuum."

Mark and Lexe burst out laughing.

"But," Heath stammered, unable to understand. "But—it looks so expensive!"

"What about the rest?" Mark pressed.

Perfidious paused to survey the remaining gadgets. "Maybe . . . maybe."

"All I need is enough to buy some flarejet parts."

"Certainly possible—before you proxy to me this big piece of junk," Perfidious pointed to the large red landracer. "This thing crush half of the good stuff! And the rest may be broke."

Something in Perfidious's overaggressive tone made Heath's ears perk up.

Mark heaved a sigh. "Just not my day, is it?"

"But that was an epic save," said Lexe. "The avalanche that landracer made—brilliant! What gave you the idea?"

Mark grinned. "That game you let me play on your Lemonsquare, Need for Nebular Speed. I won a tier 1 engine upgrade, remember? The scramjet?"

"So you weren't out to save us!" Lexe teased. "You just saw that landracer and wanted its engine for your flarejet!"

# "YOU TRYIN' TO KILL ME?"

"Well, I—erm—the opportunity," Mark stammered, turning red.

"Yeah, yeah, yeah," said Lexe, grinning.

Funk, making a show of sweeping all the 'junk', said, "Now landracer is yours. You take it out of here."

"We will," said Mark.

Heath, who had been scrutinizing the black market dealer, spoke up. "We'll also take all this junk, so don't worry."

"Oh, yes, mmm," Perfidious paused, "leave it here! I will clean, I will clean."

"No, no. We'll take it. We've caused you enough trouble. We'll clean up. Right guys?" Heath looked at his two friends, who returned only puzzled expressions since they were perfectly fine not doing extra work.

Perfidious fidgeted. "You kids need to study. Not clean messes."

"But we dumped this mess of junk here, so we'll clean it. I insist."

Mark and Lexe saw then that something was going down between Heath and Perfidious Funk. The business-minded boy and the black market dealer were staring at each other, eyes narrowed. It seemed they both knew something and were trying to see how much, exactly, the other guy knew. It was like watching a game of chess and poker mashed together.

"Fine," said Perfidious Funk, throwing away his broom, "I give you five percent wholesale for everything."

"No good," said Heath, his olive colored eyes bright with business.

"Ten percent wholesale. No more!"

It dawned on Mark. "So this stuff is worth something?!"

"I'll get twice that at Santo's," Heath continued, locked into a pokerlike stare with Perfidious. "Or maybe triple at the Sub-orbit Markets?" He laid down his poker cards. "Then there's always Lucy Creven's and her fence contacts on—"

## CHAPTER 9

"OK, OK," said Perfidious Funk, caving to Heath's better cards. He waggled a finger at Heath, "you smart boy, Mr. Dodger Robinson. I give you thirty-five percent."

"Tell you what," said Heath, clapping Mark on the back. "Mark here will give you a list of all the other parts he needs. You get the best rigging you can for him, right?"

"No engine," said Funk.

"No engine," said Heath. "Apparently that landracer has one we'll use."

Perfidious looked beaten. He thought for a moment and then consented with a nod. "OK, OK. I will look."

"Within the month, Funk," Heath pressed. "Within this month."

"OK, OK."

Heath beamed triumphantly at his friends. Mark felt so happy he hugged the guy. Lexe smiled and nodded. They all exchanged the fist bump of respect.

Perfidious interrupted them. "What about this dead autopilot bot? What you do with him?"

Leaning against the far corner wall was the now torn and leaking pilot they'd saved. Its neck had frayed wires and a green fluid dripping out. Those cameralike eyes remained blank.

"No getting information from it?" said Heath with a little bit of hope.

"No," said Funk.

"Can you hold it here for a bit, then?" Mark asked. "I don't want to give Lloyd a reason to be suspicious of me."

The swarthy shopkeeper considered it. "OK. But not for long!"

Heath looked around. "Where did that demented creep-droid go?"

"I put in trash-compactor," Funk replied and went for his broom.

That reminded Heath of his first question. "So if they only attack other androids— why did they chase us?"

"Was it the proxy ports?" Lexe added.

# "YOU TRYIN' TO KILL ME?"

"No, no," Funk replied with a firm head shake. "They make mistake. They think you have something very very powerful."

"Was it this?" Lexe said and pulled the little jagged cube from her pocket.

Perfidious Funk stared at the glinting blue edges. His dark brown eyes sharpened and narrowed. The rich crimson of his sleeve fell in ripples as his hand reached to touch the aggressive blue. Inches away, he recoiled.

"Where from this—this . . . ?" he said, finger trembling as he pointed.

"The Seven Site," said Mark.

Perfidious's eyes snapped onto Mark's. "Explain."

"A laboratory room at Shattered Sky Interspace. This was powering everything."

"No."

"Yes."

The four of them stood staring at the six sided cube on Lexe's outstretched palm. It cast a cold, clear blue light. Every crease of her fingers and all the ridges of her fingerprints stood in sharp definition.

"What is it?" she asked.

The unscrupulous, short little man who ran a black market corner store at the back end of the Port District took in a trembling breath. "Technology of the Syn'Crux."

A silence followed his words. Nothing changed, not the sound of the steady drip of green fluid from the autopilots torn face nor the acrid air with its mixture of burnt plastic and extinguisher foam. The bright florescent lights overhead didn't flicker or dim and the world wasn't any colder. But Mark felt colder. And for some reason, he wanted the cube even more.

"What does it do?" Mark asked, the hunger creeping back in.

## CHAPTER 9

Funk only frowned and shook his head. "No." He turned to Lexe. His gaze fixed onto her with honesty. "Destroy it. Burn it."

"But what does it do?" Mark pressed.

"It—it controls energy, electricity, power. Something like this."

"Controls . . . ?"

"Uses, controls. Something like this. It understands and it knows. It controls. Like nothing before—like nothing before. . . ." His dark brown eyes met each of theirs one at a time. "Destroy it. Burn it."

Mark knew the cube was just a thing, inanimate and lifeless, but he could've sworn it flashed with anger at Funk's words.

"Is it dangerous or something? Is it Illegal?"

"It is Syn'Crux," replied the trader of unlawful and criminal things. "It controls and it is without control. . . ."

"Is it rare and valuable then?" Heath asked.

"No one will buy. No one will touch," replied the dealer of illicit and stolen things. "This technology even few Syn'Crux possess. It is made from Crylite. It is refined from unnatural blood."

At these words, Lexe's palm began to tremble. Her violet eyes were frightened as they asked Mark and Heath for help. Mark found a small metal box on the floor and picked it up and brought it over. She tilted her hand. The cube tumbled down into the box and shot a bright blue spark when it hit the metal bottom.

"Syn'Crux technology?" asked Heath. "At the Seven Site?"

"The Syn'Crux—they are in such places. They are everywhere, working chaos."

The four of them now stared at the closed metal box in Mark's hand. There were no more questions; there were no more answers. Perfidious Funk started sweeping again. The small box in Mark's hand grew cold. He could see little frost crystals forming around the edges. His fingertips felt numb as they held the box.

"Come on guys," he said. "Let's get going."

Leaving the shopkeeper to aimlessly sweeping metal bits around with a stiff broom, they stepped out and onto a street slicked with cold rain. That neon triangle across the street buzzed and flickered and flashed, reflecting in all the slush puddles made of grit and winter.

"What are you going to do what that?" Lexe asked with a quick glance at the box in Mark's hand.

He held it up. Each raindrop that fell onto the box began to roll down the cold metal edges until, just before falling away, it froze. His green-blue eyes were steeped in a battle that made his hands want to toss the thing as far away as he could, and, at the same time, keep it close. The guilt and hunger and wanting were rising again. "I don't know."

Heath, not as affected by the cube, said, "Well, Funk did suggest burning it...."

"Mmmm, true," said Mark. The rain had soaked his dark brown hair into a darker shade and water dripped from loose strands. A drop fell from his hair into his eye. He awoke. "Ah, I'll figure it out later." He pocketed the box. "Let's get some grub!"

"How about a zippy?" said Heath.

"Zippies!" said Mark and Lexe.

They all agreed this was the best idea yet and promptly picked up their skyboards and kicked off to fly through the falling rain. Mark soon became distracted by thoughts of spicy Zippies warming his empty stomach. He thought the Port District must be happy for the rain, washing away the grime and the grit from the streets and from the air. Truth was, the Port District hated the rain, being perfectly content in its mud and its muck. So as the three friends zoomed away to Canapki's Deli to fill their starving bellies—chatting energetically all the while about their dangerous escapades—the Port District bid them good riddance.

## CHAPTER 9

Two weeks passed. One morning, Mark became so lost in daydreams of flarejets that he didn't really "wake-up" until lunch.

"Wake up!" said Lexe, punching him in the arm. "You just ordered a cinnamon bagel with flarejet flavored cream cheese and a tall glass of 'awesome-I-want-that-one.'"

"Oh!" said Mark and pressed cancel at least five times.

"Too late," said Heath as Mark's lunchbox buzzed.

"Oh my," said Mark as he peered inside. The lunchbox had made a normal bagel smeared with abnormally orange colored cream cheese and a big fat cup filled to the top with absolutely nothing at all. "That's—different."

Gus leaned in from out of nowhere. "I'll eat that for a quark."

"Where?" said Mark, looking around, "did you . . .?"

Lexe waved the curly red-haired kid away and asked Mark, "You look beat this week, still haven't recovered?"

"Huh?" said Mark, still looking around for an explanation to Gus's seemingly magical appearance. "No it's not that. It's my alarm clock. I tried hitting it with a shoe a few days ago. I missed. It woke me up last night with a charging rhinoceros at 2 A.M., a volcano at 4 A.M., and finally at 7:30 I woke up in a cold sweat to the heat and roar and burning smell of a five-alarm fire."

"Yeah?" Heath chuckled.

Mark stopped searching and heaved a sigh. "Just—where was the fire—you know?"

"Perhaps this'll cheer you up," said Heath. "Funk had the landracer delivered to Otto's hangar today."

Mark's eyes doubled in size. "How many flarejet parts along with?"

"None yet, it's only been two weeks."

"Right, right," Mark said, slipping back into his tired stupor.

"Hey," said Lexe. "Let's go there before class starts!"

# "YOU TRYIN' TO KILL ME?"

That idea woke Mark up a second time. They packed and left the crowded Mess Hall. The hallways were empty, save for a few miniature starfighters zipping around. They soon reached Hangar Bay 15. Inside, their half-augmented teacher bustled around, lifting large mechanical parts with his hydraulic right arm. The class had moved on from studying the general structure of a starfighter to examining components in detail.

"Hey, hotshot," he said as they drew closer. "Thanks for the landracer. It won't help your grades none, but I've always wanted a cherry red Neotsu Zero."

"Ah, ummm," stuttered Mark, "the scramjet inside it. I thought I could, we could—hhmmm." He stammered, unsure how to say he wanted to use the landracer for parts.

"It's right rusted apart," continued McMaluch as he led them to the red landracer sitting by the giant hangar bay door, "but there's nothing I love more than restoration projects!" He slapped the curved red metal fender when they arrived. "One of my favorite hobbies."

"Oh—oh, yeah," Mark nodded, at a loss for words.

Otto grinned down at him for a few moments. Then gave a hearty laugh and clapped Mark on the shoulder, hard. "I'm just wrenching your bolts. I figured you'd wanted to use it for your flarejet."

Mark heaved a sigh and laughed a little. "Man, had me thinking I wouldn't have an engine to use!"

Otto's large, good natured face faded into a reluctant grimace. "The thing is, lad," his gray eyes bore bad news, "the scramjet in that Zero is made for surface running in the atmosphere."

"What does that mean?" Mark asked.

"This is a turbine-based engine; it runs by combusting an air and fuel mixture. It's an air-breather. No air, no go. And up there, above Crescent City where the Wargame is fought—there is no air."

## CHAPTER 9

Mark's stomach began to hurt. "The Wargame is fought above Crescent City? What, in space?"

"Yes, of course. Cadets must know how to fight, to battle, in space. That's where all the action happens."

"And a scramjet—can't do that?"

"No lad, it can't," said Otto.

"I'm confused," said Mark. This information sat in his gut heavier than a rock.

"A scramjet works on land. A flarejet works in space."

"So—so you're saying I did all that for nothing?" Mark said, voice cracking like his spirit.

A silence settled down between the four of them. Mark stared at the large turbine engine sitting snug in the Neotsu's sleek red metal frame.

"Could it run on airless fuel?" Heath asked.

Otto frowned in thought. He scratched the black stubble on his chin. "Airless fuel eh?"

Heath looked between Otto and Mark. "Yeah, I'm taking flux fuels this semester. Mrs. Duboush keeps talking about reusing old air-breathing engines in space. She keeps making us study these new airless fuels. Claims they're the future."

Otto chuckled. "Ah Ethyl, she's a character after my own soul, she is. She'll make you something to dissolve engine grease and cure your gall stones in one swig," he concluded with laugh.

"Awesome! Let's go see her!" Mark turned and marched towards the door.

"Say hello to that wonderful woman from me, will ya?" said Otto.

They quickly made their way down a few halls with Heath leading the way.

"Here we are," said Heath as they stood in front of a door made of glass test tubes and beakers and Bunsen burners. The door dissipated as

# "YOU TRY!N' TO K!LL ME?"

they walked in, closing behind them as they went to stand against the back classroom wall.

"Wow," Mark whispered. The classroom was a large circle with crescent shaped desks around a square workstation. The curved walls were plastered with every conceivable warning label known to man. He saw yellow triangles cautioning not to mix strange chemicals; he saw red danger signs warning not to eat anything; he saw curved black symbols of biohazards, radioactivity, and nine different types of ways to die from explosions.

Each table had three students. They stood in front of beakers and curved glass tubes filled with liquids of swirling indigo and smooth vermillion.

"That's Mrs. Duboush," said Heath and waved to a woman with gray hair so frazzled, it look as if she had just stepped out of an explosion.

She stood behind the square workstation at the center of the classroom. Seeing them, she lifted a flask in acknowledgement. It was a small round fuel cell, red with another yellow triangle, this one warning of—unsurprisingly—more explosives.

"Listen up, people!" she said in a strong voice. "Wrap up your rocket fuel mixtures for the day. Remember to handle the glyceride carefully. Remember what happened to Jimmy," she cautioned with her sharp brown eyes. "I'll be by each table to make sure you've mixed the nitrous oxone thoroughly."

Mark watched the students, all a few years older, mixing their chemicals from behind rubber gloves and thick goggles. Professor Duboush, however, wasn't wearing any gear. In fact, as she made her rounds to each student's little lab, she checked their rocket fuel mixture by dipping her finger into the simmering liquid—and tasting it.

"No," she was saying to a tall kid in a white lab coat, "too much hydrazine." She moved on to another group and dipped and tasted and said, "no, too much tetroxide, much too much." A few more groups

## CHAPTER 9

failed her taste test until she stopped in front of a group of only two kids; one brown-haired boy wearing a lab coat burnt at the cuffs and a blonde girl with glasses whose white lab coat appeared well loved from chemical spills. Ethyl picked up their beaker and swirled the glowing vermillion mixture in the light. She took a sip right from the glass. She coughed. "Yes, good. Very good!" Another swig and another cough. "Good good, mmm very good," and she poured a fair amount into her red fuel cell shaped flask. "But remember," she cautioned, "what happened to Jimmy." Capping her bottle, she kept on "grading" the remaining groups' concoctions.

Mark leaned in to Heath. "What happened to Jimmy?"

Heath solemnly shook his head. "We don't talk about what happened to Jimmy."

Mark's right eyebrow crawled upwards.

Professor Duboush finished her rocket-fuel taste test with a sip of the last group's mixture and an approving cough. She looked over her students. "That's it, my little mad scientists, good work! Clean your labs before leaving. Today's homework: fifty pages in Various Volatile Combustibles and How to Mix Them. Tomorrow, be prepared to mix two of them to see what happens." She smiled. "I won't say which two and they will not be labeled, but do bring your blast shields."

The general commotion of student's packing up filled the chemical-laced air. Glass beakers plunked into drawers, lab coats ruffled off and into backpacks, excited chatter about the end of the school day floated around.

Mark crossed the bustling room to the frazzle-haired lady.

"Hi," he said with an extended hand. "My name's Mark, I'm Heath's friend." He thumbed at Heath, who was walking up along with Lexe. "Professor McMaluch sent us."

Ethyl's warm brown eyes chuckled along with her generous sized voice. "Did that half-rusted gorilla send you kids to fetch more oil for his tea drinking habits?"

Mark smiled at the thought of Otto pouring petroleum into his tea. "That is something he'd do, huh?"

She smiled warmly. "On a regular basis. Tells me it keeps his gears gyrating."

"Actually, professor," Heath piped up, "my friend, Mark, he wants to build a flarejet—"

"Do you?" Ethyl interrupted, turning an intrigued gaze at the messy-haired boy in question.

"Yes ma'am," Mark replied, standing a bit taller. "I'd like to compete in the Wargame this year. And I already have a frame and parts ready to build."

"I see, well, that's only three months away."

"Yes, and the only problem, Miss Professor," continued Mark, "is that I picked up a scramjet."

"Ah…"

"And Otto, I mean Professor McMaluch, said it won't run in space, up above Crescent City."

"That's correct, yes."

Heath jumped in. "I suggested using those new fuel mixtures you've proposed, professor. The airless ones."

"Mmmmmmm," she replied, brow knitted in thought. "Yes," she said and lifted the flask to her lips, then paused. "Yes." She took the swig. "What type of scramjet are we dealing with?"

Mark drew a blank, looking at Heath for help. But he didn't know either.

"A Yazda-5 sitting in a Neotsu Zero landracer," said Lexe without a pause.

## CHAPTER 9

They looked at her, surprised.

She shrugged. "It's in the game, guys."

Ethyl became lost in her chemistry-minded thoughts. Calculations were being made, discarded, and remade in her distant eyes. Every few moments she'd absently take another swig from her red fuel cell of a flask.

"No," she shook her head, slow and firm. "That engine couldn't handle it."

Mark's eager hopes began sinking into his stomach again. "It can't be done?"

"No. Scramjet fuel systems are built very different from flarejet engines."

Mark sighed. But he had promised himself he would find a way. Somehow, somehow he'd make it happen. So he kicked his hopes back up into his brain and squared his shoulders under the burden of his dreams. "That's all right. Do you know of any other way?"

Ethyl saw his spirit struggle up again, resolute. This impressed her. The corner of her lips twitched in a smile. "Not one to be stumbled so easy, huh?" She took a last swig and capped the bottle. "The problem is the fuel delivery lines." Her hands began an elaborate explanation. "A scramjet runs cold fuel from the tank all the way to the combustion chamber where it mixes with incoming air. That's where the heat happens." She paused to make sure they understood. "Now, the airless fuel in a flarejet runs hot right from the tank, backside of the sun kinda hot. It'd melt through the fuel lines and start turning your toaster into a noodle strainer."

"Whoa," said Mark.

"Yes, exactly," Ethyl nodded.

The four of them stood in her now empty classroom, each with their own frown of dismay. But then Lexe piped up. "What if we replaced the fuel lines?"

"Yes," said Ethyl. "I wondered the same. But the only material that could handle such heat would be industrial ion. So you see. . . ."

Mark didn't know what industrial ion was, but from everyone's reactions he guessed this wasn't a good sign. Heath stood back from the table with a heavy sigh. Lexe looked down at her shoes. But Mark sensed another challenge and asked, "Another Seven Site adventure?"

Heath met his curious eyes. "No. industrial ion is a highly regulated, rare, and expensive material." He paused and frowned in thought.

"We couldn't find it?" said Mark, trying to keep his hope afloat.

"Not a chance," said Lexe.

Heath shook his head in disbelief about what he was going to say. "Let me talk to a few people about this."

"You know a way?" asked Mark.

"I might, I might, but don't get your hopes up."

Professor Duboush raised her flask. "Cheers to that! Let me know when you find something."

The three young researchers crossed the room. Mark's hopes were kept buoyant by the creative ideas of his two friends; and his friends were kept eager and resolute by how hard Mark kept fighting to become a FlareRider.

But when the classroom door dissipated and they stepped into the empty hallway, there were five people waiting.

"Hello, Mark," said the blue-eyed, dark-haired, superman-faced wing leader of Alpha Squad.

Mark stopped and raised an eyebrow. "Hello, Lance."

The fading echo of students happy to go home was a distant sound as Heath and Lexe stood next to Mark. The hallway suddenly felt narrow and cramped. Lance continued to lean, arms folded, against the opposite wall. He was flanked by four older boys, though he was still the tallest.

## CHAPTER 9

Mark's heart raced. He felt like a kid in one of those movies who gets stuffed in a locker for saying what he was going to say next.

"I see you're taking your hamsters for a walk this lovely afternoon. They do look in need of exercise—vitamins too."

Lance laughed and then put a hindering hand on the rounded shoulder of the big guy to his left, who had squared up and stepped forward. "No need to be abrasive, kid. My compatriots and I were simply curious about your conversation with the good professor."

Mark's stomach clenched. These guys were out looking for hurt. "I didn't realize you ran the local sewing circle. Looking for more gossip to share over prune juice and high-fiber cookies?"

The tall thirteen-year-old laughed again, then stood and unfolded his arms. "Talk like a one man army, Earther. But look, I'm no bully. I'm the hero around here. Right?" he asked his squad mates, who nodded and snickered.

"What do you want?" said Mark.

Lance stepped forward. "I've heard some—pretty crazy rumors." He chuckled in disbelief. "You're trying to build a flarejet?"

"He is," Heath confirmed in a firm voice.

Lance's eyebrows rose in mock surprise. "Really? Wow, OK. Well, that's very admirable." His white teeth shone through a big smile not real enough to reach his eyes.

"Right?" said Lexe, reflecting Lance's fake smile. "Maybe you guys could help out, ya know? Stand behind the engine when we fire 'em up? See if they work?"

Lance chuckled while his squad mates scowled. "I think we'll pass on that, babe. But hey, quick question, where are you getting the parts?"

"From a reliable source," said Heath, standing tall.

"OK, OK, great. And each of these parts, these components, have been tested to meet our school's minimum safety standards?"

"YES, ONE TRYIN' TO KILL ME?"

"Yes, one hundred percent," Heath lied.

"Perfect!" Lance went on, flashing his sparkly white teeth. "One speed bump over. So whoever is building your junkjet — ermm, sorry, flarejet — is a licensed technician right? Able to prove you won't die or kill anyone else when you compete in the Wargame as a junkrider—oh, sorry again, my bad—FlareRider?"

Mark went along with this and showed his own teeth in a big fake smile. "Indeedy doo! Professor McMaluch is better than ten technicians!"

"Oh, I don't know about that. I thought he was just a subpar, half-shifted, tea sipping mechanic of rusted bits. But there you go. I must be wrong." Lance's eyes twinkled above his pearly whites. "In fact, I must be wrong about lots of things. Up until a few months ago, I thought Earthers were a primitive, backwards, hopeless bunch of savages. But here's one going to my school, stealing my flarejet so he can show off in front of all the girlies, and thinking he can run with the big boys. I applaud you, I really do, Mark from Earth," he said, clapping in mockery.

Mark made his face muscles keep a big grin. "Thanks, man!" he said with a thumbs up.

Lance playfully smacked Mark on the shoulder. "I tell you what, if you and whatever crapsack of a squad you're assigned to ever want to get schooled. Well then, I have the best squad around," he smiled and spread his arms to indicate the guys around him. "You nearly met Dinsdale here," he said and clapped the big guy on his left, "by way of his fat fists. Haha! Oh don't look so cross Dinzy! There is a time and place for everything." Lance comforted the greasy double-chinned kid with another clap on the shoulder. "Mr. Dinsdale Mueller is Alpha Squad's vaporizer. Nothing like a solid defensive in the form of a wall; a wall made out of bullets, am I right?" Lance laughed at his own joke. "And to his left is one Mr. Jet Chan, our vanguard; fastest gunner and the most efficient medic." Lance gave him a fist bump. Then, draping an arm around the shoulder of the

## CHAPTER 9

kid to his right, a blonde boy with an angelic face, he said, "And this is my right hand man, Mr. Cruise Galantine," Lance clapped the smirking boy on the chest. "He's our valiant. His offensive skills are so crushing—we've taken to calling him Fistbreaker." Lance finished with an offhanded wave to the last guy, a portly young boy with an eager face. "That's just Carl. He isn't in our squad, but his fetching skills are unmatched." The young boy beamed like a happy dog.

"That's totally rad!" said Mark. Then flipped his sarcastic smile into a solid stare. "But you mistake me for someone who gives two brown corn-crusted butt bricks." He stepped up into Lance's face. "I will build a flarejet. I will fly against you. I'll win so hard that you're supermanish face will look like a girl just kicked you in the nuts."

Heath and Lexe snickered. Lance and his squad mates scowled. A bare knuckled brawl was brewing. Yet while Lexe clenched her fists and flashed her violet eyes at the boys who were squaring up and stepping forward, Heath took Mark by the shoulder and said, "Come on man, save it for the Wargame."

Mark didn't budge, locked into a stare with Lance, whose smile had turned into a sneer. Mark didn't care that they outnumbered him in size and number. But Heath tugged at him until the determined thirteen-year-old relented and followed.

Lance broke into a laugh, joined by his squad. "That little Earther thinks he'll beat me! The wing leader of Alpha Squad! Laugh with me boys!" he said and joined his squad mates in a loud round of laughter that reverberated down the hall in tidal waves of prejudice.

Lexe and Heath had to grip Mark by the arms as they walked down the empty hallway to keep him from getting two black eyes and a broken ribcage. After a few quick turns, rows of lockers, and calming words to their hot-headed friend, they arrived at the skyboard racks outside the school.

# "YOU TRYIN' TO KILL ME?"

"There you are, rotten little weasel!" shouted a tall college boy next to the entry doors. "You were supposed to be standing out front!" the black-haired boy continued to shout as he barreled towards them. "I told you to stand out front!"

Lexe scowled. "Guys, I'd like to introduce my ogre of a step-brother, Ripley."

Ripley reminded Mark of the term poser—the college boy wore clothes with brand names emblazoned across every inch of shiny fabric. He swayed as he walked and his hair was slicked into the latest style, as advertised by grocery-counter magazines.

Mark sneered and growled, "Another guy who thinks he's the turd that floats on top."

Lexe tried to hold in her laugh, but snickered anyway.

"What're you laughin' for?" Ripley demanded, stopping in front of them. When he only got more snickering in response, he grabbed Lexe by the arm, not caring that she winced. "I told you to stand out front."

"I had school stuff to do!" she shouted back.

"I don't care," he said and pulled her away by the arm.

"Hey!" shouted Heath, "it wasn't her fault!"

"Piss off!" Ripley shouted back and kept pulling her towards his hovercar, a bright canary yellow two-seater. It looked like him, covered with a bunch of cheap tacky mods that he thought made it look "H-core," instead of what it really looked like: an attention starved toddler.

Heath and Mark could do nothing but stand and watch as Lexe's step-brother dragged her away. She did turn once and wave goodbye, trying to smile. They waved back with sympathetic smiles.

"What a jerk," said Heath.

"I'd put Legos in his shoes," Mark agreed.

"Put what?" Heath turned a raised eyebrow at Mark.

## CHAPTER 9

"Legos—small plastic bricks your imagination builds with? Never mind."

After the yellow poser-mobile zoomed away, they walked towards Heath's stored skyboard. They talked about life with brothers and sisters. Heath didn't have any, but said his parents were thinking of raising a bigger family once they lived somewhere nice. Mark talked about Nick, his older brother, who was best buds with his dad and worked side by side with him every day, sharing brews and barbequing ribs in the summer.

Heath asked what a barbeque was. Mark described the old metal barbeque his dad filled with coal and hickory bark; how dad would marinate steaks in a secret sauce made with a bunch of spices and chopped herbs mixed together; and then how his dad knew just the right temperature to grill the steaks and ribs so that they'd be slightly crunchy on the outside but juicy and full of wood-smoked flavor inside. Last year his dad had taught these things to Nick, while Mark watched from the kitchen window.

"All right, man," said Heath, breaking Mark's homesick daze, "I've got my board and my folks are waiting."

Mark hadn't realized Heath had hopped onto his skyboard already. He said Goodbye and waved as Heath flew down the slope and away across the elegant homes and shopping centers of the West Hills towards the gray concrete blocks in the distant Port District, which his family called home.

Mark let out a heavy sigh and sat down on the concrete steps that overlooked a shimmering neon metropolis.

The taste of sauce slathered ribs returned to him. He saw his dad cracking jokes over a plate of rib bones and his mom laughing and digging in too. Homesickness pinched him for the first time in months. He'd been so busy. Memories of home had been shoved away every day in this new world.

## "YOU TRYIN' TO KILL ME?"

Sitting there as two weeks of night fell across the sky, Mark's heart felt gripped with longing and confusion. He hadn't even started building his flarejet and already a tiredness had sunk into every muscle. Self-doubts, courtesy of the well-funded, multitalented wing leader of Alpha Squad, were beginning to burrow into his mind.

What had Lance been going on about? These safety standards and licensed specialists and all. What if he spent all this time and effort and hope on building a flarejet only to have it suck?

He wished he could throw all these thoughts away like skipping stones across a fast river.

"Eff all this!" he said to the long colors of the sunset sky. The vivid green and blue in his eyes intensified. "There are butts out there that need kicking!" He stood up and dusted his jeans. "And I know several posteriors in particular that need a strong boot up the backside—even if my own butt gets punted across the field."

# CHAPTER 10

# CHAPTER 10
## WHEN ALARM CLOCKS ATTACK

Two weeks of dark, a fortnight, did not fly by so quickly. In fact, Mark got to wondering if the sun would ever rise. Winter had begun in full force. The days without snow were bleak and gray, numbing his fingertips and his mind. But the days with snow were glorious. Seeing the snow-covered skyscrapers in the distance outside his small round window was breathtaking; watching all those hovercars streaming through blizzards in the darkness was mesmerizing. His mind reeled each time he realized Earth, his home planet, was nothing more than an anthill in a big city.

That mind-bending realization increased to a head-splitting level in Pan-Galactic history. Dr. Barrie had decided to demand three full essays written during the final exam; all because Tara Leevy had dared Gus to eat one of the professors shiny paper awards. The professor had a difficult time staying cheery while he glued the chewed up bits back together.

At least in jump point calculations his head wasn't splitting open from trying to understand just how large their galaxy was. Then again, it was splitting in other ways. Lieutenant Landeth finally allowed the use of calculators; but only because the equations got so complicated that a couple guys started to cry. Mark got to wondering why she didn't allow calculators from the start, since they'd use them for the rest of their lives. He was told something along the lines of "you need to learn the fundamentals first," and "solving problems by hand helps you appreciate math."

## CHAPTER 10

It was safe to say that his spirits had sunk somewhat. And the alarm clock, noticing Mark's melancholy mood, took full advantage of the fact.

"Your eyes match my hoodie!" Lexe exclaimed with a big grin. She wore a red and white zip up sweater with decals from one of her favorite games, Sky Scrolls, sewn onto it.

"Ayup," Mark nodded in a slow, sleep-deprived way as he moved soggy fries around his lunchbox.

Heath arrived and sat down at their table. "I'm jazzed to the nines! Guess what I just traded that pair of Outlaw headphones for?"

"What?" Lexe said, genuinely happy, owing to the fact she had spent the entire first half of lunch trying to beat a high-level boss, and won.

"A watch!" he replied, olive-eyes alight, as he held up a dark metal wristwatch that had an open face with glowing gears inside. "It's Lycra's Leviathan Edition. This rich kid's dad got it for him. Turns out, all he really wanted were some Outlaw headphones."

"It's beautiful," she said, admiring the fast moving gears inside before handing it back.

Heath showed it to Mark.

Mark nodded drowsily and said, "Yeah, looks sick."

Heath raised a disappointed eyebrow. "Whoa there, don't get too crazy excited all at once, guy."

"I'm sorry, Heath, it's just," he pounded the table with both clenched fists, "that alarm clock is the devil!" he was wide awake now, as were several nearby kids who hadn't been the slightest bit sleepy. "You know what it did this morning? Can you guess?"

Lexe shook her head, eyebrows slightly up. Heath put away his new watch.

"Four A.M.!" Mark spat out. "Four flippin A.M.! I wake up to the sounds of a back alley cat fight! Some yowling cats just spitting and hissing and pissing all over the place, right?" Mark was getting worked

# WHEN ALARM CLOCKS ATTACK

up and livid. "I throw my last shoe at the clock, k? And go back to sleep. Then, hour later, when I'm asleep again, I start dreaming up this great gym-sock powered invention in class; but in my dream, the container filled with ratty old socks flippin' explodes! I can smell it, man! I can smell it! And everyone who isn't gagging is laughing! I wake up in a cold sweat. Turns out the alarm clock had filled my entire room with the most putrid, rotten stank that ever creeped out Satan's toilet!"

"Seriously?" said Heath, trying hard not to snicker. Lexe, however, had moved her hand from covering up her giggles to holding her stomach from the pain of laughter.

"YES. And then you know what? I'm lying in bed, freezing because I had to open the window to vent all the noxious stank, and I start drifting off. I'm in that funky state between awake and asleep. You know, where you barely notice you're drooling on the pillow?"

Heath nodded, biting his tongue. Lexe put her head on the table, shoulders shaking.

"So I'm almost asleep and I hear the faint sound of babies laughing. No, no it's not funny dude. It's not. Because by that time I'm strung right out, k? I'm wired and loopy and seeing things and I swear—it's the creepiest thing I've ever heard. I mean—why are they laughing? Why are babies giggling at five thirty in the morning. WHY?"

Mark's blood-shot eyes were wide open, panic stricken, and darting between Heath and Lexe for answers. He didn't get any from Lexe, who had started hiccupping in between fits of laughter. Heath was also laughing pretty hard, but at least he placed a comforting hand on Mark's shoulder and said, "That's rough, bro."

Mark sighed heavy and let his woozy head crash onto the table. He slumped back into tiredness. The Mess Hall was loud and it hurt his ears.

"Hi! Are you Mark?" asked a girls voice.

## CHAPTER 10

Mark's bloodshot eyes peaked out above his folded arms. An auburn-eyed girl with very curly dark hair stood opposite the table. Next to her stood a boy whose small glasses didn't match his square face.

"My name's Zaza. This is Torvan. We heard you're building a flarejet. That true?"

Marknodded and mumbled, "Yeah."

"Awesome!" said Zaza and sat down along with Torvan across from him.

"We're also part of the Support Crew," said Torvan, probably just as eager as the curly haired girl, but keeping himself more composed and serious. "Need any help or anything?"

"Help?" said Mark, bewildered by their offer.

"Yeah," nodded Zaza. "I'm training to be a hydraulics technician and Torvan here is—"

"Going to be a master mechanic," he announced proudly.

"Why?" asked Mark, then realized he might have come off as rude. "Sorry, I mean, why help? This whole thing might be nothing more than a spectacular fart."

Zaza smiled. "Maybe, but it'd be pretty cool if it wasn't."

Torvan agreed. "Plus it'd rock if a kid from the Support Crew got a chance to take a swing at those snobs in the Cadet Core."

Mark was taken aback and sat in silence, his red eyes looking back and forth between these new people. "You're serious?"

Heath, who wasn't surprised at all, said, "'course they are! They're from the Crew, like us."

"And the Wargame's only two months away," Lexe added. "We'll need all the help we can get."

"Wait," said Mark and looked between Heath and Lexe now. "You guys want to help too?"

WHEN ALARM CLOCKS ATTACK

Lexe scoffed. "Insulting!"

"What'd you think?" asked Heath, just as insulted.

"Well," said Mark, not quite able to find a good reason. "There's no pay in this, and it's after school, and it's—it's—"

"It's fun!" said Zaza.

"And awesome," added Torvan.

"And let's face it," Lexe shrugged. "This isn't so easy a caveman could do it. And you are a caveman, Mark."

He scoffed, but chuckled too. Weeks had passed since he had smiled like this. It felt nice.

"All right," he said, sitting back up. "Meet us outside the school at the end of the day. We'll ride over to Otto's shop, check on the parts."

"Cool, thanks!" said Zaza and got up. Torvan smiled and shook Mark's hand. Then they walked back to their lunch table.

"That was awesome," said Mark, feeling a new found relief.

"Yeah," said Lexe, opening her lunchbox.

"We might just make it," said Mark.

"'Course we will," said Heath, taking out his lunchbox too.

Heath and Lexe started eating. Mark looked around the busy Mess Hall. The majority of these kids were Support Crew. A wave of something like hope washed over him, and he smiled.

■ ■ ■ ■ ■ ▬ ■ ■ ■ ■

After school that day, the five of them rode to Otto's Hovercar Repair. They were each wrapped up in thick sweaters underneath big coats. They didn't want to freeze from the cold air as they zipped along on their skyboards. Diving into flurries, they competed to see who could get the most snow on their face.

## CHAPTER 10

"So people from Earth chop a tree down, haul it into their living room, and hang colorful balls from its branches?" asked Torvan, completely fascinated by the notion of Christmas.

Mark laughed. "Ornaments, they decorate the tree in ornaments. But yes."

"And they hang big fake socks from walls for little tiny gifts?" asked Heath, who was flying close to Mark's other side.

"I'd want all those beautifully wrapped presents under the tree!" said Lexe, zipping around them.

"Everyone does," Mark chuckled.

"But I wouldn't want to ruin the pretty wrappings!" said Zaza as she chased Lexe.

"Why are they under a tree?" asked the boy whose glasses were frosted.

"Well—because—hhhmm, I'm not quite sure."

"Why a tree in the first place?" said Heath with a confused frown.

"You know what I want to know?" said Mark to both of them. "How have you guys never heard of Christmas? Won't the school be decorating for it during winter break?"

"The school doesn't decorate for anything," said Torvan, surprised by the notion.

"Well, that seems kinda lame," Mark commented.

"But think about," Heath rejoined. "Remember how many different cultures we've studied about? Each with their own traditions and holidays? If a school celebrated one, or even several, that would still be unfair for a whole lot of people with different traditions."

Mark frowned in thought. He felt that pressure inside his skull again that came from trying to picture how unfathomably gigantic the galaxy really was. "So many people!"

They flew on. Lexe challenged Torvan to a four block race where they had to zigzag between tall brick buildings. She won. Then Zaza challenged her. The girl with the curly hair won this time and made a few happy loops while Lexe blamed the cold air on giving her a coughing fit midway through. Heath politely declined all race invitations, saying his board could barely keep him in the air as it was. Mark tried out a few new tricks. One had him make a snowball out of only the snow you grabbed by speeding through flurry after flurry; Torvan called it the Face Freeze. Another was to have a snowball fight using only the snow you could grab from off window ledges as you flew by; this one was called The Scavenger.

Eventually, with cheeks stinging red from snowball fights and noses full of sniffles, they arrived at Otto's shop, grinning from ear to ear. Mark pounded on the metal garage door. Miranda threw it open and went back to work wiring a sleek sports hovercar. Mark grinned as he watched Torvan and Zaza's awed expressions as they walked through the shop. The place smelled of fresh coolant leaking out of newly opened hovercar engines. All the blowtorches were keeping the garage warm and toasty. Mark waved to Phil, who did his hand-into-tools trick with a big smile; Ratchet was busy hoisting another heavy truck engine and nearly dropped it when Topps—who waved at them rather energetically, paint sprayer in hand again—sprayed a fine mist of baby blue onto Ratchet's bald head.

Otto had seen them from his office. The stairs creaked as he walked down to meet them with open arms. "Well if it isn't little hotshot and company!" he said in a booming jolly voice that covered up Ratchet's angry shouts at Topps.

"Hi Otto," said Mark with a happy grin.

"We talked to Professor Duboush," said Lexe, eager to say everything.

"And brought some great news!" Mark concluded.

"And some new grease monkeys, I see," said Otto in a warm voice.

## CHAPTER 10

"Zaza Rayn," said the curly haired girl, introducing herself. "I can help with hydraulics."

"Torvan Thomas," said the boy in glasses, returning Otto's strong handshake. "Master mechanic in training."

"I know of no flarejet that ever flew without the expertise of such professions," said McMaluch with a stout nod. "Good to have you on board!" The gears in his right arm whirred as he clapped them each on the shoulder. "What news from our good lady in science?"

"Professor Duboush said she could mix up a fuel that'd run an air-breather in space!" said Mark.

"But the fuel would come superheated, so it'd burn straight through the fuel lines," said Lexe.

"So she said that if we can get some industrial ion, we could make fuel lines that could run superheated fuel," Mark concluded.

Otto, who had been nodding in approval during this outpouring of excited words, frowned at the last statement. "Industrial ion, eh?"

Heath piped up, "I know it isn't cheap, but I may be able to find some."

Otto's grizzled face made one of those bemused frowns where just the corners are turned up to match the raised, skeptical eyebrows. "That right?"

Heath nodded, firm in the belief he could.

Otto considered him, then rubbed both hands together and said, "Well all right then! I won't pry or ask questions that need no asking." He beckoned them to follow. "Here's the flarejet frame I told you of," he said as they trailed him to the back of the shop. "It's a late model u-frame. The control cab sits up and back from the engine. It's nothing fancy, but it's clean. Not a speck of rust. I had Phil and Ratchet drop the scramjet into it." He turned to Mark. "So, how you like it, hotshot?"

Eyes wide in wonder, the boy from Earth stood mesmerized. Had he ever, ever seen anything so beautiful? Forget Lance's sleek, dark, shadow of high-end technology; this incomplete, bare metal, raw machine smelling of oil and iron was a sight to inspire. He stammered, not knowing what to say.

Lexe did though. She went up and ran a hand over the scramjets bristling side. "It's incredible," she breathed.

Her motion was like momentum. Everyone went up to the mess of pipes, turbines, and circuit boards sitting exposed in a dull gray, swept back, U-shaped steel frame. They murmured their amazement in quiet whispers.

Mark, however, hadn't moved. He stood still. The potential, the possibilities, overwhelmed him. His dreams of soaring through nebulas and dodging meteors came rushing back. When Otto asked again, what Mark thought, all the kid could say was, "It looks like a lawnmower used to trim fluffy white clouds by angels in heaven."

Otto roared with laughter. "I've never heard a description quite like that!" His mechanical right arm landed heavy on Mark's shoulder. "Now come on, your black market salesman left a large delivery out back while I was away."

Mark pumped his fist and went to follow Otto.

Heath caught him by the arm and whispered, "Hold up, I have some news."

Mark, startled, looked at him. Heath held Lexe back too. Torvan and Zaza kept following Otto with eagerness.

"What?" said Mark. "I want to see what our loot bought us."

"That hawk ship we sunk at the Seven Site," said Heath. "It's been found."

"Really?" said Lexe.

"Yeah," Heath said with a nod, indicating that they should follow Zaza and Torvan, but at a distance and out of earshot. "Investigators pulled it out of the acid a couple days ago. It's more than half corroded, but they'll still be looking for evidence."

## CHAPTER 10

"How'd you find out?" Mark asked.

"My dad does deliveries for a friend of his who is a reporter for Nexus News, and, get this, the reporter guy was actually on that starliner when it got hit."

Lexe walked slower and whispered, "Do you think they'll figure out the deathwish was fake? That all of them have been fake?"

"They can't" said Mark. "We took the autopilot."

"Think they'll find us?" Lexe whispered, even though Otto and his two new mechanics enthusiasts were out of earshot and going out the back door. "Find out we took it? Should we give it back?"

"No," said Mark. "It's dead now anyway."

"Wouldn't matter if it wasn't," said Heath. He stopped by the back door, not going out to join Otto just yet. "The investigators found other evidence. They think Commander Exor is trying to cover something up."

The three of them stood at the back door, exchanging silent looks of worry.

Zaza flung open the metal door and pocked her head back in the shop. "Come on!"

They exchanged another silent look, then followed her out to a heap of parts stacked against the back wall.

"Whoa, that's a lot of stuff!" said Mark, leaving footsteps in the powdered snow.

"Good stuff too," said Otto, heavy breath misting in the cold air. "Not anything high-end, mind you, but it'll do you good."

"Wow," said Heath, who had stopped just after exiting the shop. He was looking out onto the large rectangular field behind the shop, "are those rows and rows of broken hovercars?"

McMaluch looked back at the snow covered hulls of stacked hovercars filling the field. He nodded and smiled. "My own scrapyard. Don't need to buy too many parts that way."

WHEN ALARM CLOCKS ATTACK

Mark didn't look, being preoccupied with all the parts. "So do I just bolt these things on the thing?"

Otto's metallic gray eyes were warm but serious. "This isn't a snap-on play set, kid." He pointed to a pair of black and yellow tubes, each the width of a barrel and twice as long. "That's a pair of IMP cannons. You'll use 'em for offensive. Each one fires a heated bolt of ionized mass. They'll need to be attached someplace where, when you fire 'em, you won't blast your own butt off. And attached strong, mind you." He strode over to the pile, his augmented arm whirring as he lifted a hexagon plate the size of his fist. "Now, there's a bunch of these in here. These are part of your shield system. You'll attach these with all your patience and all your skill, symmetrically, all over the flarejet. This is important, are you listening?"

Five heads bobbed in the affirmative.

"Good, because you have no armor."

Mark's eyebrows scrunched together, hard.

"Yeeesh," said Torvan. The others also wore grimaces.

"That's not good, is it?" said Mark, remembering the words live ammo and missiles tossed around earlier. "But you said that FlareRiders are out of the game when their flarejets' shields hit five percent. Why would I need armor anyway?"

"Sometimes shots get through," said Torvan

"And sometimes shields don't work right," added Lexe.

"That is why," Otto picked up the conversation. "You will spend the majority of your time—everyone's time—calibrating and recalibrating the shield envelope generator. If your SEG fails, you fail." He paused to ensure the weight of his words sunk in. "Fortunately, Mr. Perfidious Funk compensated for your lack of armor with a very strong SEG system. It's one of Orion Industries best against bullets, burners, and bombshells. It'll even bugger off a missile or two."

"Awesome!" Mark exclaimed, enthused again. "What else?"

## CHAPTER 10

"That's the basics," said McMaluch, trudging through the snow back to them. "We'll go back in and I'll give a rundown so you know what's what. It'll be a lot of electrical and computer work."

"I'll do that," said Lexe.

"The scramjet's hydraulics will need to be cleaned and tested and made fully functional."

"That's me!" said Zaza, rubbing her hands from the cold as well as the excitement of it all.

"And parts will need to be made custom to hold everything together."

"I'll do my best," said Torvan, following them into the shop.

"And you," McMaluch said to Heath, "do whatever it is you need to do. Get that industrial ion. Without it, this bird won't fly high enough to drop a duce."

"What'll I be doing, then?" asked Mark, feeling left out.

Otto stopped in front of the bare flarejet frame and placed both hands on Mark's shoulders, looking him square in the eyes. "You will build the thing. Nothing but grease, welding, and muscle-aching labor in your future, laddy. Every day after school for the next two months." The grizzled mechanic emphasized this by leaning down to Mark's eyelevel. "Believe me, boy, you won't have the time to take a whizz. Because that's what it takes—you hear? Or else you'll be nothing more than a laugh."

Mark responded with a stout nod. He would build until his fingers bled, and then build some more. Dreams aren't achieved by hopes and wishes made on dandelion fluff blowing in summer breezes, or by eyes shut tight as pennies fall down wells. No, dreams are waking up to ash and dust; dreams are fighting through sweat and blood and rust.

## WHEN ALARM CLOCKS ATTACK

# CHAPTER 11

# CHAPTER 11
## HOW TO BUILD A FLAREJET

Winter was in full flurry throughout the neon city. Mark awoke each morning with eager feet, ready for jamming into shoes, rushing down hallways, tapping under classroom desks, shuffling under the lunchroom table, running back into classrooms, and then jumping onto his skyboard so that he could zip over to Otto's shop and continue building his dream-maker. But before all that, he would always sit up in bed each morning and look out the frosted round window of his dorm room. Nothing he'd ever seen could compare to the sight of fat snowflakes enshrouding the distant sapphire skyscrapers in the city center, the ruby red office buildings in the valley, and the nearby homes, all aglow and blurred like emeralds scattered in a snow-covered field. He was thankful to be able to enjoy all this; thankful, especially, to Zaza, who had given him a fish bowl and then helped trap his alarm clock under it.

"Pass me that wrench?" asked Mark, flat on his back beneath a platform suspended in midair.

Lexe, who was sitting on the platform and using the wrench to bolt a control panel on, said, "get your own," and kept working.

"Here," said Torvan, who tossed over a wrench from the toolbox on the floor next to several scramjet parts he was repairing.

Mark thanked him and started installing the steel brackets that would hold the platform to the scramjet engine.

## CHAPTER 11

Work went on at a steady pace for some time. Everyone was wrapped up in their jobs. Lexe began installing navigation software onto the control panel she'd bolted on; the beeps and blips it made blended into the clicks of Mark's wrench and the pings of Torvan's hammer. From the main garage floor the grinding buzz saws and hissing blowtorches added an industrial flavor to the sounds echoing off the garage walls. It was like listening to music, Mark thought, and his right foot, sticking out from beneath the platform, began tapping a beat.

"Yaaaaaaahhhh!" came Zaza's happy battle cry from nearby as she dashed in from outside.

"Ouch!" Mark responded, having slammed his head on the bottom of the platform.

"Snowball fiiiight!" Zaza screamed, and began chucking globs of packed snow.

Lexe yelped and jumped off the platform to hide behind the half-built flarejet. Torvan laughed and joined Lexe in dashing round and round the scramjet engine trying to escape the curly-haired girl's armful of wintery ammo.

Mark, rubbing his head and wincing, rolled out from under the platform. "What's with all the crazy?" he shouted. His question was promptly answered by a slush ball in the face.

"That's what!" shouted a furiously happy Zaza, who ran outside to make more. Lexe and Torvan made a mad dash to join her. Mark stayed put, sitting on the floor and blowing the wet snow out of his nose, a dazed look on his face. He didn't have time to stand up and catch a breath before all three rushed in and made the back of his head look like a snowman. This time he rushed out with them, beginning the first of many snowball fights that winter.

HOW TO BUILD A FLAREJET

The month passed by with a backdrop of snow storms interrupted by clear cold blue skies, as the five Support Crew students of SPIFF built a flarejet. It was slow going and no easy task.

For weeks there were wires in tangled jumbles sticking out at the back of the cylindrical engine. Lexe worked on attaching them, one by one, to all the computers and systems inside the control capsule. This was a painstaking and time consuming process, which put her somewhat on edge; especially whenever Mark would absentmindedly trip into the organized mess. Moments like those would often end with everyone rushing over to help pull him out of the bramble bush of wires. Lexe would follow this up with a polite suggestion that he "stop frumping around and stick to making fires and grunting."

But these weeks were not all fun and games. Mark always arrived before everyone and left after everyone; most days there wasn't anyone there. Torvan came for an hour or two later in the evenings after piano practice, Zaza could only be there for an hour after school because her parents wouldn't let her stay out later, and Heath—who had to help his dad unload trucks most days and left in search of industrial ion the other days—was almost never there. Lexe helped out the most; she couldn't always be there, but she tried. Mark didn't know if that was because she was eager to help out or because she wanted to get away from her house, but he felt grateful either way.

Word had also started to spread through the school that a kid from the Support Crew was building a flarejet, and that he planned to compete in this year's Wargame. Mark, ever an optimist, had thought most of his fellow students in the Support Crew would be jazzed, just like Torvan and Zaza. A few students were, yes, but more than half didn't think he stood the smallest chance, and the rest didn't believe his flarejet would even fly.

## CHAPTER 11

Lance made sure to keep his Alpha Squad mates in check, not letting them insult Mark or laugh at too many jokes. The blue-eyed boy wanted his squad to remain respectable and heroic, going as far as defending Mark, telling kids to "quit picking on the guy," and to "quit doubting him and his intrepid efforts to bravely build what no man has built before: a fully functional flarejet out of scraps and garbage."

Fortunately, one day after school, when Lexe was concentrating on reprogramming the IMP cannon targeting system, and Torvan was focused on hammering the cannons back into place, and Zaza was busy reattaching the ammo holder, and Mark was coughing and wiping black soot off his face while being lectured by McMaluch not to test fire anything explosive inside, Heath ran in with some great news.

"I got it!" the sandy-haired boy said, pausing to catch his breath as he stood in front of everyone. "I got enough industrial ion to make all the fuel lines you'll need!"

Everyone stopped. All eyes turned to the long tube Heath had carried in. He set it down, grinned and said, "check it out," and removed the round lid.

"Give it here, lad," said Otto and picked up the tube.

They gathered round, hopeful and eager, as Otto tipped it over enough for several strands of translucent, dim-red material to slide out. Mark pulled out a handful of strands, each one long enough to reach his feet. It felt like holding a bunch of those mechanical pencil lead refill things, they were so thin. He separated one from the rest and it lost its dim red hue, appearing a ghostly pale in the light.

"Spiders Silk," said Otto, his gray stubble parting for a broad grin as he shared in their excitement. "I don't know how you got these, lad—and I won't ask," he chuckled, "but this deserves some celebration!" He tipped the long tube back up. "I popped by the Tempestuous Tealeaf the other day and bought an Indigo tea that bubbles like champagne." He tucked the tube under his mechanical arm and led the way to his office.

As they turned to follow him, Zaza and Torvan both gave Heath a high-five; Lexe gave him a fist bump and a "nice job," and Mark gave Heath a handshake that turned into a fist-grip that became a thumb-war.

"Hey," said Mark to Heath, lowering his voice as they followed Zaza and Torvan, who were both up ahead listening to Otto talk about his new tea. "Anything else on that hawk ship investigation?"

Heath shook his head. "No, but people are talking, reaching the same conclusion: Exor may be the daemon."

"Is it so surprising?" said Lexe, who had hung back to talk to them. "Exor is ruthless enough to be one. He killed every one of those slavers hiding in the Vol system a couple years back."

"Yeah, but those slavers were praying on colonization ships with tons of people."

"He killed their families too, Heath," said Lexe, staring at him. "Slavers sure, but their kids too?"

Heath just hung his head. "I know."

"Besides," said Mark, "you said Exor has Syn'Crux powers."

Heath looked up to defend his words. "That he stole."

Lexe stopped them at the bottom of the stairs and, turning to them, said, "Or did he?"

Heath just shook his head. "You know, if it's true, and Exor found out we spoke to that autopilot—we'd have a fleet commander after us."

Mark started to truly worry. "Yeah, having a daemon hunting us would not make for a happy ending."

"What do we do?" said Lexe, sharing his concern.

None of them had an answer.

"What can we do?" added Mark, voice a bit hopeless.

Another blank stare passed between them.

# CHAPTER 11

Then Heath shrugged it off. "Forget about it, guys. Exor isn't a Syn'Crux, and even if he was—there's nothing we could do." He turned to Mark and clapped him on the shoulder. "So, let's build this guy the most awesome flarejet that ever awesomed!"

Lexe smirked and said, "Yeah, let's get our favorite caveman up into space, flying like no caveman ever dreamed."

"Heh," said Mark. After a moment he let the worries drop too. He couldn't help but smile. "You guys are the best, you know that?"

And with that they left their worries at the bottom of the stairs and went up for tea.

A wondrous elixir, tea, whether served hot with a lemon drop or served sugared on ice with a peach slice, it must have been tea, tea that flowed through the fountain of life, Mark thought. And his very next thought was that he should write that down and send it to a tea company. He'd become filthy rich, instead of just filthy—as he was right now, head and arms inside the large exhaust of the scramjet's turbine. The old fuel lines spidered throughout the entire engine, making their replacement a grueling job.

Almost another month—twenty nine days to be exact—had passed since Heath brought the strands of industrial ion. Mark was feeling the burn. Exhaustion had set in. His eyes were always itchy, his fingers were always aching, and his stomach was always sour. He felt that, most times, a hot cup of tea at the end of the day was the only thing keeping him alive.

At days end, Otto would brew up a new hot tea and Mark would set up a couple lawn chairs just inside the open garage door. They would sit and drink hot tea from mugs made out of hollow engine pistons. The half-augmented man would point out snow covered hover cars driving on the nearby flyway, naming their make and model and how each compared to another, performance wise. Mark soon made a game of it: who could spot the most of a certain type first. Loser had to refill the tea cups. That winter, Mark made a lot of trips back to the dismantled engine block that Otto used as a tea kettle.

Then, almost two months after Mark had bolted on the first bracket to his flarejet, he welded the last fuel line connector. Earlier that Saturday afternoon Lexe had finished installing and checking the last set of flight software; she was now out front talking to Torvan, who had also finished with a final check of the fuel pump he'd made himself. Zaza and Heath were due back any minute, having gone to tell Professor Duboush that the flarejet was nearly done.

"That's it," said Mark to himself, moving the welding goggles from his eyes to his forehead. He took a few steps back to look at the now complete flarejet. Everybody was either outside or away. This moment of completion, of hard work, perseverance and dedication was his alone. "I did it."

He put down the welder and went up to the beastly machine. Laying a hand on top of the bare engine, so large he couldn't see over it, a feeling of exhausted triumph washed over his body. He stood, living hand on cold metal, for a few quiet, meditative, beautiful minutes.

"We'll make it," he whispered to the newly created flarejet. "We'll dodge hundreds of meteors and scream ourselves hoarse skimming Saturn's rings. We'll loop the loop around blazing comets during solar eclipses in space and—and—" he placed both hands on the machine of his dreams. "And we'll race that pompous, frump-faced, swag-turd of a golden boy—and we'll win."

Mark stood, head down, hands on metal, for a few more quiet moments, dreaming and dreaming.

"Who ordered the hot sauce?" said Professor Duboush from the garage doors. Heath and Zaza followed her in, each carrying a fuel cell

## CHAPTER 11

plastered with warning labels. "Nearly melted through the floor before I could cork it!"

Mark looked over with bright enthusiasm.

"Side note, I've run a few calculations. With this fuel in play, don't fly around in the air too much. Stay as long as you want in space, but fly up there and back quickly."

"Why, professor?" said Mark.

"Too long and too fast in the air and that scramjet will ignite. You'll go faster and faster and you won't be able to stop until the engine explodes."

"Ah," said Mark. He'd keep that in mind. Going out in a blaze of glory wasn't in the plan. "Well thanks for making it!"

"Don't thank me until you smell the exhaust fumes, kid," she said with a clap on his shoulder. "Now go pour the fuel in before it melts through those buckets your friends are hauling."

Mark took Zaza's fuel cell and went with Heath. They followed Zaza to the flarejet. She stood on tip-toe and unscrewed a metal cap. Heath set his fuel cell down and helped Mark tip up his. They both scrunched their noses and averted their faces as a blistering hot yellow liquid poured into the tank. After emptying the second cell, Zaza replaced the cap and they stood back with the others.

A brief moment of silence passed before Otto leaned over to Mark and said, "It's not going to start itself, lad."

"I know," Mark replied, "It's just . . ."

"Fire it up!" Lexe shouted, having come back in with Torvan. The others cheered.

Mark clambered up to the open control cabin. He swung onto the seat and the oval glass canopy slid over him. There was no sleek glass panel in front of him, like in Lance's Blacknova, just a cluster of switches and buttons around two big square gauges (for speed and direction); there wasn't even a fuel level indicator. He loved it.

# HOW TO BUILD A FLAREJET

"Fire it up! Fire it up! Fire it up!" chanted his friends while the teachers stood watching.

Mark's finger hovered over the start button for only a second before he jammed it. Without hesitation, the turbine began to rotate. The high-pitched whine of gears spinning filled his ears. A muffled rumble followed. It sent shudders through the engine, and through him. He tightened his grip. A second rumble. He felt the accelerating pace of his heart; it pounded harder and harder as adrenaline began filling his veins. Everyone was watching. He looked over and grinned. For some reason, McMaluch was frowning at him and making a twisting motion with his hand.

The young Earther didn't understand and looked back in confusion.

BANG.

A loud backfire shook the entire garage. Mark's pounding heart crashed against his ribs.

"No," Mark whispered, hope sinking as the engine made a last cough and the high whine of the turbine reversed.

The old mechanic strode over, not caring about the heat pouring from the flarejet. He looked up as Mark opened the glass canopy. "Crank the throttle, lad," he said, making that twisting motion again. "This beastie hasn't run for decades. Crank the thing. Pour that liquid hellfire into it!"

Mark nodded, brow knitted, palms sweating, and closed the canopy. McMaluch stepped back. Mark punched the button again. The turbine began spinning again. The high whine started filling the air again. A muffled rumble sent shudders through everything. And Mark began cranking that throttle hard.

His eyes brightened, watching the bright yellow fuel race through dim red fuel lines. The colors blended into a harsh, burnt orange. Everywhere he looked, aggressive orange lines ran around solid steel pipes, brackets, and welded parts. He was thankful, in that moment, that no armor was

## CHAPTER 11

covering his modified scramjet engine. The thing was beast. It was raw. It was real. It was, by sight and feel and sound—alive.

The pounding rumble became a steady roar. "It's alive! It's allliiiiiive!" he shouted, throttling the gas with his right hand. The engine responded with low throaty growls. Everyone broke into cheers and clapped—none of which he could hear.

"Good! That's good!" shouted Otto above the rumbling noise. When he saw Mark couldn't even hear him, he made a "shut-it-down" motion with his hand.

Mark flipped the kill switch. He waited a minute for the turbine to slow enough so that he could jump down without getting burnt by the exhaust.

"Congratulations, hotshot, you've got a working, running, flying machine," said Otto, offering a proud smile. "I'll inform Captain Zumski that he can expect a new trainee for SPIFF's Cadet Core."

"Yes!" is all Mark could say, still reeling.

"In fact, seeing as this year's Wargame is only a month away, and you'll need all the training you can get, I'll have your flarejet delivered to Sergeant Hammerstrom tomorrow."

Mark's smile vanished. The congratulatory pats from his friends went unnoticed. "Sergeant Hammerstrom? Why? Why him? What for?"

Otto had to chuckle at Mark's panicked response. "He runs the Cadet Core. You'll be in his class. No choice on that. He had all the other instructors fired a long time ago. Aaaahhh, don't look so deflated, if you can build a flarejet, you can survive that old ballistic missile."

Encouraging words those may have been, but they did nothing to alleviate the rock of doubt and accompanying stone of worry that sunk in Mark's gut. Professor Duboush directed them to stand in front of the flarejet for a picture; Mark smiled alongside a beaming Lexe and Heath, and next to a waving Zaza and Torvan with his arms crossed.

# HOW TO BUILD A FLAREJET

Then another picture of Otto with his mechanical right arm on Mark's shoulder. But the whole time, visions of the bellowing sergeant and Lance's smug face floated around his head. He was happy, he really was; having finally completed building the flarejet was something amazing—and that it worked, actually worked, was a ridiculous miracle—but what would happen tomorrow?

## CHAPTER 12

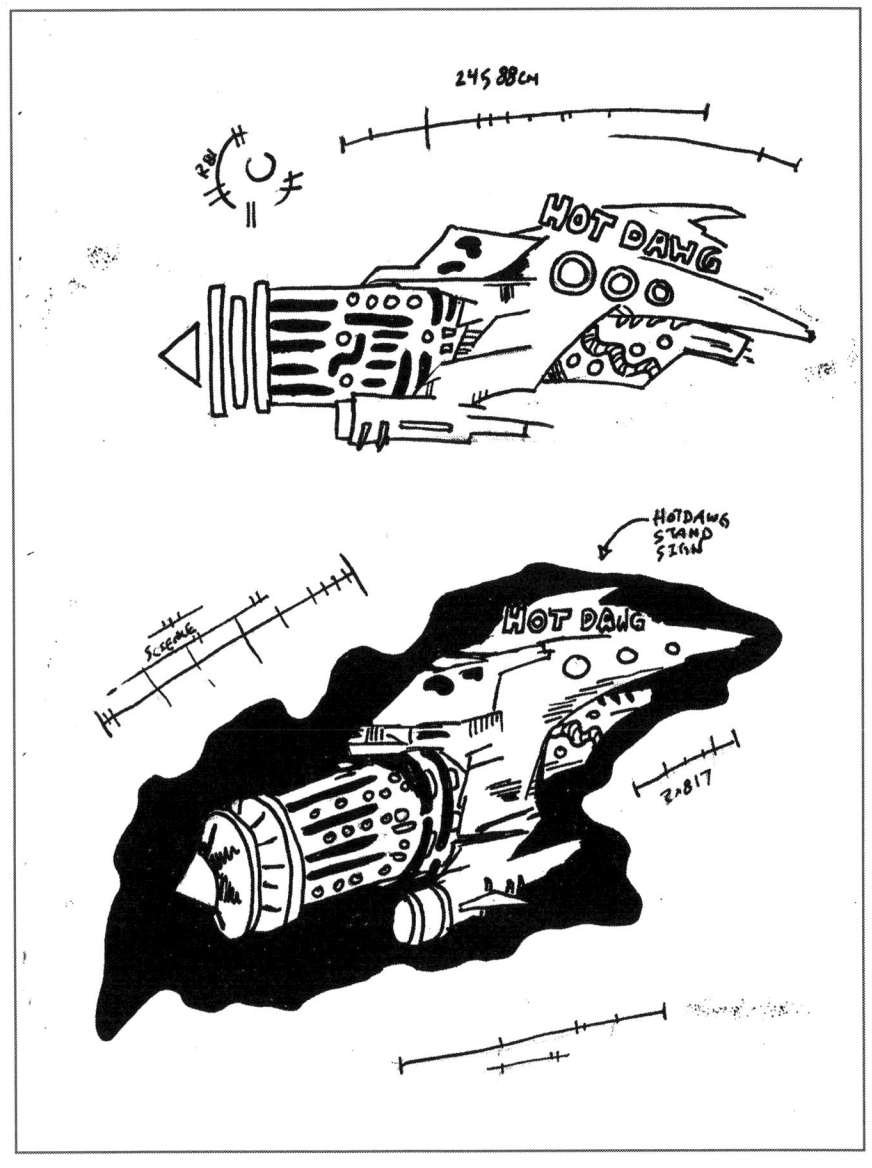

# CHAPTER 12
## JUNKRIDER

"Who let this rusted piece of glued together garbage in here?" shouted the sergeant.

"Yup," Mark muttered, having just entered Launch Hangar One to a scene of cadets encircling his flarejet. "I'm reliving my nightmare."

"You, Conley, is this your idea of a practical joke?" The sergeant continued to shout, this time at a young cadet who was trying very much not to wet his trousers.

Mark squared up and made strides. "That's my flarejet, sir."

"Yours?" shouted the bald-headed wolf in military uniform.

The other cadets parted for Mark, many snickering, as he went to stand in the face of the wolf.

"What is the meaning of it?" he growled. "Are you playing at a dumb joke or having a laugh? I'll see you expelled for both!"

"That's my flarejet. My name's Mark. I'll be the new cadet in your class."

"Insulting," said the wolf with a sneer. "I don't accept talentless, unskilled, wannabe's who'll endanger my students with heaps of welded junk."

Mark shrugged. "Tough. My flarejet is fully functional, I'm in your class, and this year—"

"I reject it," he interrupted. "I reject your flarejet and I reject you."

Mark stood his ground, looking up at the man's snarling face. "And this year," he continued, "I will be competing in the Wargame."

## CHAPTER 12

Sergeant Hammerstrom's scowl smoothed into a vapid smile. He stepped forward, towering over the young Earther. "And where do you get these delusional ideas, boy?"

The furious heat rising through Mark's veins began coloring his cheeks red. He tried to keep from kicking the man in the shin.

"From me," boomed an old, knotted, and familiar voice.

Captain Stanislaw Zumski strode towards the group.

"Sir," said the sergeant with a salute, "permission to speak freely."

The captain responded with an offhand wave. "Permission denied."

"But Captain, this—this—"

"I said permission denied!"

All chatter ceased. The only noise in the tension-filled room was the sergeant's grinding teeth. The captain surveyed the students present. His old brown eyes locked onto Hammerstrom. "This young man's flarejet qualifies. It meets minimum safety standards. You will respect that. You will also respect my decision to enroll Mark as a trainee into our Cadet Core."

Sergeant Hammerstrom looked the part of a furious and frustrated wolf cornered by an old grizzly bear. His upper lip curled in a disgruntled sneer and his dark eyes flashed. Everyone waited to see if the wolf would slink its tail or show its teeth. Straightening his dark-brown military jacket so that all the little medals jingled, he spoke his mind.

"Sir, I must object. This—this—junkjet, is a disgrace to my Cadet Core, to our school! This Earther is unqualified and unskilled and talentless. He brings nothing but a reckless stupidity to the Core I have built. Your decision, in my professional opinion in all my devoted years of disciplined service, is a meritless and biased one. I don't know how this Earther weaseled his way into your good graces, but it is shameful, sir."

The grizzled old bear stood, bemused and considering which paw to slap the wolf with.

"Thank you sergeant, for speaking your mind with such arrogant buffoonery," said Captain Zumski, stroking his short salt and pepper colored beard. "Your concerns have been dually noted, highlighted in triplicate, and promptly forgotten. Furthermore, I put it you, sir, that your words are a hot air balloon I want to shoot down with an oversized field cannon." He held a hand towards the door. "Now, march away with the swiftest of speeds. I want to hear all your little medals jingling louder than backwoods grasshoppers porking each other's brains out."

Hammerstrom stood, mouth working without sound and eyes bulging.

"That is an order, sergeant."

Every student in class stood silent and still. The air felt tense and heavy. And then the sergeant's rage exploded.

"This is outrageous! Absolutely outrageous!" fumed the balding wolf. "I'll speak to the admiral of this!" and he made good on that threat by marching away. "I'll have the qualifications inspectors reject that flarejet and that boy!"

The whole class watched him stomp off. Nobody knew what to do.

"Cadets! Attention!" said Captain Zumski.

Everyone lined up and stood to attention.

"Today's class will carry on as usual. Get into your squads and practice maneuvers. Mark will be joining Foxtrot Squad, as I have word they have an opening." He surveyed them once more. "Dismissed."

Most of the cadets began milling around and talking about what just happened when an assertive voice spoke up above the rest. "Captain Zumski, sir."

Zumski turned to consider the wing leader of Alpha Squad. "Yes, Lance?"

"I don't mean to be disrespectful, sir, but Mark's home built flarejet poses a risk to us and even himself. It is not a manufactured, certified,

## CHAPTER 12

approved machine. It could harm us or even him when it malfunctions. It is a clear and present danger to me and to our Cadet Core."

Stan wore a closed lip smile as he walked over to the blue-eyed boy and ruffled his perfectly combed dark hair. "Indeed it is young man, indeed it is."

Lance didn't know quite how to respond. He stood there with a dumbfounded blank stare. "Um, yes sir," is all he could think to say. Then he left with his squad mates, grumbling all together.

The captain stood for a minute surveying the hangar, which was full of various flarejets and their pilots. Then he turned to Mark.

"Listen," began the captain, indicating that they should walk while talking. "You pose a danger to the over-inflated egos of these Malopien mules. If any regular kid can build a flarejet and enter their exclusive club, well, their peach pearl pudding won't taste quite as exotic now, will it?"

Mark stopped walking when the captain did. He felt the old man's hand rest on his shoulder with certainty. But a frown of doubt weighed Mark down. He looked up as Stan continued.

"To them, you're different, and that's dangerous. You're in for a world of hate. Are you ready?"

Mark's brow scrunched. He never wanted to be the trail blazer, shouldering all the hurt and all the hate. But he would. "I will try to be, sir."

"There was a very wise, very old friend of mine who once said, 'do or do not, there is no try.'"

Mark smiled at the movie reference. He then frowned. What if that classic science fiction movie was actually based on real life? After all—just like he was starting to learn—the galaxy is big enough and certainly strange enough for it to be true.

"Now," Captain Stan continued, "I have my own slice of cheese to add to this motivational sandwich. And that is this: remember, success is not in the flarejet," he pointed at Mark's chest, "success is in the FlareRider."

Mark laughed. "That is pretty cheesy, sir."

"I know," the old captain said with his own smile, "but it works, eh?"

Mark nodded, feeling just a bit better.

"Good. Now go get square with Foxtrot. They are," he glanced around and then pointed to four cadets talking together on the right side of the hangar bay door, "right there."

"OK," Mark replied. "Thanks for everything."

Stan tapped his captain's cap and went on his way.

Mark inhaled and walked towards his new squad mates. He wondered what they were discussing. Probably how to get him kicked out, or maybe fun new insults.

"Hi guys," he said, trying to keep his voice nonchalant.

There were two guys and two girls in the squad. Each looked one to three years older than Mark. One of the guys—who was the oldest but not the tallest—spoke up.

"Hey it's our apple marmalade!" His offensive tone reflected in his sharp, dark brown eyes. "The buttercup to all our troubles."

Mark, quite tired of this, lashed out. "I've shoveled enough steaming stank today to—"

"Enough. The captain knows what he's doing," said an older girl with short brown hair. She stepped forward and offered Mark a hand. "The name's Samantha Stockton. I'm the wing leader of this squad."

"Hi," he replied, reluctant at first, but finding himself trusting her honest voice and firm handshake.

"We're not much to look at, but we do try."

The others murmured in agreement.

"Well," Mark shrugged, "I'm not much either, but I'll fight. I'll bleed with you guys."

Samantha gave a soft laugh. "We fight often and hard. But we try not to do too much bleeding."

# CHAPTER 12

The others chuckled quietly, agreeing there too.

"Come on," she made a short wave to her squad mates, "let's check out the miraculous heap of scrap metal this kid built."

Mark tagged along beside Samantha as they made their way over to his flarejet. His stomach felt full of butterflies on sugar highs.

"So," she continued as they walked, jutting a thumb at the other girl in the squad, "this is Keera Lenz. She's our defensive end, our vaporizer." The red-haired girl gave Mark a fist bump. "And she lives up to that title by never letting go of her triggers."

Keera smiled at Samantha's ribbing complement. She then pointed to the flarejet they were passing. It looked like a narrow seat surrounded by guns. "My baby. A Hurricane Cat. Six missile silo's rocking Kuan-8 warheads and—"

"Later, Keera, talk the rookie's ears off later," said Samantha, politely interrupting, and then looking back at Mark. "You've heard Derrick's opinion," she turned as they walked and indicated the older boy who looked like a high school sophomore. "He's our valiant. Don't be offended by his talk earlier. He's just as offensive inside the game as he is—well, all the time."

Samantha went on. "And last but never least, Marsel McMillan, our vanguard." She pointed to the chubby blonde boy. "He's supposed to be frontline with guns and medical—"

"But I don't like guns," said the big-eyed boy with an emphatic shake of his head.

"No," Derrick scoffed, "you prefer rushing in with a big bandage to cover up the hole from your lack of support fire."

Samantha pointed at Derrick. "He's saved your Talon-T2 and your impulsive butt from the trash compactor many a turn."

Derrick shrugged.

They soon stopped in front of Mark's flarejet.

"This is it guys!" said Mark, unable to keep pride from his voice or suppress the zealous smile beaming from his face.

His new squad mates didn't say anything right away, except for Derrick, who whistled in mock amazement.

"Yeah," said Mark. "I know it looks like some kinda brandura, but it kicks the fun buns."

"Brandura?" Samantha asked in a curious tone.

"Just something my granddad used to say," replied Mark with a short laugh. "It means 'piece of junk.'"

"You can say that again," replied Derrick, eager to start something.

"Hey," Samantha cautioned. "Cut it."

Derrick grinned and added two pumps of his eyebrows. Then he went back to walking around the flarejet, looking for more trouble.

"Whoa," said Keera, wide eyed at the strange engine. "What kinda cooker is that?"

"It's a scramjet," said Mark, all excited to see his new squad piling around for a look.

"I thought scramjets were air-breathers only," said Marsel, surprised by this revelation.

"They are," said Mark. "But this one's been modded to run on airless fuel. I just can't stay in the air too long."

"That right?" said Samantha, peering into the turbine. "Interesting. Hey, if it flies, it flies. The captain looked it over, and he knows what's good."

"It'll do more than fly!" said Marcel, hand on the scramjet as if it were a rare and beautiful thing. "Scramjet's like these were built for speed."

"One of my friends, Lexe, said it was a Yazda-5," said Mark.

"I know," said Marcel in an exceedingly nerdy way. "It stands for Yazda- zajebista acceleration to the fifth degree. You know, if it weren't for heat venting and all that air resistance, these types of engines would dominate everything."

## CHAPTER 12

"We'll have to test that out," said Samantha in a tone of suppressed enthusiasm. She still had to act like a leader, after all.

Derrick's voice cut in to their excited curiosity. "Why don't you have any dinnerware on this thing?"

"Any what?" Mark replied, confused.

"Armor plating," said Keera. "You've got not a single plate. One shot slips through and you're right bumbled."

"Yeah, I know. I couldn't get any in time. But I've got an Orion Industries SEG."

She nodded in approval. "Not half nitty. That'll eat a lot o' hurt."

"Look at this!" said Derrick from the side of the flarejet. "He's got Yellow-Jacket IMP cannons! What are you, a pirate?"

Marsel, who was standing by Mark, spoke up in his defense. "Ionized mass projectile cannons have the best damage-to-weight ratios."

"Only if you rail them right," said Keera, then shrugged. "But cans are cans. They pack it."

Mark's new squad mates kept walking round and inspecting. Finally Samantha came up to him with an approving smile.

"Lookin' good, rookie. Everything's in place and solid." She paused, and then nodded to affirm that idea. "Right then, let's get you briefed on our Wargame strategy and then up above for some maneuvers."

They took the brief walk back to Foxtrot Squad's flarejets. Samantha had them stand in a circle around an empty spot on the concrete floor. She took out her Lemonsquare, flicked through a few apps, and then tossed it towards the floor. It landed an inch above the concrete, hovering in place. A holographic projection streamed up from it. The projection filled the emptiness within their circle. It was like they were looking down onto the neon city from way up in space. The city was the size of a disc; the rest of the space above the city was dark and filled with tiny points of light to mimic stars. The group looked into the void.

"This year's Wargame is simple," Samantha began. "Two squads fight it out. One squad will be the 'guards' and the other will be the 'raiders.' "

Derrick heaved a sigh and shoved his hands in his pockets. "It's an Arcturian Blitz, isn't it?"

"Yes," Samantha nodded. "A merchant ship will be passing through," as she said this a small holographic model of a merchant ship floated into the dark. "The guards will accompany the merchant, protecting it from an attack." A squad of holographic flarejets cruised into view behind the merchant.

"Are we the guards?" asked Keera, hoping to unleash her vaporizer fury in full defensive force.

"No," Samantha replied. "We will be the raiders. Anyway, the win condition for the guards is protecting the merchant through the area; and the win condition for us is stealing the cargo and getting it eight clicks away. Standard rules apply: automatic win if one squad obliterates the other, points based on number of hits, triple bonus for disabling an opponent's flarejet, and a tie if the merchant ship gets destroyed."

Mark piped up, wanting to show he was paying attention. "So we'll be waiting up above Crescent City for the merchant ship to cruise in, then we blow through the guards, jack the cargo, and book it for the win?"

"No," said Samantha. "We're going up against Alpha Squad. We need to get in as many shots as we can before they take us out."

"What, why?" said Mark.

"No, we'd get creamed. They have too much firepower, too much defense, too much—everything!"

"But—"

"No. We're done. It'll be over quick. We get as many points as possible with as minimal damage as possible and then forfeit the game. Everybody got it?"

## CHAPTER 12

They all nodded, everyone except Mark, who asked, "How can I help, then?"

The hologram disappeared as Samantha picked up her Lemonsquare. "I have no idea what you can and can't do, rookie. So get into that flarejet you've built and get into space. We're going on maneuvers."

Minutes later and Mark, hollering in pure joy, followed his new squad mates as they rocketed out of the hangar bay doors and up into cold gray skies. Once more, he was soaring through the clouds, but this time he felt so much more. His flarejet didn't have the luxurious quiet of Lance's Blacknova. Instead, Mark bounced around on his seat as turbulent winds tossed his flarejet around; he gulped as the rapidly changing air pressure plugged up his ears. He couldn't stop smiling. This was infinitely better than the cold, plastic silence of Lance's flarejet. Breathing in deep, the smell of heated engine grease made his nose twitch. Little lights on the brushed steel control panel blinked and clicked; fat round gauges rattled in their holders and the little gauge needles jiggled as he flew higher and higher. The dark void of space was fast approaching. He squared his shoulders in anticipation.

The GSS Final Frontier became a spec among tiny buildings as the city fell away below them. In a moment, all the noise ceased. No rattling, no rushing, nothing but the steady clicking of little indicator lights. He had flown into the void. Nothing remained but the feel of the engine working and the sight of burnt orange fuel coursing through glowing veins of industrial ion.

"All right, rookie," came Samantha's voice of the intercom. "Let's see what you got."

He looked around to see his squad mates sitting in their flarejets. They had maneuvered to each side of him, waiting for something exciting or new from this kid with a self-built ship.

Mark's smile slipped into a serious frown. He pumped the throttle. Those fuel lines intensified as superheated liquid rushed into the scramjet's turbine. The turbine responded by shuddering in anticipation.

"Let's see those taillights!" shouted Keera. "Burn the fusebox!"

Mark did. And his "brandura" accelerated into the stars so hard, leaving a blaze of orange light so intense, that even Derrick said, "Whoa."

■ ■ ■ ■ ■ ■ ■ ■ ■ ■ ■

Mark trained for the next twenty-one days. He trained hard. A normal day consisted of waking up early for dodge and roll training with Samantha, followed by eating lunch with Marsel while sitting in his flarejet and learning all the controls, then after school being chased by Derrick in an attempt to learn escape tactics and how not to punch Derrick's insulting mouth, and finally having some measure of fun with Keera as she taught him to aim properly, stack his cannon fire, and blast holographic targets into itty bitty pieces. At the end of each day, Mark would stumble into his dorm room, flop on his bed, and start drooling on unfinished homework.

"There he is!" came Heath's hearty shout over the Mess Hall din as Mark walked over to their usual lunch table. "It's been a month since we saw you!"

"Uhhhh." Mark heaved a sigh and plopped down by Heath, who had made a space between him and Torvan. "I've been flying, man. Flying like a boy wizard who just got his first Nimbus 2k."

"Nimb-what?" asked Torvan.

"Just another Earther reference," said Mark with a tired smile.

"Hey," said Zaza from across the table. "Is it true the sergeant caught you using your flarejet's afterburners to roast hundreds of marshmallows?"

Mark returned her question by raising a confused eyebrow.

## CHAPTER 12

"We've been hearing some crazy rumors about your training," said Heath with a suppressed grin.

"No," said Mark to Zaza with a chuckle. "But I did forget to unhook an extension cord from my shield batteries last week. When I flew out the hangar, the cord ripped out of the wall, dragged a dozen toolboxes attached to it across the floor, and sailed into space behind me like a long, flapping scrap of toilet paper hanging off my flarejet's bum."

Everyone at the table laughed.

Torvan posed the next question. "What about you bulldozing into professor Nauka's class in the middle of the three-hour final exam?"

Mark sighed and nodded. "Ayup. I forgot I was in reverse."

A fresh round of laughs went up.

Mark felt his cheeks coloring. Eager to change the subject, he said, "I can't believe winter's almost over. I didn't even get to enjoy it."

"Don't worry," said Lexe, "we made a bunch of snowmen in your honor. In fact, I made one you'd really appreciate."

"Yeah," giggled Zaza from across the table. "It had a big forehead and big black eyebrows like bushy caterpillars!"

Lexe put on an air of philosophy. "It symbolized your cavemanlike brain."

Mark snorted, but then when Lexe showed him pictures on her Lemonsquare, he had to laugh.

Heath leaned in and prodded Mark with an elbow. "Did you see the news?"

Mark looked up at the large screen on the wall. It was looping the news. He couldn't hear anything but the subtitles read: Search ongoing for missing Director Ernest Shaw. A video appeared of a Director Shaw, showing a jolly man in his late fifties, dressed in bulging clothes and wearing a warm smile. Last seen at the Atlas Convention with Eli Exor. A video followed of Eli Exor, who appeared tall and sharp with deep eye sockets and a long, gaunt face. The Atlas Convention was called to discuss relocation plans for the Obliv. Various officials of the Alternate Weapons Agency were present along with—

"How did the Director disappear?" said Mark. "Was it the Syn'Crux?"

The table went quiet. Even Zaza, who was normally full of life, sat picking at her food.

Heath responded, grimacing and pausing between strings of words. "A day after he went missing—they found—carefully placed on his seat with a Syn'Crux symbol carved into it—a severed human tongue."

Mark grimaced. "Why would the Syn'Crux do that?"

Zaza, moving her distraught eyes to Mark, said, "It's a sign. It means they got him to talk—and he told them all they needed to know."

"So the Syn'Crux got the Obliv location from him? Did they steal the Obliv then?"

"Apparently not," said Torvan. "In the event of the Director's death, the location is passed on to the overseer of Shattered Sky Interspace. The overseer—Nona Kine—raised suspicions about Exor's constant hounding for the Obliv. She refuses to give the location until the investigation is over." Torvan shook his head in anger. "So Exor went ballistic and is demanding the Obliv before the Syn'Crux steal it."

"He is, is he?" said Mark, a gleam of knowing in his eyes. "Almost as if he's growing more desperate while trying even harder to seem innocent—wouldn't you say?"

Lexe locked his gaze and shook her head slowly, indicating this was not the time or place for their theory. Heath apparently agreed, because he cleared his throat rather loudly.

"It's supposed to hail tomorrow," said the sandy haired boy, quickly changing the subject. "So try to get above the weather quick. Hailstorms make a mess of any kind of shield system."

## CHAPTER 12

"That's right!" said Zaza, perking back up. "The Wargame's tomorrow! You'll be flying and we'll be watching!"

Mark looked at Lexe and Heath before finally relenting about the Eli-Exor-is-a-daemon theory. He turned to Zaza and tried a smile. "Yup, yup! Foxtrot squad up high trying to steal away a merchant's loot and treasures!"

"You know who you'll be up against?" Torvan inquired.

Mark winced. "The Alphas."

"Oh . . ." said Torvan.

"So no stealing loot and treasures?" said Heath.

Mark shook his head. "No, our wing leader wants us to get a bunch of points and then forfeit."

"What position does she have you playing?" asked Zaza.

"She said I'd be their rogue."

"What's that?" asked Zaza.

"Like a scoundrel ninja, with guns!" Mark replied with comical affect.

Zaza stared at him, clearly not getting it.

"It's mostly a support role. I dive in for a few quick pot shots and then speed back out."

"Why a support role?" asked Heath, himself intrigued.

"Samantha said I don't have the aim yet for any major offensives or the defensive skills to last through a long dogfight. But I do have a good engine. Turns out the acceleration is a kick in the pants," he said and laughed.

Soon Mark's time and thoughts were preoccupied with answering the questions his friends were asking. A few more students from the Support Crew sat down to talk about his custom built flarejet. A few kids even stopped by just to say hi and wish Mark the best of luck tomorrow.

That night was a restless one, and the sleep he did catch was filled with disturbing dreams. There was one where he flew into a million pieces of jagged hail, only to have his glass capsule crack and let out all the air; he woke up gasping for breath, face buried in the pillow.

There was another one where deformed Syn'Crux shadows and dozens of those rusted Seven Site droids chased him in the middle of a jungle until he fell into a mess of tree vines, unable to move as the Syn'Crux came for his tongue; he woke up jumbled in his blankets and trying to yell.

But the weirdest of all was a horrible dream where he fought in the Wargame until his flarejet exploded with the sound of a small fishbowl breaking. The flaming glass pieces then became Seven Site droids that swam through space making dolphin sounds. And when he tried lashing out at them, arms all sluggish as if he were punching underwater, they became tall, faceless Syn'Crux that crept up close to his face and breathed out the most fowl breath smelling of rotten eggs. He woke up from that, reached under his pillow, grabbed a shoe, and chased his newly-freed alarm clock round and round and round the room.

## CHAPTER 13

# CHAPTER 13
## WARGAME

The next day arrived—unstoppable and without mercy for his lack of sleep. School was canceled all day so everyone could watch the Wargame. And so, as he walked to Launch Bay Three (which had been converted into a stadium) through crowded hallways filled with excited shouts and tumultuous chatter, his head felt like a split melon.

But when the crowd pushed and shoved and moved him through the stadium doors, every headache and grumpy feeling fled in an instant. The sheer size of the cavernous Launch Bay Three was overwhelming. Mark felt as if he had walked onto a large covered football stadium.

He stood agape as the crowd tumbled all around him. This was a big event. Kids were running around on the grass by the bleachers until their parents yelled at them to take a seat; students were sitting in groups with their phones out, sharing holographic pictures and videos of previous Wargames. There were vendors of all kinds of foods and candies walking up and down the stairs shouting if anyone wanted Candy Clouds and getting in arguments with dads over the "outrageous" prices; there was even a guy pushing a hot dog cart around with a big orange sign that read Hot Dawgs. All this pandemonium made Mark grin.

He took a deep breath and walked to the opposite side of the field where the bleachers were covered in silver and gray decorations, the colors of Foxtrot Squad. He glanced over at the side of the field where the other squads had their flarejets lined up. His stomach lurched as a

## CHAPTER 13

mixture of anxiety and determination jumbled together. A familiar sleek black shadow stood with three other flarejets against a background of shimmering gold flags. The Alphas were out in full parade.

Samantha caught sight of him and ran up. "There's a problem. Sergeant Hammerstrom's got the Wargame Inspectors here and they're digging around your flarejet and—"

Mark didn't say anything. He broke into a run, arriving to find the sergeant along with three men and two women dressed in the same official suits and speaking in an official manner to Lexe, Heath, Torvan, and Zaza. It looked like an interrogation to Mark, and that made his fists clench.

"Hi," he said, walking up, brisk in step and firm in voice. "I'm Mark. How I can help you?"

The person in charge—a balding middle-aged man with a sallow face—looked down his round nose at Mark. Then, he ignored Mark and spoke to Hammerstrom. "Ah, this is the young Earther in question, yes?"

Mark's face felt flushed. "Listen, my flarejet qualif—"

"Hot dogs!" interrupted a loud grating squawk near the bleachers. "Hot, hotty, hot dogs!" shouted the man pushing the cart, his neon orange Hot Dawgs sign blazing.

"My flarejet qualifies!" Mark repeated.

The official ignored Mark and looked to Hammerstrom, who said, "He has built this disgraceful contraption along with his inept friends. You can imagine, sir, how dangerous it must be for everyone. It can't even fly in the air without the risk of accelerating into explosions!"

"Indeed!" rejoined the inspector official while his inspector colleagues murmured their agreement.

Lexe, who was already angry after a long interrogation, raised her voice. "We aren't—"

"Hoooot dooooogs!" shouted the vendor, closer and more annoying than before.

"We aren't inept," Lexe repeated.

The officials enjoyed a round of chuckles.

"Dear child," said an older female official, "you're a bright, young thirteen years of age. How could you know the first thing about building such a complicated machine?"

Torvan responded with firm conviction. "Our teachers and our profess—"

"Get your pipin' hotty totty doggies heeeere!" the vendor squawked, louder and closer, his triangular neon sign blaring in a rude and obnoxious manner.

"And our professors," Torvan continued, teeth grinding, "taught us well."

"Be that as it may," said the second male official, "flying this self-built machine with its untested air breathing engine and hazardous, highly explosive fuel clearly violates our safety standards."

"But I tested it!" said Mark. "I've flown my flarejet every day for the past month. I've refueled and recalibrated and retested every piece in every system in every area of my flarejet! All my friends double and triple and quadruple checked everything down to the very last bolt!" He paused to catch his breath. "And, AND, Professor McMaluch not only supervised the whole thing, but calibrated all the major safety systems himself! So today, today, there is no way any of you are stopping me from joining my squad and—"

"HOT JUICY MELTY CHEESY PUFFY HOT DOOOOOOGS!"

Mark whirled towards the vendor with his fists clenched. Thankfully, Heath was there with a restraining arm and calming words.

"You're hard work and efforts are praiseworthy indeed," said the fat-nosed official, "as are those of your charming young friends here.

## CHAPTER 13

Regrettably, and remember that this is for your own good, we must reject you and your flarejet this year. Perhaps next year when you have a proper flarejet."

Mark exchanged several frustrated and heartbroken glances with his friends. They were all exasperated and without a single idea of what to do.

Then, an authoritative and dominating female voice broke through all the noise. "Sergeant Hammerstrom."

The man's medals clinked as he whirled to face the tall, raven haired woman. Hers were a set of piercing green eyes set in a classic, commanding, ageless face. She stopped in front of the officials, who all bowed deeply. The sergeant, who had been happily sneering at Mark, snapped instantaneously into a straight-backed salute. "Admiral."

"Sergeant," she continued with a gentle smile, "this young man will fly with his squad today."

"Yes, Admiral."

"Dismissed."

The sergeant went away, quickly and with all haste.

"Inspectors," she said to the still bowing officials.

"Yes, Admiral," they said in unison without looking up.

"This young man's flarejet qualifies in full."

"Yes, Admiral."

"Dismissed."

The five officials scurried away faster than roaches afraid of the light.

The admiral turned to Mark and his friends with a small, genuine smile on her lips—even though her sharp green eyes were cold from years of politics and strife.

Mark couldn't help quickly blurting out, "Thank you, Admiral!"

"Thank those who believe in you," she said in a warm, serious tone.

Mark stole a glance towards the bleachers. Otto McMaluch noticed and nodded in acknowledgement. Then he tapped Captain Zumski on the shoulder, which interrupted the man's argument with a beer vendor. The captain waved at Mark with his free hand, the other being busy holding a cone of Cloud Candy.

"Now all you need to do," the admiral continued, "is not go flying into any more classrooms."

Mark, surprised by the admiral's sense of humor, didn't know how to reply. They watched her direct, graceful strides as she left the field. For a few moments no one spoke. Then everyone started cheering.

"You're in!" cried Zaza.

"Officially in," added Heath.

"Good to have you gunning with us," said Keera with hearty slap.

"Let's get flying!" said Samantha to her squad.

"GET YOUR HAAAAT DAAAAGS HEEEEERE!" went the crazed vendor.

Each cadet jogged over to their flarejet. Mark exchanged a few fist bumps with his friends as they followed him to the pile of beastly junk they all felt proud to have helped him build. He climbed into the cockpit, sat down, and was about to close the glass canopy when Lexe stopped him.

"Wait! I've thought of the perfect name for our hotshot caveman!"

Mark and Heath exchanged puzzled looks as Lexe grabbed a couple portable blowtorches. She tossed one to Zaza and told Torvan to follow them.

"What are they doing?" Mark asked Heath, watching them run away alongside the bleachers.

Heath shrugged as the trio reached the hot dog vendor. Then he saw what they did, which made him wince and say, "Wow."

"Saucy!" said Mark with a grin as Zaza ran back holding both blowtorches while Lexe and Torvan ran close behind, holding the Hot Dawgs sign they had just cut off the top of the vendor's cart. In the distance the

## CHAPTER 13

man was screaming obscenities from behind his cart and throwing hot dogs after them.

"Close the canopy!" Zaza shouted as they drew nearer.

Mark pressed a button and crouched down as the glass canopy closed over him. Heath, guessing what they were going to do, grabbed two ladders and leaned them against the glass. Lexe and Torvan climbed up and began welding the triangular orange sign onto the metal strip above the glass canopy. When they were finished, Lexe busted off the S at the end of the sign. Now, Mark's flarejet had a long fin emblazoned with its new name: Hot Dawg. He had to laugh. "So cheesy—so perfect."

Heath removed the ladders and everyone backed away with encouraging waves. Mark waved back, made a thumbs up, and pressed the button that would start the engine.

"Yes," he said to himself as the turbine whirred to life. The now familiar rumble of the scramjet starting was a great comfort. Veins of burnt orange began to glow as superheated yellow fuel coursed through dull red lines. A haze of heat made the air over the bare engine shimmer. His grin widened as the launch doors yawned open. Outside, a menacing gray hailstorm poured down. He didn't care, he'd soon be far above and flying—in outer freaking space.

"Here we go, people," said Samantha over the intercom. "Follow my lead." Her swept-back, swan like Apex-9 floated up and zoomed out the doors.

Mark respectfully waited for the rest of his squad to jet before he grabbed the controls, lifted off, and roared out into the storm.

"Wwwooo yeah!" he hollered. Hail the size of golf balls mashed against his shields as he craned upwards. Rushing up through the storm he heard the growl of the scramjet working, the lashing wind outside, and the smashing hail. Then he broke through the clouds and soared into the empty nothing; and then, so fast his ears began to ring, silence enveloped him.

"All right," came Samantha's clear voice, "we will hide and hold formation at our ambush point. When the Alphas are in range, give it all you've got. We need to rack up points and then forfeit or we'll get creamed. So bug out when your shields get to twenty percent. You'll need it to run with. If they get your shields down to five percent or lower it's an automatic kill and they get triple bonus. Don't. That's it. Just don't. Got it?"

Everyone replied the affirmative. Radio silence followed as the five flarejets left fading streaks of color. Soon they were in position. They stayed hovering in place, in silence, waiting. Mark tilted slightly to the side so he could look down. The angry hailstorm obscured the majority of the city below. Mark wondered how everyone in that stadium could see the Wargame.

If he had been sitting in the stands with Heath, Lexe, and the others, he would have found out. After Alpha Squad had flown out, a gigantic holographic projection filled the whole stadium. The floor, walls, and ceiling vanished; even the long rows of bleachers disappeared. Everything was replaced by the illusion of sitting on absolutely nothing while floating in space and watching as a merchant ship drifted into view.

"Here we go, here we go!" Samantha's voice warned as Mark saw the merchant and its Alpha Squad escort. His grip tightened; his heart hammered; for a brief moment he thought of home: the warmth of the Australian sun, the buzz of beetles in tall stalks of grass, and his moms cinnamon-scented apron when she hugged him. "I wish mom and dad could see me now," he whispered.

"Break ambush on my signal," said Samantha.

Mark waited, eyes focused on the four distant Alphas and one merchant ship. Any minute he'd be charging in gripping both triggers.

## CHAPTER 13

But then something they hadn't expected happened. Three of the four guards shifted course. They came charging straight at them!

"Brake and scatter! Brake and scatter!" Samantha yelled and flew at full throttle. The rest of Foxtrot followed suit, scattering in different directions.

"How did they know where we were?" shouted Derrick's angry voice.

"Yeah," agreed Keera, "I thought we were supposed to have the element of surprise or something!"

"Forget that. Scatter!" shouted Samantha. "Make them split up!"

Mark focused on a point and flew away, just like he'd been taught. He had a steady burn going and was feeling comfortable when a loud boom twisted his whole flarejet into an uncontrolled spin.

"Shields at eighty-six percent," a digital female voice informed him.

"What the hell was that?" he yelled, frantically trying to regain control.

"Hard left! Burn hard left!" Keera shouted over the com.

Mark yanked left and looked right. A white multifinned missile blitzed by.

"Get out of there!" She continued yelling. "Three of the Alphas are swarming your six, nine, and twelve o'clock!"

Pulling up, he sped vertically. A stolen glimpse revealed Lance, Jet Chan, and Cruise gunning after him from different directions. His head snapped forward, eyes fixed on the stars. "Eat my afterburner."

Mark twisted the throttle. A surge of superheated fuel rushed through those red veins like the adrenaline surging through his heart. The beast came to life.

Back at the stadium, people went silent. Antsy kids stopped squirming, hardcore fans stopped arguing, and even the food vendors stopped yelling. Everyone watched Mark's flarejet. Its holographic projection filled the middle of the stadium. And when Mark cranked the throttle, nothing remained but a dark orange streak against the night.

"Whoa," breathed Torvan.

"Yeah," agreed Heath.

Zaza bounced on her seat. "He's going to win!"

Lexe nodded with pride. "Yeah he is."

Mark looked unstoppable. His flarejet raced across the void with effortless speed. But going in a straight line would not save him. It only made him an easier target.

"Eff," he cursed as streaks of burning metal began blazing past him. Jet Chan had locked on with those sniperlike guns.

Mark cursed again, throttling down so he could bob and weave like Derrick had taught him. He tried to be a moving target. That didn't help. Chan's long range shots were accurate enough to shoot the wings off flies in midair. Each hit sent shock waves down Mark's shield.

"Eighty-four percent," announced his SEG. Then, "eighty-one percent—seventy-eig—seventy-f—seventy-two percent."

"Guys!" he yelled. "I'm getting rocked over here!"

"Keep burning!" said Keera.

"Burn harder, burn harder, buttercup," Derrick added.

"I can't outrun bullets!" Mark shouted back.

It wasn't enough. Lance and Cruise soon had him in range of their guns. Lance's sporadic fire from his Cold Plasma Cannons kept missing—but Mark soon learned why Cruise was called the "fistbreaker."

"Holy burning laser storms!" Mark shrieked as hundreds of electrified yellow beams hit his shield, the cool blue surface splattering and waving like a lake during a lightning storm.

"Shields at sixty-eig—bbbzzzz—fifty-five."

"I'm getting owned out here! Where are you guys?!"

"Keep them in play!" came Samantha's excited voice over the intercom. "They've left the merchant with one guy! Derrick, Keera and I are railing him and Marsel's going in for the cargo!"

## CHAPTER 13

Mark growled, banking a hard left out of a vertical burn. Lance and his squad mates followed, hunting with pleasure. An idea ran through Marks mind. Swerving right, he led them in a zigzag. Then he slowed down. They began catching up. Their guns cut his shields down to 44 percent. That's when he broke pattern, burning hard in reverse until he flipped upside down and jammed the throttle on full.

"Haha! Suck it!" he yelled triumphantly as his flarejet, still upside down, rocketed right over their heads.

This strange maneuver bought him some time away from their guns. Not enough time, though. Wrenching around, they gave chase.

He dove, fighting for survival once more.

"I'll be space junk soon," he grumbled as ice-pale plasma shots, laser fire, and heated lead began raining into his shields. He tried the Avus Fake Out and then four other escape tactics. Each one worked for a brief instant, helped by his immense acceleration, but he couldn't outrun their guns for long.

He tried a dodge and burn that Samantha taught him. His scramjets quick acceleration left his stomach lurching. He made abrupt changes in direction, going up and down and side to side. His vision became a blurred mess of stars and bullets.

But Mark knew he couldn't keep this going. Burning, dodging, escaping every which way, he still had three superior flarejets eating his tail, and they found pleasure in putting up entire walls of hurt.

He watched his shields flickering and faltering with each shockwave; he felt each hit in his flarejet, and he hurt as it took hit after hit, shuddering from the force; he heard the SEG count down the remaining shields from 44 to 32. He felt powerless and helpless and beaten. This made him angry.

Another storm of pain rocked his flarejet.

"Yeah?" he shouted, nearly ripping the controls off while turning around. "Oh yes?" he yelled, twisting his entire flarejet to face them, head on. All three Alphas reflected in the whites of his eyes. "Eat your medicine!" he shouted at them, triggers stuck on full. "Eat it!"

SHUNK, SHUNK, SHUNK, SHUNK. Mark's IMP cannons began firing lava-colored bursts of ionized mass. The heavy thumps sent shivers down his spine, the good kind of shivers. He loved the way the burning red blasts surged from each side of his flarejet, spitting out into space like cannon fire from a volcano. Each round blasted into Lance's Blacknova, dealing massive damage. But at the same time, Mark was being punished by all three Alphas.

Back at the stadium, Zaza gasped, Torvan frowned, and Lexe was shaking her head and saying, "only a caveman—only our fuzz-for-brains caveman would play chicken."

The stadium filled with a close-up of the scene: Mark's flarejet charging against three superior machines, a flood of neon fire between them.

"That's one angry kid," remarked the announcer, a local news guy with a full head of hair and a penchant for one-liners. "But if he doesn't get out of the frying pan soon he'll end up—in the fire. Ha! Ha!"

"Right you are, Joe," replied the announcer sitting with him, a serious woman with curly blonde hair. "His shields are already at nineteen percent and dropping fast. Any more of this punishment and he'll drop below five percent."

"And as you know, Jenn, that's an automatic kill for the Alphas. Mark will be required to forfeit and fly home with clipped wings, wounded in spirit no doubt, like—a bird. Ha! Ha!"

"Oh! There he goes, Joe!" she said, watching with everyone in the stadium as Mark pulled up enough to jet right over the three Alphas.

"Let's leave the hunt for a moment here, Jenn, and focus in on the scene of the struggle at the merchant ship." The stadium wide projection blurred out and then zoomed in on the main fight. "Looks like the three Foxtrot FlareRiders are still being held back by the lone Alpha vaporizer."

## CHAPTER 13

"True," she replied. "But their constant fire has been successfully bleeding Dinzdale's shields, which stand at twenty-two percent." Then, "Look there!" She pointed to Marcel, who had been floating close to the merchant. "He's lifting the cargo off the merchant ship! Any minute now the symbol will touch Marsel's flarejet. Foxtrot Squad will have stolen the merchant's shipment."

"A tense moment for all of us watching, I'm sure. Remember, though, Jenn, that those foxes will need to get the cargo eight clicks away. You could say they need to—tuck tale and run. Ha! Ha!"

"Wait! Lance stopped hunting Mark!" she said as the action filling the middle of the stadium zoomed out to include Mark and the three Alphas. "Lance and his two squad mates have broken the chase! They are speeding back to the merchant ship. Will they make it in time to stop the cargo from being stolen?"

The news guy laughed. "Jenn, Jenn, Jenn, those three are the best FlareRiders in our whole solar system! They'll make it," he said with a proud nod.

"You may be right. Looks like the Alpha's charge ripped through Foxtrot Squad."

The action in the stadium reflected her words as Lance, Cruise, and Jet slammed into Samantha and her squad. Pale plasma bolts and laser fire smashed into Foxtrot from the front and Dinzdale's solid lead kept hitting from behind.

"But look at their strategy here," said Jenn. "Samantha is leading Lance away into a dogfight. Derrick is doing the same with Jet Chan. This leaves Keera to protect Marcel against Dinzdale and Cruise Galantine."

"The fistbreaker and doomsday are a powerful one-two punch, Jenn. I wouldn't be surprised if Keera was—floored! Ha! Ha! "

"Look there!" she interrupted, excited. "Mark is swooping down with cannons ablaze!" She clapped as Mark entered the stadium's view from the top right.

"Uh oh! All the Alphas seem to be making a straight shot for Marcel," said the news guy as Lance and Jet broke away from their dogfights. "Could this be the famous Alpha Annihilation tactic?"

The whole stadium watched, breath caught and hearts pounding. Everyone's eyes locked on the holographic cargo symbol so close to Marcel. The audience collectively gasped as they witnessed Jet and Dinzdale and Lance and Cruise all turn against the shy boy.

The entire Alpha Squad aimed their guns at the kid, ripping, tearing, and cutting with all hellish pain. The boy and his medic-class flarejet were being torn apart.

Every Foxtrot Squad member tore back at the Alphas, trying to get them away from Marcel, but the Alphas ignored it all, concentrating everything on Marcel.

The boy's flarejet wasn't built to take so much damage. His shields disintegrated in wisps of misty blue. Several shots slammed into his machine before he could even hit the forfeit button. And when he did, the Alpha's simply stopped and turned back to attacking everyone else again. Marcel's flarejet, engine broken, began slowly tumbling away in a helpless drift. The cargo remained, blinking, just outside the merchant ship.

"Yes it was!" the announcer guy crowed. "The Alpha Annihilation! Boy, what a show, what—a—show."

"It's not over yet," the lady persisted. "Any one of the FlareRiders from Foxtrot could swoop in for that cargo."

"They could, yes. But who would be crazy enough?"

As if in answer to this question, which he could not possibly have heard, Mark hatched an insane plan and dove at the glowing cargo.

# CHAPTER 13

"There he goes!" the blonde lady shouted. The audience joined her in a cheer as Mark snatched up the cargo and slammed thrusters on full.

"What is he thinking?" said the biased news guy. "He knows he doesn't have the firepower or the shields to win this thing—so why is he fighting?"

She turned and looked Joe straight in the eyes. "Maybe because that's—one angry kid."

Joe scowled at her for mocking his one-liner signature.

Lance saw Mark steal the prized cargo. He gave furious chase.

Mark noticed. "Time to make good on my threats." He aimed his flarejet for Crescent City and dove.

Laser fire joined the streaks of cold plasma raining around him, announcing that Cruise had joined Lance for this last hunt. Mark kept the throttle twisted as the tops of Crescent City's gray hailstorm clouds drew closer. With each hit, his shields suffered. From 16 to 9 percent. Any second now and the game would be lost.

"Let's see if the prof's warnings were real," he said as his flarejet broke into the dense clouds.

His intercom crackled and then popped as someone switched into it. "You can't do that!" came Lance's angry yelling. "You can't go into Crescent City! It's out of bounds!"

"I'm a raider, so yes I can!" Mark shouted back.

"No. You can't. It's against the rules!"

"The only rule down here is no shootin', Tex."

"You're endangering civilians!"

"There aren't any civilians up he—whoa!" He shouted, yanking the flarejet left, just missing a hazel-haired girl on a skyboard, her eyes behind her rain-soaked glasses just as wide as Marks.

"See? SEE?" Lance screamed!

"That was one time," Mark retorted.

"You'll end up hurting somebody!" Lance yelled at him.

"Yeah, your ego," Mark shouted back, and then dodged a building.

People going about their daily lives on the streets and in the office buildings of the East Ridge were treated to a spectacular show that day. Some random desk worker would be sitting, filing spreadsheets, when he'd hear the distant roar of a turbine engine drawing closer; then a flarejet would blitz past his window, right at eyelevel, rumbling the desk and spilling coffee everywhere. Then, just when he'd finish cursing and wiping his pants, two more flarejets in hot pursuit would blitz by, shattering the windows so that the desk worker could lean out and shake his fists.

Mark's intercom popped and switched again. Samantha's confused voice filled the control cabin. "What are you doing, rookie?"

"Those braggarts can't use live ammo down here," he lied, hiding his true idea. "You guys rack up as many hits as you can up there. I'll keep 'em busy."

"That's insane—but OK!"

Everyone back at Launch Bay Three was going nuts. Half the stadium was yelling in protest, infuriated and calling for the rule book. The other half was yelling and cheering, not giving a damn about the rule book.

Meanwhile, sweat dripped down Mark's forehead. Dodging buildings was pretty easy, they were stationary, but when it came to darting between flyways filled with hovercars that turned and swerved and nearly collided when they saw him rocketing towards them—well, that was tough. To add to that, the rain had mixed in with the downpour of hail splattering across his shields, blurring everything.

The anxious voice of Professor Duboush sounded over the intercom. "I told you to stay out of the atmosphere, kid!"

"I remember," he said as he burst around the side of a building.

"Then get back up into space!" she hollered.

## CHAPTER 13

"How long until my turbine fires up?" said Mark, his eyes focused on not plowing through skyscrapers that appeared out of the hailstorm at random.

"It doesn't matter!"

"I'm doing this."

The professor switched off.

A moment later Samantha switched on. "You're crazy! The prof told me you'll explode! Get back up here!"

Mark's voice remained calm. "How are you guys doing up there?"

"Good. Derrick rescued Marsel and Keera is fighting Chan. I almost have Dinzdale at five percent, so just get up here and we'll collect our points and be done."

"No," said Mark, determined to risk it all.

Duboush's voice came firm and threatening. "Get out or we'll be picking up pieces of you!"

Too late. The engine gave a loud spit and backfired. Mark's teeth rattled as the whole flarejet shuddered and lurched. Everything shut down. It was like a flashback to so many months ago, when he went skydiving in a stunt plane. Everything had gone eerily quiet, even though the neon city kept rushing by. He twisted the throttle, nothing. He pulled up, nothing. He pushed down, nothing. Every switch he flicked was dead, every knob sunk without resistance, and the hydraulic controls felt weak, slack, and powerless.

Mark combed a sweaty palm through his hair. "That better not be it," he whispered.

The scramjet responded by showing this was just the beginning. Thin tendrils of air began weaving in through the front. They were binding together into a massive cord. From silence to the searing sound of a hurricane, life blurred. Careening faster and faster, accelerating exponentially, he went tearing through downtown.

"Erp." His lungs tried collapsing. He looked down at the speedometer; this made his eyes blur again. The flarejet was accelerating so fast that the digital numbers were a whirring green blob. He looked up and decided not to steer, fearing that the gentlest touch would mess him right up.

Heart racing as fast as his flarejet, he couldn't resist crowing, "The g-forces, man! The g-forces!"

"You've left Lance in the dust!" came Samantha's excited shout. "I can see you guys on my scope. You're three clicks ahead and gaining!"

Mark laughed. "There's no stopping me now!" Then he realized what he just said and frowned. "Literally."

Otto's firm voice rattled the intercom. "Try to steer out of Crescent City. You'll run out of air out there. Go for a soft landing. We want you back in one piece."

"Will do!" Mark shouted back, thankful that Otto was there.

"You're five clicks away!" Samantha shouted.

Back at the stadium things had quieted down considerably. Everyone's eyes were glued to the close-up of Mark in his flarejet. Some people were whispering to each other and speculating if he'd make it; others were placing bets. Most people, though, were sitting in anxious silence.

"Seven clicks! You're going to win this thing!" said Samantha, updating Mark and everyone listening in.

Mark grinned and, in a whisper no one else could hear, said, "This is for you, Mom."

"Eight clicks!" she shouted. "You did it! You did it Mark! We won the Wargame!"

The stadium erupted with cheers and hoots and hollers. Lexe was high-fiving everyone, Zaza was hugging everyone, Torvan was grinning, Heath was saying "I knew he could," and Mark's beaming face filled the projector. Everything was right with the world—and then his flarejet exploded.

## CHAPTER 14

# CHAPTER 14
## WORLDS APART

People watched in silence and horror as debris rained down from a rising pitch black cloud. Some falling metal chunks glowed, others smoked, all were in little bits. Soon everyone could see the empty space where Mark used to be. The view inside the stadium panned up and down and side to side trying to find something, anything; but it looked as though Mark and his flarejet had simply evaporated.

"Whhhooooo yeeeaaahh!" could suddenly be heard. A control cabin fell out of the gray sky. It streaked down the screen and disappeared. The view adjusted downwards. There, on the pavement, lay an intact flarejet capsule sporting a big triangular fin with orange letters that read: Hot Dawg. The glass canopy opened. Mark stepped out. He pumped both fists in the air. A thunderous cheer filled the stadium.

A medic crew rushed to pick him up and make sure he was all right. Nothing broken, they tossed a blanket over his shoulders in case he was in shock and flew him back to the stadium.

Mark was in shock. His flarejet had just exploded. But, he'd also won the Wargame. The very thought made him dizzy. No sooner had the medics released him then the media descended.

"Congratulations, kiddo! You won!" said the first news reporter to corner him, which happened to be one-liner Joe. "How do you feel?"

Mark's face beamed. "Like I just WON."

## CHAPTER 14

Joe flashed a smile at the camera. "Ha! Ha! I guess you could say Mark feels—YES WHAT IS IT?" he finished with a snap at an assistant with an info tablet. "Oh, I see" he said, reading it. "I see, I see," he murmured to himself before looking up directly into the camera. "Ladies and gentlemen," he began with a dramatic tone. "I have just now received breaking news." His second pause was for no other purpose than more drama. "This young man," and he placed a hand on Mark's shoulder, "has been disqualified."

"WHAT?" screamed Mark.

"Yes, tragic," said John in an offhanded way to Mark before turning back to the camera he loved. "Yes, you heard it here first, folks. This young Earther and his Foxtrot Squad mates have been disqualified."

"WHY?"

Mark continued to be ignored as the reporter continued. "The panel of judges has determined that this young boy's reckless flight through our beloved city violated numerous rules and, in fact, several city ordinances."

Mark, exasperated, chuckled in disbelief.

"This decision is not final. The awards ceremony will be postponed until the judges have reached a decision. The judges will also confiscate and examine what remains of Marks flarejet. However, for now, his disqualification stands. Therefore, due to this upset, the win automatically goes to Alpha Squad."

"Yeah," Mark nodded. "I'm done. I'm done with you people." He started to walk away.

"Here to comment is the Alpha Squad wing leader. Hello Lance!"

"Hello, Joe!" said the tall, blue-eyed boy striding into frame. He clapped Mark on the shoulders and, in an obnoxiously friendly way, dragged him back to the camera. "I've just heard the news myself."

"And how does that make you feel?"

"Well, Joe, our beloved city is a beautiful metropolis teaming with honest, hardworking civilians. I could have shot Mark down at any time with only a few squeezes of my trigger. And you know what Joe? I did think about it. I thought that shooting him down would avert any disasters to the city and the people we love."

Joe beamed at Lance and clapped him on the back. "Noble, quite noble of you indeed. Yes, you were in the right."

Mark scowled. He tried to pull away, but Joe and Lance had him pinned.

"But I didn't, Joe," continued Lance. "Do you know why?"

"Why is that, Wing leader Lance?"

"Because I was afraid, Joe," said Lance, becoming dramatic. "I was afraid that one misplaced shot—I don't miss, Joe, but I still worry—one of my shots could have hurt somebody. And I just could not bear the thought, Joe. I couldn't."

"Ladies and gentleman, here, right here before your eyes stands a real hero," said the camera-loving reporter in a swelling of pride. "I am honored to be standing here with this gallant young hero, reporting to you of his well-deserved win today."

"Thank you, Joe. But I do want to say one more thing."

"Yes?"

Lance draped an arm around Mark's shoulder. "This young champ fought for the first time today. And even though the judges will sternly discipline him, I believe he played a great game. And I am thankful the little guy is A-OK."

"Heroic and humble!" Joe cheered. "You are a marvel, Lance. Indeed, we are all thankful for the young boy's safe escape after he destroyed his own flarejet on that rampage."

The camera followed and zoomed in on Joe as he stepped to the side.

"And now we go to our stadium side cam to hear what the people on the street have to say."

## CHAPTER 14

Mark shook Lance's arm off his shoulder and said, "Ass," then walked away.

The stadium side camera projected a life-size holographic view of Joe next to a man standing by a food vender cart.

"Sir," said holographic Joe, "I understand that your hot dog cart was vandalized just before the Wargame started."

"Yes, that is correct," said the hot dog vendor, making a hot dog out of habit to calm his anger.

"And how did this happen?"

"Let me tell you!" He slapped mayo on the dry bread. "These kids, they ran—I was selling hot dogs—and they ran up to my cart here," he patted his hot dog cart as if it were his only child, then smothered the hot dog in gunky relish. "They ran up here—with blowtorches—and they CUT," minced onion fell out of the bun as his hands started trembling with rage, "my sign right off. And they dragged it," the ketchup he squirted missed the bun and splattered onto the floor, "to that dumb kid's junkjet!"

"And how does that make you feel?" Joe interrupted.

The hot dog in the vendors hands trembled violently now. "It makes me feel—" he grabbed the hot dog in both hands and squeezed. "It makes me feeeeeel—like I'm going to kill that little whelp!" he bellowed and ripped the hot dog in half.

"Whoa, take it easy! Take it easy!" shouted Joe, backing away even though he was a holograph. "Let's go to our other stadium side cams."


Two months passed. The snow became sleet; the sleet turned to slush; and the slush slowly washed away in the cold rains of early, gloomy spring. After being disqualified, Mark had hoped every day the judges would reverse their decision. After a few weeks the hope turned into wishing for at least some news. It seemed like an eternal wait. For more than a month he had been on edge, expecting. Lunch conversations revolved around nothing else. He wanted to know, one way or the other, if he was a winner or a loser. Then, one day, he stopped caring. He hated getting up each morning. His friends didn't say anything at first—but after a while, they called him out on it—because that's what friends do.

"Two months," Heath began, trying to get Mark fired up again. "Two whole months since the disqualification and still nothing."

"Yuuup," said Mark, picking at the same lunch he'd ordered every day for the last couple weeks.

After a pause, Torvan took a shot too. "Man, the whole decision is unfair. Ridiculously unfair!"

"Yuuup," said Mark, going through the motions of chewing.

A longer pause followed. Then Zaza piped up with a different idea. "You wanna go boarding today? We can all play suckerpunch!"

"Nooope," said Mark, sucking juice from a straw in slow, lazy gulps.

The longest pause yet sat between them. The Mess Hall was packed as usual and cheerful chatter mixed with gossip and mini food fights. But at their table, only Lexe's game made any sounds. Zaza poked her in the ribs and pointed at Mark.

Lexe shrugged. "He doesn't want to talk—look," she faced him. "Hey, Ernest Shaw's body was found last week. No tongue. Syn'Crux symbol carved into his chest. Police say all the burns look like those caused by Commander Exor's stolen Syn'Crux powers. The inspectors found and raided a Syn'Crux lab too."

"Cool beans," he said, staring out at the rain.

Another moment of silence passed before Heath, quite irritated, spoke up. "What's with you, man? We used to get all riled up and rail against the stupidity of those judges! Now you just don't give a flying dump! We used to high-five all those people from our Support Crew who sided with

## CHAPTER 14

us and thought it was all unfair. Now you just pick fights with everybody! We used to cuss out the people who made fun of you. Now you just ignore them." He paused and frowned. "I mean, I guess that's good, teachers tell us to ignore all the haters—but it's not like you've thickened your skin—you just gave up. What's going on?"

Everyone at the table kept looking at Mark, and he felt it. He looked at their faces, each filled with genuine concern and friendship. He figured he owed them some truth, some honesty.

He shrugged and hung his head over the mish-mashed plate of food. "I got knocked out. I fought my hardest, sacrificed my flarejet—the flarejet we all built together—just so I could fail. I failed. TKO. Uppercut to the face. Ding, ding, done."

A different silence now, one of friendship opening, could be seen in the eyes of those around him. They were thinking about what to say.

Heath spoke up again. "Dude, you got knocked down. You didn't get knocked out."

Lexe also tried to be encouraging, but in her own way. "Yeah, I've heard cavemen have thick skulls. Harder to knock out."

Half of Mark's frown turned into a small smile. But then he scoffed. "No. I killed my flarejet. My dream. I blew it back to rusted scraps and junkyard metal. It's gone and I'm done, just done."

"We can always rebuild stuff," said Lexe, and everyone murmured in agreement. "But we can't rebuild you. Only you can do that."

"Listen," said Heath, "go talk to the captain. He'll know. Seriously, talk to him."

Mark looked up at Heath. He saw the honest concern. He looked around the table at his friends and saw the same light reflected in their faces. "Yeah, I guess I've been a bit of a weed, huh? Sure, what the hell. I'll go after school."

The day passed as it always did these past several weeks—blank and boring. His language professor was constantly sympathizing with his loss, in twenty different languages, which had begun to grate on his nerves; there were so many new solar systems being plotted in the waypoint class that it was stupid confusing. Dr. Barrie took every opportunity to correlate Mark's disqualification to historical, losing dogfight battles; at least the lieutenant remained cold and apathetic and focused on teaching, which was somewhat comforting.

The day slid by and Mark found himself sitting in Captain Stanislaw Zumski's office. The man was currently preoccupied with his mid-afternoon bowl of soup. Mark's aimless gaze wandered around the cluttered office. It sat at the top left of the GSS Final Frontier. It had once been used by many a captain during the galactic starships deep space missions. Mark could see out of the large curved window. It overlooked the Crescent City valley and some of the neon lit skyscrapers downtown. The office was cluttered with displays of strange cooking utensils, empty bottles of exotic spices, and several autographed chef hats.

"So," the captain began with a loud slurp of his soup, "your face is drooping low enough to touch your shoes."

Mark sighed. "Any news from the judges?"

Zumski slurped his soup. "No."

Mark turned back to the window. Zumski found a chunk of potato and began chewing it.

"Captain," said Mark, still gazing out the window, "you ever sit and look out the window?"

"Only when I'm not eating," Stan replied, a twinkle in his crinkled brown eyes.

Mark was silent, looking out over the neon city. "All those people," he mused, "all with a destination—a purpose." He turned his eyes to the

## CHAPTER 14

wise, old captain. "Sir—why did you pick me? I mean, why did you offer me this opportunity? I'm not nearly as good as Lance or—anyone of the other FlareRiders."

"No," replied the captain, "you're not. Lance is the best FlareRider our school has seen in decades. The young man has a protégé talent. He's a hero. Got the wealth, looks, skill—the whole enchilada!"

"So why am I here? What good am I?" Mark demanded.

The captain kept chewing his potatoes, pausing only long enough to say, "Think about it, ace."

The boy from Earth thought about all the movies he'd seen and books he'd read staring a kid as the main character. "Some sort of prophecy? Am I some kind of secretly orphaned hero destined for great things?"

Stan chuckled.

"That's got to be it," Mark insisted. "I'm a nobody right now, but soon I'll get superpowers or something and rock everybody, right? You've seen this in a vision or foretelling or divination or something. . . ."

Stan was having a difficult time eating while chuckling so much.

"What?"

"No."

"No?"

"No."

Mark sat back in his chair with a thump. He heaved another sigh. "So what then? I'm a nobody? I'll stay a nobody forever?"

Stan stopped eating and looked at Mark for a while. He moved the soup bowl away and folded his hands and cleared his throat. "I knew a kid like you once," he began, eyes intent on Mark. "The kid had no talent. Zero. No skill either. His parents lived their whole life in a small town, doing small things, for small pay. He didn't have any dashing good looks to speak of either—well, he thought he did," said Stan with a nostalgic grin, "but he didn't," he shook his head and chuckled. "No, the only thing he had going for him was an obstinate stubbornness, like a goat. Now, he thought he had heart and spirit too, you see. The bold, beating heart of a Borian-system bear-shark; a free spirit like that of a Surrealian sky-lark—was his airheaded self-image—but no, nothing of the kind. Just the goatlike stubbornness of a fighter." Nostalgic memories overtook the man and he sat, scratching his short, square gray beard in an absent-minded manner.

"What happened to him?" asked Mark, eager to know this kid's fate.

The captain gave a derisive snort. "Starved through ten years hauling tinfoil on a merchant rig before he saved up enough to buy a crapsack starfighter. Then he joined up with that infamous mercenary core: the Three-O-Three. After that," Stan leaned back, making the chair squeak, "he spent the next couple decades protecting civvies and getting into fights all the way from Beta Centauri to Orion's Halo," he picked his bowl back up, "and he sampled the galaxy's most delicious foods."

Mark's eyes went wide as he realized who the kid was. "That was you?"

The captain slurped a spoonful and thumbed at the jacket hanging on the wall behind him. Mark leaned to the left to see it better. It had to be the coolest leather jacket he'd ever seen. It was of simple design, like a modernized version of the aviator jackets he'd seen in old European war pictures. It was made of dark, tanned leather and the cuffs and collar were scuffed and faded as if had been worn every day with love and pride. The number 303 was imprinted on each shoulder sleeve. The front had the simple red and white symbol of the Three-O-Three Squadron.

Mark squinted to read the words below the symbol. "Ace of Aces." He sunk back into his chair, dumbfounded to have learned the old man had such a wild past.

## CHAPTER 14

The captain finished his soup and dropped the spoon into the empty bowl. He sighed, content, and pushed the bowl away. "Listen, I'm not going to tell you why you're here or, for that matter, why you're anywhere." He got up and went to the window. "Look here," he said and pressed two fingers to the window. Moving each finger away across the glass brought the distant crater ridge into focus, as if he were zooming in on a screen. "You see?"

Mark had gotten up to look. "What is that place?"

"It's an old oak tree up on the North Ridge. Been there since the founding. Few people know of it because of the old cemetery below. So, sometimes, when life is buggered, I go there to think."

Mark kept staring for a while. Stan took his fingers away and the tall tree disappeared into the distance. The young Earther thanked the captain and took his leave. He walked through the silent hallways until he was outside, and then, stepping on his skyboard, he pointed it towards the North Ridge.

It was an early spring night scented with rain, even though the clouds had cleared. The ride there wasn't short, but it seemed so, due to the abundance of thoughts clogging his mind.

He had been so wrapped up in thoughts and memories that he simply let his skyboard take him there. During the whole ride his head had been down, eyes unfocused in a blank stare at his shoes. So when he saw a blur of tombstones on the ground beneath, he was brought back with a jolt.

"Whoa," he breathed as he sped up the ridge. He stared at the sleek tombstones below, all in neat rows and columns, each one aglow with a single neon blue stripe around angular edges. He began to feel a bit creeped out as he kept gliding over the large cemetery. The North Ridge was steep and high and seemed to rise forever. Seeing row after row of graves beneath uncut grass as he rose higher and higher was unnerving, and he thought of turning back. The board was tilted at a sharp angle upwards and his sides were starting to hurt from leaning forward to keep his balance. Turning back sounded good. But the ridge was in sight now; the tall branches of the old oak were visible. He tipped forward, rushing to the top.

The old oak towered into view. He pulled up at its base and hopped off. Standing the skyboard up by the tree, he turned around. The view rushed into every corner of his vision.

"Intense," he whispered. His vision filled with all the life before him. Homes of the wealthy perched on the ridge became homes of the middle-class near the valley floor, which in turn became the apartment blocks of those who looked up at the expensive homes on the ridge, and then went to work. Further on loomed the skyscrapers; their neon angles and corners and curved dimensions cut into the night sky. But that's not what had Mark's eyes. No, the boy from Earth had all his rapt attention focused on the planet that loomed over the neon city like a rising full moon.

He could see Earth from up here! Not the whole planet, only about half, but what a sight! "I can see Australia," he whispered, dumbfounded.

"Those are the Brisbane and Sydney city lights. And that's Melbourne down there!" He said with an excited voice and pointed, even though no one was around to see.

The young Earther sat for some time, watching the world turn ever so slowly. "That's my home," he said to himself. "My home planet," he whispered with a disbelieving frown. "Such a weird thing to say—home planet." He mulled over those words and the feeling of immeasurable distance they brought.

His eyes darted up into the bejeweled night sky. "So many home planets," he said in awe and wonder. "Home planets filled with people like me." The size and scope of the galaxy began to rush into his head, making his brain swim and slosh around as if at sea. He raised a single finger. "And I'm only a single, solitary, little one. . . ."

## CHAPTER 14

Mark sat down at the knotted trunk of the old oak.

"I wonder if anyone cares about me?"

Amazing, how a single set of words can invoke emotions that seem to shift reality. To Mark, that question changed so much of what he saw. Crescent City, with all those homes scattered down the ridge and across the valley, with their inviting porch lights and warm windows, held perfectly happy families and perfectly loving parents—and none of them were his. All those cars on the flyways held kids and their friends being carted around to the mall or to the movies or someplace fun—and he didn't fit in with any of them. Mark's eyes dropped to his shoes and he rested his chin on his knees. He moved his fingers through scraggly blades of grass and, from time to time, ripped up a handful to hold for a moment. Then he'd tilt his hand and watch the grass flutter away in the light spring breezes.

"Mom cares about me. . . ."

These words were different. They returned a bit of hope to his heart. He thought for another moment and then said, "And I care about me—I think."

These words, different even from those before, returned a bit of faith to his spirit.

His eyes returned to the horizon where Earth met Crescent City.

"I miss you Mom," he said to the spot on Australia she might be at right now. "I'm not doing so great up here. You told me to do my best—and I'm trying, I really am—but it's not good enough, not up here." He paused and sighed. "There's this kid, Lance, who is the best FlareRider—it's a person who flies these things—, well, you'd have to see them. But then I guess you'd never let me fly 'em if you did," he chuckled to himself. "Anyway, he's the best in decades or something. Everybody loves him, just, everybody. Because he's talented and skilled and a whole long list written on toilet paper. But I don't care. The thing is," Mark shrugged in exasperation, "and I know I just started but—but I really thought I could do it, I could make it, you know?" His eyes fell again. "If I just worked really hard and trained and did my best like you said—I could kick his prancing posterior from here to Jupiter." He looked up. "But I didn't, Mom—I didn't." His hands kept busy tearing up grass.

"We built a flarejet. Me and my friends, we put together a bunch of scraps and junk from this crazy dangerous abandoned site that was illegal—erm—long story. But you should have seen my new friends, Mom." He chuckled at the memories. "They're awesome. You'd love 'em. Probably invite their parents over for dinner and all." The smile faded into a frown again. "But we built this flarejet and I flew it in this Wargame thing. Then crazy junk happened and I ended up winning. But my flarejet exploded. Don't worry though, I was OK. But after that the judges disqualified me—me and my whole squad, Mom," his face sagged in disappointment.

After a pause, he sighed and continued. "Things have calmed down but," he shook his head and looked up again. "But it's been two months and—and I'm still angry!" the frustration reflected in his eyes. "I'm defeated and disappointed and—angry!" He threw a clump of grass. He watched the scraggly blades spiral down. He unclenched his fist from the next clump he was about to tear up. Another heavy sigh followed.

"Also," Mark continued, changing the subject, "There's this captain. You remember? The old guy with a short gray beard who recruited me?" Mark continued. "I talked to him about all this stuff. I talked to him and, I don't know if he gave me advice or just told me a story while eating soup. But he did tell me I was stubborn, like a goat—or a fighter, I guess." Mark paused with a half-smile, half-frown. "He also told me I won't be getting any superpowers anytime soon, and there's no prophecy about

## CHAPTER 14

me. I'm not an orphan either. Which, that makes sense. And I didn't think so anyway. I look like you and Dad, after all. . . ."

He exhaled long and loud. He left grass stains combing through his hair. "So I guess I'm a goat. A fighting goat," he shook his head with a rueful grin. "But so is the old captain. He fought through a lot of BS in his life," said Mark, fingers shuffling the grass again. "And I you have too, huh, Mom?" His eyes stayed fixed on the glowing spot of light on the Australian continent that hung just above Crescent City. "You don't talk about it or show it. You just keep on fighting for your family." A moment of thought and a lot self-reflection passed before his brows knitted in an honest realization. "I guess that means that I should get back up and keep fight too, huh?"

Ideas began pouring in as he let his mind break free from a self-made prison of doubt, anger, and defeat. Clues began coming together and the puzzle pieces began falling into place. For some time Mark leaned on the old oak, tearing up grass and looking out over the neon city. After a while he stopped and said, "and I know exactly what I need to fight for—Eli Exor's capture. Ruthless bastards like that can't go running free. Now when I know the truth."

Standing up and brushing the blades of grass off his pants, he went over and grabbed his board.

He turned one last time to the tiny city floating on a continent on a single planet that itself floated in an unfathomable swirl of planets. "Thank you, Mom, for listening."

Standing for a short minute to let the feelings of gratitude and love and just a little bit of longing sink into his heart, he moved to get on his skyboard. A sudden rustling in the leaf covered branches above startled him. He looked up. The shadowed foliage and thick, bent oak limbs made his eyes strain to see. A few leaves fell around him.

His heart drummed behind his ribcage. He stood, frightened but stubborn, for a moment. Nothing moved. His eyes narrowed. There was a human shape on a branch way up high. Or maybe his eyes were just playing tricks, either way he decided it was time to get going.

■ ■ ■ ■ ■ ■ ■ ■ ■ ■

In a bare concrete storage room, where a harsh fluorescent light shone on steel barrels and industrial boxes, a soldier stood holding Commander Eli Exor's black jacket. The stench of sweat and blood made the air stale. A cry would echo in the empty room from time to time. The soldier paid no mind, waiting only to hand the gold embroidered coat back when his commander asked for it.

Eli, with white shirt unbuttoned at the top and sleeves rolled up, made a round-house kick at the large punching bag hanging by a heavy chain from the ceiling. His foot collided into the worn leather with a dull thunk, puffing out a cloud of chalk.

"Commander," said a middle-aged man dressed in sleek clothes. "I urge you to denounce these rumors of you being the new daemon. A press release stating your innocence of the director's death would be only beneficial."

"No," said the Commander. "I will not even dignify such idiotic rumors with a response." He clenched his fists and struck at the punching bag. "I am the Hunter of the Syn'Crux. I am the daemon killer."

"Commander," repeated the well-groomed adviser. "The people are beginning to believe you are the new daemon. They are beginning to believe you faked your own deathwish to look innocent. That because you already possess the key, you need only the Obliv. And you tortured the director for it."

## CHAPTER 14

"Nonsense," Eli replied with unconcerned pride. "Only the weak minded would believe such drivel. I will not acknowledge these feeble rumors, these weak lies, these," he struck the leather bag with ferocious, disciplined force, "idiotic accusations." He stood back and snapped his fingers at the waiting soldier. "Do not worry, Advisor Larson, I will soon find this new daemon—and kill him."

The soldier marched to Exor, handed him his coat, and marched to the leather punching bag. In one quick motion the soldier unzipped the bag. An augmented left arm fell out, followed by a body.

"Another round?" Exor asked of the badly beaten and bruised man who had fallen out. "Or will you tell me who your new daemon is?"

The Syn'Crux man who lay in a heap, groaned. His augmented legs were fine, being made of metal, but his ribcage appeared so broken, it had sunk in.

Exor leaned down. "Save yourself the pain. Tell me, and I will let you die now."

The man, eyes swollen, looked up at Exor with a sneer and spat in his face.

Commander Exor picked up the man's detached metallic right arm. Then, he straightened up and looked at his advisor. "Who inspires such loyalty?"

Advisor Larson's face remained blank.

Exor tossed his black coat back to the waiting soldier. Then, he turned and considered the beaten Syn'Crux man. "Such loyalty—beyond the pain of death, must be rewarded." He gripped the man's detached metallic arm like a club. He looked down at him, and swung hard.

# WORLDS APART

# CHAPTER 15

# CHAPTER 15
## "LET'S-GET-DANGEROUS."

Mark stood, hands in jacket pockets and hood up against the mist of cold rain, waiting. The buzzing neon triangle across the street from the Black Pearl Bazaar turned off and on, and off and on, its reflection bright in the rain-slicked street. He looked up toward the sound of a skyboard getting closer.

Heath soon flew down. He stopped, flipped his skyboard up, and then went to lean it next to Mark's board that rested against the exterior brick wall.

"Where's Lexe?" Heath asked, shaking the rain off his coat and joining Mark under the Bazaar's short purple awning.

"Said she'll be here," Mark replied and greeted him with a fist bump.

The loud whine of a tricked out, two-door, bright yellow hovercar made them look up. Ripley's highly modded ride came zooming down from the nearby flyway. It landed so hard on the street in front of them that its flux field sent a wave of dirty street water all over the storefront and all over Mark and Heath too.

They stood, drenched and cold, in shock as the hovercar revved once, shut down with a loud sputter, and the driver's door opened.

"Got you gooooooood," said the obnoxious college guy who stepped out. Two of his friends got out too and joined him in a round of laughter. Then Lexe climbed out from the back seat.

# CHAPTER 15

"Hey, guys," she said, looking both embarrassed and angry.

"Don't go anywhere else!" The pumped-up jock shouted at her. "You hear? You stay right here until I get back." His nostrils flared as if to make a point. Then, he waved to the other two guys and they followed him down the street, making crude jokes.

Lexe watched them go before turning to Mark and Heath. "Sorry about that," she apologized, ashamed.

"Aahh," Mark replied, still wiping water from his eyes. "Don't worry about it. Karma gets people back for being gasbags."

"Who's Karma?" asked Lexe. Then, in a vehement tone, "and when's she going to destroy his car?"

Mark chuckled. "Soon, I hope, soon."

"Why didn't you board over?" asked Heath, shaking the water from his jacket.

"My mom took my skyboard away. She said I've been gaming too much."

"So your step-brother offered to drive?" was Heath's skeptical reply.

"No," she scoffed. "I told him there were bars around here that wouldn't look at the fake IDs him and his drinking buddies made. I hope they get caught and locked up with a crazy homeless guy named Burly Bob."

Her frustrated wish was so honest that Mark and Heath had to laugh.

"So why are we here?" she asked.

"Come on," Mark said and opened the door to the Black Pearl Bazaar.

The three of them were greeted by the familiar smell of desert sands from distant planets and strange, soft music from even further solar systems.

"Aaahhhhh!" said Perfidious Funk from behind his counter. "My favorite customers," he added with open hands raised out of large, billowing purple sleeves.

"Hi, Funk," said Mark as they greeted him.

# "LET'S-GET-DANGEROUS."

"Come to make me good deals?"

"Not today," Mark replied. "We need to look at the autopilot."

Heath and Lexe stared at Mark.

Funk's thick black eyebrows furrowed. "Behind the store. Left side."

"Thanks," said Mark, leading the way through the beaded curtain to the hallway.

"And you get that Syn'Crux autopilot out of here already!" Funk shouted as they left. "Bad for business!"

"What are you doing?" said Lexe.

"I was thinking, last night," said Mark as they went down hallways lined with storage doors on the right and crates on the left.

"That's never good," said Lexe.

"I was thinking about how much time and work we put into that flarejet—only for me to fail."

"You didn't fail," said Heath, trying to be comforting. "It's just the judges are unfair and Lance belongs up a donkey's—"

"I did fail, though," Mark interrupted, turning to look at them while walking. "I failed. . . ."

"But the awards ceremony is tomorrow," said Heath. "You missed the announcement today. The judges reached a decision about the Wargame winner. The admiral will announce it at tomorrow's ceremony. Maybe you won."

"Lance won. And you know it," Mark retorted. "Anyway, I talked to Stan, like you suggested. And then I took a walk."

They let Mark walk on in silence. He was deep in thought. Soon they stopped at the stores back door. Mark opened it and they stepped out. The cramped alley behind the Black Pearl Bazaar was dirty. The light evening rain did nothing to refresh the smell of old brick buildings and nearby dumpsters. A haggard raven flew away, cawing a warning to its kind.

## CHAPTER 15

"Over here," said Mark, going around a pile of stacked crates.

Heath and Lexe joined him. Sitting against the old brick building was the Syn'Crux autopilot they had rescued. Its neck, still partially severed, had green fluid congealed in stiff streams down its plastic chest.

"Whoa, check out these skyboards," said Lexe, admiring three long, powerful boards propped against the corner of the back wall a few steps away from the autopilot.

"Huh," said Heath. "The third one looks modded right out." He pointed to a black and red skyboard made of sweeping rough curves and three thin engines.

"These don't look like Funk's boards though," Lexe commented. "They look like they're someone else's."

"It is dead," said Mark from his crouch next to the autopilot. This snapped them out of admiration. He pulled a small metal box out of his pocket.

"You still have that Syn'Crux cube?" said Heath, surprised once more.

"Yes," said Mark, not meeting Heath's disapproving eyes. "It's Syn'Crux tech, just like this autopilot." Taking the cube out, he placed it in the palm of his right hand. He didn't wince as much this time. The jagged blue cube went unfolding into digitized blue and purple squares. A few drops of rain fell onto his glowing blue hand, freezing upon contact. He extended his hand towards the autopilot. A spark of charged electricity left his palm, racing into and through the Syn'Crux android.

"Hello, world," it said, lenslike eyes focusing and refocusing.

Mark looked between Heath and Lexe. "See?" His hand stayed on the pilots shoulder. Then, "The deathwish, why is it fake?"

"Retrieving," The pilot replied. "Error: 401. I am unauthorized to access."

Mark heard Heath's sigh. He pressed on. "Who is the Syn'Crux daemon?"

# "LET'S-GET-DANGEROUS."

"Retrieving," it replied. "Error: 403, forbidden."

Heath placed a hand on Mark's shoulder. "Come on. It's not going to happen."

"No." His eyes were intent on the broken android. A feeling of anger began welling up. The melted cube spoke of using that anger. After all, he was confused. He was frustrated. He was a failure out to prove himself right. Anger was justified. Wasn't it? "I'm going to force it out of him."

Dark arcs spun out from his right hand, lancing into the autopilots plastic body. Its eyes began snapping open and closed like camera shutters gone haywire. Flashes of blue lit up this dark corner of a back alley.

The pilot spoke. "Obliv location acquired. Swarm 9 prep for off-world transport at Spaceport Docking Bay Zero. Swarm 1 prep to guard. Exor en route with Obliv key tonight."

Mark's hand jerked back. Silence followed. The three of them were left stunned, not knowing quite how to react.

"This is proof. Right here," said Mark, feeling staggered by this revelation. "The fleet commander killed Ernest Shaw to find the Obliv. Now he knows where it is, and he's bringing his key to take it away—tonight."

Heath squared his chest and said, with great conviction, "We have to tell an adult."

Lexe stood up from her crouch and said, with just as much conviction, "We can't."

"Why?" he demanded.

"What are we going to tell them, huh? Hey look, we found this android lying around the Seven Site quarantine and hacked it and it told us a bunch of stuff. Oh by the way, it's the autopilot from the deathwish ship you're investigating, you know, the one you found months ago—missing its autopilot."

## CHAPTER 15

Heath paused with a blank stare, but then reaffirmed his trust. "No, they'll believe us."

"No," said Mark, slowly standing up. He looked from one worried face to the other. "We fight Eli Exor."

His words brought on a fresh wave of shock.

"Really?" said Lexe. "I mean—really?"

Heath tapped the side of his own head, saying, "He's off the nut."

"Yes. We get there before him," said Mark with serious conviction. "When he arrives at Docking Bay Zero, key in hand, ready to steal the Obliv—we shut him inside and we call the cops. Criminal with the evidence. Boom. Done."

Heath kept shaking his head through the whole thing. "That's stupid dangerous."

Lexe nodded. "That's crazy dangerous."

"Well then," Mark responded with a straight faced stare. "Let's—get—dangerous."

Nobody blinked an eye for half a minute. After that, they busted up laughing.

Lexe was still trying to control her laughing fit when she said, "you've been waiting to use that one, huh?"

Mark could only nod and wipe his eyes.

"But seriously," said Heath with fading chuckles.

Mark coughed the mirth away. "I am serious."

Heath's face dropped.

"Stan told me I was stubborn, like a goat," said Mark, facing them.

Lexe and Heath shrugged and murmured in agreement.

"So last night I decided to stop Exor from stealing the Obliv. Hopefully with you guys."

"What?" said Heath, shocked.

"Why?" said Lexe, equally surprised.

# "LET'S-GET-DANGEROUS."

"Because nobody else will. And because we can," said Mark, going back towards Funk's shop.

Lexe whispered to Heath, "You're right. His coconut is cracked."

Heath didn't hear her, jogging up to Mark instead. "No, Mark. We can't. These are Syn'Crux. If we die, we die. And that's the end. What I'm afraid of, is getting hurt. I don't want to get hurt."

Mark stopped and faced him. "Heath, if we all lived in fear of getting hurt, nobody would get up off their couch—ever."

For a minute, they stood silent, looking at each other and thinking. Were they really going to stop a Syn'Crux daemon as ruthless as Eli Exor?

"They're coming," interrupted the autopilot from where they left him.

Mark, Heath, and Lexe looked back at the sprawled out android. Its eyes were turned up, lost in the sky.

"They're coming to take me home," it said, robotic voice making those words all the creepier.

"Who is?" said Mark.

The android's eyes shut off. A strange wind began to howl. It began gusting down the side alleyways of the Black Pearl Bazaar. Then, a short, magnetized rushing noise reverberated down each alleyway.

"That sounded like something heavy landing really fast," Lexe whispered.

They slunk up the left alley. Leaning out the end, they saw a large gray hovercar made of straight angles inset with rectangular, dark tinted windows. It sat, waiting. Another rushing noise began. Looking up, they saw three similar hovercars roaring down from the nearby flyway in a rage of magnetic noise and electrical arcs.

"Syn'Crux?" asked Lexe.

"Who else?" said Heath, worried and angry. "We just broke into their android using their technology."

## CHAPTER 15

"Let's go," said Mark, ripping the cube off his right hand and slamming it back into the metal box in his pocket.

"But my board—and yours—is out there next to them," said Heath. "And so is Lexe's brother's car."

"And so are four Syn'Crux cars with twice that many tongue-ripping murderers inside," Mark replied, turning back down the alleyway.

Heath and Lexe followed him. He stopped by the three skyboards leaning against the corner. "We're borrowing these boards."

"They're not ours," said Lexe as Mark locked his feet into the black and red board, and Heath took the sleek, expensive one.

"We'll return them either way," Mark reassured her. "But right now—"

He was cut off by the back door flying off its hinges.

"We're out!" He dropped the third board at Lexe's feet. It started with a dark green glow and she jumped on. The three of them raced up into the sky.

"They're following us!" said Heath.

Mark and Lexe stole a glance. Four bulldozer-sized hovercars were rumbling and rising from the street, giving off heavy electrical arcs. They rose into the sky and accelerated at them.

"Move!" said Mark and leaned forward. But he wasn't used to this new board. It had power, an insane amount of power. The dark, serrated skyboard blitzed forward. "Holy flying garbage monkeys!" he yelped with arms flailing like windmills, his body pushed back as if someone had shoved him.

"Wait for us!" Heath shouted angrily after him. They had to lean forward all the way just to not fall behind. Speeding after Mark, who was crouching and gripping onto the red board with both hands, they went careening towards the local hovercar flyway: five full lanes, all stacked on top of each other, each going in opposite directions.

## "LET'S—GET—DANGEROUS."

Mark, unable to control his flight, sped straight into the lowest lane. Car horns, rushing winds, and curses accosted the boy. Lexe and Heath followed him in, deftly maneuvering between cars. Further back the four gray hovercars slam on their brakes, skidding stop from colliding into traffic.

Mark's board jetted him out the other side. The calm night air enveloped him again. He looked back. Their hunters had flown down below everything. Hurtling upwards, they resumed pursuit.

"We need to lose them," he whispered to himself, trying to stand on the twisting skyboard. "We need to get back to all that noise."

"What's he doing?" shouted Heath, watching Mark speeding towards the lowest lane at a steep angle.

"Don't know," Lexe replied, kicking forward and zooming after him, "but it looks fun!"

Mark's eyes wanted to shut tight as he headed for the transparent flyway street. He could see the blurred sides of dozens of speeding cars. He pressed on through the dizzying spell of noise. A rush of static electricity made him shiver as his body burst through the first floating street. Car horns began to blare. The second street above felt the same. But after cutting through the third street level, he decided to fly along with traffic. Looking back, he saw Lexe following in absolute glee. Heath darted his skyboard between cars in a clearly terrified way.

"Get outta traffic, you little snot!" yelled a bald man leaning out his car window.

Mark didn't hear him, too focused on trying not to end up a bug on some trucker's windshield. He looked back.

The four pursuing hovercars had dived in after them. The first one had plowed through the lowest level, crashing into a truck. The second one had dodged around the cars and raced up to Mark's level. The remaining two were flying outside traffic on the sides of the lane, boxing them in.

## CHAPTER 15

Mark weaved in and out of cars, clipping mirrors and getting honked and yelled at. His feet were adjusted to the board, but not fast enough to avoid scraping paint off large vans and bouncing off the roofs of smaller sports coupes. Lexe and Heath were also bouncing around traffic, the only difference being Lexe cussed right back at people and Heath profusely apologized.

Mark caught site of something in the distance. An idea sparked to life. "Hello, tunnel," he said and grinned. All five lanes were leading straight into a vertical rectangle of a tunnel. The tunnel cut through a skyscraper, and Mark planned to go right in.

"I'm not going in there!" Heath screamed as he saw Mark point to the vertical tunnel ahead.

Lexe didn't hear the sandy-haired boy's terrified voice or see the panic in his olive-colored eyes. She was too busy telling an angry fat man driving a convertible to take his fake wig off and eat it with garlic.

The three of them went racing through the multicolored tunnel. Mark remained in the lead. Behind them, the two gray hovercars on the outside were forced to squeeze into traffic. Now there were three bulldozers chasing them in the tunnel. This was good.

The tunnel would soon end. Mark could see more neon skyscrapers ahead, just outside. The flyway went weaving on into them. But he planned to exit far sooner and leave those bulldozers behind.

"Hey guys," he shouted back towards Heath and Lexe. "On my signal, we dive down to the first level!"

"Why?" said Heath, even more panicked about diving through traffic while in a tunnel.

Mark's eyes snapped forward. The exit loomed. "NOW!" he yelled.

All three skyboards dove in unison through the third level, then the second, and burst out the bottom of the first lane just as the tunnel ended.

# "LET'S—GET—DANGEROUS."

Two of the Syn'Crux hovercars, trying to chase down after them, crashed. One of them slammed into a semitruck, bounced off, and went skidding across the sidewall. The second smashed into the bottom of the tunnel, exploding and scattering glass and plastic out the tunnel exit in a rain of flaming metal pieces. This caused an instantaneous pile-up on two of the five flyway lanes, causing the third gray hovercar to be locked in traffic.

The three daredevils stood on their skyboards, floating hundreds of feet in the air, looking up at the chaos in the tunnel.

"Whoa," said Heath, watching the explosive spectacle.

"Beautiful," Lexe added.

"They miscalculated a bit, huh?" said Mark, then twisted his board around and pointed down and to the right at the spaceport below. "And guess where we ended up?"

Heath's eyes widened at the comet-shaped spaceport they happened to be so close to. Then his eyes narrowed at Mark. "You planned this, didn't you?"

"I've got an idea," said Mark. "And I remember it being parked in hangar forty-two." He looked towards Lexe. "Lead the way?"

"Sure." Pulling out her Lemonsquare, she found the hangar in question, then darted downwards.

Mark tilted forward, following her to Crescent City Spaceport. So did Heath, who started to say something but stopped and followed out of curiosity.

"You know," said Mark as they glided down, a small smirk highlighting his thoughts, "I feel a bit of hero right now."

"How's that?" said Heath. "Because you're breaking and entering to do something the police should be doing?"

Mark shrugged and grinned. "Maybe."

## CHAPTER 15

Lexe led them to Hangar 42. The overwhelming thunder of spaceships blasting off made them cover their ears. They stopped by the half-barrel structure, kicked off their boards, held them under their arms, and walked in through a side door.

All the noise faded to a distant rumble, which they could still feel beneath their feet, when they stepped inside. The air smelled of clean metal.

Mark walked up to the spacefighter Lieutenant Landeth had brought him in. The rigid angles and beastly nature of the machine made him smile. He reached up to place a hand on the nose.

"When I first saw this baby, it looked like a boring old tractor," Mark began. "Then with the flick of some switch, boom, it became this beast."

"It has a UBF-generator?" said Lexe. "Sweet."

"Very," said Mark. "That's how we're going to get past everyone. Syn'Crux, guards, and door-mice alike. Lexe, can you find it and remove it?"

"Easy," she said, walking over to the starfighter with her eyes focused and searching.

"Even if we get past everyone," said Heath. "We don't know where Docking Bay Zero is."

"Your dad does deliveries to the Spaceport, right?" Mark asked.

"Yes. Oh, I get it. I'll use his access codes to get the Spaceport maps."

"Even better!" said Mark. "I was going to suggest—hmmm—anyway, your idea is less illegal."

A metallic wrenching noise followed by a pop and a fizz came from the back of the starfighter. Lexe walked around the side, triumphantly holding up a book-sized box.

She brought it over and handed it to Mark. They huddled close. She pressed a combination of four different buttons. A bubble formed around the generator box. It expanded to envelope all three of them. Then it misted away.

"LET'S-GET-DANGEROUS."

"Is it working?" Heath asked.

"Don't know," Mark replied. "Here, let's scoot over to those chrome sheets of metal."

"Wha hahaha!" Lexe chortled. "Heath! You look like a boring book writer! And Mark, you're a short, fat, spaceport security guard! Holding a sub sandwich instead of the UBF box!"

Heath was laughing too. "Said the girl who looks like a stuffy, old art critic lady!"

The three of them stood, laughing and pointing out how boring they each appeared.

"Allright, let's get crackin'," said Mark. "And if anyone stops us, just say that I'm the security guard who is escorting you two crazies to your private jet or something."

Heath led them to the large hangar bay doors. After Mark helped him open them, Heath pointed to the center of the spaceport. In the middle of the launch and landing area was a squat, single-story hexagon shaped building. Surrounded by glass, it looked like one of those towers at an airport, only very short. "Maps are in that control tower. I'll use my dad's access codes when we're in."

The three of them stayed in a huddle, rushing across the spaceport tarmac looking like three very random, very boring people. Starships were blasting off and landing on each side of them. The air, thick with spent rocket fuel, made them choke as they ran on ground that constantly shook.

Mark was the first to burst in through the door. Heath and Lexe followed but almost ran into him, since he'd skidded to a halt. They soon knew the reason why.

The door at the opposite end of the room swung closed. Three other people had come inside. They were intimidating by appearance, unapproachable and menacing. The tall woman at the front had a blue

## CHAPTER 15

Mohawk and tattoos of artistically inked exotic animals down her arms. Her tattoos moved and crawled beneath her skin. To her right stood a short, gruff, burly man from a motorcycle gang. His beard grew out long and knotted and had the color of fire. To the woman's left stood another intimidating woman; she wore modern business clothes that spoke of prestige, sophistication, and power.

"Hello," said the short, fat mall cop who was Mark.

"Good afternoon," said the tattooed woman whose sharp blue eyes pierced.

The mall cop cleared his throat, which made his stomach jiggle. "Well, don't mind us! We're just here for normal reasons — to do normal stuff."

"Yes," she replied with a chilled demeanor, "as are we."

She made the mall cop feel insecure and a little frightened. His eyes couldn't hold her steady gaze. He brushed imaginary crumbs off his big belly and turned to the boring book writer. "Well, Humphries, we need those — erm — direction providers."

"I concur, Bob," the author in sweatpants said. He walked over to the central control panel.

But at the same time, so did the burly biker. The two stood by the controls and stared at each other with perplexed expressions. Then they each turned back to their leaders with silent pleas for help.

"Excuse us," said the beautifully intense woman to the mall cop, "we have business here. Wait until we finish."

The mall cop furrowed his bushy black eyebrows at her. "We do too, lady. Deadlines and all that," he said while waving his sub sandwich around.

"You can wait. We cannot. Tell your friend to back off," she said and took a menacing step closer.

"I would if I could, lady, but I can't. Tell your bearded biker to step aside so we can do our thing." He too stepped closer.

# "LET'S—GET—DANGEROUS."

The two adults stared at each other, unyielding stubbornness in their eyes.

"Don't be childish," she said, crossing her tattooed arms so that the inked creatures slithered. "Our matters are urgent."

The portly fellow folded his arms, crushing his sandwich. "So are ours!"

"You're trying my patience. We were here first."

"No! We were here first!"

"I remember setting foot before the door opened for you."

"That's funny, lady, because I remember the same—except opposite!"

"How dare you call me a liar!"

"How dare you—dare!"

"What an unimaginative thing to say."

"Yeah? Well you're a crazy weird person!"

"Heh. Am I supposed to be insulted? I've never been so bored!"

"And I've never been so badgered by such a freakish pain in—"

"Hey, Bob?" interrupted the balding book writer at the same time as the biker turned to the woman and said, "Eleanor?"

"Yes what is it?" said Bob and Eleanor, rounding on their friends.

"We found what we needed," said the biker to the woman.

"I've got the maps," said the author to the short, fat man.

The two bickering adults stared at their friends with blank looks. Then, instantly went back to staring at each other, hard. Daggers could have flown from their stubborn eyes.

The burly man placed a gentle hand on Eleanor's arm and led her away while the boring author led Bob aside.

"Dude," whispered Lexe from her art critic disguise, "what's wrong with you?"

The boy disguised as Bob glared after the tattooed woman. "She makes my toe's curl up into fists."

## CHAPTER 15

"Well cork it," said Heath disguised as Humphries, "Docking Bay Zero is down through that elevator." He pointed at the elevator door on the left wall.

"Let's go," said Bob.

The three of them walked over to the steel door and stopped, surprised. Those three intimidating-looking people had walked over and stopped by the door too!

Bob and Eleanor opened their mouths to hurl more insults. Fortunately, their friends held them back with fast whispers of caution.

A ding and the door opened. All six adults crowded in. Nobody said anything. They all tried to get as much personal space as possible. Bob and Eleanor stood with such stiff, straight backs that anyone would think they were fence posts. The elevator music sounded cheery, upbeat, and sickeningly bubbly.

A second ding and the doors opened onto a security checkpoint at a lower floor. All six adults rushed out. They got into their two groups and conferred about where they needed to go next. Then, after a brief moment, they all walked over to another door. It buzzed and said, in a digital male voice, "Please enter password and complete passpuzzle."

The tattooed woman turned and began whispering to her group.

Bob turned to his group too. He whispered to the art critic in old-fashioned glasses. "Lexe, can you get through either of those?"

"My name's Liz now, I've decided," she said with a critical tone and fling of her hair.

"Liz, can you?"

She adjusted her horn-rimmed glasses and searched the room. Her eyes landed on a box of powdered white doughnuts perched on the empty security guards desk. "Yes. I can hack the passpuzzle on the door."

"OK, make it fast. I can't stand being in the same room as that infernal woman."

# "LET'S—GET—DANGEROUS."

The art critic went over to the door, which had a glass display that lit up in myriads of dots.

Bob looked over at the tall, tattooed woman who made him feel light-headed and dizzy. She stood with her two friends by the guard's computer. He felt like saying something provoking.

"What are y'all doing by the guard's computer? Hacking it?"

Eleanor whipped around and glared at him. Then said in a mocking voice, "What are you doing by that security door? Trying to break it down with your big fat butt?"

His cheeks colored red. "You're more suspicious looking!"

"I beg your pardon?" she said and straightened up.

"You heard," he said and stepped forward. "And we were here first!"

"You wouldn't be first anywhere but the ice-cream truck."

"Well you're a freak!"

"And you're a boring, talentless, unskilled laborer!"

Meanwhile, in the corner of the room that wasn't a raging temper-tantrum, the art critic and the author were trying to figure out the passpuzzle to the security door. Dozens of glowing dots covered the glass door in neat rows and columns. It wouldn't open until the dots were connected in the right pattern.

"Here are the powdered doughnuts you wanted," said Humphries, handing the box over to Liz.

"Thanks. Now just stand here and block their view," said Liz and took out a white powdered doughnut. "Check this out," she said and lifted the pastry to her pursed lips. Aiming at the glass door, she blew. A fine mist of powdered sugar puffed off like talcum powder. "Watch it settle on the grease spots."

Sure enough, the fine powder settled like a mist on the glass. But it only stuck where the glass was greasy.

# CHAPTER 15

"See? Every time the guard swipes his finger across the glass and connects the right pattern of dots, he leaves a fatty streak. The start is where it's greasy the most."

"That's the passpuzzle!" said Humphries.

"Right. Now go get our fearless leader before he starts throwing toys and crying."

The balding man rushed over to the squat, red-faced mall cop, who seemed happily engaged in the most frivolous of arguments.

"Lady, I tell you right here, surfing a cresting wave is the best thing on Earth!"

"False! Snowboarding the powdered slopes of a mountain is the best!"

"Umm, Bob," the author said, trying to interrupt.

"Woman," continued Bob without a pause. "Quit being a right pain and admit that surfing is the best."

"Better idea," said the challenge-seeking woman, "You quit acting the goat and admit that snowboarding is the wildest."

"Surfing!"

"Snowboarding!"

"Eleanor," said the burly biker, trying to interrupt her.

Eleanor and Bob looked at their associates, then back to each other. They both harrumphed at each other and walked away with their friends.

"Have fun throwing a fit over there?" asked Liz.

Bob sighed and shook his head, confused about the feelings his gut was giving.

"I've solved it," she continued. "So let's go." She swiped a finger in the greasy pattern.

"Access granted," responded the digital male voice, and the door slid open.

# "LET'S-GET-DANGEROUS."

"Huh, I guess we didn't need the password," Humphries commented.

The door had opened onto a small square chamber with two elevators, one on the left and one on the right.

"Which one do we take?" asked Bob.

"Uuuuhhh," Humphries replied, uncertain.

The three intimidating-looking people walked into the chamber behind them. For a brief moment nobody did or said anything. Then, at the same instant, both groups walked to opposite elevators. They politely ignored each other until the elevator bell rang and the door opened. Each group stepped in to their own elevator.

"Bye, freak!" said Bob to the lady in the other elevator.

"Ta-ta, ya creep!" she responded.

"No," said Humphries, pulling Bob's arm down before he made a very rude hand gesture.

"Where do you think they were going?" Liz asked.

Humphries shrugged. "Don't know. There's dozens of floors from here to where we're going."

"Where's that?"

"The lowest level. That's where Docking Bay Zero is."

Those few words reminded each of them why they were here. Nobody knew what lay ahead. They each stood in silence as the elevator descended. The cheery elevator music droned on.

"Do you think we'll really beat Eli Exor to the Obliv?" Liz wondered out loud. "Or have to fight him in a dangerous, all out, bleeding confrontation?"

"Either way," said Bob, "We will win! Soon as that traitorous fleet commander walks in through the doors—we lock the place down, call the cops, they arrest him, and we bask in the triumph of being heroes!"

"With healthy rewards, I'd imagine," said Humphries.

## CHAPTER 15

The three young would-be heroes looked off into the distance, imagining away. The elevator sunk ever lower, playing that positively tooth-aching happy music.

Liz's smile sunk first. She had been thinking about dangerous things when she'd realized something. "Strange, don't you think?" She said to them while staring into her disturbed thoughts, "that we haven't seen any guards?"

Humphries smile fell. "True. There were none at the control tower."

"Or at that last security checkpoint," said Mark, his smile being the last to fade.

These ominous words hung in the elevator as they continued their descent. Nobody said anything until they reached bottom. The door opened with a pleasant ding!

They stepped out of the cheery elevator and into a hauntingly empty tunnel. It led away in opposite directions to their right and to their left, curving in a long arc of bare concrete and harsh florescent light. None of them said anything. Their eyes roved around, trying to understand where they were. Harsh vapors hung in the air, burning their noses. The walls were streaked with black burns.

Leaving them to their perplexed shock, the elevator's optimistic tunes faded as the door shut. A dull whir and the elevator began climbing away. Where were all the security guards?

"LET'S-GET-DANGEROUS."

CHAPTER 16

# CHAPTER 16
## THE OBLIV

"All right, I'm taking this thing off," said the mall cop. He pressed a button on the sandwich. The uber-boring field surrounding them evaporated. All three adults disappeared, replaced by three kids.

"Left or right?" said Mark, covering up his nervousness with determination.

"Doesn't matter," said Heath. "Both tunnels lead to Docking Bay Zero."

"Right then," he said and marched down the fluorescent lit curve.

Heath and Lexe looked all around, then at each other, following after sharing a frown.

This far below the spaceport and nothing could be heard of the ships taking off or landing above. No roar of engines or smell of spent rocket fuel; no blinding bursts of light or signs of life. Occasionally the sloped tunnel walls would rumble and concrete dust would fall from the ceiling; that's what made the gritting and grinding noise underneath their feet. At least the lights didn't flicker.

Mark arrived at a security booth. It stood empty on the right side of the tunnel wall. He opened the door and walked in. On his left were two large windows that looked onto the tunnel. On his right stood a wall lined with empty gun racks. During a normal day, someone would walk up to the windows, check in, and continue down the tunnel. But this was no normal day.

## CHAPTER 16

One of the two office chairs had been knocked over. One monitor showed the well-lit tunnel behind them, the other three screens showed a dark tunnel ahead. One window was clear and intact, the other was broken to pieces. Someone had left the microphone on, and it buzzed on and off, and on and off again, filling the empty room with echoes of static.

"Guns were used here," said Heath, touching several scorch stains on the wall. "In self-defense, it looks like."

"The guards trusted whoever did this," said Lexe, tracing her fingers over a panel on one of the desks. "Nobody pressed this lockdown button."

"It has to be Exor," said Mark, with mounting conviction. "Turn your flashlight on, Lexe, and come on." He marched out the second door and into darkness.

Lexe took out her Lemonsquare, turned on the small orb of light, and jogged after him.

Heath joined them. "You know this means Exor's already here?"

"Yes," said Mark, not stopping his march down the curved dark tunnel.

"What if he tries to kill us?"

Mark, still striding forward, reached into his pocket. The soft white glow from Lexe's Lemonsquare illuminating that familiar dented metal box.

Heath slowed down. "That's a bad idea."

"No—it isn't," said Mark. A cold rage burned in his eyes. His heart wanted to use power, immeasurable power. "I will use it for good. Use it against evil. Give them a taste of their own pain."

"Look," said Lexe, trying to change the subject. She pointed to a glowing red Docking Bay Zero sign just ahead. It floated above the outline of a door.

They quickened their steps but hadn't gone far when Lexe stopped with a sudden jerk. Her light pointed at the floor. All three pairs of feet became rooted in place.

"What's thahhh…" Lexe trailed off, voice trembling. "What's that red streak on the floor?"

The three kids stood still. None of them took their eyes from the shimmering red stain. The darkness seemed to be eating at the weak little light beam. The air felt as if had begun to move, and choke itself down their throats.

A single metallic whir broke the silence. Lexe jerked her light upwards. A hard plastic pair of backwards bent legs; a glossy plastic and metal chest; long, thin, powerful hydraulic arms; and a flat featureless face with seven haphazard holes for eyes and no mouth. It had been watching them.

Krreeeeeeeeeevvvvvvv!

Its earsplitting robotic scream drowned out their screams.

They ran. Screeches began chasing them through the dark. The droids hands and feet tore into concrete walls and floors in its hunger for them.

Lexe's light was a treacherous thing. Swinging her arms as she ran, the light would blind them on the upswing and plunge them into darkness on the downswing. The droid, lopping after them like an animal, appeared in flashes.

Their hearts were pounding, bursting; their sides were stitching, cramping. There, just ahead, stood the security room. Refuge and hope waited.

Lexe dived in first. Mark followed.

"Aaaaahhhhh!" Heath screamed as the droids metal claws ripped into his shoulder. Steps away from safety, he crumpled to the floor, a long bleeding gash across his right shoulder.

Mark rushed over, pulling him in. Lexe bolted to the controls and punched the lockdown button. Heavy steel shutters fell, covering both doors and the broken window. The steel shutter over the second window closed only halfway, jamming in place. A second later, the seven-eyed

## CHAPTER 16

droid slammed into the door. It screamed in frustration, ripping at the metal shutters.

"Help me with Heath!" Mark shouted, taking off his sweater.

They quickly tied the sweater around the boys bleeding shoulder. When they finished they both took him by the arms and sat him in a chair.

"Keep pressure on it," Lexe said to Heath.

The sound of metal scraping against glass made them all wince and turn around.

"Why didn't the shutter close over the second window?" Mark shouted, watching the metal skeleton run another finger down the glass.

"I don't know," said Lexe as she punched the lockdown button over and over again.

The droid backed up. It came rushing at the pane of glass.

"Holy shi— " Mark exclaimed, flinching backwards as the droid slammed it's whole body into the window. The glass shook.

They watched the steel-framed creature slam into the window two more times. It screamed in frustration. After that it took a few steps back. Its seven beady eyes darted, looking at the strong glass window as if it were—thinking.

Lexe, backed up against the wall, whispered, "it looks like one of those Lurks from the Seven Site."

"Yeah," Mark replied, "but not broken or rusted."

"No, just demented," she scoffed, eyes locked on the droid in apprehensive fright.

"Doesn't look like it's getting in."

"I think it knows it too."

They watched as the tall droid turned and disappeared into the shadowed tunnel, its feet scraping against the concrete floor. The darkness soon enveloped its hard plastic and metal body.

"Damn it," said Heath, angry from the pain. "I told you, I told you both this was a stupid idea!"

Nobody said anything. They watched the darkness.

"It's gone," said Lexe. "It's gone and we need to get gone."

"No," said Mark. "We press on."

"I'm going to slap you," said Heath, huffing from the pain. "I am going to walk over to you, and I am going to slap you."

"Docking Bay Zero is just down the hall," Mark pressed. "We'll lock the metal doors and be safer there."

"Safer?" Heath winced as he stood. "Did you NOT see the streak of blood? Someone died on the way there! Probably one of the guards!"

The grating sound of metallic feet slowly scraping the cold concrete floor interrupted their argument.

"It's back," said Lexe.

Mark squinted. "What the hell is it dragging?"

They leaned forward to look out the solid glass window and into the dim tunnel.

"It's something heavy," said Lexe.

They watched the seven-eyed droid. It walked forward at a slow but steady pace. Its left hand wrapped around an ankle.

"It's dragging a security guards dead body," Heath whispered.

Shocked, they stood still, staring at the gruesome spectacle. Harsh florescent light glinted off the steel framed droid as the darkness parted for it and its previous prey. The white concrete floor made for a disturbing contrast to the shimmering crimson streak left by the guard's large, muscular body.

Lexe voiced the only question on all their minds, "Why?"

The droid stopped in front of the shutterless glass window. It reversed its grip on the dead guard's leg. It aimed. In one fluid motion, it swung the whole carcass over its shoulder.

## CHAPTER 16

Thunk.

The corpse hit. The room shook. And the guard's body slid down with a stomach-turning squeak, leaving a smear.

"I'm going to be sick," said Lexe.

Heath averted his eyes and didn't say anything.

The seven-eyed droid, having trouble with its grip on the dead man's ankle, wrapped its other hand higher up the leg. Turning sideways, it swung the body again.

Thunk.

The glass quivered. The smear lengthened. The body thumped on the floor.

Marks face screwed up in disgust. "It's using the guy like a club."

Once more the droid adjusted its grip. Once more the corpse hit. Once more the body squeaked down the trembling glass. This time a small crack spidered around the point of impact.

"Guys," said Heath, refusing to look at the window. "Guys, we need to get out of here."

Thunk.

The droid aimed the dead man against the smooth glass again, cracking it again, bleeding onto it again.

"I'm getting sick of this," said Mark, rage boiling in his eyes. His hand dove for the metal box in his pocket. But it wasn't there. "It's gone!" he shouted, frantically digging around in his other pockets.

Thunk.

"It fell in the hall," said Mark. "Lexe, give me your Lemonsquare and open that door."

"Don't be a dumbass," is all she said.

Thunk.

"Exor must be controlling this droid. I'm going to stop him," said Mark, anger burning in his eyes.

"Still sound like a dumbass."

"Open the door," he said and grabbed her Lemonsquare off the desk. Thunk.

"Don't do this," said Heath, gripping Marks arm.

"It'll rip us apart," he replied, darting a glance at the cracking glass. "Go!" he shouted to Lexe.

She opened the shuttered doors. Mark ducked out. She closed the shutters.

Heath held his bleeding shoulder as they watched their friend run as fast as his feet would take him.

Mark heard the thud of the dead body being dropped. He heard the droid give chase. Running straight into the darkness, he held the Lemonsquare and its glowing orb low to the floor without glancing back. Those robotic screams began following him. He could hear metal feet dashing against concrete floor. A surge of energy made his feet fly as he imagined being used as a meat club against his friends.

He saw the dented little box on the floor. Scooping it up, he ran on. The screams and scraps and scratches were on his neck. The glowing red Docking Bay Zero sign flashed just ahead, appearing above the outline of a door.

"Yes!" he yelled, slamming into the door. It burst open. He rolled into Docking Bay Zero, shot back up, and smashed the door shut. Then he punched the red button on the nearby panel. The little screen buzzed red and flashed the word Locked. He heard the heavy thud of the droid slide into the door.

"That's right! Who's the chump now?" he shouted at the door again, kicking it. Then he realized there were two other people watching him. He made a slow turn. Eli Exor stood in the center. A hazel-haired girl stood by a door that clicked shut.

## CHAPTER 16

Eli Exor, tall and gaunt in face stood in his black military jacket, shocked to see Mark and this girl.

The thirteen-year-old girl with shoulder-length hazel hair—who looked like she had run in from a different door at the exact same time as Mark—stood looking at the boy from Earth, mirroring his own surprise.

"What are you kids doing here?" Eli Exor said, deeply alarmed and angry. He had turned away from the control panel encircling the Obliv. The Obliv appeared to be a large dark sphere sitting in the center of the cavernous, shadow-steeped docking bay.

Mark heard nothing. Instead, he gawked at the girl.

"Hi," said the girl.

"Hey," said Mark.

The Fleet Commander's brow furrowed.

"My name's Mark," said Mark, walking over with an extended, sweaty hand.

"Mine's Ella," said Ella, meeting him halfway for an awkward handshake.

"Children!" said Exor. "It's not safe for you here!" He stood, impatient and annoyed, left hand gripping the spherical Obliv key.

During the clammy handshake, Mark bravely looked at Ella. The shadows filling the corners of the poorly lit docking bay cast everything and everyone in a dull light. But he still noticed her eyes. They were a dazzling blue-green. They made him think of those rare moments surfing under the crest of a huge wave; he'd look up, the ocean curling above him, and see sunlight dancing through the water, just before he wiped out. Suddenly his heart wanted to mash his face right into hers. His eyes darted down and away.

"Hey!" Exor shouted. "Get out of here before you get hurt!"

Ella thumbed towards the man. "Are you here to stop this grassbag?"

"Yeah," said Mark with a curt nod.

"Me too," said Ella with conviction.

"Remove yourselves before I remove you by force," growled Exor. "That's an order."

"You're not taking the Obliv!" said Mark, whirling to face him and sticking out his chest so Ella would notice how brave he was.

"And stop that stupid droid from hurting my friends!" said Ella.

Mark turned to her. "Your friends are being attacked by a droid too?"

"Yeah," she nodded. "Seven eyes, super creepy. It killed a guard to get to us to split."

"Listen, you little fools," the man continued. "I am taking the Obliv and I am killing the daemon." Then he showed his teeth in a snarl of a smile. "If you'd like to wait and watch, please do—but stay out of my way!"

Ella rounded on him. "You're the Syn'Crux daemon! You killed Ernest Shaw for the location," said Ella. "I found the evidence in one of your Syn'Crux labs."

"I also found evidence," added Mark. "The autopilot revealed it. The one you ordered to crash into your starliner and then suicide itself into the Seven Site."

Exor's pale eyes boiled with indignation. "Such insolent mouths on the pair of you! I am Fleet Commander Eli Exor. I am the hunter of Syn'Crux. I am the daemon killer."

The kids couldn't keep staring at his burning eyes. They darted glances at the large sphere behind him.

The Obliv took up the whole center of the docking bay. A menacing sight, devouring light into all those sharp red and blue fissures that covered its dull black metal surface. In the gloom of Docking Bay Zero, it appeared ancient and of dark purpose.

Mark and Ella exchanged a confused look. Eli's tone may have been harsh, but it seemed genuine.

## CHAPTER 16

"Why are you trying to take the Obliv, then?" said Mark.

"And who's the daemon you're fighting?" Ella added.

The fleet commander placed the Obliv key on the control panel. He took off his black jacket and folded it, setting it by the key. Rolling up his sleeves, he began approaching them. "I don't need to explain myself to anyone, let alone children." He took a coal black stone from his pocket. It began glowing a menacing purple in his right hand. "Children don't know any better. Children don't see the gray areas. Children shouldn't be here."

Mark felt a sudden jolt of panic as Eli advanced on them. His throat went dry and he backed away along with Ella. But where to? Should they fight? Would they win? Would they even survive?

A light, clear woman's voice broke the rising panic. "You'd go this far, then?"

Eli whirled to face the shadows behind him.

From wisps of darkness, a person emerged. She walked in silence. She moved with purpose, comfortable in each step.

She wore authority. It suited her well. Sharp black hair framed her persuasive face. She could have been a beautiful, powerful woman—yet she was something more. A jagged network of digitized lines radiated out across the skin of her high right cheekbone. These thin, angular lines slanted away from her right eye, like a tattoo, though deeper and real. The woman who would inspire loyalty until death had arrived.

"Kine," growled Exor. "Nona Kine—"

"Eli," she said with a touch of a smile.

THE OBLIV

# CHAPTER 17

# CHAPTER 17
## MISTAKES

Nona Kine had a beautiful smile that she used often enough, though never in warmth, above which were two eyes unlike any. Both were a heavenly blue, and both were broken. Each pupil, each center, appeared cracked. Veins of darkness seeped from her pupils into her surrounding sky-blue irises. She continued her ominous approach.

Commander Exor snarled and attacked her. His feet slid across the smooth concrete into a firm stance. His right arm swung wide, the black stone in his fist radiating. A charge of dark purple energy surged from his fist. It hissed through the air, blasting towards the woman.

Nona crossed her arms in front of her face. The torrent broke like a wave and washed around her. As the arcs of energy dissipated, everyone saw her standing, feet apart and beautifully wicked eyes narrowed in malice and forethought. The skin of her forearms had several thin cuts, trickling blood from Exor's attack.

"Mistakes, Eli," said Nona, uncrossing her bleeding forearms. "You keep making them."

He pivoted his feet and swung his fist to throw another bolt of energy at her.

She dashed it to the ground. "In your mad desire to be a hero—you've forgotten that you're only human."

He scowled and swung his fist towards the ground in front of her as if throwing a hammer. A river of purple fire charged at her.

## CHAPTER 17

She flicked her fingers, tearing it apart.

"And the fact that you stole your powers from us," she continued, the room darkening. "And the fact that my Syn'Crux powers are woven into my blood," Jagged black triangles multiplied across the woman's whole left arm and sharp purple squares digitized her whole right arm. "Should accelerate your survival instincts into understanding how human you really are."

"You will die as your predecessors died," growled Fleet Commander Exor, rays of dark purple light radiating from between the fingers of his clenched fist. "By my hand!" He balled his fists and thrust them forward, yelling loud enough to match the roar of the inferno he had created and cast at the woman.

Mark had seen this cataclysmic attack before. Eli had used it to incinerate the gray man, the previous daemon. Now, the same blistering tidal wave of rolling lightning burned the ground towards Nona. It electrified the very air with the smell of acid and sounds of fire.

"No." Her broken blue eyes snapped onto the charging inferno. She raised her digitized hand.

Mark winced and cupped his ears as a shrill sound began to rise. The river of lightning slowed. It crawled through the air, shrieking as it froze just a few inches away from the woman. Silence.

Tense moments passed as Mark and Ella watched the collision of power. They could see fury in Exor's gritted teeth and his hatred for Nona in the swollen veins of his straining arms. More than this, they could see Exor's arrogance faltering, his pride trickling away in each bead of sweat that ran past his snarling mouth to drip onto the gray concrete. His heavy breathing echoed in the silent cavern.

In this brief moment of peace, Nona considered the frozen lightning. It pulsed with energy, still alive. She sneered, locked her gaze on Eli's disbelieving eyes, and clenched her digitized hand into a fist. Detonation.

Before Mark could shut his eyes, burning light blinded him. A wave of heat singed his hair. The blast of lightning being shattered apart punched his chest, rocketing his body backwards.

Mark and Ella, coughing from the pain of breathing the heated air, tried to stand up.

Nona opened her fist. A storm of black, gold-edged triangles rushed forward. It slammed into the fleet commander, cutting through his white shirt and burning his skin. She then raised her open palm. Exor, yelling in rage and pain, began rising off the floor in a whirlwind of broken black triangles.

Mark and Ella, paralyzed from shock and confusion, could only watch. They saw the man who had threatened their lives be raised off the floor, screaming from the force of his spine arching backwards at a painful angle, arms being pulled from their sockets, ribcage bulging against his tattered white shirt. Mark gulped and Ella squirmed as Nona Kine lifted Eli Exor higher and higher in the storm of jagged glass.

Mark's mind swam in a queasy kind of fear. He gripped the pitted metal box in his pocket. It felt cold from the cube's power. Could he help Eli? He tried swallowing to ease the nervous tension. Did he want to?

"Stop it!" Ella shouted.

Mark glanced at her. Her cheeks were red and a frightened anger filled her eyes.

Nona looked at them. She sighed. A twist of her left hand and Exor was left floating high off the floor in a slowly rotating, spherical prison.

"You know," said the woman as she turned to them. Her black and purple digitized arms returned to a normal skin tone. "I didn't expect kids to be here." She began a slow, purposeful stride towards them. "I guess that's my mistake." Reaching into a pocket, she withdrew a little black leather book. "So the question becomes," She opened the book. "How do I learn from my mistake?"

# CHAPTER 17

They felt numb, watching the striking woman stop in front of them, take a yellow number two pencil from behind her ear, and begin writing in the crisp white pages of her small black book. The pencil ended three fourths of the way up in a jagged break where the eraser used to be.

"You're not going to just murder Eli in front of us and walk away!" said Mark, his fist clenched the cold metal box so hard his knuckled cracked.

"You want to save the man who would hurt you?" said Nona with raised eyebrows, even though her focus remained on writing.

Mark looked at Eli. The fleet commander kept pounding his fist against the slowly rotating prison. Each strike sent ripples across the topaz-crystal surface. He seemed enraged, hurt, and desperate.

"Yes," said Ella, her voice touched with the same pity that Mark felt.

The woman punctuated her written thoughts with a flourish and clapped the book shut. "Are you two some sort of plucky young heroes?" she said in a tone of fascinated amusement. "Is this some sort of heroic story playing out inside your head?" She leaned down to look at them, her hands on her knees as if she were lecturing children. "Most important: Do you believe this has a happy ending?"

They both stammered out nothing in response.

She turned to the trapped fleet commander. "Let's find out."

A snap of her fingers and the rotating sphere blinked away. Eli thudded to the ground. He lay where he'd fallen, breathing heavy with one arm under his chest and the other splayed out.

"My dear fleet commander." Nona began walking towards him. "If you die for these children, I will preserve your good reputation." She stopped in front of him. He did not look up from the pool of sweat and dust he lay in. "However, if you make the mistake of trying to be a hero again—and you fight me," she leaned down, "I will take everything from you—and you will watch these children suffer."

His eyes snapped up to her, a snarl smeared his face. "Damn the children!"

Nona Kine staggered backwards as Exor sprung up and slammed his fist into her stomach.

Ella darted a glance at Mark. Neither of them knew what would happen next, or what to do. But it looked like the fleet commander would win after all. Wouldn't he?

In one powerful motion Eli Exor struck Nona across the face. She staggered back, her black hair swaying in front of her broken blue eyes. She stared at Exor, her face blank.

"I will end you, Nona," Exor growled. He swung another roundhouse punch. It landed right above Nona's cheekbone, snapping her head downwards and making her stumble further.

She looked back up at him.

He strode towards her with white knuckled fists. "I will destroy you, I will destroy the Syn'Crux," he made to swing at her, "and I everyone will praise me as a he—"

Nona Kine's left hand shot up and clenched his throat. He choked.

Mark started breathing hard. Ella stepped forward and glanced over at him, as if they were supposed to help Eli. But what could they do?

Panic widened Exor's dirty silver eyes. His hands began beating against Nona's outstretched arm.

"Eli," said the woman, disgust in her steady voice, "you disappointment me."

Exor sunk to his knees, hands clawing at Nona's arm.

Nona's mouth made a little frown of thoughtful contemplation. "Now if I'm going to arrive a smidge too late to save those kids from the Obliv," she wondered out loud while choking the fleet commander. "But just before our traitorous fleet commander is able to escape—I better make him look like we fought a little."

## CHAPTER 17

Mark blanched. Something bad was about to happen. He didn't know what to do. A glob of spit welled up in his throat. He didn't know what to do.

Nona's left hand held Exor's head up while she raised her right hand, which she tightening into a fist.

"Let's put some bruises on that face."

Mark flinched and shut his eyes just as Nona's fist hammered down. He tried to shut his eyes tighter. Shutting his eyes didn't drown out the sounds though. He winced every time he heard her knuckles crunch into the man's face. A nose broke. A jaw cracked. A silver eye was bruised black.

Mark shivered. The bile rising up from his stomach burned. No. This wasn't right. His eyes snapped open, filled with anger. This wasn't right. His hands trembled as he rattled the jagged cube out of its metal box and onto his right hand. Cold pain stabbed through his palm; he didn't care. He stole a glance at the girl. To his surprise, her left hand gripped a palm-sized red stone. It glowed in ferocious black and pink hues. Her left hand and forearm were being covered by jagged triangles. She clenched her fist; wisps of pink and black rose from it. Her fierce blue-green eyes were on fire. She looked sickened by Nona.

"Stop," they both said, voices cracking. "Just stop it. Stop it!"

Nona stopped. Her haunting eyes met theirs before returning to Eli. "He didn't want to save you after all, did he?" She let go of Eli's throat. His head sagged to the side as his paralyzed body crumpled to the floor. She approached them, slow, menacing, and absently examining the knuckles on her right hand, which were beaten and bleeding. "Perhaps you still think I'm the villain," she said, then showed them the back of her hand as droplets of her own blood fell to the floor. "But look—I bleed just like you."

Mark quickly lifted his right arm, aiming his digitized palm at her as she advanced on them. But she could see his hand trembling. She could see panic creeping inside. She could see his shallow, erratic breathing.

"We don't need anyone saving us," said Ella, her red fist raised. But her hand shook just like her voice.

"You haven't learned?" Nona's eyes showed her disappointment with them. "Being a hero is a mistake."

Without realizing it, Mark's digitized blue squares were charging for attack. He wished his hand would stay steady. It trembled more. "Yeah? Well—have fun in the hospital!"

A surge of blue lightning arced from his open palm.

Nona stopped and flicked two fingers on her dark left hand.

Every ounce of power instantly reversed. The back shock hit, rocketing him backwards and bouncing his limp body off a wall. He fell to the floor, lungs collapsed. Broken squares rained around him, burning his skin. Laying on the floor, dazed, ears ringing, his breath came in rasps. His vision swam in a blurry mess. He felt as if he'd placed his right hand on an open car battery. And he wanted to puke. Above all, he wanted to puke.

From what seemed a great distance, a girl shouted. He groaned. Neck rigid with pain, he tried looking up.

A flash of light. A dull rumble shook his body. Then a few minutes of silence. He could hear his own heartbeat. His vision slowly came back. Ella stood in front of him. Her left hand held onto a palm-sized red stone. It glowed in ferocious black and pink hues. Jagged triangles covered her left hand and forearm.

His voice came out hoarse and ragged. "Ella."

She did not hear him. Her focus remained on protecting them. A dark orb circled and flowed all around her and Mark. Like a sinkhole made of

## CHAPTER 17

gravity, it was slowly ripping up the floor, crushing nearby columns, and consuming Nona Kine's attacks. Chunks of concrete and steel whirled around their protective orb. The air felt thick and smelled acrid.

Mark saw the effort in Ella's face. Her hands shook as if she bore a heavy burden. He gritted his teeth. He had to get up. In painful effort, he tried to lift himself off the floor.

"Get behind the column," said Ella, her voice exhausted.

Mark tried to stand up. No. Walking there wouldn't work. He started dragging himself there.

Ella fell to one knee. "I can't—"

In an instant their defensive orb blinked away. Nona Kine's dark gold torrent struck Ella, blasting her back in a river of power.

"No!" Mark screamed, watching Ella's limp body slid away to crumple against a far wall. His legs still weak, he gritted his teeth and hobbled over to her. Kneeling down, he saw she was still breathing. He choked down an angry sob as despair rose from his fear stricken heart. This wasn't how it was supposed to go! Not waiting for the girl to come to, he stood on weak legs and faced the woman.

Nona Kine had stopped attacking. Beautiful mouth curled in a sneer, she had turned to the fleet commander. "Are you watching, Eli?" she asked him.

He coughed up blood.

"I will take everything," she continued. "You will not die a martyr. You will die a betrayer, a traitor, and a coward."

Eli's eyes drifted up to her, nothing left of his pride but fear.

Mark clenched his fists. This wasn't how it was supposed to go. His breathing came out erratic. Wasn't he supposed to beat the bad guy, save his friends, and be the hero? "I could," he whispered to himself. He looked down at his fingers, flexing the jagged little squares. "Save my friends, save Ella, be a hero," he whispered to himself—or was it the cube whispering to him? "Let go. Consume. Breath."

His right hand lifted, open and out and ready. Let go, came the whisper. You will be the hero, it promised. I will breath.

The blue squares began flaking up and off his hand. No skin beneath, only a bleak darkness. All the rubble began vibrating off the floor. Metallic groans came from iron beams bending. Concrete columns began shredding apart. Mark felt alive, so very alive. He could see and touch everything. His heartbeat pulsed in the straining steel ribs holding up the high ceiling; his blood rushed through the liquefied metal swirling around his palm; his eyes, his eyes could see each breath on Ella's lips and each atom of the Obliv's construction. Burning neon embers whirled in front of his hand. He looked at Nona Kine.

The woman's eyebrows arched up, but only slightly. She raised her dark, misting left hand in response.

With a light push, as if a whispered breath, Mark attacked. The sharp little embers surged forward. His attack flowed fast, a digitized river of glass.

Nona created a black-and-gold shield. Marks torrent poured into it, hissing as shards of sharp blue squares struck the shield and evaporated. Like sparks falling from a welding torch, splashes of gold went cascading onto the ground. The sharp sizzle of raw blue squares smashing into a boiling gold and black mist sounded horrid and smelled of burning metal.

Through all this, Nona stood calm.

Mark could barely breathe. His right hand began going numb. All his anger, all his confusion, all of him kept trying to sustain the digitized torrent. His arms visibly shook. A fleeting tremor of panic made him grimace. He heard a ragged gasp behind him. Ella was waking. How much longer could he hold the hurricane?

## CHAPTER 17

He looked at Nona Kine. It didn't matter how much longer he could hold it. The woman was barely trying; her left hand raised, blocking everything, with her broken eyes on Mark, she remained relaxed, and relentless. Then, deciding the lesson was over, she made a slight flick of her wrist. His crude torrent of embers began to wobble.

"No," Mark breathed as his torrent of jagged blue glass began collapsing in on itself. "No, no, no!"

An ear-splitting boom followed. Shards of plasma and matter fell in a fine mist across Docking Bay Zero.

Mark collapsed, lungs rasping, steps away from Ella.

"Have you learned your lesson about the whole hero thing?" Nona asked.

The boy and girl remained silent, filling their lungs with charred air. They watched the woman walk back to Eli Exor's paralyzed body. She pried the black flowstone from his hand.

"I do hate it when people make the same mistake over and over and over again." She crushed Exor's stolen power in her fist. Fine black sand poured from her fingers. Then, she walked to the control panel and picked up the Obliv key.

"Mark, we can't win this," Ella whispered to him as she sat up against the scorched wall.

He rolled onto his back, looking sideways at her. He knew the truth of it. More than that, he felt it. The cube's cold had stiffened his knuckles. He winced trying to flex his fingers. "We don't have a clue what we're doing, huh?"

They looked over at Nona. Her back was to them as she lowered the Obliv key into a small hollow. A pulse of silver electricity encircled the Obliv. The ancient metal sphere began rotating.

"What do you think she'll do to us?" said Mark, wincing as he sat up.

Ella didn't answer. Her eyes were focused on the Obliv. "You know," she said, her voice full of churning thoughts. "If we destroy the Obliv, we could still win this."

Mark's eyes lit with hope. He stood up next to her. "All right, you get Exor and I'll destroy it!"

Ella frowned. "No, you get that guy. I'll take care of the Obliv."

Mark felt that protective stubbornness welling up. "You saw what I can do. I've got this."

"Don't worry," said Ella, her voice showing her own stubbornness. "I'll destroy it."

"I'm not worried. I'll destroy the key and get us out of here."

They stayed locking down in their stubbornness for a full minute, staring at each other.

"Seriously," said Ella, "Trust me on this!"

"How about you have some faith in me on this!"

"How about you quit acting the goat, then!"

"You're a right pain, you know that!"

They both decided to act in a rather rash manner. Ella stood up and aimed her nearly burnt left hand at the Obliv key. Mark bolted up and raised his nearly frost-bitten right hand in the same direction. They lashed out.

Two forms of power cut across Docking Bay Zero. One, a digitized bolt of blue electricity, crackling forward in a torrent of jagged chaos; the other, a burning surge of raw red energy, searing forward in a rush of devastation. Both would have destroyed the Obliv, had Nona Kine not interceded.

In one fluid motion she turned to face Mark and Ella, aiming both open palms at their attacks.

Mark's bolt crashed into Nona's left hand. Ella's surge crashed into Nona's right hand.

## CHAPTER 17

"One more lesson?" said Nona Kine. "OK, but this is the last one." She curled her fingers as if they were claws sinking into flesh and tugging gently.

Panic screwed up Mark's face. He tried stopping his attack by closing his hand. That's when he realized he couldn't feel his hand.

"Ready?" said Nona.

For a moment, the stillness of every air particle became absolute. The air hung heavy in their lungs, clouds of concrete dust stood transfixed around them, and neither a breath nor a heartbeat could move.

A dark gold pulse sprung from Nona's outstretched palms. It flowed into Marks electrified torrent as well as Ella's misting surge.

Mark stood breathless as Nona's dark-gold torrent slithered towards him, breaking and devouring every arc of lightning like a venomous snake. Within seconds the gold flow reached Mark's hand. It bit into his palm. He shuddered. Paralysis seized his heart. He tried tugging his right arm free.

"I can't," said Mark, breath catching in terror, "I can't let go!"

"I can't either!" Ella yelped, tugging at her left arm with her whole body.

"Haaahhhh," Mark breathed, ripping at his right arm with his left hand. The cold blue squares were draining down his forearm, leaving pale skin. It looked hypothermic and dead.

"She's tearing out my flowstone!" Ella screamed as Nona's powers slowly extracted the red stone that Ella had sunken into her skin.

Mark stopped. He stared at the back of his hand. A small vortex of twisted blue squares had formed in the center. His lungs seized. He understood. Nona Kine was taking the jagged blue cube right out of his hand.

When the last few digital drops drained out through Mark's palm, he screamed. Ella's screams mirrored his own. Their Syn'Crux powers had been torn away.

They crumpled to the ashen floor. It smelled of the sweat that had dripped from their faces.

But Mark and Ella did not die. Nona Kine had chosen otherwise.

Satisfied, she lowered her hands. Her right arm misted a digitized purple and her left glowed a burning black, neither were damaged in any way. For her, this had been simplicity itself. She strode over to them, those silver lines on her face fading back to the color of coal. Her arms faded to their natural skin tone. She looked down at the boy and the girl. They tried to look up, but had not the energy. So the woman with the beautifully wicked eyes knelt down beside them, in order that they might hear her.

"We aren't heroes—we are humans."

She allowed time to pass, so that they might understand.

"Do you know what that means?" she asked, knowing they had not the breath to respond.

Mark's eyes were unfocused. His ears hurt. His mouth tasted of iron, like blood.

"It means we make mistakes," she continued as she rose, elegant in meaning and purpose. "All four of us made mistakes today. Proving to ourselves how human we really are." She beckoned to a tall metal figure. It began walking to them, scrapping its feet. Nona looked back down at them. "That's why I urge you to keep a little notebook in your pocket." She took out that little notebook of hers again and tapped the slick black leather cover with a finger. "You can jot down all your human fallacies in it, all the mistakes you've ever made. It'll remind you of your humanity."

They could not move. Mark's limp hand lay in front of his blurred vision. It looked gruesome. In the center, an angry red scar had puckered the skin. It looked as if a burning metal rod had been stabbed through the middle of his palm, leaving the imprint of a dark vortex. His cube was gone. His fingers were pale and felt numb from cold. His body felt

## CHAPTER 17

stiff, ridged, and bruised all over. He saw Ella, lying crumpled next to him, her ocean eyes half closed and sweat and blood in her tangled hazel hair. He choked down a painful sob.

Nona Kine felt pity for these children. She crouched back down next to them and gently placed her hand on Ella's forehead. "Have hope." She placed another hand on Mark's forehead. "For there will come a day when no one will ever make a mistake again." Her broken heaven-blue eyes twinkled with zeal, reflecting her drive and intent. "After the Obliv serves its piece among pieces, after Crescent City yields to me, after the Earth is made ready—I will bring an end to all mistakes—and we will all get together and light a big bonfire and burn all our little lies, stumbles, and betrayals. We will burn all our little books, all together. We will burn our mistakes."

Nona stood. The tall, seven-eyed droid picked up Mark and Ella by their collars. She turned and began leading the droid to the Obliv. Fear and anxiety slushed in Mark's lurching stomach as he swayed from the droid's iron grip. The words Nona Kine had spoken had the dark confidence of a death noel. Like a heavy bell rung from a tall church steeple, the certainty in her voice sounded ominous, brave, and unstoppable.

"Until I bring about such a day, however, we must learn from our mistakes," said Nona.

Ella's response came out rather slurred. "I'm going to learn how to kick your ass."

Mark wanted to join in too, so he slurred out a, "Yeah, next time—next time I'll punch your nose holes."

Nona ignored their weak words. "I'm learning from my mistakes—with you two. Into the Obliv you'll go. And when you come out, all the media will think I saved you. And you're going to believe them."

"Nobody will believe you," Mark growled at her.

Ella spat on the floor, leaving a blood-soaked splatter. "I know I won't."

Nona simply smiled. She stopped by the control panel and picked up the spherical key. Then she noticed Eli's black military jacket. Tracing the gold filigree around the coat's collar with her finger, she said, "Do you see what happens—when we refuse to learn from our mistakes?" She casually tossed the coat in Exor's direction.

Mark's eyes followed the coat as it unruffled in midair and settled on the man's cracked ribcage. The once powerful fleet commander lay crumpled on the stained concrete floor where he'd fallen. Only his silver eyes moved, watching the consequences of his arrogant pride. Mark scrunched his eyebrows. Was someone humming? Who was that? Nona?

Mark's eyes darted back to look at the woman. Her hands floated over the controls. A pulse of silver electricity encircled the Obliv. A deep, reverberating hum sent tremors through the floor. The ancient metal sphere began rotating slower.

The Obliv filled his vision now. Its surface radiated energy and beckoned. Panic gripped him. He looked away from Nona, away from the Obliv. Trying to calm his mind, he focused on his body. Moving his tongue in his bloodied mouth was difficult, it felt swollen and dry. The tips of his fingers were regaining heat, making them itch. A realization darkened his eyebrows. She was humming. A song. A familiar little lullaby.

His eyes darted to Nona. Her striking face seemed calm and content. Her focus remained on the controls as the beautiful, other-worldly song rolled from her lips, happy yet haunting. A listing verse, a lulling melody, it reminded Mark of a family long broken apart, of childhood memories shattered at heart, of an unforgiving past that would never depart.

Where had he heard such an unforgettable melody? Who had sung these heart-wrenching verses? A flash of a starliner being hit by a hawk-class ship. No, before that. A recollection of the captain pointing to a star-chart and talking about Earth. No, after that. Yes, a memory of

## CHAPTER 17

falling asleep while galaxies filled his mind and wondering—wondering if he'd ever see a vertical horizon.

His eyes widened and his breath caught. He stared at Nona Kine.

"You're Lieutenant Landeth's sister!" he blurted out at the same time as Ella exclaimed something, though he was too shocked to hear it.

Nona's fingers stopped hovering over the controls. She looked up and into the distance, a small, nostalgic smile at the corners of her lips. "Yes," she said, voice touched with sadness. "Though they wouldn't know it."

Mark, reeling from the realization, didn't see that the Obliv had stopped. A line broke the dark surface. It formed the shape of a long, thin door. The door slid upwards to reveal a clean brightness.

"But the Syn'Crux took you . . ." Ella trailed off.

"How are you a daemon . . . ?" asked Mark.

Nona's nostalgic smile turned sour. Her shattered eyes held acidic memories. She nodded at the seven-eyed droid.

The white metal droid moved towards the thin door. Mark and Ella both made weak attempts at pounding their fists against its steel arms and kicking its plastic body. It threw them deep into the machine.

The curved door began to close.

"No, no, no," Ella yelped, as they both crawled back to it. It closed before they made it. Mark beat his fist against the soft brightness.

A dull white glow began surrounding them. Silence. They stopped struggling and sat down.

Mark could hear Ella breathing. He could hear his own heartbeat. Besides these, there was nothing.

Ella broke the silence. "What do you think's going to happen?" Not a single note of fear tinged her voice, but rather a calm confidence.

Mark thought about what to say. Her eyes really did remind him of surfing under a cresting wave. He decided not to lie about 'everything going to be alright". She'd see right through that crap. So he decided upon the truth. "Can I hold your hand…one last time?"

She searched his eyes, gave a sad smile, and said, "yes."

He intertwined his fingers between hers.

The dull white glow increased. A deep reverberating hum. A sharp, caustic smell. A deep white light. Memories began to flash like a movie. The white light burned the film. Mark thought he was screaming, but he wasn't sure. Ants went crawling inside his mind.

# CHAPTER 18

# CHAPTER 18
## THE FIGHTER

The young boy from Earth, with dark brown hair and the stubbornness of a goat, awoke. He opened his eyes to a different hue of white and a different smell of clean. Tiles of a calming cream color lined the ceiling. The bed sheets wrapped around him felt soft and snug. He felt comfortable and warm and safe. As his ears adjusted, he could hear the sounds of heart-rate monitors, hospital equipment, and—someone slurping soup.

Mark tilted his head towards the noise. Captain Stan sat by his bedside, a cup of chunky vegetable soup in his left hand and a spoon in his right.

"Hey there, ace," he said, continuing to slurp soup.

"Hello, sir," Mark replied, feeling groggy.

"How's your head? Still attached?"

"I dunno," said Mark, so out of it he thought it was loose. "I think so."

The captain gave a warm chuckle. "When you're feeling up to—"

Mark bolted upright. "Are Heath and Lexe okay?"

"Yes, yes. They are quite all right."

A wave of relief hit and he sunk back into bed. Everything hurt, especially his head.

Stan noticed Mark flexing his fingers. "How's the hand, then?"

Mark took his right hand from underneath the covers. Shock, confusion, fear, worry, all flooded his mind. He stared at his palm. A black scar in the shape of a dead vortex darkened the skin at the center. He yanked his other hand out from the covers so he could trace the scar. It felt like

## CHAPTER 18

a scar, with skin healed in small ridges the color of charcoal. It also felt slightly sunken in. He rotated his right hand slowly. The jagged vortex was mirrored perfectly on the back.

"It hurts," said Mark, flexing his fingers, "and it's kinda cold."

"Yes," said Stan, putting away his soup. He gave his full attention to the boy. "But the pain will fade—in time."

Mark kept rotating his hand and tracing the scar. The shock had worn off, but not the confusion or fear.

Stan saw this and put a comforting hand on the boys shoulder. "Don't remember, huh?"

"No," Mark replied. He tried to remember, but winced, gripping his forehead. He wanted to curl up in a ball from the pain.

"Don't try to remember. It'll increase the pain. Your mind needs to heal."

Mark rubbed his forehead. He sunk back down under the gentle pressure of Stan's hand on his shoulder. Laying there, looking up at the ceiling, he said, "It feels like something was burned out of me—and I don't even know what it was—someone just took it, and it's gone."

Stan gave the boy a few moments of sadness, knowing grief needs to play its part.

"You did a brave thing," he said, gripping the boys shoulder.

Mark sighed. He looked at the captain's kind face with its wrinkled eyes and square salt and pepper colored beard. "Lexe and Heath are really OK? That's the last thing I really remember. Us in a—messed up room—a weird skeleton trying to break in," He winced again, rubbing his forehead.

"Yes, they are. They'll be waiting for you at school. Which reminds me, there's the Wargame award ceremony to get to. The doctors have you cleared, so whenever you're ready."

Mark frowned. "But what happened? How did I get here?"

The captain thought for a moment. Many of his old friends had suffered through wounds. Whether true or not, he always thought corny laughter was the best medicine. So in a lighthearted tone he said, "An Ambulance."

Mark chuckled. "Well yea, but who brought me?"

"Ambulance people," Stan replied, continuing his prescription of cheesy medicine.

Mark laughed and shook his head.

Stan smiled. "I'm happy to see you can still laugh at my cheesy jokes." But then the old captain's smile faded into seriousness. He pressed a button at the side of Mark's hospital bed. The wall opposite the bed faded and became a large screen. The screen had depth, as if they were looking into the living room of a TV set. Two chairs faced each other in interview style. In one of them sat a handsome blonde man in a serious suit who looked like a news anchor.

"Ladies and gentlemen, we continue our coverage of this breaking news story," said the serious-faced man from his comfortable chair. "Shocking, appalling, disturbing. These are the words our viewers have used." He paused for drama. "We saw him hound Ernest Shaw, our director of Lunalife, but we still trusted him. We knew he was at the same conference from which Ernest Shaw was taken and tortured—but we trusted. We heard reports from the starliner crash investigation and the raided Syn'Crux lab pointing to a deathwish cover-up—but still—we trusted." The anchorman paused again. "Ladies and gentlemen—we were deceived. Our beloved white knight—Fleet Commander Eli Exor—was a dark horse."

Mark looked to Captain Zumski with excitement. "It's on the news!"

"Yes," the captain replied in a voice urging caution. "One thing I've learned in all my years—is that people love a good betrayal story. Tell

## CHAPTER 18

them someone good was really an evil criminal and they eat it up, eager to tell their friends 'I told you so.'"

Mark frowned, not knowing quite what the old man was implying.

"Now, here for an exclusive interview," continued the serious newsman, "is the person who stopped the traitor, the woman who kept the Obliv from the Syn'Crux, the hero who saved innocent children," He turned to the right side of the stage, "the overseer of Shattered Sky Interspace—Miss Nona Kine!"

An elegant woman walked onto the set. Her right cheekbone and surrounding skin were etched in a beautiful, haunting digital web of angled lines. The camera wasn't close enough for Mark to see her eyes, but he was sure they were a shattered blue. He blanched.

Stan observed the boys changing reactions from shock to fear to confusion. His voice was gentle when he asked, "are you all right there, ace?"

Mark held his stomach. "I—I don't know—I think so," he tried looking at the woman again. "I see her—and, I don't know why but—I'm afraid—and I want to puke."

The old captain's eyes wrinkled in thoughtful worry. He looked at the woman, and considered.

"Good afternoon, Overseer Kine," said the host and sat back down after she did.

"Good afternoon," she responded in a voice both dark and authoritative.

"This breaking news is simply amazing. Please tell us the depth of Exor's depraved deception."

"Naturally," said Nona Kina, beginning with a smile. "As you recall, Exor's constant hounding for the Obliv's location made Ernest suspicious." She paused to affect warmth on the former director's name. "Now, he didn't feel the need to dig deeper, but I did. My search intensified after Mr. Shaw went missing. He is—was—a very punctual and cautious man." She seemed to show some grief. "When I heard that the hawk-class ship involved in Exor's near fatal crash had been located and was under investigation, I rushed to the Chief Inspector's office. He informed me that a Syn'Crux lab had also been uncovered. In the subsequent raid the investigators found additional evidence."

"And what did the evidence from these two sources show?"

"It was inconclusive, but it may have shown one fake deathwish among many."

"Shocking!"

"Yes. And I could not understand why. Eli Exor, as fleet commander of Crescent City, took an oath to serve and protect. How could he have been a Syn'Crux daemon all along?"

"It is so shockingly simple," marveled the newsman. "He had the means: he already had the key to unlock the Obliv. He had the opportunity: torturing the location out of Mr. Shaw at the conference. And he had the motive: to use the Obliv." The man shook his head while Nona looked on with a grim frown of agreement. "And he tried to cover it up so beautifully—by faking deathwish attempts on his own life."

They both gave a dramatic moment to the audience, allowing it all to sink in.

"Do, please, tell us what you did after realizing this horrifying truth."

"I never hesitated," she replied. "I opened the confidential communications that Ernest Shaw left for me in the event of his death. It showed the Obliv's location. I went there straight away to remove it."

"And you interrupted Exor's attempt to steal it."

"Correct. In fact, Exor was in the process of using the Obliv on a child from a group he had captured earlier. He planned to hold them hostage in case of being captured."

"Revolting," said the anchor man so his audience could see he was in touch with their emotions. "Do go on."

## CHAPTER 18

"I confronted him—"

"Yes?" he said, leaning forward in his chair.

"Yes," she replied, calm as ever. "I tried to reason with him; children's lives hung in the balance, after all."

"Very kind-hearted of you," the man murmured.

"He refused to see reason—"

"Horrible man."

"He chose to fight. I was able to get the upper hand and free the children."

"A heroic victory!"

"Yes."

"Shocking, absolutely shocking. And yet not surprising. A wise man once wrote, 'watch out for the best of us, for sometimes, they are the worst of us.'"

Nona Kine simply smiled.

"What are your plans for the Obliv?"

"Ah," said Nona, folding her hands in her lap. "I have heard the outcry from the good people of Crescent City. I will personally oversee the Obliv's removal to a highly secure, militarized location."

"Well," said the news anchor with a confident, flashy smile. "I just know the citizens of our fair city will feel relieved to hear that!" Then he turned to the audience and took a serious, ominous tone. "Yet, we are left wondering—who will hunt the Syn'Crux now? Who will stand against the next daemon?"

Zumski turned off the holographic television. The woman and the newsman and the interviewing room disappeared. Mark was left staring at a blank hospital wall; his mind felt just as blank.

"So Eli Exor was a Syn'Crux daemon! He tried to kill me in the Obliv!" Mark raised his hand and stared at the scar. "That's why I have this scar—isn't it?"

# THE FIGHTER

"The news would have us believe so . . ." came Zumski's distant reply.

Mark thought about the captain's skeptical tone. "You don't believe that?"

The old captain thought for a moment, and then looked at the boy. "Eli Exor made a solid fleet commander. He was an honest man."

"You don't believe he was a Syn'Crux daemon who tried to steal the Obliv and kill me?" said Mark, genuinely curious.

The captain looked at the young boy from Earth with seriousness in his weathered brown eyes. He placed his callused, worn left hand on Mark's scared right hand and pressed for emphasis before letting go. "I believe there are difficult times ahead," said the old captain. "Fortunately, there are those who will rise to the fight."

Mark frowned. Something inside him whispered that fighting wouldn't work. His voice came out tired and discouraged. "But I don't feel like being a hero much anymore."

"Ah," said the wise man. "But there is a difference between being a hero and being a fighter."

"I don't feel like being a fighter either," Mark grumbled. He felt rather empty. He kept rotating his hand and looking at the scar that penetrated his palm. "I don't want to get up anymore. I don't want to fight. I don't want to make that mistake again." The nothingness inside his head hurt. He felt like a failure. "I just—I just want this scar to go away!"

The old captain saw the pain and anger building up inside the boy. He thought for a moment, and then said, "Back when I served in the forty-second platoon, I got to know a certain fellow—went by the name of Tommy B. He was a boxer. Legal, illegal, didn't matter, he'd sign up looking for hurt, and he gave hurt back. And when the medics tried to heal any fresh scars he got, well, Tommy declined." Captain Zumski looked at Mark, a wise kindness in his old eyes. "Now, when someone sees that man's slanted nose that didn't heal right and the scar above

## CHAPTER 18

his eye and that offset chin—they know he's a fighter, sure—but more important, they know he's a fighter who stands back up."

Mark had to smile, imagining himself with boxing gloves in a boxing ring. He saw himself being knocked down and standing back up and getting knocked back down again only to stand up again. That made him feel tough. And feeling tough made him feel all right. He liked thinking of himself as a tough boxer with scars, getting back up after every fight, win or lose. He decided to get up then, and get going.

Captain Stanislaw Zumski and the boy from Earth arrived at the SPIFF Mess Hall just as the Wargame awards ceremony was wrapping up. All the tables were piled with food and packed with students. The wall of windows had a short stage set up in front of it where the awards were being announced; the wall at the opposite end had several long tables of food—to which the captain excused himself—and the two side walls displayed highlights from the Wargame. A short hush would pause all the conversations and noise as the announcer gave out each award. Then the hall would fill with sound once more as the student who won an award would walk over to claim it. Mark made his way amid the noisy ruckus and intermittent food fights to the regular table he sat at with his friends. He grinned when he saw everybody there. He decided to sneak up and sit down so they wouldn't notice.

"Hi guys," he said, trying to be as cool as possible.

"Hey!" they all erupted in excited shouts.

His attempt at trying to seem like a cool tough guy broke the instant they all tackled him.

"You're alive!" shouted Zaza from underneath a bear hug.

THE FIGHTER

"How'd you survive?" asked Heath with a handshake turned fistbump.

"These two crazies have been telling us stories about fighting demon androids!" said Torvan, pointing to Lexe and Heath.

"He survived by using that cavemanlike skull," said Lexe with a grin.

Mark felt overwhelmed, and his smile showed it. The first thing he said was, "Thanks guys. No, I really mean it. Thanks for being awesome."

"Ah, you're the best," said Heath with another fistbump.

"No, you guys are the best!" said Mark to all of them.

An announcement interrupted their happy reunion.

"The Top Cadet badge goes to — Lance, wing leader of Alpha Squad!"

A cheer went up. But not from everyone, only a few tables belonging to Lance's own squad and their friends.

"What're these awards all about?" Mark asked.

Heath scoffed. "Just a bunch of pompous peacocking."

Mark laughed. "So they didn't call our names or anything, huh?" He looked at them with a mixture of sarcasm and, deep down, a little hope.

Lexe shook her head. "Noooope. They just finished. The Top Cadet is the highest honor, and the last. Figures that golden boy would get it."

"Meh, forget about it," Mark said with a shrug. "Who needs awards?"

The table murmured in agreement, but it was half-hearted.

The superman-faced boy strode down from the awards platform, a bounce to his step. He made sure to look over at Mark's table and wave at all of them.

Mark gave him a lampooning smile and mocking wave back.

Zaza gasped when she saw Mark's right hand.

"What happened?" she said and pointed.

"Oh," said Mark, not quite sure how to explain it all as everyone looked at his hand. "I—wait," he glanced from Lexe to Heath. "What happened to you guys after I left?"

# CHAPTER 18

"Not much," said Lexe with a disappointed shrug. "That pyscho droid didn't come back. We waited until the medics arrived for Mr. Trippy here," she said and thumbed at Heath.

"Your shoulder all right?" asked Mark.

"Oh yeah. Just a scratch, actually," he said, a tad embarrassed. "But your hand, that's a right gnarly scar, that is."

"Yeah," Mark replied, inspecting it again. "I'm not even sure how I got it."

"Not sure?" said Lexe with a raised eyebrow. "I'm not sure what I had for breakfast this morning. If I suddenly had a wicked scar like that—I'd at least make something up."

"I just—I don't remember," he replied, a painful confusion in his eyes.

The five friends huddled around the circular table and talked. They talked about Marks scared hand and his strange lack of recent memories; they talked about Eli Exor and his plot being all over the news; they talked about the Obliv and Nona Kine transporting it someplace safe; they talked about what was good and what was gross up at the buffet tables.

"Good afternoon, students," said a clear voice.

Everyone in the Mess Hall quieted down. All heads turned to their admiral.

She stood on stage to a backdrop of a blue-skied Crescent City. Her strong green eyes swept over everyone in a commanding way. Her presence could be felt in the sudden silence.

"Another season has been well played. Our Commander's Club has demonstrated superior leadership and earned ten badges; our Cadet Core has flown with fearlessness, earning eight; our Support Crew has earned three badges of honor." She surveyed the hushed students. "All that remains is the matter of who won the Wargame."

THE FIGHTER

Mark sat up taller. For some reason he thought if he sat up higher to see better, he could hear better too. But the pounding of his heart in his ears made listening difficult.

"Before I declare the winner, an announcement: the faculty of SPIFF, judges of the Wargame, and city officials have ruled that Crescent City airspace is, from hence forth, restricted."

A cheer went up from Alpha Squad, the Commander's Club, and half the Cadet Core. This was followed by buzzing conversations.

Mark looked at his friends in knowing disappointment. They looked back at him, equally frustrated.

"Quiet please," said the admiral. "I would like to add a personal announcement."

The jam-packed Mess Hall fell silent.

"I have served as your admiral for many decades. I have seen many acts of bravery, loyalty, and valor in my time both in the Space Force and here at SPIFF." She affected her pause by looking over the crowd of young faces. "Yet, this year I witnessed certain students put forth such earnest effort, such true ingenuity, such courageous valor—that my own faith was strengthened. For even I doubted one of these students, which is something no educator should ever do. Happily, there were other teachers who fought my cynicism." The admiral gave a warm nod to Captain Zumski and Otto McMaluch, who smiled in thanks from where they sat at the faculty table. "Now, I would like to recognize those few students." The admiral's green eyes made sure she had everyone's full attention. "Torvan Thomas and Zaza Rayn, you scarified your time and put forth exceptional effort in helping a fellow student. We thank you."

The Support Crew cheered. Zaza bit her lip and looked down at the table. Torvan tried to be professional like the captain by nodding once, but he couldn't hide a smile.

## CHAPTER 18

"Lexe Haxler," the admiral continued. "For your tireless work and loyalty to a friend in danger—we thank you."

Another cheer. Lexe smiled rather sheepishly, and brushed her yellow bangs from her shy eyes, which looked funny coming from such a constantly sarcastic girl.

"Heathcliff Dodger Robinson. You demonstrated acute business acumen and stuck by your friends in spite of fear—for this, we thank you."

Several Support Crew students shouted his name over the cheers. Heath, sitting up straight through her words with a gigantic grin, nodded several times.

"And finally," said the admiral. "For his creative solutions, his stubborn tenacity, and for standing back up after people kept knocking him down, I am pleased to accept Mark into the Cadet Core and—"

Her words drowned in a sea of applause.

"And," she continued, "because the airspace ruling is new—technically—the Wargame title goes to Squad Foxtrot."

A roar, a deafening roar erupted to fill the entire Mess Hall. The Support Crew was by far the largest of the three groups, and everyone in it jumped to their feet, whistling and clapping and high-fiving each other.

Mark was floored. He sat on the bench at the table like a dumbstruck lottery winner. Zaza kept hugging him, Heath and Torvan kept high-fiving and low-fiving everyone, and for some reason, Lexe tousled his hair. He could not stop grinning.

The only people not celebrating were the cadets of Alpha Squad and a few of their friends in Beta Squad and the Commander's Club. Their heads kept darting around in dumbstruck confusion at all the noise crowding them in. Jet Chan sat stone faced with arms crossed; Cruise Galantine's soft facial features were screwed in a mixture of disbelief and horror; Dinzdale had a piece of barbeque chicken hanging from his gaping mouth, it fell on his sauce slathered plate with a splat; Lance stood and yelled his protests using certain words quite unbefitting a Top Cadet.

"Great jive in the bucket brawls, eh?" came Keera's happy and confusing words.

Foxtrot squad had come over for some high-fives and fist bumps.

"Ah, I guess you're not so bad, muffin man," said Derrick with a bone crushing handshake.

Samantha and Marsel were there too, talking and laughing with everyone.

Then Mark heard the hiss of hydraulics and felt a metal hand rest on his shoulder. He turned around.

Otto McMaluch and all his whirring gears and clicking cogs and oiled machinery stood with the biggest of smiles across his scraggly face.

"Listen!" he announced in a proud and happy bellow. The gears of his right arm turned as he swept his arms wide to encompass the Mess Hall. "Listen to them cheer! This is the first time in decades that someone from the Support Crew—one of their own—has changed his stars." He looked down at Mark with a proud shimmer in his eyes. "You made it, hotshot."

Mark didn't know how to react. Those words rung deep within him. He made it. He made it. . .

"Thank you, Otto," is all he could say as he stood up and hugged the burly man who smelled of diesel and engine grease and tea.

Otto's big belly shook with a heartfelt chuckle. "Oh, get on with ya," he said.

Mark stepped back, all he could do was keep grinning like a fool and looking around, letting everyone's laughter and happiness carry his soul away.

# CHAPTER 18

When Mark stumbled into his dorm room that evening, he was still grinning. He didn't even care that the alarm clock saw him and preemptively struck by blaring the sounds of a five alarm fire at a fireworks factory. He just patted the little robot on its spider head and went to stand by his bed. The clock, suddenly confused, stopped raging and tilted its front sensor the way a confused owl tilts its head, and watched Mark as he gazed out the window.

Mark's large grin had worn down into an exhausted smile. Hands in pockets, he looked out the small circular window of his escape pod dorm room. The dusk of another late spring fortnight fell through the sky in darkening colors. The advancing night spoke of the coming darkness, but Mark could see the stars begin to light, and he knew the day would always dawn for another fight.

Those adventuresome green-blue eyes roved over the neon city, watching hovercars zip across long stretches of flyways, watching skyscraper office lights dim as people left work for home, and watching the embers of suburbia begin to glow as families reunited. There were untold adventures out there, and he wanted to be part of every single one.

The exhausted smile disappeared, replaced by a confused frown when he realized he'd been clenching and unclenching his right hand. Taking his hand out, he held it up to the light of the round window and stared at the small scar shaped like a broken vortex.

"How the hell did I get this?"

He stood still, turning his hand from one side to the other. "And why do I feel like I'm missing something—and someone." He looked out the little round window for a few quiet moments. "I wonder if that woman who saved me knows. I should find a way to ask her." A vision of Nona Kine's shattered blue eyes flashed. He winced from the pain and shut his eyes. "Every time," he whispered. "Every damn time."

He grimaced, rubbing his dry, aching eyes. Then, with a sigh, he looked back out and over the neon city. "I wish I had that cube right now." He flexed the fingers of his right hand in an absentminded way. "I could fix all this with my little blue cube. I could live again." He winced and shook his head. "What am I saying?" He scrunched his eyes closed, scowling as he pushed a strange hunger away.

"Ahhhh," he said, shrugging several times and rolling his shoulder blades as he took the few steps to his desk. "My friends are safe and happy, I'm finally in the Cadet Core, and we won the Wargame!" The chair swiveled when he flopped into it. "Everything's going to be jazzy fizzle down at the boondocks!" He folded his hands behind his head, leaned back in the chair, and kicked his feet up onto the old escape pod control panel with a happy sigh. "First thing tomorrow, I'm having a zippy!"

As it turned out, his feet landed on the dusty buttons in the perfect order. Right foot on the big red eject button and left foot on the combo of buttons to activate it. A loud unlocking clunk, a thunderous roar from the single booster, and the boy from Earth and his whole dorm room made a shimmering fiery arc across the beautiful evening sky of Crescent City.

■ ■ ■ ■ ■ ■ ■ ■ ■ ■

Far into downtown Crescent City, at the heights of the Shattered Sky Interspace corporate tower, the light from a pearl blue Earth and its celestial crown of stars and galaxies poured in through a high glass dome. The dome encircled a cavernous chamber, illuminated only where the glass sunk into the floor by a harsh cyan light. The toxic air held the smell of a city at midnight—buzzing neon, artificial life, and insomnia.

Nona Kine's entrancing voice echoed in this hallowed chamber. "I have hunted the Syn'Crux hunter."

## CHAPTER 18

The Obliv turned with lazy rotations behind her. Arcs of silver light shone from its myriad fissures.

Her tone carried absolution and atonement. "I have killed the daemon killer."

One hundred Syn'Crux, men and women, old and young, spliced and shifted people representing every hidden Syn'Crux enclave throughout the living galaxy looked upon her with fortified hearts and loyal spirits. Their upturned faces were illuminated by myriad colors of power. The power radiated from their hands.

"Eli Exor is dead. We control the Obliv." Her shattered eyes held the gathered crowd. "What say you, Harbinger?"

A tall, handsome man with the demeanor of a vice president and the dark, sleek clothing of a prophet parted from the crowd. He strode to the steps that lead to Nona. The features of his stoic face were illuminated by the silver energy emanating from his right hand. He stopped halfway up the steps and turned to address the Syn'Crux representatives. In a deep, reverberating voice, he spoke.

"We are witness to your ascension, Daemon Kine."

Silence. Then, the Earth and stars beheld one hundred Syn'Crux as, in one motion, they raised their radiating fists. A new daemon has risen.

# THE FIGHTER

# About the Author

Rafael G. Hauxley hails from Rzeszow, Poland. He immigrated to Salt Lake City in 1990. There, he learned English by reading Asterix & Obelix, Tintin, and Calvin & Hobbes. Since then, he's bounced between three colleges, sold motorcycles, and trekked around Europe. In 2009, encouraged by an amazing professor, Rafael closed down his architecture business. He had decided to write.

Rafael currently lives in bookstores and libraries around Portland, Oregon. He goes there to smell books. Smelling books causes him to contemplate life, the universe, and how much mischief, exactly, could be made in a galaxy filled with quirky people, wild adventures, odd inventions, and strange foods. He plans to discover the answers through fourteen books spanning two intertwined series: Mark From Earth and Ella From Earth.

Read his ramblings and musings on Facebook.com/markfromearth. Also, please pester him to finish writing the sequel. He spends too much time following Finn & Jake, rewatching old Monty Python skits, and thinking of funny words…like lollygagging.

COMING SOON....

# ELLA FROM EARTH